RANDOM
HOUSE
LARGE
PRINT

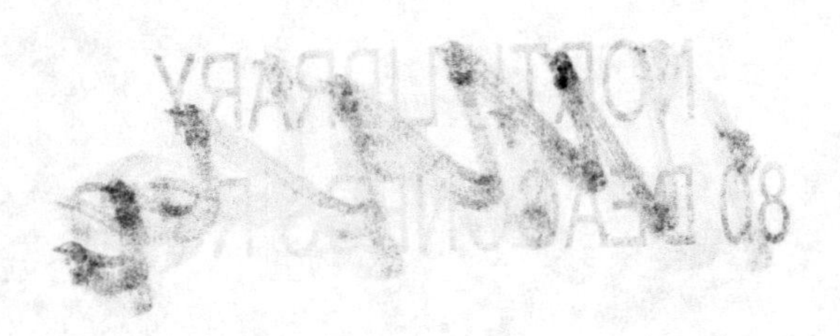

THE SMOKE JUMPER

NICHOLAS EVANS

For Harry, Max and Lauren

Acknowledgments

Many thanks to those who helped in the research: Priscilla Robinson, Rob Whitty, Huw Alban Davies, Suzanne Laverty, Dave Mills, Bruce Weide, Pat Tucker, Jeanette Ingold, Jim Marks, Bob Maffit, Dan Plerscher, Dave Friend, Chris Thomas, Jeremy Mossop, Janey King, Sam Davis, Geoffrey Kalebbo, Philip Jones Griffiths, Charles Glass, Gavin Smith, larry Stednitz and Garrett Munson of Alternative Youth Adventures, For their support and encouragement and much more besides, thanks to Linda Shaughnessy, Larry Finlay, Sally Gaminara, Irwyn Applebaum, Nita Taublib, Tracy Devine, Caradoe King and Charlotte Gordon Cumming.

Finally, for help and patience far beyond the call of duty, special thanks to two fine Missoula smoke jumpers, Wayne Williams and Tim Eldridge.

THE SMOKE JUMPER

No man may earn his heart's desire
Lest first he brave the smoke and fire.

PART ONE

ONE

THE IMPORTANT things in life always happened by accident. At fifteen she didn't know much, in fact, with each passing year she was a lot less clear about most things. But this much she did know. You could worry yourself sick trying to be a better person, spend a thousand sleepless nights figuring out how to live clean and decent and honest, you could make a plan and bolt it in place, kneel by your bed every night and swear to God you'd stick to it, hell, you could go to church and promise properly. You could cross your heart seven times with your eyes tight shut, cut your thumb and squeeze it and pen solemn vows on a rock with your own blood then throw it in the river at the stroke of midnight. And then, out of the black beyond, like a hawk on a rat, some nameless catastrophe would swoop into your life and turn everything upside down and inside out forever.

Skye later reckoned that on the night in question that old hawk must have been outside sitting up on the roof biding his time and watching the rat have a little fun, because it all started in a real low-key kind of way when those two women came sashaying into the bar.

She didn't know who they were but what they were was plain for all the world. They were wearing more make-up than clothes and she could tell from the way they swayed on their high heels that they were already hazed with drink. They both wore tight little tops, one red, one silver and fringed, and the woman in front, who had long black hair and breasts propped up like melons on a shelf, had a skirt so short she needn't have bothered. The music in the bar was thumping loud and the black-haired woman tried a little shimmy to it as she walked and almost fell.

The men they were with were close behind them and obscured, steering them through the crowd. Both wore cowboy hats and from the corner booth across the room where Skye and her friends were sitting, she couldn't make out their faces. Not that she was remotely interested. She was more than a little hazed with drink herself. The lights were dimmed to a dull red glow and through the hanging curl of smoke all she registered was a couple of sad forty-something-year-old guys chasing their youth and doubtless cheating on their wives. Skye looked away. She picked up her beer and drank, then lit another cigarette.

She watched them mostly because she was bored, which was kind of sad too, considering it was her birthday. Jed and Calvin were slumped stoned and speechless beside her, Roxy was still crying into her hands at something Craig had said to her, and Craig was still cussing on and on about his goddamn heap of a car breaking down. Another great night in fun city, Skye said to herself and took another swig. Happy birthday to me.

The bar was a godforsaken dump so close to the railroad that the bottles shook and clinked whenever a train went by. For reasons that weren't too hard to fathom, the cops left the place alone and so long as you weren't in diapers, the staff turned a blind eye to underage drinking. Consequently much of the clientele was around the same age as Skye. A lot younger for sure than the four who had just walked in. They were at the bar now and stood waiting to be served. They had their backs to her and Skye again found herself staring at them.

She watched the tall man's hands moving on the black-haired woman's hips and on her ass and up her spine to her bare shoulders and saw him lean in close, nuzzling her neck. God, he was *licking* her. How gross some guys were. What was it with women? How could they stand being slobbered over by jerks like him? The whole sex trip was something Skye still didn't get and doubted she ever would. Oh sure, she *did* it. Everybody did. But she still couldn't figure out why it was cracked up to be such a big deal.

The man must have whispered something dirty because the woman suddenly threw back her head laughed raucously and made a playful attempt to slap him. The man laughed too and swiveled to avoid her and his hat fell off and for the first time Skye could see his face.

It was her stepfather.

In those few moments before his eyes met hers she glimpsed in his face a look she had never seen before, a kind of inner face that was still just a boy's, loose and joyful and strangely frail. Then she saw him recognize her and saw the boy vanish as swiftly as he had appeared. His face clouded and clenched and became again the one she knew and feared and loathed, the one she saw when he came back in the early hours to the trailer seething with drink and fury and called her mother a squaw bitch and beat her until she howled for mercy and then turned his foul attention upon Skye.

He straightened up and put his hat on the bar and said something to the woman who turned to consider Skye with a look that lay somewhere between disdain and disinterest. Now he was heading toward the booth. Skye squashed out her cigarette, hoping he hadn't seen it. She stood up.

"Let's go," she said quietly.

But she was trapped in the booth. On one side Roxy was sobbing into Craig's shoulder and hadn't heard and on the other Calvin and Jed were still out of it. Her stepfather reached the table, his eyes taking in the evidence: the beer bottles, the brimming ashtrays, the comatose bums she chose to hang out with.

"What the fuck are you doing in here?"

"Come on, it's my birthday." It was pathetic but worth a try. She even thought of calling him "Dad" as she briefly had when he and her mom married, before he revealed just what a mean, disgusting sonofabitch he really was. But she couldn't bring herself to utter the word.

"Don't give me that shit. You're just fifteen years old! What the fuck do you think you're at?"

"Aw, give her a break, man. We're only having a little fun." It was Jed, who had resurfaced. Skye's stepfather leaned across and grabbed him by the throat, hauling him halfway across the table.

"You dare talk to me like that, you little slice of shit."

Jed's weight made the table tilt and everything on it except for him slid off onto the floor in an avalanche of breaking glass. Craig was on his feet now and he tried to grab Skye's stepfather by the arm but her stepfather twisted himself around and with the hand that wasn't throttling Jed punched the boy full in the face. Roxy screamed.

"For godsake," Skye shouted. "Stop it! Stop it!"

She was aware that everyone in the bar was staring at them. One of the waiters was coming over along with the man her stepfather had arrived with.

"Hey folks, let's cool it here, shall we?" the waiter said.

Skye's stepfather shoved Jed back into his seat so hard his head slammed against the back of the booth. Craig was on his knees bleeding from the mouth and Roxy was sobbing over him, trying to help him. Skye's stepfather's chest was heaving and his eyes were narrowed and dark and he turned them on the waiter.

"Did you serve alcohol to these kids?"

The waiter held up his hands. "Sir, let's keep things calm now, please."

He was slightly built and about a foot shorter

than Skye's stepfather. He had long hair tied back in a ponytail.

"Did you? Did you serve them alcohol?"

"They said they were twenty-one."

"And you believed that? Did you ask for their I.D.?"

"Sir, could we talk about this—"

"Did you?"

Skye stood up and pushed her way out of the booth.

"Look, we're going, okay? We're going!"

Her stepfather spun around and lifted his hand to hit her and although all her instincts told her to cower, somehow she managed not to and instead stood her ground, glaring at him. She could smell his cologne and it was so cloying and the memories it stirred so foul that it almost made her gag.

"Don't you dare lay a finger on me."

It was little more than a whisper. But it stopped him or maybe it was all the eyes upon him that did it. Whatever it was, he lowered his hand.

"Get your ass home, you little Indian whore. I'll see to you later."

"The only whores in here are the two you came in with."

He made a lunge for her but she ducked out

of his reach and ran for the door. Over her shoulder she saw that his friend and the waiter had grabbed his arms to stop him coming after her. She burst into the night and started to run.

The air hung hot and humid and she could feel the tears running on her cheeks and it made her almost choke with anger that she should be so weak as to let that bastard make her cry. A freight train was going by and she ran alongside, watching the lights beyond it strobe between the wagons. There were lights on her side of the rails too, strung on a wire above her, each with its own frenzied aura of insects. The train seemed many miles long and from afar, already out of town, she heard the mournful wail of the engine like a verdict on the sorry place through which it had passed. Had it been traveling more slowly she would have climbed on board and let it bear her wherever in the world it was headed.

She ran and ran like she always ran. And it didn't matter where because wherever it was couldn't be worse than where she was and where she had been. She'd run away first when she was five and done it many times since. And it always got her into trouble but, what the hell, what kind of trouble was there that she hadn't seen already?

She ran now until her smoke-seared lungs could take no more, and as she stopped, the train's last wagon went by and she stood slumped with her hands on her knees, gasping and watching its taillights grow smaller and smaller until the night swallowed them as if they never had been. Somewhere way off in the darkness a dog was barking and a man yelled for it to cease but it paid no heed.

"Never mind. You can catch the next one."

The voice startled her. It was male and close at hand. Skye scanned the darkness around her. She was in what appeared to be an abandoned lumberyard. She couldn't see him.

"Over here."

He was sitting on the ground, leaning against a stack of rotting fence posts overgrown with weeds and he looked as if he might almost have melted out of it for his hair was long and tangled and so was his beard. He was a white boy, older than Skye. Eighteen or nineteen maybe and very thin. He was wearing torn jeans and a T-shirt emblazoned with a roaring Chinese dragon. A dust-covered duffel bag lay on the ground beside him. He was rolling a joint.

"Why are you crying?"

"I'm not. What the fuck is it to you anyhow?"

He shrugged. For a while neither of them spoke. Skye turned away as if she had other things to do or think about. She wiped the wet off her cheeks, trying not to let him see. She knew she should probably walk away. All kinds of freaks and psychos hung out down here by the railroad. But something within her, some hapless craving for comfort or company, made her stay. She looked at him again. He licked the cigarette paper and sealed the joint, then lit it and took a long draw. He held it out to her.

"Here."

"I don't do drugs."

"Sure."

THE CAR THEY STOLE belonged to somebody with small kids. There were little seats fitted in the back and the floor was littered with toys and picture books and candy wrappers. The boy knew what he was doing, for it took him only a couple of minutes to pop the door lock and get the engine going. They stopped after a few miles so he could switch the plates with another car.

He said his name was Sean and she told him hers and that was all they knew about each other except for some common hurt or longing that didn't need uttering. Nothing else seemed to matter, not where they were going nor why.

They drove north until they hit the interstate then headed west with a river to one side and the dawn rearing in a widening red scar over the endless plains behind them. Neither of them spoke for a long time and Skye sat turned in her seat looking back and waiting for the sun to show itself and when finally it did it set the land aflame with crimson and purple and gold and flung long shadows from the cottonwoods and rocks and from the black cattle that grazed beside the river and Skye thought it was the most beautiful thing she had ever seen in her whole life.

On the floor she found a picture book that she remembered from elementary school. It was about a little boy called Bernard whose parents always ignore him. One day a monster appears in the backyard and Bernard runs inside to tell them but still they just ignore him. The monster eats him and goes into the house and roars at the parents but they think it's Bernard fooling around and ignore him. And because they're not scared, the monster loses all his confidence. Skye turned to the last page which always used to make her feel sad. The poor old monster has been sent to bed and is sitting all alone and forlorn in the dark, feeling a total failure.

They pulled off the interstate to get gas. There was a diner there that was just opening and they bought coffee and muffins and settled themselves to eat at a table by the window while an old woman mopped the floor around them. While they ate he asked her how old she was and she lied and told him she was seventeen. She said she'd been born in South Dakota and was half Oglala Sioux, on her mother's side, and he said that was cool but she told him that she didn't think it was and anyhow she didn't know anything about that people or their history except that it was full of pain and misery and she already had enough of both to be getting along with, thanks very much.

He told her he came from Detroit and that his parents and his older brother were all in jail though he didn't say for what and Skye didn't ask. When he was fourteen he had taken off and for the last three years had been traveling all over. He said he had been down to Mexico and Nicaragua and Salvador and said he'd seen things he never could have imagined or believed.

"Like what?"

"Magic. Shamans. People walking through fire and not even being marked by it. People dying on account of being cursed. I saw a dead woman brought back to life."

Skye asked him about it but he didn't want to tell her. She asked why he had come to Montana and he said it was because he wanted to meet a grizzly bear in the wild. He said he had learned in Mexico that it was his spirit animal and that he had been a bear in another life. She laughed because this skinny kid was about as unlike a bear as a person could get. A stick insect maybe or a giraffe or something, but a grizzly bear? No way. He looked hurt and went all quiet on her and so she apologized and, finding it hard to keep a straight face, asked him how he planned to go about finding a grizzly. He conceded that it wasn't going to be easy but figured they should head for Glacier Park, which he'd been told was a good place to start looking.

Skye nodded, trying to look serious.

"Right," she said.

"You got a better idea?"

She could think of about a hundred.

"Whatever," she said. "I don't give a shit."

They drove the rest of the day while the sun swung over them, heading like them for the snow-capped mountains that loomed ever larger before them. In the afternoon it got so hot they pulled off the interstate and meandered along narrow roads through a forest humming with insects. They found a creek with a swirling pool and swam naked and unashamed in the cold clear water then lay in a meadow full of wildflowers and dried themselves in the sun while butterflies danced around them. He said she looked pretty and she thought he might want to touch her and half wanted him to but he only stared at the sky and smoked another joint and seemed hardly to know she was there.

By the time they got back on the interstate the western sky was filling with great gray thunderheads among which the sun crazed fitfully, pale and cold and metallic, while lightning flickered from their roiled bellies to the mountain mass below.

She saw the police car before he did. Something made her look back and as she did so the cop turned on his flashing red and blue lights. Sean looked in the rearview mirror and said nothing. He didn't look scared or even worried, just stoned. He slowed and pulled onto the shoulder and the police car behind did the same. The cop sat there awhile, no doubt checking them out on his radio.

"What do we say?"

Sean shrugged.

The cop got out of his car and walked slowly toward them. Sean lowered the window, watching him in the side mirror all the way. As he came alongside, the cop bent so that he could get a look at Skye. He was young, in his mid-twenties maybe, with a neatly trimmed ginger mustache and blue eyes that were wide-set and friendly. He touched his hat and Skye gave him her best smile.

"Howdy. Where you folks headed?"

"Glacier," Sean said, not looking at him.

"Great. On vacation?"

"Yeah."

"This your vehicle?"

"Belongs to a friend."

"Uh-huh. Okay. Well, I'd like to see your driver's license, registration and insurance, please."

Sean turned to reach for his bag. Skye suddenly had a bad feeling that he had a gun in there and that he was going to do something dumb and dreadful. But he seemed to change his mind and turned back to the cop.

"I forgot. All that stuff got stolen."

Something shifted and hardened in the cop's eyes.

"Would you mind stepping out of the vehicle please, sir?"

He straightened up and reached for the door handle and in the same moment Sean gunned the engine. The cop yanked the door open and tried to grab Sean's shoulder but the car was already moving and he lost his balance and fell and in the fall his arm went down behind Sean's seat and twisted and got trapped. He cried out.

"Stop!" Skye shouted. "Stop!"

There was a loud crack and Skye knew from the man's scream that it was the sound of his arm breaking. But Sean either didn't hear or care. He just hit the gas pedal harder so that the tires squealed and smoked and the car snaked its way back onto the highway dragging the cop beside it yelling and shrieking. Skye screamed.

"Are you crazy? Stop the car! For godsake, stop!"

But he didn't. She reached over to try to knock the shift out of drive but he shoved her violently back across the car and her head cracked against the passenger's side window. With his left hand, he was trying to unhitch the cop's arm from behind his seat but it wouldn't come free. The door kept swinging open and slamming shut again on the poor man's arm and when it opened Skye could see his face above the sill. There was a bloody gash all down one side of it and his eyes were glazed with fear.

The car was swerving across the lanes of the highway and Skye became aware of the blast of horns from other vehicles. They were passing a pickup truck and there was a big brown dog standing in the back and the driver was hooting and yelling at them and the dog was barking, trying to keep his balance as the truck lurched away to avoid them.

"You idiot!" Skye shouted.

"Shut up!"

Suddenly there was the tearing sound and

then a loud thud and Skye looked back to see the cop's body bounce and twist and tumble across the road behind them.

"You stupid fucking idiot! What are you *doing*?"

The cop's severed arm was still jammed behind the boy's seat and he wrenched it free and threw it clear and slammed the door. Skye screamed and started to hit him and he struck her hard in the mouth. She felt a tooth break and blood start to flow and that made her want to hit him all the more and with all her strength and anger she lashed at him and tore at his face and hair until finally he punched her so hard she felt something give in her head as if she were being swallowed from inside and she slumped in her seat watching the world twirl away from her in a red benumbing mist.

TWO

THE DAY that Edward Tully met the love of his life began badly. Snow had been falling all week and he had been looking forward to some good weekend skiing. But in the early hours of Friday morning the snow turned to rain and by daybreak (if one could so call such a minimal transition) Boston was knee-deep in gray sludge. As if to make doubly sure, it was raining indoors too. Around midmorning the heating and water for the whole apartment building went off. When Ed went to investigate he found the elevators were out of action, water cascading down the stairwell and the lobby full of wet-legged people yelling at each other.

The building was being remodeled and for the past two months the construction crew had proved daily more adept at upsetting the residents. This morning, it emerged, a carpenter had severed a power cable and a water pipe in one surgical flourish of his power drill. Mr. Solomon, the lugubrious old widower who had the apartment next to Ed's, said an ambulance had just taken the guy away. How badly injured, Mr. Solomon didn't know, but he trusted it was nothing trivial.

Ed had been working most of the night on the second act of his new musical, the one (he allowed himself no doubt on this matter) that was going to make him famous. It was going well though he was increasingly aware of how the construction work was infusing both music and lyrics with a darker, more menacing tone than he had intended. When he squelched in his soaked shoes back into his apartment he found there had been a more literal infusion. The ceiling had sprung a leak directly above the piano. The piano itself, an old upright of uncertain parentage that needed tuning so often it wasn't worth the effort, seemed undamaged. But the stack of music sheets that lay upon it, Ed's entire night's work, was sodden. There was another leak in the closet where he kept his climbing and skiing and fly-fishing gear and he had to clear out the entire contents and pile it on his bed. He sat down in a huff on the couch, right on top of his trendy new Calvin Klein spectacles that he'd gotten only last week and cost a fortune. They were totaled. There was plainly some sort of cosmic conspiracy going on.

Then the mail arrived, returning to him, with thanks, not one but two rejected scripts and demo tapes of his last musical, the one that clearly wasn't going to make him famous. One of the accompanying letters, from a big Broadway producer, penned, no doubt, by a minion, damned him with faint praise then said the work "owed perhaps a tad too much to Sondheim," which sent Ed into a whirlpool of brooding self-criticism for several hours.

Now it was late afternoon and he was sitting at another piano, much grander and sleeker and more tuneful than his own, listening while his least favorite pupil slaughtered an innocuous and none too taxing piece of Chopin. The kid, a deeply unprepossessing ten-year-old who went by the name of Dexter Rothwell Jr. was dressed entirely in black except for his sneakers which were silver and gold and probably cost enough to feed an average family for several weeks.

What Ed found most irritating of all was the baseball cap the boy always wore. It was also black and, of course, worn back-to-front and had DEATH ZONE—CREW MEMBER on it as if written by a hemorrhaging spider. Ed was not by nature a violent person, quite the opposite. But sometimes the urge to remove this cap and with it whack young Dexter Rothwell around the ears was almost overpowering.

Since finishing college three years ago, teaching piano was how Ed made enough money to keep on composing. During the winter his only other source of income was from playing every Friday night in a downtown bar, which despite being paid little money and less attention, he still enjoyed. With his teaching, quite unintentionally, he seemed to have cornered the market in the spoiled offspring of the city's most graceless high-achievers. He had been teaching this particular brat for six months now and not once had the kid smiled or even looked him in the eye.

Ed stared out of the window, trying to detect a trace of Chopin amid the faltering cacophony that filled the Rothwells' manicured drawing room. The January darkness that had barely lifted a corner all day was closing in again and the rain was still coming down. He watched it making rivulets on the waxed finish of Mrs. Rothwell's black Mercedes convertible that basked in the driveway beside Ed's rusting Nissan. The boy's streak-blond, spandex-clad mother was, as usual, working out in the gym across the hallway, wearing one of those headphone radios, presumably to drown the horrors of Dexter Jr. at the keyboard. She was a thin, small-boned woman with a pointed face and whenever he caught a glimpse of her through the doorway, pounding away on the jogging machine, Ed was reminded of a demented mouse trapped in a treadmill.

Dexter Rothwell Jr. finished and slumped back from the keys.

"Chopin sucks," he said.

"You think so? Really?" Ed tried to sound light, amused even.

"Yeah."

"You've obviously been too busy to practice since last week."

The boy grunted and began to pick his nose. They sat for a moment listening to the muted thump-thump-thump of Mrs. Mouse clocking up the miles across the hallway. Ed took off his glasses, the old ones with the Scotch-taped hinge, and gave them a polish. It reminded him that he couldn't afford, literally, to be impulsive here. He took a deep breath and put them back on.

"Okay. What shall we play, then? Want to try some more Led Zeppelin?"

He wasn't kidding. In a desperate effort to engage the boy's interest two weeks ago he'd had him play "Stairway to Heaven" and a couple of Rolling Stones numbers. There had been the faintest flicker of interest.

"That sucks too."

"Wow, they all seem to suck. Chopin, Mozart, Led Zeppelin."

"Yeah, right."

Ed let the silence hang for a moment. The boy was glowering out at the rain, still picking his nose. Ed studied the sullen, slack-jawed profile and made a few rapid calculations about the damage he was about to inflict on his already parlous finances. Well, so be it. He stood up, plucked the music from in front of Dexter's nose and stuffed it into his briefcase. The boy looked up at him.

"What's going on?"

"Nothing, Dexter. And that's the problem."

"We only just started."

"Yep and I'm through. I'm out of here."

He opened the door and came out into the hallway just as the boy's mother emerged from the gym, toweling her face with care so as not to mess up her lipstick. She frowned.

"You two done already?"

"Yes, ma'am. Done and dusted."

He picked up his coat from the chair by the front door. Dexter stood shiftily in the drawing room doorway, shrugging and mugging at his mother as if the world had gone crazy. Mrs. Rothwell looked at her watch.

"But it's only—"

"The thing is, Mrs. Rothwell, you're wasting your money and I'm wasting my time."

"Why? Isn't Dexy making progress?"

Ed looked at the boy. He was standing there, twisting his fists into the belly of his T-shirt and scowling at the floor like a jilted Neanderthal. It was a pathetic sight and for an instant Ed felt an inkling of pity.

"No, ma'am. He isn't. In fact, frankly, Dexy sucks."

THE ELATION LASTED only until he got home. The heating was still off and water was still dripping into the garbage bin that he'd placed where the piano used to be. He showered in cold water, singing to keep himself from freezing and from thinking too much about what a reckless fool he had been to give the Rothwells the bullet. Then he made himself some hot chocolate, microwaved half a pizza left over from last night and ate it huddled in his overcoat in front of the TV news which chronicled nothing but doom and disaster and though his own paled by comparison, his mood remained resolutely grim.

They liked him to show up at the bar at eight even though the place never got crowded until much later, so around seven-thirty he again braved the rain out to his car and set off across town in one long and gloomy crawl of traffic.

The bar was called Ralff's, though who Ralff was and why he spelled his name like that, Ed had never been able to discover. It stood near the waterfront on the fringe of a jauntily revamped area that was thronged with tourists in summer but on a winter's evening such as this seemed like a sad mistake. Apart from Ralff's the only reason for going there was the movie theater just across the street, which was good for business but bad for parking. Tonight, however, Ed was in luck.

Through the smear of his windshield as he came around the corner, he could see a Jeep pulling out of a space right outside the bar. He signaled right and stopped to let it leave. The car behind honked though it must have been obvious why Ed had stopped. He looked in his mirror and saw a beaten-up white VW bug. It honked again.

Ed shook his head. What a moron. The Jeep vacated the space and Ed moved forward so he could reverse into it. He assumed the VW would either pass him or wait for him, but as he shifted into reverse and turned in his seat he saw it nip sharply into his space. He couldn't believe it. There was no way he was going to take that kind of asshole behavior from anyone. He switched on his hazard lights and got out.

Two people were getting out of the VW. The driver was a young woman and as Ed stomped toward her, she flashed him a smile of such dazzling innocence that he thought for a moment she must be looking at someone behind him. He looked briefly over his shoulder to check but there was no one there. The woman was wearing a red ski jacket with the hood turned up over a mass of thick, dark hair. The passenger was a man, taller and broader than Ed, a fact that perhaps should have struck him as relevant but didn't. All Ed noticed, through his rain-streaked glasses, was that the guy was grinning. Which didn't do much to endear him. The rain was now a monsoon.

"Excuse me," Ed said in as level a voice as possible. "That's my space."

The woman looked at her car then looked back at him with that same infuriating butter-wouldn't-melt smile.

"No. It's ours."

She locked the car and zipped up her jacket.

Even with steam coming out of his ears, Ed recognized that he was confronting an extraordinarily good-looking woman. She was olive-skinned, with a wide mouth and perfect teeth. Her eyes were big and dark and flashing now with amusement. And because there was no other likely cause for it but himself, this served only to fuel Ed's rage.

"Listen, you knew darn well what I was doing. I stopped to let the guy out, I signaled, I pulled forward so I could reverse in and you snuck in behind me. You can't do that."

She shrugged. "We can. We did."

"Damn it, you can't!"

He was sounding shrill now and to restore an appropriate posture of manly threat he shot a withering look at the woman's creep of a boyfriend who was still grinning like an ape as he came ambling around the back of the car toward them. Ed could feel the rain soaking though the back and shoulders of his coat. An icy trickle ran down his neck. He could hardly see a thing through his glasses now, but he thought he caught a first faint look of embarrassment on the woman's face. She turned to the ape boyfriend for support.

"Please don't become abusive," the ape said.

"I'm not!"

"You just said 'damn it.' "

"Jesus—"

"Nuh-uh, please."

He held up his hands, palms out, in warning. Then suddenly he smiled and frowned and looked maddeningly sympathetic.

"Hey, man, I'm sorry. But listen, life's a jungle. In a few thousand years the only drivers will be those whose ancestors first learned how to nip into other people's parking spaces. It's called survival of the fittest. It's tough but that's evolution. Now, please excuse us or we'll be late for the movie."

And with another smile, he took the woman's arm and steered her off across the street, leaving Ed standing there, drenched and tongue-tied and totally futile.

"You inconsiderate pair of—"

A car whooshed past, drenching his legs with spray. Another car was honking at him.

"Hey, man, move your car. You're blocking the road here."

"Oh . . . get lost."

Ed trudged back to his car and got in and dried his glasses. He had to cruise the area for twenty minutes to find another place to park and during all that time thoughts of revenge swirled darkly in his head. Eventually, he found a space just a few cars along the street from the woman's

VW and as he walked back past it he had the idea. It would be a perfect reciprocal act.

He went into Ralff's and apologized to Bryan, the manager, for being late. He'd had a bad day, he said. Bryan shrugged and said who hadn't? The place was almost empty so Ed didn't feel too bad. He went quickly behind the bar and by the cash register found a piece of paper and a pen.

"Hey, come on," Bryan called. "Let's have some music!"

"I'll be two minutes."

He scrawled something on the paper then found some wrap and carefully sealed it so the rain wouldn't get to it. He headed for the door, calling to Bryan that he'd be right back.

Outside, the movie theater crowds had disappeared. Apart from the occasional car swooshing by in the rain the street was deserted. Ed went straight to the VW and leaning over the hood carefully disengaged the wipers. They came off easily. He inserted his wrapped note under one of the arms. He stood back with a satisfied smile. Vengeance, he concluded, sticking the wipers into his coat pocket, was a dish best eaten wet. He turned and headed back to the bar.

"In a few thousand years," the note said, "the

only drivers will be those who learned how to steal the wipers of the parking space thieves. It's called survival of the fittest."

DESPITE THE DAMPNESS of his clothes and the miserable day he'd had, he played well that night. Around ten, the place started to fill. One of the tables applauded every number and it caught on with the others. He racked his brain for songs about rain and they went down well. "Stormy Weather" even got calls for an encore. He didn't have a great voice but tonight he seemed to be getting a cold so it sounded deeper and, in his opinion anyway, kind of sexy. Leanne, one of the waitresses on whom he'd always had something of a crush, kept bringing him drinks and, maybe it was just his imagination, but she seemed to be looking at him in a totally different way.

Every time the door opened he was gratified to see that it was still raining. It was pathetic, he knew, but he kept imagining the woman coming back to her car and finding the note and he only wished he could be there to see her face. The movie must have finished by now and he wondered if she might show up and what he'd do if she did. But Ralff's was a drinkers' place, all low lighting and red velvet banquettes, and though all he knew about her was that she stole parking spaces, he imagined she was more the healthy type, yogurt and yoga classes, and probably wouldn't be seen dead in a dump like Ralff's.

But he was wrong.

He had just taken a fifteen-minute break before his last set. He'd gone to the restroom and on the way back been cornered—willingly, enthusiastically cornered—by Leanne, who told him how much she'd enjoyed his playing tonight, especially his new sexy voice. So when he settled back at the piano, Ed was feeling pretty pleased with himself. He sat down and was just taking a drink, when he saw her. It was the red ski jacket he noticed and had he looked a moment later he might not have recognized her, for she was just taking it off. Under it she was wearing a cream-colored sweater. Her boyfriend (who, to be fair, didn't much resemble an ape after all) was ordering drinks and while he was busy doing that she sat upright on her stool, stretching her back and long neck and looking around the room. Ed watched her.

She stretched her neck and dragged her hands back through her hair in a gesture that presumably had some practical purpose, such as untangling it perhaps, and another woman might have made it look like preening. But with her it seemed entirely without vanity. And one of the sexiest things Ed had ever seen.

Suddenly he realized that she was staring right back at him and a slow smile of recognition spread across her face. And, in what he would later call a moment of pure genius, Ed started to play a number from his last (never performed and doubly rejected) musical. It was a smoochy, late-night love song that "owed perhaps a tad too much" to Tom Waits. It was called "Your Place or Mine." The chorus went:

We've finished the whiskey,
Let's finish the wine.
I feel kinda frisky,
Is it your place or mine?

He kept his eyes on her while he sang. Her boyfriend didn't seem to mind. He was enjoying the joke too and when Ed had finished the guy raised his glass in a toast and sent Leanne over with a drink. Ed went on with the set, playing any song he could think of that was vaguely relevant, changing a lyric here and there to make her laugh. He played "We've Gotta Get (You) Out of This Place" and "Somewhere There's a Place for (You)" from *West Side Story*. He felt inspired, empowered. The audience was great, joining in a joke they didn't even understand. He was playing only for her, the woman whose wipers he still had in his coat pocket. So he was more than a little disappointed when he was just halfway through "Lovely Rita, Meter Maid," to see her stand up and start putting on her ski jacket. Then he saw they were coming toward him.

They waited on the far side of the piano until he'd finished. She looked sheepish. Ed finished the song and while the applause rippled around them he nodded at her.

"That was funny," she said. "You're good."

"It's true, I admit it. Thank you."

"Listen, I'm really sorry about what happened. I don't know what came over me. I've never done anything like that before in my life."

"It was my fault," the boyfriend cut in. "I made her do it. It's just, you know, we were late for the movie and, well, anyhow, we're . . . sorry."

Ed nodded without looking at him. He couldn't take his eyes off the woman. God, she was gorgeous. Then he realized they were waiting for him to reply.

"Well, thanks," he said. "I mean, hey, look at it this way. I got a free biology lesson."

His coat was hanging on the back of his chair and he reached into the damp pocket, found the wipers and held them out to her.

"Here."

She frowned.

"You haven't been back to your car yet?"

"No."

"Well, I think you'll find you need these."

She gave him a wry smile and took them. The boyfriend laughed.

"Quits?" Ed said.

She narrowed her eyes at him. "Well, we'll have to see about that."

"I tell you if you didn't have such a big boyfriend, you'd have really been in trouble."

"This is my cousin David."

They were the sweetest words Ed had heard all day. He held out his hand.

"Edward Tully. Pleased to meet you."

David said he was pleased to meet him too. The guy had a handshake like a steam press. Ed turned to the woman with whom he was already in love and offered his hand and she took it in hers.

"Rita," she said.

Ed hesitated, holding onto her hand. It felt cool and delicious. Rita? Was it possible? She laughed.

"Okay, Julia. Julia Bishop."

"Hey, Ed!" Bryan was calling from the bar. "If music be the food of love, get the hell on with it."

"He's such a romantic," Ed said.

She smiled and said sorry again and then they all said goodbye and she and her cousin headed for the door. Ed started to play a John Lennon song he hadn't played in years. But if she knew it, as surely she must have, for it was named for her, Julia showed no sign of recognition. She simply walked out into the night with her cousin and didn't once look back.

Half of what I say is meaningless,
But I say it just to reach you, Julia.

When Ed got to his car half an hour later, still cursing himself that he hadn't had the sense to get her phone number or at least ask where she lived or worked, he found his wipers had been removed and a note tucked under one of the arms. "I learned," it said on one side. Ed turned the note over. On the other side was a phone number.

It had stopped raining.

THREE

IT WAS nigh on noon when the smoke jumpers came. They plummeted in pairs on each pass of the plane, their bodies jolting as the parachutes cracked open and filled and left them floating like medusas in an ocean of sky. Now and then the chutes masked the sun that flared harsh and white and unforgiving behind them, making shadows of their downward drift on the veil of smoke that shrouded the mountainside.

They were a crew of six men and two women and every one of them landed safely in the jump spot, a narrow clearing not forty yards wide. They shed their parachutes and jumpsuits and stowed them, then unpacked their chainsaws and pulaskis and shovels from bags that were dropped separately and soon they were ready to start cutting a fire line.

The peak that watched over them while they worked was called Iron Mountain. Its western shoulder was thickly forested and had no ready access by road. The fire had been spotted by a ranger that morning and, fanned by a strengthening westerly, had already taken out more than a hundred acres. If it continued to head east or switched to the north there was little risk. But to the south and west there were ranches and cabins and if the wind shifted they would be in grave danger, which was why the call had come for the smoke jumpers.

They cut their line along a limestone ridge that ran along its southern flank. The line was a yard wide and half a mile long. They worked in waves, keeping a good ten feet apart, sawyers first, then the swampers to clear the felled trees and branches, then the diggers. They sawed and hacked and scraped and dug until the ground was cleared to the mineral earth so that when the fire arrived it would be starved of fuel. By the time it was done, they were soaked in sweat and their yellow flameproof shirts and green pants were blotched like camouflage with earth and ash and debris.

Now they were resting, each in his or her own space, some squatting, some standing, strung along the ridge like weary infantry. None spoke and but for the rumble of the fire beyond the ridge the only sound was the harsh staccato babble of their shortwave radios.

Last in line, some twenty feet below the others, stood a young man with straw-colored hair that was matted and tangled with sweat. He was tall and lean and his ash-covered face was striped black like an animal's where the sweat had run. Even his pale blue eyes looked somehow feral. He had set his pack and hardhat beside him on a slab of rock and was carefully wiping clean the steel head of his pulaski. When he had it gleaming he leaned the shaft against the pack and took off his fire gloves and laid them on the rock too, then dragged his hands through his hair and wiped his brow and unhitched his canteen.

He was twenty-six years old and his name was Connor Ford and though he was tired and sweaty and dirty and his lungs were sore from the smoke, there was nowhere in the world he would rather have been. It was his first jump of the season. Squatting in the doorway of the DHC-6 Twin Otter a few hours earlier, watching forest and mountain and canyon tilt as if unhinged from the earth fifteen hundred feet below and seeing the blue and white and yellow canopy tops of those who had jumped before him drifting down and away, he had felt something not far short of ecstasy. And then the slap on his left shoulder from the spotter telling him to go and the leap into blue infinity, tucking himself in and counting to five and then the jolt as the chute snapped open and there he was, suspended in that wondrous arc of silence, neither man nor bird but something of sky and flesh and earth combined.

The water in his canteen tasted warm and metallic. It was only the end of May but it felt like high summer and Connor figured the temperature had to be well into the nineties. It had barely rained all year and the air was as dry as tomb dust. If things kept on this way it was going to be one hell of a summer for fires. Back at the base in Missoula, some of the jumpers were already fantasizing about how they were going to spend all the overtime and hazard pay. He'd called Ed in Boston two nights ago and told him to put down a deposit on the new car he'd been promising himself. Ed and that fabulous girlfriend he'd been going on about for months were arriving in Montana the coming weekend. It was the first time ever he'd missed the start of a fire season, which only went to show what a sorry effect a woman could have on a man.

From above him up the slope now he heard Hank Thomas, the incident commander, give the word to move on. Connor took one last swig from his canteen then fastened and stowed it. He was about to shoulder his pack when he heard a strange sound. It was only faint, like a strangled cry, and it seemed to come from over the ridge where the fire was. He looked and for a moment saw nothing. Then, just as he was about to pick up his pack, he saw what at first he took to be a flaming branch rise above the pale spine of rock. It took him several seconds to recognize that it was no branch.

It was a large bull elk, but like no elk Connor had ever laid eyes on. Every hair of its coat had been burned and its skin was charred black. Its great rack of antlers flamed like a torch. The animal scrambled up onto the ridge, dislodging a clatter of falling stone, and just as it found its footing it saw him.

For a long moment the two of them stood quite still, staring at each other. Connor felt like a pagan before some ancient demigod or devil summoned from a world beyond. He felt the sweat chill on his neck.

Slowly, ever so slowly, he reached for the small Leica that he kept in his pocket and at the same time felt the wind around him lift and swirl and he saw the flames on the elk's antlers dance and fan sideways and he heard the fire beyond it bellow as if in some dread conspiring chorus.

The animal was in his viewfinder now and it raised its muzzle proudly as if posing for a portrait and suddenly it occurred to Connor that there was a message here, though what it was and for whom he had no idea. He pressed the button and at the sound of the shutter the elk turned and vanished and Connor stood wondering if it had all been but a trick of his imagination. Distantly he heard a voice calling him.

"Hey, Connor! We got a fire to fight here."

He looked up the ridge. The other jumpers had gathered their gear and were ready to move off. Nearest to him was Jodie Lennox, a tall, red-haired midwesterner who'd been in the same rookie class as Ed and Connor two years earlier.

"Did you see that?" Connor asked quietly.

"See what?"

He paused. It seemed that the message, if that's what it was, had been for him alone. He picked up his pack and swung it over his shoulder.

"See what?"

"Nothing. Let's go."

THAT NIGHT THEY SNATCHED a couple of hours sleep in a sheltered shoulder of the mountain through which the fire had already passed. They worked shifts, checking for hot spots where the fire still smoldered in roots and stumps and crevices. The beams of their headlamps sent shadows jagging on the blackened earth as they made their slow patrol among the barbed wire tangle of charred scrub, scanning the ground like ghouls and scavengers in a war zone. And all the while the fire kept up its muffled roar around the corner of the mountain, telling them it was not yet done.

Connor woke around one o'clock, feeling hungry and cold. Two hours earlier the sky had been choked with orange clouds but while he slept the wind had shifted, carrying the smoke away, and now the universe spread unraveled above him. He pulled his sleeping bag around his shoulders and lay on his back, deciphering the constellations in the way his father had taught him.

He found the Pole Star and traced the spine of the Little Bear. From there it was only a hop to her big sister who Connor always thought looked more like her other names, the Plow or the Big Dipper, but which his father always called the Great Bear. Then in turn he traced her spine to the Northern Crown with her trailing kite and Arcturus at its point burning like a torch. Then he followed the broad river of the Milky Way until he found Scorpius who had stung Orion, the great hunter, which was why you couldn't see him anymore. Another hunter was there instead, Sagittarius, who was half man and half horse and was standing there in the water, getting ready to shoot his bow and arrow while Aquila the eagle flew away in fear downstream.

"The sky's full of stories," his father used to say. "Thousands of them. All you have to do is look up there and read them."

Connor remembered that first lesson when he was only four years old. His father had woken him in the middle of the night and told him to get dressed and to be quiet as a mouse so as not to wake his mother. The two of them walked out under the stars in their stocking feet to the corral where his father's bay mare stood waiting and his father hoisted him up into the saddle and told him to hold on tight to the horn while he swung himself up behind. They rode at a slow walk up through the meadows with the cattle moving away like shadowed ghosts and the cottonwoods along the creek glowing silver in the starlight and stirring not a leaf in the still night air.

His father had to reach around him to hold the reins and Connor felt warm and safe yet full of adventure and could even now, all these years later, almost summon the smell of the man, of leather and hay and cows and sweat and tobacco, in a blend that was all his own. They rode to the crest of the butte where you could look down on the little ranch house and there they left the horse to graze while they lay side by side on their backs and studied the stars with the smell of fresh sage wafting sweet and smoky around them and an owl calling somewhere below in the trees.

Connor was fourteen when his father died, leaving him and his mother greatly in debt. But there wasn't a day since gone by that he hadn't thought of him and felt the loss of him nor a night such as this when he hadn't traced the stars and recalled their stories with the echo of his father's voice to guide him.

The image of the burning elk had haunted him all night. He had fallen asleep thinking of it and now it came to him again, imposing itself upon the stars. It bothered him that the animal's antlers had been so big, for by this time of year it should have shed them and any new growth would be much smaller. Maybe it was just a trick of the light, but still he couldn't stop wondering what the apparition might mean and why he should think it had meaning at all. His father had never had much truck with superstition and Connor himself had never felt the need of it either. The here, the now and the visible seemed sufficient. His mother, on the other hand, was a walking almanac of omens. She said it came from her Irish ancestry and that her parents and grandparents before them had been worse with it than she was.

In her day she had been a minor celebrity on the women's rodeo circuit and before every ride invoked a litany of ritual and incantation to keep bad luck at bay. Even now the sight of a lone magpie sent her into an elaborate mutter of exorcism which involved asking after the creature's health as well as that of its absent partner and offspring. She always burned a sprig of sage the night before Connor left for his summer of firefighting and once he had overheard her quietly reciting some kind of prayer over it. She pretended it wasn't serious, but he knew it was. So it bothered him that he felt the way he did about the elk. Perhaps some ancient Celtic gene had woken in his veins and he would forever, like his mother, be its slave.

The sky was starting to fill again with clouds. They were sliding in like a vault from the west and the nearest were already tinted amber by the fire on the mountain. Connor studied the slow eclipse of the stars. He wondered if the elk had lived and if so what lonely vigil it now kept and where. Then he cussed himself again for allowing it such rampant access to his thoughts.

It was with relief that he heard Hank Thomas starting to wake those who were still asleep.

Connor sat up and rubbed his eyes. He fitted his headlamp and switched it on, then hauled himself out of his sleeping bag and set about organizing his gear.

"How you doing, cowboy?" Hank called.

"Okay. I could handle a steak and a beer."

"I'll get on the radio right away."

Others chimed in with their fantasy orders while they packed their gear. Ice cream, pizza, chocolate milk-shakes.

"So when's that lazy good-for-nothing musician friend of yours going to grace us with his presence?" Hank asked.

"Flies in Saturday."

"I hear he's in love."

"I figure he must be. He's bringing her with him."

"Poor dumb bastard."

"Poor dumb woman," Jodie said. There was a cry of sisterly support from Donna Kiamoto, a "snookie," or second-season jumper, from Wisconsin.

"Is she a firefighter or what?"

"Got enough on her hands fighting Ed off," Donna said.

"No," Connor said. "She's a teacher. She's going to be working on some wilderness program or something. Kids who've gotten in trouble with the law."

"I know it," Hank said. "Out of Helena. They're a good outfit."

Hank's radio squawked into life and everyone hushed to listen. A helicopter was on its way to make a water drop on the flank of the fire nearest to them. Hank reported that he and the crew were moving out to cut another line. Soon they were all packed and ready to hike. Their headlamps angled fitfully while they checked each other over, the beams panning and shafting the charred darkness around them, glinting on their tools and sometimes catching the white of an eye or a flash of teeth in the black of their faces.

"Okay, boys and girls," Hank said. "Unless anyone wants a shower from that helicopter, I suggest we get our backsides out of here. I want to be home for breakfast."

THEY DIDN'T MAKE IT back to Missoula in time for breakfast. Nor for lunch nor supper. Once the fire was dead, it took them three hours to hike out with all the gear to the nearest road where the bus stood waiting and by the time it dropped them back at the base it was just before midnight on Friday. Driving back into town Connor was so tired he almost fell asleep at the wheel of his truck. He collapsed on his bed still wearing his clothes and boots and reeking of fire and slept the dreamless sleep of the dead for twelve hours.

He and Ed were renting the same apartment they'd taken the previous summer. It was on the top floor of a ramshackle pale blue clapboard house on the east side of town, just over the river from the university. It was two bedrooms, a kitchen and a bathroom and even a tourist from another galaxy might have guessed that for the rest of the year it was inhabited by students. The floorboards creaked, the doors didn't shut properly, the plumbing had a mind of its own and the walls were all scarred with Scotch tape and painted in various combinations of deep blue and purple, except for the bathroom which was entirely painted black. When Connor arrived the previous week, the only residents of the monster antique refrigerator had been an onion in its seventh stage of growth and a tub of apricot yogurt with enough green fur on it to upholster a small sofa.

He opened his eyes just past noon and found himself again under the scowling scrutiny of his least favorite rock group. They were on a poster he kept forgetting to take down. He'd never heard of them but they were clearly exponents of some dark and esoteric zone of metal. They were all half naked and pierced in so many peculiar places with rings and chains and studs and bolts that it made you wince even to look at them. They didn't look too happy about it either.

Connor got up and walked to the window. It was another hot and cloudless day but at least there was a breeze ruffling the cottonwoods along the Clark Fork. Through a gap in the flutter of leaves he could see an old man in the shallows teaching a young girl to cast a fly. The sun was bouncing off the water behind them and it looked pretty enough to send Connor off to get his new Nikon. He changed the lens to a 200mm zoom and finished the last few frames on the roll. It reminded him that the roll of film he'd shot with the Leica on the mountain was still in his pocket. Maybe he'd have time to go to the studio and process both rolls before Ed and Julia flew in.

He took off his smoke-scented clothes, showered, shaved and dressed again in some old but clean blue jeans and a white T-shirt. And after he'd made himself some coffee and then cooked a death-defying brunch of ham and eggs and fried potatoes, it was getting on for two o'clock.

Outside the heat was shimmering off the sidewalks. He dropped a bundle of dirty clothes at the Laundromat by the gas station. Mrs. Tyler, the old woman who ran it, had a collie-cross that Connor always made a fuss of and he spent a few minutes hunkered down, stroking the dog's stomach and telling the woman about the fire on Iron Mountain.

"They say it's going to be another big year for fires," she said.

"It's getting pretty dry out there."

"Where's Ed? Isn't he jumping with you all?"

"He gets in later today."

"I thought it'd been a tad too peaceful. You tell him hi from me."

"I'll do that."

He walked along Front Street toward North Higgins, hugging the shade where he could find it. It felt good to be back in Missoula. It was an easygoing place where you could be what you were without others rushing to judge you. Much of the laid-back atmosphere flowed from the university across the river. The town was always full of students, even now, with the summer vacation already under way. And sometimes this made Connor feel like an outsider, reviving in him a twinge, more of regret than of envy, that he'd never gone to college himself.

In recent years the town had become a magnet for those who were tired of city life but weren't yet ready for the log cabin and hauling water from the creek. In Missoula they found the perfect balance. They could be in the mountains in minutes and still have at hand all those truly crucial things in life—like shopping malls, the latest Hollywood movies and a good cappuccino. Living alongside them were the environmentalists: from full-blooded eco-warriors who ate loggers for breakfast to more mild-mannered bunnyhuggers, hippies and assorted hangers-on who, at the drop of a recycled paper hat, would hug almost anything and anyone. Then there were the culture-vultures and counterculture-vultures, musicians, painters, sculptors and writers of every description. Ed, always a fountain of useless but often intriguing information, claimed there were more writers per acre in Missoula than in any other place on the planet.

The darkroom Connor used was tucked among some garages in a backstreet off North Higgins. It was one narrow room with a studio at one end and the darkroom area boxed off at the other. There were drapes along one wall and rolls of different-colored paper that could be lowered to make backgrounds for portraits.

The place belonged to a photographer called Trudy Barratt who worked mostly for *The Missoulian*, the local newspaper. She and Connor had met two summers ago when the paper used some of his forest fire pictures and they'd started an affair that lasted the rest of the summer. It faded in the fall when he went back over the mountains, as he always did, to spend the winter on the ranch. But the two of them had remained friends. Trudy had helped get him commissions and given him a key to the studio so that he could use it whenever he liked.

Connor let himself in and switched on the lights. The air was hot and dank and smelled of chemicals and he left the door open until he'd gotten the air-conditioning going. He took down a set of wedding prints that Trudy had hung up to dry and laid them carefully on the worktop. There was one among them that Connor knew was destined for what she called her "whoops album": pictures her clients wouldn't want to see. In this one the bridegroom was kissing one of the bridesmaids in a way that didn't seem to impress the bride one little bit. It was an image that might prove useful come the divorce.

When everything was ready, Connor shut the door, turned out the main lights and took the two rolls of film from his pocket. He worked carefully, taking his time. He had always enjoyed this part of photography. The womblike intimacy, the aloneness, the ghostly red of the safe light that somehow suspended time.

He had taken pictures ever since he was a

child. His father had given him a used Pentax SLR for his ninth birthday and later helped him rig up a darkroom in a corner of the barn. In those days Connor liked to take pictures of animals and when he was twelve, one he'd taken of a black bear standing on its hind legs in the creek won a competition in a wildlife magazine. In his late teens and early twenties he made a few dollars here and there selling skiing and climbing pictures to one or two magazines who liked his work. But it was smoke jumping that gave him his first big break.

It had happened three years ago, his and Ed's rookie season and as fine a baptism as any jumper ever had. It turned into one of the driest summers on record and forest fires became big news all over the country, especially the ones sweeping through Yellowstone Park. Connor always took a camera with him—nothing special, just a cheap pocket snapper. And one day, almost by accident, he took this breathtaking picture of Ed, alone on a ridge, swinging his pulaski, silhouetted against a wall of flames that must have been two hundred feet tall.

Trudy Barratt put him in touch with a photo agency in New York and the picture was printed on the front page of *The New York Times* and in newspapers and magazines all over the world. It earned Connor more money than he'd ever seen and with it he paid off all the debts that had accumulated on the ranch and still had enough to buy himself some new cameras and lenses. *The Missoulian* ran a feature piece about his success with a picture of him looking absurdly glamorous in his smoke jumping gear, which earned him much ribbing from every other jumper on the base. He even got a couple of fan letters which made Ed jealous as hell. Back in Boston that fall, Ed had the Yellowstone photograph of his silhouette blown up five feet wide and hung it on his wall. He claimed it worked wonders for his love life.

The two of them had met some years earlier when Ed was a freshman at the university in Missoula and Connor was wondering if he was going to be a ranch hand all his life. Every summer, throughout the West, the Forest Service took on casual "pounders" to fight backcountry fires. Pounding was a lot less glamorous than smoke jumping but you had to do it for several seasons before you could even apply to be a jumper. It wasn't everyone's idea of the perfect summer-vacation job. The young men and women whom it attracted came from many different backgrounds. But whether for the rest of the year they were cowhands, students or ski bums, they all had that same itch to find something with a little more adventure than washing dishes or waiting table.

Connor and Ed had found themselves side by side, cutting line on the same crew, and Connor, who already had a season of pounding under his belt, had gone along with the tradition of giving the college-kid rookies a hard time.

In the macho world of firefighting Edward Cavendish Tully was an easy target. He was from a wealthy family in Lexington, Kentucky, and was studying music and, at first, for both these facts, along with his slight southern drawl, the round gold-rimmed spectacles and aristocratic good looks, he was mercilessly teased. But he was as fit and tough as the best of them and took the taunts with such good humor that soon he was liked by the whole crew.

Connor was even more impressed when he found out that since the age of six, Ed had been diabetic and needed to inject himself with insulin before every meal. On top of all this, it turned out that this classical music scholar also played lead guitar in a college band and could do more than passable impressions of anyone from Van Halen to Hendrix. Getting to know him taught Connor the fallacy of judging people by their background or wealth or whatever other label happened to hang around their necks.

It was a classic attraction of opposites: Ed the extrovert intellectual, always ready with a joke or a story or an opinion on anything and Connor the level, laconic one. Connor wasn't a great one for analyzing these things, but he recalled Trudy Barratt once saying that he and Ed each had those traits that the other lacked and aspired to and that if you could forge one person from the two of them, the result would be a really great guy. Connor wondered if that was supposed to be a compliment and concluded that it probably wasn't.

What they undoubtedly did share was a passion for the outdoors. On their days off they would go climbing or fly-fishing or canoeing. The fires they fought that first summer forged a deep and durable friendship. They even invented their own private ritual. It came about when they were cutting line one day and the wind changed and the fire blew up and they suddenly found themselves, just the two of them, surrounded by flame.

"Hey, man!" Ed called. "We're in the heart of the fire!"

And for some weird reason, without any kind of rehearsal, they had both put their clenched right fists to their chests and solemnly declaimed "Hearts of fire!" and then given each other a high-five. It was only a kind of mock macho joke and they laughed about it afterward. But they'd done it ever since before every fire they'd fought.

Connor had other friends, of course, mostly around Augusta and Choteau and a few in Great Falls, kids he'd grown up with and been with at high school. Then there were his climbing and skiing buddies and one or two other firefighters he met up with from time to time. But there wasn't one among them he could call close. As an only child he'd always been something of a loner. His mother used to call him The Watcher. Once, only half joking, she'd said that he was happier looking at life through a camera than actually living it. The truth was, Ed was the only real friend he'd ever had.

After he graduated, Ed had moved back east, to grad school in Boston where he'd stayed ever since. Yet every summer he still somehow managed to come back to Montana and the two of them would spend some months together, fighting fires and having fun. Ed loved to help out on the ranch. It was only a small spread and since Connor's father died, mother and son had had to handle pretty much everything on their own. It was the main reason Connor had never gone to college.

Ed's family raised thoroughbreds and he would tease Connor's mother about the ranch horses, telling her how slow and clunky they were and why didn't she go to Kentucky and get herself something half decent. She would pretend to be cross but it was clear she adored him. She had once even referred to him as her second son. The only thing she had never been able to understand was what possessed him and Connor, two otherwise seemingly sane young men, to make them want to spend their summers putting out fires. Connor could remember the evening when they'd told her over supper that they were going to sign on as smoke jumpers.

"We're going to be Zoolies, Ma."

"What in heck's name is a Zoolie?"

"A Missoula smoke jumper, Mrs. Ford," Ed said. "They're as cool as it gets. Even cooler than being a hotshot."

"Oh, really. And what the heck's a hotshot when it's at home?"

"They're ground firefighters, Mrs. Ford. They're like the marines or something, I guess. Or think they are. Hotshots think they're cool and are always boasting about it. Whereas smoke jumpers really are cool and don't need to."

"There's only four hundred smoke jumpers in the whole country," Connor said.

"There's that many idiots, huh?" she said.

"Let me get this straight. You get to go way up high in a little airplane, you find a fire and then you jump out and land in it. Is that the idea?"

"Ma, they do give you a parachute," Connor said.

"Oh, well. That's okay then. You boys must be out of your minds."

Ed frowned. "Mrs. Ford? I forgot. How many years was it you rode rodeo?"

"That's totally different."

"Yeah," Connor said. "In rodeo you don't get a parachute."

As it turned out, Ed had something of a struggle persuading those in charge of selection at the Missoula base that his diabetes wasn't going to be a problem. But he excelled himself in training and with the help of a compliant doctor (a close family friend who didn't quite lie but didn't quite tell the truth either), managed to persuade them that his condition would in no way interfere with his ability to do the job. By now they were more than glad to have him.

Back in February, Ed had called to tell Connor about this new girlfriend he'd started dating. The guy clearly had it bad. Over the years there had been a number of girlfriends (mostly Ed's) and one or two had even lasted more than one summer. Last year Connor had been heavily involved with a six-foot-tall hockey champ from Seattle by the name of Gloria McGrath whom Ed had nicknamed Darth. When these affairs happened, the two men happily gave each other space. Ed was a congenital romantic, forever falling in love and declaring every time that this, hand on heart, was the one. Nevertheless, listening to him going on and on about her over the phone, Connor had gotten the distinct impression that this Julia woman actually might be the one.

"You remember Natalie Wood in *West Side Story*?"

"No."

"Connor, really, sometimes, man, I despair of you. It's a classic. You must have seen it on TV—you know, that little square thing that stands in the corner of the room?"

"So, she's beautiful."

"Yeah, but you know how some beautiful women know how beautiful they are? Well, Julia doesn't. She's totally natural. And you know what? She likes to climb, she can ski like a dream. She's smart, funny, artistic—"

"Doesn't the halo get in the way?"

"No, the wings do a little but they're kind of sexy. I tell you, man. This is it. I want to have her babies."

"I don't think it works that way around."

It was quite a buildup. Connor was looking forward to meeting her.

Both of the rolls of film that he was processing now were black and white. He often shot color too, especially when he'd been commissioned, but when he was shooting for himself he usually preferred black and white. The shots he'd taken of the old man teaching the girl to cast were a washout. There were one or two others on the contact sheet that were perhaps worth printing but he wasn't going to bother now. He was too interested in the other roll, the one he'd shot on Iron Mountain. In truth he was really interested in only one frame of it.

His heart had beaten a little faster as soon as he held the negative up to the light and saw that it was there. He didn't even look at the other shots. The moment the negative was dry enough he had gone straight for a ten-by-eight print. It was in the tray now and as he rocked it, letting the developer swill slowly to and fro across the paper, he could see the elk starting to appear, as if through a haze of smoke, just as it had on the mountain.

In that fraction of a moment when he had taken the picture, the animal had lifted its head and turned it to a three-quarter profile and in so doing had sent the flames leaping from its antlers in a furious jagged swirl.

But it wasn't this, nor the ripple of flames along its charred black back, that made Connor shiver again. It was the look in the animal's eye. There was a rim of white along its lower lid and the message it conveyed was not of fear itself but rather of some fearful admonition.

FOUR

ONE OF the many things that she admired about Ed—and perhaps the only thing she envied—was the effortless way he fell asleep. No matter where he was, no matter how much noise or motion or fully-fledged chaos was going on around him, he could just close his eyes and rest his head and before you could count to twenty he was away. On this occasion, the resting place was Julia's shoulder. He had taken off his glasses, kissed her neck and nestled there shortly after the flight attendant took away their barely touched meal trays and even though she was now finding it a little uncomfortable, she didn't want to wake him. She liked the feel of his breath on her neck, rhythmic and warm and shallow as a child's.

Ed had insisted she take the window seat so she would have the better view of Montana when they flew over. They were on the north side of the plane and for the past hour she had been watching its shadow glide across mile after mile of dun-colored prairie and across badlands riven with the ragged scars of waterless creeks.

It was more than four months now since Ed had called to claim his wipers. And although she would happily have consigned the whole saga of theft, reprisal and counter-reprisal to deepest history, never to be mentioned again (for she was still mortified over what she'd done), the story of how they met had already become legendary. Ed had told all of his friends about it and all of hers too—at least, all those she'd allowed him to meet. And during the telling, if she was present, Julia would dutifully grin and hang her head in comic yet heartfelt shame.

If she was shocked at herself for stealing Ed's parking space, she was almost equally shocked at how quickly the two of them had become what her mother, with a somehow disparaging tone, called "an item." Since breaking off her engagement to Michael the previous spring, Julia hadn't dated anyone and was enjoying a life free from any whiff of romantic complication. She had devoted herself to her work at the institute, gotten many early nights, read more novels than she had in years, even done some painting. If she went out, it was only ever with girlfriends.

And on the sole occasion she'd broken that rule and gone to see that godawful movie with her cousin, wham-bang, there she was, back in the tangled land of love.

Her mother had doted on Michael. He was at Harvard Law School and was pure WASP—handsome, blond and brilliant, with a smile that came straight out of one of those magazines you found in dentists' waiting rooms. Crucially, from Julia's mother's point of view at any rate, he was also seriously rich, or one day would be, when his inheritance came through. It was an inheritance which, like those of most noble families, had murky origins and as far as Julia could establish, without being unduly nosy, had something to do with diverting rivers and chopping down millions of trees.

If not dazzled by all this, Julia had, for a while at least, been sufficiently distracted so as not to notice another of Michael's attributes. He was boring. Not just a little boring, now and again, the way that most men were and for which, by and large, one forgave them, but boring on a colossal, stratospheric scale.

Her best friend and roommate, Linda Rosner, not known for her mincing of words, had pointed this out the very first time she laid eyes on Michael and broke open the champagne when Julia broke off the engagement. The whole experience probably accounted for why the next man in Julia's life should turn out to be a passionate musician from the South who in his spare time liked to parachute onto forest fires. Life with Ed, of course, brought the ancillary risk of terminal exhaustion, serious injury and even violent death. But not, she could already attest, of boredom. He could be a little moody sometimes and, occasionally, make some clever quip without realizing it was hurtful. But he had a heart the size of a pumpkin and, most important of all, he made her laugh.

Until the night they met, the only time she'd ever been serenaded was by one of those balding fiddle-players who hovered in suspect Italian restaurants. Michael had paid him right away just to get rid of him. The effect of Ed playing those songs just for her, even though there had been a good deal of irony involved, had been devastating. She was an instant pushover. Well, almost instant. They had gone to bed on their third date, though had he asked—and had Linda not been sitting there all eyes and ears pretending to read the newspaper—Julia would have happily succumbed when he showed up for his wipers.

Like Julia, Linda was a New Yorker, born and

bred, though from a much wealthier family. She rolled her own cigarettes using licorice paper and smoked more than she ate. She was never more than a size eight and only five feet one but a little went a long way. They had met at art college where Linda was a founding member of the Neo-Gothic Radicals, a concept which Julia had never quite grasped but which seemed to involve wearing a lot of black lipstick and dressing up like a distant cousin of the Addams family. After two years as a struggling artist, during which time anything remotely associated with making money was considered "moronic capitalist shit," she had decided that if she couldn't beat them then she might as well join them. She'd dumped the weird clothes and black lipstick and gone to law school. The plan was to land a job on Wall Street and buy a black BMW instead.

The moment Ed stepped into the apartment that night, Julia knew he had Linda's seal of approval. They opened a bottle of wine and then another and sat talking until two in the morning. Ed spent a long time looking at some of Julia's recent paintings that were stacked against the wall. They were the result of a two-month trip to Kenya that she had made the previous summer. She had fallen in love with the elemental space and imagery of Africa, but although she'd taken a stack of photographs, when she got home she found that she couldn't recapture the spirit of the place on canvas. She felt her paintings were clichéd. But Ed kept saying how great they were and singled out as his favorite the only one she liked, a huge close-up of a zebra, its coat so magnified that the picture looked almost like an abstract.

He had them both helpless with laughter about the flood at his apartment and with his impersonation of the appalling Dexter Rothwell Jr. And when he told them that as well as being a musician and composer he was also a smoke jumper Julia thought Linda was going to swoon. When he left, the two of them stood dazed and grinning at each other like a pair of schoolgirls.

"Well," Linda said. "There you go. A poet-warrior."

"What do you think?"

"What do I *think*? Babe, if you don't stake a claim pretty damn quick, I will."

Now, four months later, Ed and Julia were still at that stage where it was hard to keep their hands off each other and the idea of being apart for the summer didn't appeal to either of them. Ed had therefore suggested that she should try to fix a vacation job in Montana. It took no more than a phone call.

When Julia was at art college she used to spend June to September working in Colorado with an organization called WAY, Wilderness and Youth. The kids who went there were young offenders, sent by the courts as a last chance. In groups of up to a dozen at a time they were taken out into the backcountry for two whole months. They were given a pair of hiking boots, a sleeping bag, a waterproof poncho and a tarpaulin and that was all. With the support and supervision of four field staff—of which Julia was one—they had to learn how to survive in the wild.

Until then Julia had always assumed that she was going to try to make a living as a painter. But what she witnessed during those three summers, the stunning transformation of some of those kids from apparent no-hopers into confident, social young adults, had such a profound effect on her that she changed her mind. She went on to get a master's degree in educational psychology and ever since had been working as an art therapist at a school in Boston for children with special needs.

Two years ago WAY had started a second center, in Helena, Montana. And in one simple phone call Julia managed to get herself hired for the summer. WAY's Colorado field director, Glen Nielsen, had moved up there to run it. He and Julia had been good friends and, had it not been for Michael back in Boston, they might have been more. When she called him, he said he was thrilled to have her back and that, if she wanted, he could even fix her up with an apartment in Helena to share with two other women on the staff. When she told Ed that she thought this was a good idea, he looked hurt. He wanted her to live with him in Missoula.

"Listen," she said. "You and Connor have got this boys' thing going there."

"Boys' thing? Connor wouldn't mind you living there. He's cool."

"I'm sure he is. He sounds like a great guy. But I really think it's better if I have my own place. Hey, don't go all mopey on me. You said Helena's only a couple of hours away."

In the end, however, she relented, though how much they were going to be seeing of each other she didn't know. The WAY staff rotated in shifts. You did eight days with your group and then another team of staff came out and took over while you took a six-day break. Ed would get either Fridays and Saturdays off or Sundays and Mondays.

She felt his head stir now on her shoulder.

"Are we there yet?" he said like a drowsy child.

"We're on our way home. You slept the whole summer."

"You smell so good."

"I'm glad. My whole left side is paralyzed. Your head weighs a ton."

"I can't help it. It's all those brains."

He kissed her cheek then put on his glasses and leaned over her to look out the window.

"We're somewhere over the Dakotas," he said. "In a few minutes we'll be over Montana. Must be why I woke up. I'm not kidding. It always happens. I wake up just as we fly over Montana. I get this, kind of, vibe or something."

"Oh, yeah?"

"I promise you. I once met this woman who was into astrology and reincarnation and all that stuff and I told her about this and she said it was because in a previous life I'd been a native Montanan."

"What, a cowboy?"

"A Blackfeet Indian. Apparently I played the drums."

"What was your name?"

"I forget."

"You're lying. Come on, what?"

Ed sighed. "Bear With No Teeth."

Julia laughed loudly. “Bear With No Teeth!”

“Go on, mock. I don’t care. It’s only my previous life we’re talking about here.”

“Why with no teeth?”

“How do I know? Maybe I sucked as a drummer.”

“What else did she say?”

“That was it. She got angry when I asked who was on lead guitar and wouldn’t tell me any more.”

They passed the rest of the trip watching the plains below give way to a land of buttes like the backs of great whales and pine-clad ridges and broad river valleys. Ed was her guide, naming the places they passed. The mountain ranges of the Rosebud and the Bighorn and the Pryor and farther to the north the sprawl of Billings and a curve of the Yellowstone River flowing the other way. He made her lean close to the window so that she could see the eastern walls of the Rockies ahead, getting larger and larger, the remnant snow on their highest peaks glowing pink in the late sunshine. And in no time at all those same peaks were dwarfed below them and they were crossing the continental divide and swinging in a slow curve along the western side, with the forest skidding by thick and many shades of green and broken only by lakes that flashed the sky back at them. And then at last the slow descent toward Missoula, with the forest softening into valley and pasture and they could see ranches and houses and horses and cattle and cars and people going about their business. And Ed said that it always felt as if he'd never been away and that the sight of this land opened something within him, a yearning space that was about to be filled.

Julia stroked his hair.

"My little Bear With No Teeth."

When they stepped out of the plane the air was laced with the smell of kerosene and sunbaked asphalt. Even so, Ed filled his lungs with it as if it were the sweetest he'd ever breathed. He put his arm around her and they walked toward the arrivals gate.

"There he is."

Ed waved and through the glass of the arrivals lounge Julia saw a tall young man with long blond hair waving a cowboy hat at them. The crowd of passengers moved slowly. There was an old man being pushed in a wheelchair ahead of them so it took a long time to get to the gate. Beyond it Connor had put his hat back on and was standing there smiling and calmly waiting. At last they reached him.

"Excuse me," Ed said. "Is this the way to the fire?"

"Too late, man. We already put 'em all out."

Connor took off his hat again and Ed opened his arms and they gave each other one of those funny man-to-man hugs that always seemed to involve slapping each other's backs.

"Hey, old buddy," Ed said. "How's it going?"

"Good. Better for seeing you. Hey, new glasses."

"Yeah. Julia says they make me look sexy."

"Well, maybe she needs some too." He turned to her. "So, seeing as ol' sexy-specs here never introduces anyone to anyone, I guess you must be the famous Julia." He held out his hand. "I've heard a lot about you."

"Likewise."

"Welcome to Montana."

"Thank you."

His hand was hard and calloused and he was fixing her with his pale blue eyes in such a direct and steady way that it made her feel almost shy, as if he could somehow see inside her head.

"And I already found a space for my truck out there, so I figure I'm safe."

Julia gave Ed a withering look. "Will I ever, ever live that down?"

Ed looked at Connor and they both considered this and shook their heads gravely and said together that they thought it unlikely. Connor grinned.

"Julia, I'm sorry. I'll never mention it again."

"You promise?"

"I promise. Come on. Let's go get your wipers, I'm sorry, your bags."

On the way to the baggage hall and while they waited by the carousel, Ed bombarded Connor with questions. He wanted to know who was jumping this summer, what fires they'd fought so far and where, what the weather had been like, what the forecasters were saying and so on. Connor answered patiently, directing his answers not just to Ed, but to Julia as well.

After all that she had heard about him, it was interesting to meet him at last. Watching the two of them and listening to the way they talked, she could understand why Ed considered Connor his best friend. There was a stillness to him, a reserve that complemented Ed's exuberance. Once while he was talking, Connor caught her staring at him and he simply smiled and she smiled back.

Their bags arrived and Ed took a quick look inside his guitar case to make sure there was no damage and then they wheeled everything on a cart out to the parking lot. Connor's truck was an old pale blue Chevy pickup which Julia declared a perfect match for his battered, sweat-stained hat. He told her the hat was entirely for

Ed's benefit and that normally, like all smoke jumpers, he dressed a lot more formally in a business suit and necktie.

"And, of course, you wear that when you're parachuting in," she said.

"No, that's when we wear the fireproof tuxedo. You never know who you might meet."

They dumped the bags in the back of the truck and climbed into the cab, where they sat three abreast with Julia in the middle. On the way into town Connor asked about her job with WAY and she told him what she knew about it from her time in Colorado. He asked her when she was due to start and she said they were expecting her in Helena first thing Monday morning. Connor thought for a while then said that if they had no other plans, they could maybe all drive over to the ranch Sunday afternoon and visit with his mother.

"Maybe I shouldn't tell you, Julia, but my ma's always had a thing going for Ed here."

"It's entirely mutual," Ed said. "I admit it. How could I not be in love with a woman who knows by heart every song in *Oklahoma!*?"

"Pretty darned easily, I'd have thought," Connor said. "So, Julia, I guess that means you must know 'em all?"

"What's Oklahoma?"

Ed groaned and put his head in his hands and Connor and Julia laughed.

They ate that night at a little upstairs diner just across the river and afterward strolled back over the bridge. It was getting dark and the giant white letter M on the hillside above the town glowed as if tethered afloat in the ink of the sky. There was a small park below the bridge where some sort of informal concert was going on. There were lanterns down there and a small crowd of people sitting on the grass and the wafting sound of guitars made Julia feel warm and dreamy and she slipped her arm inside Ed's and leaned her head on his shoulder as they walked.

When they got back to the apartment, Connor made some coffee and they sat around the kitchen table talking for a while. Ed asked how the photography was going and Connor said he'd had a couple of commissions lately but on the whole things were quiet. He went across the room and came back with a large brown envelope, pulling a picture from it which he said he'd printed only that afternoon. He handed it first to Ed, who was sitting across the table from Julia, so only he could see it. His eyes widened.

"Wow. What on earth is that? Is it an elk?"

"Yeah. He just stepped out of the fire."

"What happened next?"

"I don't know. One moment he was there and the next he was gone."

"Connor, man, that's one hell of a picture."

Ed handed it to Julia. It took her a moment to focus and when she saw what it was she took a sudden sharp breath.

"It's terrible."

Ed laughed. "So much for compliments."

But Connor wasn't laughing. He was staring hard at her as if he knew exactly what she meant. She shook her head and handed him the picture.

"I'm sorry, but I can't look at that."

Connor took it from her without a word. He slid it into its envelope and took it back where he'd found it. Ed made a joke about Julia being a tough critic of his music too but she was too shocked by what she'd seen to catch it. She stood up. Ed looked suddenly worried.

"Julia? Are you okay?"

"I'm sorry, I'm just so tired. I'll leave you guys to it."

She kissed Ed on the top of his head. He said he wouldn't be long.

"Goodnight, Connor."

" 'Night, Julia."

She brushed her teeth in the black bathroom, which Ed called "the suicide cell," then went to their bedroom and undressed. Connor had given them the bigger room and thoughtfully pushed the two single beds together. There was a wooden rocking chair, a bedside table and a lamp with a frayed purple shade and in the corner stood a big old closet with one handle missing. There were dust-rimmed rectangles on the walls where pictures or posters used to be. Bugs were clattering against the screen of the open window and a few of the more enterprising had found a small tear in one corner and were doing demented loop-the-loops above the lamp.

She got into bed and opened her book. She was reading *Anna Karenina* for the third time and was more moved by it than ever. But now she found herself reading the same paragraph over and over again and soon she gave up and switched off the light. She could hear the rustle of the river outside and the muted voices of the men in the next room and although she knew it was warm, she pulled the covers up over her shoulders against the chill she still felt within her since seeing Connor's photograph. She couldn't get the image out of her head. Ed had called it "one hell of a picture" without realizing that was literally what it was. But Connor had understood.

She must have dozed off, for the next thing she knew, Ed was lying naked behind her, kissing the back of her neck. He wanted to make love and when she murmured that she was too tired he acted all hurt, saying it was going to be days, maybe even weeks, before they might see each other again. So she turned and let him stroke her and soon the image that had so troubled her melted and was gone. But in the soft collusion of their limbs there was that night, for the first time, a trace of sadness.

FIVE

THE EAGLE rose in languid circles on the thermal, its shadow sliding across the canyon wall that glowed like baked ochre in the afternoon sun. In places the rock face was stained darker with patches of rust where winter water had run and parched tufts of scrub sprouted from its cracks and ledges like hair from an old man's ears. Slowly now, as the sun lowered itself behind the canyon's other wall, this tableau of color was being swallowed in a rising tide of shadow. Every so often the eagle called and the sound wafted away down the canyon in an echoing lament.

What, if anything, the bird made of the straggled band of beings many hundred feet below was impossible to tell, but the woe of its cry was never more apt. They came trudging along a trail that wound beside the bed of a dried-up creek. Their heads were bowed, their shoulders slumped, their faces caked with dirt and sweat. The trail was steep and their progress painful and slow and the dust they kicked rose in clouds around their knees. They were like pilgrims who had lost both their way and their faith or forlorn refugees from some distant atrocity, stripped of all but grief and self-pity. Which was what, in varying degrees, all but four of them were.

They were passing through a tangle of dead pines that had been ripped from their roots by the torrent of snowmelt that had raged down the canyon in early spring. And here they halted while one of their number stumbled away from the trail and hid herself behind a clump of willow scrub.

"Let's hear the call, Skye!"

There was a pause. The eagle called instead. One of the boys sniggered.

"Come on, Skye. You've gotta call your number!"

Behind the screen of scrub, Skye McReedie, half-breed, cop killer and all-around no-hoper, squatted with her teeth clenched and her pants hitched around her knees, peeing into the dust. She was damned if she'd play their dumbass kids' games.

"Skye, if you don't call it, we'll have to come looking."

Skye closed her eyes to contain her anger. It was so humiliating. You couldn't even take a piss without them being on top of you. That stuck-up little missy-prissy Julia, the so-called "senior staff," the one yelling at her right now, was the worst of all. She was always so goddamn nice. Skye had been trying hard to get a rise out of her, to make her lose her cool for a moment, but so far no luck. You'd think, being a woman, the bitch would understand how tough it was for her. There were ten kids on this fucking chain gang and Skye was the only girl.

"Okay, sorry, Skye, but I'm coming in there!"

"Fuck you," Skye muttered. "Seven!" she shouted.

"Thanks, Skye. Keep it going."

Skye angrily hauled up her pants and fastened them.

"Keep calling it, Skye."

"Seven! Seven! Seven! Seven!"

She stomped out from behind the bushes and kept shouting her number all the way back to the others, until she was standing right in front of Julia and shouting it a foot away from her nose.

"Seven! Seven! Seven! Okay? Is that okay now?"

"Yes, Skye. That's fine. Thank you."

Mitch, the self-appointed bigmouth of the

group, made some smart remark about how pissed Skye was and she wheeled around and told him to shut the fuck up or she'd kick his fucking face in.

"Okay, okay, everybody," Julia said, raising her hands. "Let's circle up, right now."

There were groans, but the other staff—Scott, Katie and Laura—started marshaling everyone and soon, for the umpteenth time that day, they were all standing in a circle looking at each other in silence. Skye just stared at the ground.

"Okay," Julia said calmly. "We all know by now what happens when someone uses abusive or inappropriate language. So, Skye, when you're ready, we'd like to hear twenty alternatives to what you just said."

"What? I just said my number. What do you want? Six? Five? What?"

"No, you said the F word twice to Mitch and threatened him with violence."

"Like, oh my, I was *so* scared," Mitch said.

"And we'll have twenty alternatives from Mitch when Skye's done."

Mitch gawped with offended innocence and there was a ripple of laughter. At seventeen he was the oldest in the group. He was tall and dark and muscular and knew exactly how smart and good-looking he was. Skye couldn't stand him. They all fell silent again. Everyone was staring at Skye and she was still staring at the ground. They waited a long time and as far as she was concerned they could wait forever.

"Well, Skye," Julia said. "You know, there are no deadlines here. We haven't got a plane to catch or anything. We've got all the time in the world, so all we're going to be late for is getting supper."

Skye sighed and threw her head back. She didn't want to make eye contact with anyone. That goddamn eagle was still flying around up there, squawking away like an idiot.

"Okay," she said at last. "Like, I could have said: 'Oh please, dear Mitch, please don't make jokes about poor little me.' "

"Good. That's one. Let's try and steer clear of sarcasm, though."

"Or. I could have said, you know, it's kind of hard if you're the only female on this gig, taking a leak in front of all these . . . boys. It's, like, totally embarrassing, okay?"

"Yes, I think we all understand that. Good, that's two."

It took another half hour for her to come up with the other eighteen. And then almost as long again for Mitch to do his twenty. And at last, after they'd all taken a drink from their water bottles and several more had been into the bushes to pee, hollering their allotted numbers like a stuck stereo, they shouldered their packs and set off again up the trail.

When the judge had told her he was going to send her on this program Skye hadn't had any idea what it might involve. All she knew was that it sure sounded better than being sent to jail like that maniac Sean. And for the first month it had been a breeze.

They'd lived in a disused barracks just outside Helena and although it was a pain being the only girl in the group and you had to get up at the crack of dawn and do all kinds of dumb things like jogging twice a day and doing P.T. and hoisting the flag every morning, the rest of the time all you had to do was sit around and be "evaluated," which meant answering the same boring questions she had been asked a million times before by probation officers and case managers and social workers and so many different kinds of shrink she'd lost count. Sometimes she just made things up to confuse them or to fool them into thinking they were onto something, but mostly she just trotted out the same old answers. About her home, her childhood, her parents and, of course, her feelings.

They always wanted to know how you *felt* about everyone and everything and they asked you so goddamn often it made you want to scream. It was like it was the only thing they'd ever been taught at shrink school or wherever it was they sent these jerks. "And how did that make you *feel*, Skye?" Like, when you'd just told them how you had to listen every night while your stepfather came home drunk and beat and raped your mom and then came looking for you. "And how did that make you *FEEL*?" "Oh, terrific, I just loved it, you know?" And they always asked it with that same look of care and concern, like they really, really understood how it must have been, like they shared the pain, like it had happened to them too, which was of course total bullshit because they were all a bunch of spoon-fed do-gooders and not one of them had lived in the real world or had the faintest fucking clue what it was like.

After a month at the barracks, suddenly, one night last week, they were given this big spaghetti meal, handed a sleeping bag and a few other things, bundled onto a bus and, four hours later, dumped in the middle of nowhere. On the journey Skye had tried to work out where they were heading but it was too dark. For two days, with barely a bite to eat, they had hiked thirty miles through the mountains which Skye figured was supposed to shock them or break them or something and because of that she just kept her head down and did it. Sometimes her lungs felt like they were going to explode and her feet got all bruised and blistered and hurt like hell but she was damned if she was going to show it.

On the third night they arrived at a clearing and there was Glen, the program director, to meet them and some other staff, all smiling and joking and slapping everyone on the back and saying how well they'd all done. The staff had buried some cans of peaches in a circle and the whole group had to find them, like it was a game you'd really want to play when you'd been busting your ass hiking for forty-eight hours. The peaches sure tasted good though.

Ever since, the food had been boring as hell, granola and nuts and raisins and oatmeal and rice, that kind of healthy shit. On that first evening, as they sat around the campfire, Glen told them that they were going to have to learn how to make fires with a bow drill, like Indians did (only he said Native Americans like people did nowadays so as not to cause offense or to try and make you feel proud or something). Glen looked like some old hippie. He had long blond hair tied back in a ponytail and this wispy beard that he kept stroking and a gentle voice that went up at the end of each sentence as if everything he said was a question. When he mentioned this bow-drill thing, he looked at Skye as if, being half Indian, she might already know how to light fires this way. Yeah, right. As if.

All of the group, he went on, would have to master the bow-drill technique. Each night it would be somebody's turn to make the fire and if he or she couldn't do it, then that night no one would get hot food. Which was fine for him because the next morning he got in his truck and went home, leaving Julia in charge.

They all had to make their own little bow-drill set after combing the forest for the right bits of dead wood and in the five days that had since passed, all but two of the group had learned how to use them. The only two who hadn't were Skye and a kid from Billings called Lester whose head was so cooked from all the crack he'd done, he'd probably have had trouble lighting a pool of gasoline with a blowtorch. Skye figured she could make a bow-drill fire easily enough, but she was damned if she was going to try. Last night it had been her turn and everyone had to eat cold food. She wasn't popular, but who gave a shit?

The hiking since that first forced march had been easier. They'd done maybe ten miles a day but with lots of stops to form circles whenever anyone cussed or did something wrong. No one told them where they were or where they were headed and whenever anyone asked, Julia just smiled that annoying, cute little smile of hers and said it was the journey that mattered, not the destination. Which was about as dumb a remark as Skye had ever heard, because who in their right mind doesn't care where they're going?

Skye was one of Julia's "primaries," which meant they were supposed to have, like, this special relationship. Skye was supposed to go to her for help, cry on her shoulder and confide her innermost secrets. Yeah, right. Julia was walking behind her now as they made their way up the canyon. In front was Byron, a boy from Great Falls who'd stabbed someone in a robbery.

He had straggly red hair and a tattoo of a tiger on his left shoulder which was supposed to look scary but somehow only looked sad. Skye couldn't stop staring at it. Beneath the layer of smeared dirt, Byron's skin was as pale as an albino's. There was a ring of pink at the back of his neck where the sunblock had been rubbed off by his pack. Skye liked him. He tried to act tough like the others but, just as you could see his pale baby skin under the grime, you sometimes got a glimpse of the sweet kid he really was. He was the only boy in the group who was at all friendly toward her. The others spoke to her only when they had to, except Mitch, who never missed a chance to taunt her, mostly when the staff couldn't hear.

The light in the canyon was fading, as if it were being siphoned out by the pale salmon sky. For half a mile the trail grew steep and treacherous with rocks that slipped beneath their boots to roll and clatter through the dry brush below. Then, as they rounded a ridge, the land fell away before them and opened into a meadow with a lake at its center. Far beyond it, the mountains they had glimpsed throughout the day were still catching the last rays of the sun and their reflection shone pink and unruffled on the surface of the lake. As if on some tacit command, the group stopped and stood in silence, gathering their breath and taking in the view. Skye was beside Byron.

"Cool place, huh?" said Byron.

Skye nodded but said nothing. She knew it was beautiful and knew that if she weren't such a freak she should be moved by it, as Byron was. But she felt nothing. It was as if the processes of knowing and feeling had uncoupled within her and a skin grown between them. She was aware that Julia had come to stand beside her.

"Is this where we camp?" Byron asked.

"That's right," Julia said.

"Cool."

"Pretty enough for you, Skye?"

Skye shrugged and fiddled with the strap of her pack though it didn't need fixing. "Why should I care?"

THEY SAT IN A CIRCLE around the fire warming their bare or stocking feet against the flames that rose tall and untroubled into the windless night. The firelight set their faces aglow and flashed in their eyes as they talked and laughed. Across the lake a horned moon slowly hoisted itself above the trees.

This was Lester's fire, started with his own bow and drill without help. And the pride he felt was plain for all to see. He sat straight, with his head held high and a permanent lopsided smile. Julia watched him across the fire and the sight of him made her feel warm inside. It was what she had always loved most about this job, seeing the self-confidence of these damaged young souls being built brick by brick with such modest acts of achievement.

Lester was fifteen years old and, with both parents shuttling in and out of jail, most of those years had been spent in institutions of one kind or another. Julia had read his case notes. How he'd stolen and wrecked his first car at the age of ten, how he'd started doing drugs then tumbled rapidly and predictably into a spiral of theft and fraud to fund his habit. Two years ago he had overdosed and spent three days in a coma that had left him permanently damaged. He slurred a little when he spoke and sometimes his mind seemed to crash like a computer while he was doing some simple task, like tying a shoelace, and he would stay frozen until someone came to help. There was a naive sweetness to him, though when roused, his temper could be wild and both these traits made him a target for teasing. Mitch, predictably, was the expert. He did it so subtly that Julia sometimes wasn't aware of it until Lester exploded. But tonight you would never have guessed any of this. Lester Whaley had made fire using just a few bits of wood, and he sat basking in his own reflected glory, beaming at the world, the undisputed King of the Bow Drill.

He was sitting between Mitch and Katie, a bouncy and slightly irritating P.E. student from Billings. She was the least experienced of all the staff but talked more than any of them. She was telling everyone about the night last summer in Yellowstone Park when a group she was with hadn't hung the bear bags high enough in the trees.

"One of the kids on this group was really big, you know, two twenty pounds, more maybe.

His name was Brett and he was always hungry and forever moaning on about how there was never enough to eat. Anyway, in the middle of the night, I wake up and see there's someone over by the bear bags, so I think, uh-huh, it's Brett having a midnight feast. So I get up real quietly and tiptoe over and I'm, like, just a few yards away and about to say 'Okay, buddy, you're busted,' when he makes this grunting noise and turns around and it's this ginormous grizzly bear, like three times Brett's size."

"So what did you do?" Byron asked.

"Well, I just got him in an armlock, wrestled him to the ground and gave him a good talking-to."

"You did not!" Lester said.

Mitch gave a mocking laugh and was about to make some smart remark until he caught the look Julia shot at him.

"No, I'm just kidding. I yelled. The bear was more scared than I was and took off. He'd trashed the whole bag but it was weird, all he ate was a tube of toothpaste."

All of them laughed. All except Skye. She was sitting between Byron and Scott and was staring into the fire as if she wished it would consume her. Scott was a philosophy major from Denver and had done three seasons with WAY in Colorado. He had a wise and gentle manner that the kids related to. During supper he had been quietly trying to engage Skye in the conversation. But she was having none of it. In the glow she looked so sad and beautiful that Julia had to fight an urge to get up and go over and hug her. Normally she wore her long black hair in a ponytail but tonight it hung loose and shone in the firelight as did her big black eyes. Since Lester succeeded in making his fire she hadn't spoken. When it happened, amid the whooping and cheering, Julia had looked around and seen on Skye's face the realization that she was on her own now: the only obstacle between the group and a hot meal every night.

Tonight's meal had now been cleared away and it was time for "group," the nightly huddle around the campfire. Sometimes they went straight into discussing the day or an issue that was bugging someone. And sometimes one of them, student or staff, would get things going with a story. Tonight Julia told one about two friends called Joe and Mo who went into a diner and ordered steaks.

"And so the waitress goes into the kitchen and after a while out she comes with the steaks and she gives them each an empty plate and then puts the dish with the steaks on it between them, in the middle of the table and off she goes. So Joe and Mo, who are both really, really hungry, sit there looking at the steaks and they see that one of the steaks is big and the other is small. So, Joe thinks, ah-ha, I know what to do. And he picks up the dish with the steaks on it and offers it to Mo to help himself, assuming Mo will be too polite to take the big one. But that's exactly what Mo does. He takes the big one and says thanks a lot and proceeds to eat it all up."

Lester laughed.

"Yeah, well. Joe didn't think it was funny at all. He's absolutely furious and he eats the little steak without saying a word. You know, there's smoke coming out of his ears, he's so mad. And so when Mo's finished he looks up and sees Joe's face and he says, hey, what's the matter with you? And Joe says, well, if you must know, I'm mad at you. And Mo says why? And Joe says because I offered you the two steaks and you took the big one. And Mo says, oh, so what would *you* have done if I'd given you the choice? And Joe says, well, because I'm polite and well brought up, I would have taken the small one. And Mo says, well, what's your problem, you *had* the small one!"

Everyone laughed except Skye.

Julia asked what the moral of the story was and they spent the next half hour talking about selfishness and generosity and about whether people are good to each other only because they want others to be good to them in return. The discussion was a success. Skye was the only one not to speak. Then Julia asked if anyone had another issue he or she wanted to raise with the group. As usual, it was Mitch who first held up his finger.

"Okay, Mitch," Julia said. "Off you go."

"I'd like to make an affirmation."

"Okay. Go ahead."

"I'd like to congratulate Lester for getting this fire going."

From all around the fire came voices of support.

"So, good for you, dude. We know how tough it was and how hard you've worked at it."

The phony sincerity and patronizing tone made Julia itch to intervene. She'd taken an almost instant dislike to Mitch. He was vain, devious, manipulative and malicious and those were only his better points. Sometimes it took a lot of effort to be professional and to keep her personal feelings in check. His "affirmation" was almost certainly a prelude to something else and she had a good idea what it was.

"And I'd like to say thanks, dude," he went on, "for making all that effort for the group.

And maybe one day soon, when someone else makes an effort, we'll get a hot meal every night."

There were calls of "support" from two of his followers, Paul and Wayne.

"That sounds more like a criticism than an affirmation," Julia said.

"You take it how you like, man."

"Well, if you have an issue to raise with someone, Mitch—and I'm not a 'man'—I think it's only fair that you should make it clear."

"I think it's pretty goddamn clear already."

"Not to me it isn't. And later on, please, we'll have twenty alternatives for that word."

Mitch laughed in contempt and looked around at Paul and Wayne. They were both grinning, their eyes darting between Mitch, Julia and Skye, who was still staring steadfastly at the fire. Julia was clenched inside with anger and it was hard not to show it.

"So, Mitch, spell it out, please."

He lifted his eyes to the stars and sighed. "Okay. It's an issue we all have—"

"Everyone speaks for him- or herself here, thank you, Mitch."

He paused a moment, clearly containing some sharper response.

"It's an issue *I* have, then. With Skye. Everybody else has gone along with this bow-drill thing except her and we're all—*I'm* getting pretty sick of it."

There were many calls of support. Mitch gave Julia a triumphant nod. For a while no one spoke. The tension seemed to find voice in the crackling of the fire.

"Skye?" Julia said gently. "Do you want to respond to that?"

Skye shook her head without taking her eyes off the fire. She looked like a lost orphan and all Julia's instincts cried out again to comfort and protect her. But it was important not to. One of the main aims of the program was to socialize these kids, to make them aware of the effect their actions had on others. The stand Skye had taken over refusing to make a bow-drill fire may have begun as an act of attention-seeking bravado. But now it had grown into a fully-fledged point of honor. And although the pressure on her to back down was now immense, so would be her loss of face if she did.

"Would anyone else like to say something about this issue?" Julia asked.

Byron held out a finger. Julia nodded for him to go ahead.

"I'd just like to make a—" He stopped. It was rare for Byron to speak in group and he was clearly nervous. He swallowed.

"An affirmation?" Julia prompted.

"Yeah. An affirmation. Skye, you're, like, the only girl out here and like you said earlier today, you know, when you had to go to the bathroom and all—"

Mitch sniggered. Julia was about to pounce but Scott beat her to it.

"Mitch, I think you should show more respect when someone's speaking. Go on, Byron, we're listening."

"Well, sometimes, I think maybe we don't all realize how hard that is for you, Skye. And maybe this whole thing with the bow drill and you not wanting to do it, is like, because we're all guys or something and it's your way of kind of getting back at us. Hell, I don't know what I'm talking about."

He frowned at the ground as if the words he was trying to find might be down there. His cheeks had turned red.

"Anyhow. I just wanted to give you this affirmation for putting up with us all. And tell the truth, I don't care if I can't have hot food when it's your turn to make the fire, because I think you have a right to your opinion and all. And I think you're a good person. And, well, that's all I got to say."

"Thank you, Byron," Julia said.

Then there was a long pause. They were all looking at Skye. She was biting her bottom lip so violently that Julia was worried she might make it bleed. There were tears welling in her eyes. Then quickly, without looking at any of them, she stood up and walked away into the darkness.

SIX

ACROSS THE red sand of the arena Connor could see in the viewfinder his mother's head and shoulders above the wooden rails of the chute. She was wearing a bright pink shirt with white trim and the battered black hat she said always brought her luck. It had a band of small silver steer heads which his father had given her for their first wedding anniversary. She was looking down at the seething horse beneath her and concentrating hard on getting into the right position.

The afternoon light was mellow with dust and barbecue smoke and the shadows were lengthening and but for the possibility that he was about to record the demise of his only living parent, Connor might have been more excited about how good it all looked. Then the sun flashed on her hat band and the old, curiously detached instinct for a good picture took over. He fired off a few frames, zoomed wider and clicked the switch on the Nikon's motor drive to be ready for when the chute opened.

"I can't believe your mother's nearly fifty," Julia said.

"Neither can she," Connor said. "That's the problem."

They were sitting in the front row of the bleachers, Julia between him and Ed, and for a two-bit rodeo like this there was quite a crowd behind them, a couple of hundred people, Connor figured, maybe more. His mother had been talked into this madness by an old friend who was on the organizing committee. He said it would be the big draw of the afternoon: a "Seniors' Bareback" event for charity. Connor's mother wasn't much taken with the "Seniors" bit, but when he called again to say her old arch rival from Livingstone, Madeline "Queenie" MacFall, was going to do it, that did the trick.

"If that talentless, horny-assed old Jezebel can do it at forty-seven years of age, I'll be damned if I can't," she said.

And despite the fact that she hadn't been on a bucking horse for five years and was starting to get arthritis from all the bones she'd broken over the years, there was nothing Connor could say to stop her.

"Honey, it's real sweet of you to worry," she said. "But it'll all be over in six seconds."

"One way or the other."

"Well, it's as good a way to go as any."

Secretly, Connor was proud of her. The only condition she insisted on was that they change the name of the event from "Senior" to "Celebrity." A little while ago, before running back to the bleachers, Connor had helped her get ready. She was still a fine-looking woman though her face bore the lines of too much sun and she stooped a little from an old neck injury. Seeing her all dressed up in her riding gear, the pink shirt and white bandanna, reminded him of when he was a boy and he and his father would travel with her on the circuit. He'd noticed even then how men used to look at her in a certain way. She, on the other hand, never had eyes for any other man but his father, either before his death or since.

When she was ready, they stood together leaning on the rails to watch Queenie MacFall last all of two seconds before being catapulted onto the sand. Incredibly, she stood up waving and smiling with nothing worse than a raw backside and a bruised ego. His mother had grinned wickedly and shaken her head.

"Well, as we used to say, fall by name, fall by nature."

Now it was her turn. The P.A. system clicked and boomed.

"Well, folks, our next rider needs no introduction, but I'll do it anyhow. We're mightily honored and privileged to have with us this afternoon one of Montana's all-time-great rodeo stars. From Augusta, number five, the sensational, the incomparable, Maggie Ford!"

"At such moments in the theater, they say 'Break a leg,' " Ed whispered.

"Ed!" Julia slapped his knee.

He held up his hands. "I'm not saying it!"

"Let's hope that's all she breaks," Connor said. "Okay, here we go."

The chute opened and the horse exploded into the arena. His mother marked him out perfectly, keeping her boots above the break of the horse's shoulders as his front feet hit the ground. She held the rigging with her left hand, her right arm caressing the air like a ballet dancer's while she lowered her legs to the horse's withers, her toes pointing daintily outward. Connor's motor drive whirred at six frames a second. There were some good pictures here. The dust was up, the shadows black and the horse, a stocky little gray, was wild-eyed and giving the performance of his life. But there was no way he was going to throw her. She was spurring now, expertly, keeping in time with each leap he made, riding the bucks as if they were nothing.

Ed and Julia were on their feet hollering beside him and everyone else seemed to be cheering too and it was all Connor could do not to join in, but he kept shooting for the whole six seconds and didn't stop until the pickup men rode up alongside and delivered her safely to the ground. Connor put down the camera and stood up to applaud with everyone else. Julia was bouncing up and down like a kid. She threw her arms around Ed and then did the same to Connor.

"That was amazing!" she yelled.

"Connor, it's unnatural," Ed said. "Mothers aren't supposed to be like that."

"Yeah, I know. I gotta get her locked up somewhere. Come on, let's go see her."

THREE HOURS LATER they were sitting in the back room of Elmer's in Choteau, with the trophy in pride of place on the table among the steaks and beers. Connor's mother had walked it with a score of eighty-five and declared it should have been ninety if one of the judges hadn't been so dumb. He didn't know his fanny from his fetlock, she said, and had marked the bronc down for being too easy a ride.

She was telling Julia about the old days now, stories Connor had heard many times before and some of which he'd even witnessed, so he knew precisely where truth ended and embroidery began. The one she was telling now was yet another Queenie MacFall story, the one in which the poor woman got attacked by a swarm of bees in the middle of being interviewed on TV. Even though Ed must have heard it before too, he looked as enthralled as Julia. The guy seemed to have an endless appetite for anything Connor's mother ever said. The steaks were enormous and nobody had managed to finish them except Ed, who was now tucking into Julia's. Connor pushed his chair back and stretched out his legs.

The women were sitting on the other side of the table, Julia opposite him. He was finding it hard to take his eyes off her. He'd found it hard since the moment they'd met. There was something about her that just hauled you in. Her laugh, her dark brown eyes and how they creased up when she smiled—Connor stopped himself, ashamed that he should even notice such things. This was his best friend's girlfriend, for heaven's sake.

It was nearly a month since she and Ed had arrived and there hadn't been many days like this when they'd all been off work at the same time. Even so, Connor felt that he knew her, that somehow he'd known her a long time. She was one of those women who touched you a lot, not as if she were coming on to you but in a natural, unconscious way. If she was making a point, she'd put a hand on your arm and although he knew it meant nothing, that it was just a friendly, sisterly kind of thing to do, it always had an effect on him. And when she'd given him that hug at the rodeo, he hadn't known where to look.

"Connor?"

He heard his mother's voice. They were all looking at him.

"Hello?" Ed said. "Is there anybody home?"

"I'm sorry. What was that?"

"Your ma wanted to know where we're going climbing tomorrow."

"Oh. I figured we'd go down to the Bitterroots."

"So you're a climber too, Julia?" Connor's mother said.

"I've done a little. I'm not very good."

"She's terrific," Ed said. "It's like watching Spider-Woman."

"I wish."

"Well, you watch yourself with these two young lunatics here."

"If you'll forgive me for saying it, Mrs. Ford, but after watching you today, it seems like it may be in the genes."

"In the Wranglers," Ed said. Connor's mother smiled.

"Listen," she said. "There's airplanes, there's mountains and there's horses. You tell me which it's smarter to fall off."

They had coffee and paid the check. Connor's mother asked if they wanted to stay the night up at the ranch but Connor said they'd better head back over to Missoula to get an early start on the mountain. They said their goodbyes in the parking lot. Connor's mother handed her rodeo trophy to Julia.

"Mrs. Ford, I can't possibly take this," Julia protested.

" 'Course you can. I got too many of the darned things already."

Julia looked at Connor.

"Take it," he said. "She means it."

"Well. Okay. Thank you." She gave Connor's mother a kiss. "I'll treasure it."

"You're welcome," she said, climbing into her truck. "If it was worth melting down, I'd have kept it myself."

They drove south with the night falling soft and blue around them. Away to their right the

Front Range stood out against the last red ribbon of the dying day like the ramparts of some dread empire. Through the open windows came the smell of cooling earth and sage long baked by the sun. Connor's old Chevy rattled and creaked its way along the blacktop following the tunnels of its own headlights through groves of cottonwood and up into the shadowed folds of the badlands.

They sat three abreast, as they now always did, with Julia between the two men. She was cradling the trophy in her lap while Ed held forth on the marvel of Connor's mother and how he was definitely going to write a musical about her. It would be called *Queen of the Red Dust*. Connor asked if that would be before or after all the others Ed was definitely going to write, the one about smoke jumping (*Hearts of Fire*) and that other idea of his about the psycho piano teacher who murders his pupils. Julia said she hadn't heard about that one and Ed started explaining it. It was called *Choppin*, he said. "Think *Sweeney Todd* meets *Amadeus*." He didn't get much further because Julia began to laugh and it was so infectious that soon they were all at it and Connor's lungs began to hurt as badly as they sometimes did when he was on a fire.

The laughter seemed to drain them for afterward they fell silent and sat as if hypnotized watching the flutter of moths in the beam of the headlights. They crossed the divide at Rogers Pass and as they rounded a bend they found a herd of mule deer, seven mothers and their young, standing in the road. Connor stopped the truck and the deer stood for a long time staring back, their eyes shining like opals and their long ears atwitch. Slowly, pair by pair, they moved off the highway and melted into the night.

They passed through Lincoln and by then Ed was snoring softly, his head propped against the pillar of the door. For some miles more neither Connor nor Julia spoke but there was nothing awkward in their silence. He'd never been one for small talk and he'd already noticed that she seemed to be the same. When at last she did speak it was to ask him, in that direct way she had, about his father. She wanted to know what he had been like and Connor told her that he'd been a good man, quiet and gentle and caring.

"I guess a lot of people thought it was my mother who was the strong one, because she's always been, you know, kind of upfront."

Julia laughed. "I noticed."

"Yeah. Well. She speaks her mind even when it might be better not to. But, underneath it all, it was my dad she depended on. After he died, for a long time she was just lost. I remember the morning of the funeral, the doctor gave her these pills, tranquilizers or something, I guess, so that she'd be able to hold it together at the service. Anyhow, she went and took too many of the darned things and so when everyone showed up at the church and came up to her to pay their respects and said how sorry they were, she was laughing and joking and saying, 'Hell, it's okay, when you gotta go, you gotta go.' "

Connor shook his head and smiled at the memory. "It was terrible. You know, kind of funny, but terrible. But afterward, for a long time, she was in a real bad way."

"That must have been tough for you."

"Uh-huh. For a while."

"You don't have any brothers and sisters, do you?"

"No. They tried, I think. For years. But it never happened. You?"

"No. Just me."

"And your mom and dad?"

"My mom lives in Brooklyn. My dad left when I was twelve years old. Just upped and went."

She left it hanging in the air awhile and from her tone he got the feeling that the loss of her father was as much of an issue for her as the loss of his own was for him. He waited for her to go on.

"He lives in Germany now, married to a much younger woman. You know, the whole cliché: younger, taller, blonder, prettier. She's probably great. I've never met her. And I haven't seen him in, God, must be five or six years now. He calls sometimes at Thanksgiving and Christmas. Sends a postcard now and again. I don't really know him anymore."

"What kind of work does he do?"

"Construction or something. I'm not even sure of that."

"Did he have more children?"

"No."

"And your mom?"

"She's a trapeze artist in a circus."

Connor looked at her. "For real?"

"Yeah, she does this act, you know? Dives through hoops of fire, that kind of stuff." She saw the surprise on his face. "Hey, why should you be the only one with a superhero for a mother?" She grinned. "Okay, she's not. She's a hairdresser. Has her own little salon in Brooklyn."

"And that's where you grew up?"

"Yeah. She's great. Very Italian. Never stops talking. Has the most disastrous love life you could imagine. She's like a lightning conductor for unsuitable men. I love her to bits."

They talked the whole way back to Missoula. And all the time he couldn't help being aware of her scent and of the warm press of her shoulder and her hip against his. They talked about his photography, about her work in Boston and about her trip to Africa the previous summer and how she'd loved the place and the people there. She said she wanted to go again one day, maybe even work there for a while. Connor said he had always wanted to go to Africa too and many other places besides and that he hoped one day he'd get the chance.

He asked her how things were going with the wilderness program and Julia told him about the Indian girl and what a great kid she was but how she was so closed in on herself that nobody seemed able to reach her. Connor said there was a smoke jumper, a full-blooded Blackfeet, whose brother worked with troubled kids on the reservation in Browning.

"I remember him saying these kids often don't have any idea about their ancestors and what a remarkable culture they had. His brother tries to get them involved in reviving some of the traditions. Apparently it works real well. Maybe he could help you out somehow."

Julia sounded interested so he promised to get

the guy's number for her. By now they were driving into Missoula and Connor found himself wishing the journey could last longer. He parked outside the apartment and switched off the engine and they sat for a moment looking at Ed who was still sleeping. Julia smiled as if to herself and in her eyes Connor could see the love she felt for his friend. He watched her lean across to kiss Ed gently on the cheek to wake him. And though he wanted to feel only happiness that these two good people should have found each other, Connor couldn't quite suppress a dull twisting inside him that was not of jealousy but of some nameless kindred yearning.

Later, when they had sorted their gear for the climb and said their goodnights, he lay alone in the darkness, trying not to listen to the intimate murmur of their voices in the next room and to the creaking of the bed and trying to banish from his mind the images it conjured. And long after they had fallen silent and all he could hear was the rustle of the river through the open window, he lay awake staring at the ceiling and at the dappled shadows of the trees.

They set out before dawn and drove south with the mist curling from the Bitterroot River on their left and the sun lighting the tops of the mountains to their right. They parked and hiked west for two hours with the sun lifting behind them and warming their backs and sparkling on the skein of dew-drenched spider webs that veiled the brush around them. At last they came to the foot of a wall of gray rock that rose from the forest, sheer and slightly concave and riven with stained cracks that looked as if they had been chiseled by giants. Julia stood gazing up at it.

"You guys have got to be kidding," she said.

Connor and Ed had climbed it several times before and they told her it wasn't as daunting as it looked from down here and she shook her head and looked less than convinced. But without another word she swung her pack off and sat down on a rock and started to take off her boots and put on her climbing shoes and the two men did the same. Ed took out the little penlike syringe he always carried and gave himself a shot of insulin and they sat and ate some of the ham and cheese sandwiches that Julia had made before they set out. They stowed all but what they would need for the climb behind some rocks then put on their harnesses and roped up.

Connor led and Julia climbed behind him, and looking down at her on the very first pitch, he could see that she knew what she was doing. She had a good upright posture and moved with a nimble confidence, keeping her hands and arms at shoulder level.

By late morning the sun was hot and they stopped on a ledge above a narrow chimney they had climbed and shed their sweaters and drank from their water bottles and rested awhile.

"Listen," Julia said. "Listen to the silence. Isn't it amazing?"

She had tied her hair in a high ponytail and was wearing shorts and a yellow sleeveless top that showed her back and shoulders and didn't quite conceal the cream straps of her bra. Her skin was tanned and flawless but for a small birthmark, like a dab of chocolate, just below the nape of her neck. She was smoothing sunscreen onto her upper arms and shoulders and talking to Ed while she did so about a tricky part of the chimney and Connor did his best not to look at her and at the curve of her breasts and instead turned to stare out over the forest that spread giddily below.

They climbed for another hour, up a second broader chimney then worked their way slowly around a massive overhang on a shelf so narrow that only the tips of their toes found purchase. After that the mountain was more friendly for a while but although it was more of a hike than a climb they stayed roped. They crossed a spine of rock to another part of the mountain with ravens swirling around them and below them, croaking in disdain. Then on they went and on and up through a field of fallen boulders strangely sculpted by the wind and rain so that they looked like a colony of sleeping dinosaurs.

The final part of the climb was the hardest and once Julia lost her grip and slipped. She gave a little cry and there was a clatter of sliding rocks, and Connor, belaying her, braced himself and called out "below" to warn Ed and the rope jerked tight and held and he looked down to see her swinging for a moment in midair and Ed's anxious face below. She had slipped only a few feet and she quickly found her footing and the three of them kept still and silent until the last echo of the displaced rocks faded far below them.

"Sorry, guys," she said.

"Are you okay?" Ed asked.

"Yeah, I'm fine."

She looked up at Connor but said nothing. She rested awhile to gather herself and then she climbed the rest of the pitch as if it were nothing. As she neared the top, Connor reached down and took hold of her wrist and she held his and he hauled her up onto the ledge. She tied off and stood there beside him, belaying Ed as he climbed toward them. She was breathing hard and her skin glistened with sweat. Connor watched her and she sensed it and smiled at him and he smiled back. When he had about twenty feet more to climb, Ed took a short rest and while they waited for him Connor squatted down on his haunches and looked out over the forest. He felt her hand on his shoulder and he looked up at her. The sun was flaring behind her and he had to squint to see her face.

"Thanks for helping me down there," she said.

"You helped yourself. You climb real well."

"Thanks."

"You're welcome."

They reached the summit an hour later. There was a small pinnacle and below it a platform of undulating rock some twenty feet across and decorated with patches of gray-green and amber-colored lichen. The platform fell away sheer on three sides and some who had climbed here before had carved their initials on the side of the pinnacle along with the dates they did it. There were higher peaks all around but still it seemed as if the entire world lay unfurled below them.

Ed told Connor to take some photographs and so he got out his Leica and lined them up in the best place, where he could look down on them a little and make the most of the view. Through the viewfinder he watched them hold each other and press their cheeks together and smile at the camera. He took three pictures, altering the angle each time.

"Now one of you two," Ed said.

Connor shook his head. "I'm the photographer around here."

He had never liked having his picture taken. But Ed insisted so he reluctantly handed over the camera and took his place beside Julia. He felt shy and awkward and didn't know whether to put his arm around her but she calmly made the decision for him and circled hers around his waist and so he put his around her shoulder and felt her move closer to him so that their hips pressed together. He could feel the warmth and sleekness of her skin all along the inside of his forearm and on the palm of his hand that cupped her shoulder and the air he breathed was laced with the hot sweet smell of her.

"Come on, man, lighten up," Ed called. "You look like somebody died."

Julia looked up at him and smiled and he smiled down at her and at that moment Ed clicked the button.

"Okay, another one," he said. This time they looked at the camera. "That's more like it."

Connor felt something relax inside him. He

told himself it was all right to feel the way he did. She was a beautiful woman and any man would feel the same. It was in no way a betrayal of Ed. He was simply aware of her, that was all. Ed took another picture and Julia let go of Connor and stepped away toward Ed, saying that now it was her turn. She had her own little camera and took a picture of the two men goofing around, striking a comic macho pose.

The camera had a timing device and she told them to stay put while she set it. They teased her for taking so long about it but at last she had the camera positioned on a pile of rocks and ran to join them and she was laughing so much she almost fell over. Connor and Ed moved apart to make space for her between them and she put her arms around them both and the camera flashed.

They settled themselves on the rock shelf and ate the rest of the sandwiches and some apples and nuts and a bar of expensive Swiss chocolate that had gone soft and sticky in the sun. Like a conjurer, Ed brought out a bottle of merlot and three plastic glasses that he'd secretly stowed in his pack and he opened it and poured the wine and made a solemn toast to friendship, which they all repeated.

After they'd eaten they lay on their backs on the baked rock and stared at the sky. Small sculpted white clouds were drifting from the west and Ed got them playing a game in which the three of them took turns naming what the shapes reminded them of. They fell silent and a little later Connor sat up and saw the two of them were asleep. Ed had taken off his T-shirt and apart from his sunburned neck and forearms his skin was pale. He had turned upon his side and was curled like a child in the shelter of Julia's arm.

For a long time Connor studied them. The rise and fall of their breathing was in rhythm and their faces, slackened by sleep, had an innocence that touched him and somehow saddened him though he didn't know why it should. A butterfly appeared over the rim of the rock and fluttered around them for a few moments before settling on Ed's shoulder. The undersides of its wings were a powdery buff but then it opened them and the tops were such a vivid red that it looked like an open wound. Suddenly it was lifted by the breeze and borne away and Connor watched it go and as it grew smaller and smaller the thought struck him that what a man allowed into his heart was a matter of choice.

And long after the butterfly had vanished he stayed staring out over the many miles of forest and mountain hazing in the heat and stretching with the bend of the earth to the horizon and to others beyond. And he banished the sadness that he'd felt and told himself that the world before him was brimming with hope and promise and that the way things were on this most golden of summer days was how life truly was and how it always would be.

SEVEN

THE CLOUDS at which they had laughed that afternoon soon had revenge. They gathered and darkened and opened and for three days there was rain without pause. The ground had been baked hard by the hot, dry days of May and June and so most of the water ran right off into the creeks and rivers before the forests had a chance to drink it. But it moistened both land and air enough to give the Missoula smoke jumpers a few days' calm.

Not that calm was ever too welcome. Rain meant fewer fires and fewer fires meant less overtime, less hazard pay and, although they had to be careful who they said this to, a lot less fun. A smoke jumper's definition of what constituted a "good" summer bore little resemblance to anyone else's, especially those for whom forest fires could spell ruin or disaster. During a "normal" summer, the Missoula base got five or six fire calls a week. A "good" summer could bring that many each day.

Until the heavens opened, ten days ago, this summer had been looking good. The rain had dampened the jumpers' spirits a little. Since it stopped there had only been four calls, all to minor fires that were quickly put out. But things were looking up. The skies had cleared, humidity was falling and the new heat wave looked set to stay. And as the barometer and fire risk rose, so did the jumpers' mood.

The smoke jumper base lay in a long and shallow valley just south of Missoula airport. It was a cluster of mundane white buildings landscaped a little halfheartedly with a few token trees and shrubs. Beyond the buildings was the airstrip where planes of different makes and sizes stood ready to roll at a moment's notice. Looming to one side, like a sinister circus of torture, were the towers and platforms and high-wire rigging of the training units, where many a young rookie had stood with a pounding heart, quaking knees and a face drained of all but fear, staring down at the ground and wondering if smoke jumping was after all quite as romantic as once it had seemed.

The epicenter of the base was known as "the loft," a warren of interconnecting rooms where the jumpers worked when they weren't on a fire. At its hub was the lounge, a long room with a linoleum floor and low armchairs set against whitewashed walls. There was a coffee machine and a microwave where jumpers could cook their own food. It was here every morning that the jumpers gathered for roll call. Leading off it were the operations room where there were wall maps on which every fire in the region was flagged, the loadmaster's where the firefighting gear and supplies were sorted and the ready room where every jumper had a bin. Then there was the manufacturing room, where parachutes and jumpsuits were made and repaired. And, finally, the tower, where parachutes were hoisted for inspection after every jump and hung from on high like the sails of some ghostly galleon.

In another building, a short walk away, was the visitor center. Here there was an exhibition where people could learn about smoke jumping and watch a video of some jumpers in action. There were life-size models, one in full jumping gear and another in firefighting gear and because the Forest Service was eager to convey the politically correct message that smoke jumping was open to both sexes, the firefighter model was a woman. The problem was, it seemed as if they'd lifted a mannequin straight out of a department store window. She was wearing lip gloss and mascara and in her spotless, neatly pressed shirt and pants, she couldn't have looked less convincing. Ed had christened her Barbie Goes Jumping and a visitor had once been heard to mutter that she'd have trouble putting out the candles on a birthday cake.

There were indeed women smoke jumpers, but not many. Of some four hundred jumpers across America, only twenty-five were women. What deterred more from applying—apart, perhaps, from a more highly developed survival instinct or plain common sense—was a matter of conjecture. But it probably had something to do with the impression, not entirely without foundation, that smoke jumping was an occupation copiously fueled by beer and testosterone. Firefighters of all kinds, from the Bronx to Bora Bora, tended toward the macho end of the job spectrum. Smoke jumpers had parachuted into an adjoining spectrum all of their own.

Not that this could have been deduced from the evidence on display inside the manufacturing room on this particular July morning. Beneath the baleful gaze of three enormous elk heads mounted somewhat surreally on the wall of the manufacturing room, as if they had crashed through the masonry and weren't too impressed at what they'd found, five Missoula smoke jumpers, all of them male, were sitting demurely at sewing machines. Ed was between Connor and Hank Thomas. Next to Hank was a rookie called Phil Wheatley, whom Hank had already nicknamed Pee-Wee, and Chuck Hamer, a snookie who'd done three years as a hotshot in Idaho and looked like a bear with a crew cut.

It was a tradition that jumpers made and repaired much of their own clothing and gear. Ed was making a new red waterproof top and feeling more pleased than he'd probably care to admit with the way it was coming along. As more than one former girlfriend had observed, Ed had always been "in touch with his feminine side." Few if any, however, knew the price he'd had to pay.

Ed's father, Jim Tully, was a self-made multimillionaire better known to the citizens of Kentucky as Big Jim, the Mower Man. He was a walking definition of what he liked to call "good ol' P.S.G."—plain southern grit. The fourth and final son of a stable hand who had deserted his family and drunk himself to death in the Depression, Jim was born with an eye for the main chance and two big hands to grasp it with.

As a child he'd had to carry his boots to school to save the soles and he vowed that no kid of his was ever going to have to do the same. Boots had straps and the only point of them was to haul yourself up. From the age of eight he mowed lawns after school, giving his mother half the money and saving half. When a mower needed fixing, he'd fix it himself until he knew every nut and bolt and screw and sprocket of every model there was. At seventeen he went to college to study business and quit after a month, concluding he already knew more than they could teach him.

And he did. By twenty-five he had his own store, Big Jim Mowers—"Show us a better deal and we'll cut it!"—and by thirty-five there was a whole chain of them all across the state and into Ohio, selling U.S.-made mowers and imports too, including his own range of Big Jim Chompers, assembled in a factory he'd built in Taiwan. His face—handsome, but not so handsome that you wouldn't trust him—beamed from billboards and TV screens, telling y'all to come along to Big Jim's "where the grass grows greener." And they did.

He built a mansion on a hill with a pillared porch and called it Grassland. There were fountains and peacocks and servants and a thousand rolling acres of pasture, where sleek horses lazily grazed and swished their tails. He bought new homes and cars for his mother and brothers and sisters and then set about finding himself a bride that suited his elevated station.

As soon as Big Jim laid eyes on Susan Dufort, he knew she fit the bill. She was pure Kentucky thoroughbred. Beautiful, cultured, sensual and witty, she was the only daughter of one of Kentucky's oldest and most revered families. Her parents, Leonard and Ernestine, were appalled. But Jim wooed them as sedulously as he wooed their daughter and soon all three succumbed. The marriage was front-page news, as were the births of their children, Jim Junior (Little Jim), Charlie, a year later, and Edward, three years after that.

Sons one and two were clippings off the old lawn. They both had their father's blond hair, the jutting jaw, the wide, toothy smile. They talked like him, swaggered like him and did all the things Big Jim himself would have done had he had their privileged start in life. Both later captained the college football team, worked hard and played harder. They had little patience and less talent when it came to the things their mother held dear.

Susan Dufort Tully could play just about any musical instrument you put in front of her, but her greatest love was the piano. She had once harbored ambitions to play professionally but her father said it was too cruel a world and populated by all kinds of predatory and unsuitable people. So instead she played for pleasure, although she still sometimes had dreams in which she was playing Carnegie Hall in a pool of light, her gown flowing in folds of red velvet on the stage around her. The only one who understood such dreams was Ed.

One of his earliest memories—he figured he could only have been three years old, maybe younger—was waking in the middle of the night and hearing piano music. His mother was a poor sleeper and had a habit of slipping out of bed and going downstairs to play the giant black Steinway grand that stood in the hall. Ed remembered tottering from his room in his pajamas, bleary-eyed and still half asleep, and out across the cream-colored carpet of the landing and looking down through the balustrade.

His mother had lit the silver candelabrum that stood on the piano and the lid gleamed and so did the polished maple floor of the hallway. It was late summer or early fall and she was wearing something ivory colored and shiny and her dark hair which she normally wore pinned up lay loose on her shoulders and that shone too. Years later she told Ed that she had been playing Chopin nocturnes and he had always wished he knew precisely which one it was. All he knew that night was that it was the most beautiful thing he had ever heard. He crept halfway down the shadowed side of the staircase to get a better view and perched himself there to watch and it seemed like a very long time before his mother, for no apparent reason and utterly without surprise, as if she had known he was there all along, looked up at him and smiled.

When she'd finished the piece she patted the long piano stool and moved to one side and Ed went down and she hoisted him up and placed him beside her. She played another nocturne and Ed watched her pale long hands fingering the keys, like a pair of graceful animals with some separate will and purpose of their own.

Although he later had many other teachers, good, bad and indifferent, it was his mother who taught him how to play and who instilled in him the notion that any kind of music could be fun. Her great passion was Mozart but she also knew all the great musicals by heart and by the time he was six or seven so did Ed.

It was around this time that he was diagnosed as having diabetes, which seemed to bother his parents much more than it bothered him. His mother made such a fuss about having to inject him that Ed soon adopted a kind of studied nonchalance and took over managing it himself.

His father's reaction to both the diabetes and the boy's burgeoning passion for music was the same: a subtle mix of pity, indulgence and a vague, unspoken disapproval. It seemed that Big Jim considered both music and any kind of physical disorder unsuitable for a boy. At least, for a Tully boy.

With the music, Ed would later wonder if it was because his father felt baffled or even excluded. Perhaps it represented some last unbreachable barrier on his great social ascent. Or perhaps he was simply jealous of how it bonded further a mother and son already linked so firmly by looks and by temperament. Whatever the cause, his attitude rubbed off on Ed's brothers, neither of whom had ever shown any interest in music. Their jibes were never uttered in the presence of their mother and were usually good-natured, as were the ones about Ed's eyesight, which was poor enough to warrant glasses while he was still in primary school. But in a fight one day when Ed was about twelve years old, over something so trivial he couldn't remember, Charlie told him to get lost and go play one of his "faggot" musicals.

It might have deterred a less confident or stubborn child. But Ed turned out to have more P.S.G. in him than his father or brothers might have credited. With his mother's encouragement he pursued his passion, stuck to his practice and became a fine pianist. They both knew, early on, that he didn't have her technical finesse. His playing was robust and passionate and where such attack was called for, he could soar. But he lacked a certain delicacy of touch with the more subtle pieces and, in any case, his instincts were more pop than classical. More Motown than Mozart, his mother used to say. More Hammerstein than Handel.

He wrote and staged his first musical in high school at the age of sixteen. It was based shamelessly (and no doubt illegally) on the movie *Alien* and the music was mostly plundered from Puccini, but it was seen all the same as a triumph. Even his father seemed almost impressed. His brothers were rather more impressed by his other musical creation: a rock band called Redneck Peril for whom Ed wrote the songs and played lead guitar, becoming almost overnight, to his surprise and delight, an object of modest rivalry among the best-looking sophomore girls.

He had never had any doubts about his sexual orientation and had long ago stopped worrying about his brother's "faggot" jibe, but he later recognized that it had probably had an effect on how he chose to spend his leisure time. Nothing could induce him to follow his brothers' example, join the jocks and play football. Instead, he developed a taste for sports that were even more hazardous, where you pitched yourself not against padded and helmeted hunks but against the very elements themselves, against snow and ice and mountain rock.

In his seventeenth summer, he went on a wilderness survival and leadership course in Montana, fell in love with the place and came home saying that this was where he wanted to go to college. The music program at UM in Missoula perhaps wasn't the best in the country, but it was good enough. His father was furious. Music might be okay as a hobby, he said. Maybe. But it sure as hell wasn't a proper college subject ("for a man," he might have added but didn't). What was more, no son of his was going to some hick, two-bit school for semiliterate cowpokes.

By then Ed actually enjoyed such battles. Over the years a pattern had developed. He stayed calm and this made his father more abusive and the more abusive his father became, the more his mother took Ed's side. Secretly she wasn't too keen on UM either. She wanted Ed to go to Ann Arbor, where she had studied, but she didn't say a word about that in front of her husband. In the end, Big Jim conceded the battle rather more easily than Ed expected, figuring, no doubt, that two out of three sons following in Daddy's footsteps was as much as a man had the right to expect. Mollycoddled by his mother and with too much darned Dufort blood in him, Ed was now officially a lost cause.

It was a relief. And since then, although—or perhaps because—they hadn't seen so much of each other, he and his father had gotten along better. There seemed at last to be a mutual acceptance of their differences. There were even times when the old alliances shifted, such as when Ed told his parents that he was signing up as a smoke jumper. Predictably, his mother was horrified and his father fascinated and enthusiastic.

"Don't be such an old fussbudget," Big Jim chided her. He slapped Ed on the back. "This here's a grown man now."

That was three years ago and neither then nor since had Ed mentioned the sewing machines. He smiled to himself now, as he sat stitching the last seam of his waterproof, imagining what his father might make of such a scene.

The siren sounded just as he snipped the thread.

"We have a jump request at the Lolo National Forest. The jumpers will be Tully, Ford, Hamer . . ."

Chuck Hamer let out a whoop and the sound of the loudspeaker was drowned for a moment as everyone leaped from their chairs and headed for the door. They didn't have to listen for they all knew who was on the jump list.

". . . Schneider, Lennox, Pfeffer . . ."

The routine was that those who weren't scheduled to jump always rushed to the ready room to help those who were. Ed ran after Connor into the lounge which was normally a quiet place but now, with the siren and the loudspeaker blaring and jumpers bursting in from every door, was more like the deck of an aircraft carrier at full scramble.

". . . Wheatley, Delaguardia . . ."

Within seconds they were all in the ready room and by the time Ed got to his bin Donna Kiamoto was already there holding out his jumpsuit for him to climb into. Ed's heart was beating fast. No matter how many times you jumped, that excited twist of nerves in the stomach was always the same. Donna helped him fasten his jumpsuit. The suits were padded and made of Kevlar. They had high collars and zippers all the way up the legs for easy exit.

"There you go, soldier."

"Thanks."

It was Donna's birthday in two days' time. She was throwing a party at Henry's, one of the smoke jumpers' favorite bars in downtown Missoula. Ed and three friends he used to have a band with had promised to play.

"If you're not back by Friday night, Tully, you're dead meat."

"Well, if it goes that long I'll be in overtime, so at least I'll be rich dead meat."

"Hey, if it happens, can I have that guitar of yours?" Hank Thomas called.

"Can I have your girlfriend?" Chuck said.

"Sorry, man, she only goes for good-looking guys."

Everyone laughed. Donna helped Ed fasten his suit and then he reached into his bin for his boots. Connor was already suited and booted and in his harness. He was bending forward while someone attached his parachute. He was always the first to be ready and was routinely teased for it.

"Hey, Connor, your chute's upside down."

"Yeah and you got your boots on the wrong feet."

Connor gave a weary smile. He clipped on his reserve chute and personal gear bag and picked up his helmet, ready to roll.

"Come on, you tired-ass bunch of slowpokes,

what's keeping you? We've got a plane to catch."

FROM THE WINDOW of the Twin Otter, the fire looked a halfhearted affair. It was six or seven acres at most, Ed figured. And with little wind, it didn't seem to be going anywhere in a hurry. So much for overtime. But then again, you never could tell.

He looked around at the other jumpers, sitting bulky in their jumpsuits on the cramped bench that ran along the starboard side of the plane. With the door constantly open, it was too noisy for much conversation and anyhow most jumpers liked to prepare themselves in their own space, finding the right frame of mind for the jump. The jumpsuits were thick and hot and Ed could feel a trickle of sweat run down his back. Connor, as always, looked cool and comfortable.

The plane made another pass over the fire while the spotter and assistant spotter squatted by the open door, hooked in for safety, trying to figure out a likely jump spot. The spotter's name was Frank Bird though everyone called him Big Bird or Bigs because he was the smallest man on the base. He was also, at fifty-five, one of the oldest and wisest and had his name on the hundred-jump list back at the base. Ed always found it comforting to have Bigs as spotter.

The pilot dipped a wing and started to circle back and Ed, quietly chewing a power bar to top up his blood sugar level, found himself looking directly down on the fire. It looked like a large arrowhead chasing the slow drift of white smoke up the west flank of the mountain. The terrain was difficult, all steep ravines and jutting crags and barely a space between the trees. Wherever Bigs chose for the jump spot, it was going to be tight.

They were flying at about a hundred and ten miles an hour at fifteen hundred feet and Bigs had to yell to make himself heard over the noise of the engines when he showed them the jump spot. It was a thin clearing that ran down the mountainside in a crooked green scar. At its widest it was no more than thirty feet across and on all sides it was guarded by tall lodgepole pine. They passed over it three more times, dropping a pair of crepe-paper streamers on each pass to measure the wind drift. The streamers were in combinations of pink and blue and yellow and weighted with sand and Ed watched them snake and flutter away below him toward the trees.

"Looks like we've got about three hundred

yards of wind drift," Bigs shouted. "Everybody see the spot? Okay, let's do it."

The jumpers were all putting on their gloves and helmets and personal gear bags and going through their final buddy checks. Ed and Connor were jumping first stick, which meant that Ed was going to be the first man out of the plane. Once they'd landed, that made him the incident commander. The last time that he'd gone first, he missed the jump spot and landed in a creek. He could feel the adrenaline begin to course through his veins and he took some long deep breaths to calm himself. There was a flash and he looked around startled and saw Connor grinning as he lowered his camera. Ed raised his middle finger. Connor stepped close so that their helmets touched.

"You okay?"

"Yeah, I'm fine."

"Want me to go first?"

"No way. You couldn't hack it."

Connor cuffed him on the helmet.

"Leave some space for me down there, okay?"

Bigs, kneeling by the door, called over to them asking if they were ready.

"Yessir!" Ed yelled.

He turned to face Connor and they put their

fists to their chests and looked each other in the eye.

"Hearts of fire!"

They said it together then gave each other a high-five.

"Go for it, man," Connor said.

"You too."

"Okay, fellas," Bigs yelled. "Hook up!"

Ed hooked his static line to the cable and inserted the locking pin into the clip and asked if he was clear. The assistant spotter confirmed that he was.

"Okay, we're going to come around on final now. Get in the door!"

Ed stepped forward and squatted in the door, putting his left foot out onto the step and flexing his right leg and foot behind him. With both hands he took a firm grasp of the sides of the doorway. The rush of the slipstream ripped in around him. He felt its cold blast compressing his face through the lattice of his face guard. He looked down at the toe of his left boot and then looked beyond it to the reeling green blanket of forest below. It was hard not to stare at it but he knew it was wrong to do so and wrenched his eyes away and locked them on the horizon.

Bigs yelled to ask him if he'd seen the streamers and gotten a good look at the jump spot. Ed looked him in the eye and said he had. He felt the plane tilt and watched the forest rotate below him as the plane came around and steadied into its final approach.

"See that first ravine? Could be a little squirrelly just as you come over there. Watch out for it, okay?"

"Got you."

"Okay, we're on final!"

Ed was still taking his long, deep breaths. He flexed his knees and the muscles at the back of his neck and he closed his eyes for a moment to center himself and to summon calm and strength and luck. It was crucial to get thrust when the spotter gave you the signal to jump. Unless you made a good, clean, vigorous exit, you could find yourself plunging headfirst with your lines tangled around your feet and when your chute opened your whole body would get cracked like a bullwhip and knock every ounce of air from your lungs.

"Get ready!"

Ed raised himself up on his left leg a little and raised his right knee off the floor to give his foot more spring. The forest seemed to be calling him, tempting him to look down at it, like a siren luring him to the rocks, but he resisted and kept his eyes on the horizon. Then it came. A sharp slap on his left shoulder from Bigs and he launched himself with all his might through the doorway and out into the thin blue air.

"One-one-thousand . . ."

He didn't know if he was counting aloud or not for the rush of air seemed to suck the words from his head.

"Two-one-thousand . . ."

He'd given himself such a thrust from the door that his body had twisted. He was staring up at the roaring white belly of the plane that was swimming away from him like a shark with the sun masked behind it.

"Three-one-thousand . . ."

And then he saw Connor jump after him and suddenly the sun flared out from the tail and he was blinded and knew nothing but the craving pull of the earth as he plunged at ninety miles per hour toward it.

"Four-one-thousand . . ."

He braced himself and an instant later he heard a whoosh and a crack and he was jerked like a fish on a line. His body skewed and straightened and he looked up and saw the white and blue and yellow dome of his canopy billowing above him. And there was Connor, higher and to his right, the lines of his chute streaming out and then the chute filling and holding and Connor's body swinging in a long curve until he was upright and steady and floating. And the plane was gone and its roar was gone and the only sound in the clear vault of air was the whisper and flutter of the two parachutes.

They circled and Connor whooped and Ed felt himself grinning like an idiot at the forest kaleidoscoping below him. He pulled on the toggles and steadied himself and steered the chute around so that he was facing the fire. And with Connor out of sight behind him he began to ride the wind down in a lazy sequence of S turns toward the jump spot and the drift of white smoke beyond.

Connor called out and told him to look to his left and he saw a herd of elk, about a dozen females and their young, crossing a ridge. The last one stopped and looked back and Ed couldn't be sure if she was looking up at them but he thought she was. And then she turned and disappeared over the ridge and all that was left were the shadows of the chutes gliding silently, a darker green on the green of the forest.

He reached the first ravine and, just as Bigs had said it would, the air around him suddenly whirled and his chute riffled and lurched and he felt himself swing to one side and then swing back again and he used his toggles and steadied himself onto a new course. He looked down into the ravine and saw a gash of white water maybe three hundred feet below him and then he was over the ridge on the other side. The wind had risen and seemed to have shifted south and the jump spot was coming up fast and Ed had to toggle hard to hold the right line.

The trees were only about a hundred feet below him now and they were taller than he'd thought they would be. They were mostly lodgepole but there were Douglas firs among them too. His heart was thumping. Hanging up in a tree was embarrassing at the best of times, but if you were first man it was downright galling and he was determined that it wasn't going happen. The idea was to fly over the spot and turn upwind then drop gently into it. At the moment he seemed well set to do just that.

No sooner had the thought passed, however, when the wind dropped and his chute flapped and he lost a good fifteen feet that he badly needed. Shit, he thought. He wasn't going to make it.

Coming up fast now, some fifty yards ahead, he could see the tops of the trees that edged the near side of the clearcut and he was so sure he was going to land in them that he started trying to pick the most friendly looking one. To hang up was bad enough without getting skewered on a branch. Then suddenly the wind whipped itself up again and he managed to get some lift, maybe just enough to make it. He could see the pale green brush of the clearcut revealing itself before him now but he still didn't think he was going to clear the final line of trees. There were a couple there that were bigger than the others and he was heading straight at them. He toggled hard to the left and saw a lower place and aimed for it. He was surfing the treetops now. His boots caught a branch and then another and he hoisted his knees but then his knees were crashing through the branches too and he started to yell and curse himself for a fool. . . .

And then he was out and clear and over the trees and floating down into the pale green calm of the clearcut with the grace of an angel.

He hit the ground with both feet and rolled and was standing again before his chute had time to settle and he half expected the watching forest to burst into spontaneous applause. He felt like taking a bow.

He looked up, expecting to see Connor, but there was no sign of him. He took off his harness and was just climbing out of his jumpsuit when he heard Connor's voice.

"Shit! Ow! OW! Goddamn it!"

There was a loud cracking and splintering of timber and then Connor's boots appeared through the branches of one of the big lodgepoles, followed by the rest of him. His parachute billowed out above the tree and slowly settled, swallowing both tree and man. Then something gave and Connor appeared again and fell and for a bad moment Ed thought he was going to fall all the way down. But after about ten feet his lines snagged and held and Connor hung there, swinging gently to and fro about seventy feet above the ground.

Suddenly everything was silent again. Ed stood looking up at him and Connor lifted his face guard and just hung there, looking back down at him. Ed was trying to keep a straight face.

"Hi," he said.

"Fuck."

"You okay?"

"Yeah, I'm terrific."

"I bet the view's really great up there, huh? You know, I looked at that tree and said to myself, is that a good place to land? And then I said, no, I think it might be better down here in the jump spot."

"Fuck you, Tully."

"Need any help?"

"Not from you, asshole."

Ed laughed and started gathering his chute. Connor found a foothold on a branch and gently tugged on his lines to test how securely they were snagged. Then he reached into his pants pocket for his letdown rope and tied himself off to the tree. The Twin Otter passed overhead and a few moments later Chuck Hamer and Phil Wheatley came gliding into the jump spot. Both made perfect landings.

"Hey, Connor," Chuck said. "You picking apples up there? You're out of luck, man, that there's a pine tree."

Connor didn't reply. He was trying to disentangle his chute. Chuck and Phil got out of their harnesses and jumpsuits and set about stowing their chutes and while they did so, Chuck kept up the ragging.

"Boy, was that an easy jump spot. What d'you reckon, Ed?"

"Yep. Piece of cake."

"How was it for you, Pee-Wee? Wasn't that a piece of cake?"

"I guess it was okay." He grinned but, as a rookie who didn't know Connor too well, seemed a little uneasy about joining in the fun.

By the time Connor was ready to lower himself out of the tree, he had a full audience. All the other seven jumpers had landed and every one of them hit the spot, looked up at him and made some smart remark. Connor gave as good as he got and, knowing him so well, Ed could tell that he saw the funny side of it and was pretending to be angrier than he was. As Connor slid down the rope they all cheered. He waved a finger at them.

"Thank you. Thank you all so much. Bunch of assholes."

When he was only two or three feet from the ground he let go of the rope and jumped and as he hit the ground his right leg buckled and he cried out and fell over. A couple of the jumpers laughed, thinking he was just fooling but Ed knew something had happened and he ran over.

"What happened?"

"My ankle. I landed on a rock or something. Shit."

He sat up and hoisted the bottom of his jumpsuit. He undid the laces of his boot and pulled down his sock and Ed saw the leg was already swelling fast.

"Hell, Connor. You're such a goddamn attention-seeker."

"I know. I just want to be loved."

They radioed for a helicopter and Connor was lifted out and the seven remaining jumpers set about putting out the fire. It wasn't too much of a contest. They got the tail under control first, then cut line along the north and south flanks. The wind dropped and with the night came air that was cool and moist and the fire lay down like a lamb. The following day they starved the head with a burnout. The lines held and the night was spent mopping up. By the second dawn it was done and dusted.

Ed and his friends played at Donna Kiamoto's party at Henry's and played so well they weren't allowed to stop. "Great Balls of Fire" got three encores. He hadn't expected Julia to be there, but it was her staff changeover day and somehow she'd managed to slip away a little early. Ed kept his eyes locked on her while he sang. She danced with just about everyone, except poor old Connor who sat at a front table, watching and drinking too many beers, his bandaged leg propped up on a chair and his crutches propped behind him. The ankle had turned out not to be broken, just sprained, but badly enough to stop him jumping for a while.

Ed and Julia helped him home, one on either side, his arms draped around their shoulders and Ed carrying the crutches. It was nearly dawn and the birds were starting to sing in the cottonwoods along the river. Connor was singing "Great Balls of Fire," slurring the same words over and over again, while Ed and Julia laughed and teased him. A police car cruised by and stopped and the cop rolled down his window. Julia turned on the charm and explained that they were smoke jumpers and that Connor had been wounded in action and the cop smiled and wished them goodnight and drove on.

They helped Connor up the stairs and he was going on about what a beautiful couple they made. He said they were the most beautiful couple in the whole world. Julia was laughing so much they all nearly fell.

"It's true, man," he slurred. "You're just . . . beautiful. Julia, you're . . ."

"Beautiful?"

"Yeah. That's right. You're beautiful. I don't mean like, to look at . . ."

"Hey, thanks, Connor."

"No, I mean . . . You are, of course you are. God, you *are*. But, hell, you know what I mean. Ed, you're real lucky, man, to have a woman like this. And Julia, you're lucky too, to have this . . . ugly old sonofabitch."

They lowered him onto his bed and Ed pulled the boot off his left foot. Connor held up his bandaged foot which had no boot and Julia began to laugh again so that she had to sit down on the bed.

"You're not wearing one on that foot," Ed said.

"What? Oh."

"You go to sleep now."

Connor suddenly reached out and held onto them both. He'd lifted his head off the pillow and even allowing for the drink there was a sad urgency in those pale blue eyes that Ed had never seen before and didn't understand.

"I love you guys. I really love you, you know?"

Ed ruffled his hair and Julia leaned over him and gently kissed his forehead.

"We love you too, cowboy," Ed said. "Now sleep."

EIGHT

JULIA HAD once heard someone at an educational psychology conference make a joke about how the first half of your life was wrecked by your parents and the second half wrecked by your children. She couldn't yet attest to the truth or otherwise of the second part of this, but after seeing so many damaged young lives in the course of her work, she had no doubt about the first. Counselors and therapists of almost every variety were encouraged to look at themselves in order better to help their clients, and in most matters Julia felt she had a pretty good handle on herself and what had made her the way she was. The one exception was her father.

When Connor had asked her about him that night, driving back from the rodeo, she had come close to tears. It was strange, for she could go for months without ever giving her dad a thought and then suddenly, out of nowhere, the loss of him all those years ago would hit her like a punch in the solar plexus. It was only later that it occurred to her that there was something about Connor that reminded her of her dad.

She had friends whose parents had been in such a perpetual state of war that when one of them left, it came almost as a relief. But with her parents it had never been like that. As far as she was concerned, they were completely happy, more than happy. Unlike other people's parents, they actually seemed to be in love. And then one day, out of the blue, her father announced that he had fallen in love with someone else and he packed his bags and went.

Julia had always adored him. He was her hero, a fine-looking man, blond and tall, with a great sense of fun, the kind of dad a young girl's school friends envied. When you told him something, even some silly, trivial thing that had happened at school, or gave him an opinion on something, he always made you feel that what you said was interesting and important.

He often used to come home late from work (Julia later discovered why) and she would lie awake until she heard his car pulling up outside and then the click of the front door and his footsteps on the stairs. He would tiptoe to her door and peep in to see if she was still awake and she would say hi, Daddy, and he would come and sit on her bed and talk with her and ask her to tell him all about her day.

And then, three days after Julia's twelfth birthday, he dropped the bombshell and vanished from their lives. Her mother almost went crazy with grief and had never really gotten over it. She loved him to this day, even though it turned out that the woman for whom he'd left her was only the latest in a string of them, stretching back almost to the year they'd gotten married. Her mourning for her dead marriage was so intense and crippling that in some odd way the roles of mother and daughter seemed to get swapped around. Julia spent the next two or three years comforting and looking after her and in the process managed to ignore the fact that she too had suffered a bereavement just as shocking.

As to the effect this might have had on her subsequent attitude to men in general, she had something of a blind spot. It didn't seem to make her either hate them or mistrust them. If anything, she just pitied them a little for the primitive waves that seemed to surge uncontrollably through their lives, particularly when they reached what her mother called "a certain age." She knew, in an academic way, the classic effect that paternal desertions were supposed to have on a young woman: by rights she would end up marrying some boring, recycled fifty-year-old father figure trying to suck in his stomach and hide his bald patch. Luckily (knock on wood), the allure of such men still eluded her, though sometimes she wondered if her engagement to the prematurely middle-aged Michael was a first scary symptom.

She had been thinking a lot about her father lately and mainly because of Skye who, she knew, had suffered a similar desertion. Julia had tried on a couple of occasions casually to broach the subject. But it was clearly as taboo as every other subject. Skye didn't talk about anything. She had reached rock bottom and the time had come to do something about it.

Julia was lying on her back in her sleeping bag, looking at the moon and listening. For the last hour or so a pair of owls had been talking to each other, one behind her up in the forest and the other somewhere away across the valley. It was starting to get on her nerves. Earlier she'd heard coyotes yipping and a few minutes ago something heavy, a bear maybe (at night everything was a bear) moving through the brush down by the creek. She had toyed with the idea of going to check that the bear bags had been hoisted high enough, but then thought better of it. For the fifth time in half an hour, she looked at her watch. It was twenty past three.

He was late.

The moon was three nights short of full and the air was so limpid she could see every blemish and ripple of its surface. It cast a pale gray light on the shoulders of the Douglas firs below the campsite and sent long arrowed shadows from them across the dry grass of the clearing where the group had camped. They lay side by side, staff and students alike, like a row of giant larvae. Their sleeping bags were wrapped in blue tarpaulins to keep off the dew which already glistened in the moonlight. The owls stopped and as if on cue, Lester started talking in his sleep.

"You do it," he said. "No, *you* do it! Come on, man. It's your turn."

He talked in his sleep almost every night. During the first couple of weeks, he used to sit up and shriek and wake everyone up but now his dreams seemed to have calmed a little. Sometimes another student who was awake would talk back to him in surreal conversation. But tonight nobody else spoke and his monologue subsided to a mumble and then to silence.

Julia was lying between Byron and Skye and by the sound of their breathing, both seemed to be asleep, though with Skye you never could tell. Sometimes Julia would wake in the middle of the night and find her staring into space with tears rolling down her cheeks. The first time she had reached out and touched Skye on the shoulder and asked if she was all right and Skye had quickly turned her back without replying.

Julia had seen that kind of crying before with other kids she knew had been abused. They didn't sob or wail or sniff, the way ordinary kids cried, kids who had parents who would hear it and immediately come and put their arms around them and comfort them and make the pain go away. Abused kids cried silently. Because if you didn't, all you got was another beating. So you learned to cry in private, in the dark, at the dead of night, when nobody could see or hear you. And you kept absolutely still, just let the tears empty out of you in a stream of silent sorrow.

Over the years both in her regular job at the institute in Boston and during her summers with WAY in Colorado, Julia had worked with hundreds of children. In their several ways all had known more than a fair share of misery and misfortune. And if you let it get to you, as a teacher, if you embraced their pain too deeply and made it your own, you were in trouble. That didn't mean you couldn't understand or comfort them. But if you were going to be of any real use, you had to keep yourself strong and centered and slightly separate. And Julia had always managed to do that. Until she met Skye.

There was something about the girl that moved her more than any child she had ever worked with. And Julia didn't understand why. In Colorado there had been three or four students, one of them a girl about the same age as Skye, who had started off just as hostile and uncooperative. But not one of them had kept it up as long as Skye. One of the basic ideas of the program was to let peer pressure work on such attitudes. Those who caused difficulty for the others soon learned the consequences of their actions. Many of these children had been so assaulted by the world in which they had grown up that simply to survive they had built walls around themselves and placed on the ramparts all sorts of subtle weaponry. And to watch these walls crumble and the weapons fall silent and to witness instead a dawning of empathy and trust was almost magical. And it was happening with this group already. Even Mitch, the one who considered himself so hard, even he was showing signs of softening.

But not Skye. For more than six weeks now the girl had kept her defenses in place, even strengthened them. She seemed to have figured out the minimum level of cooperation and stuck to it. She spoke only when spoken to and with no elaboration. She was now an exile, a stranger among friends. Not once had Julia seen her smile, except early on, in mirthless sarcasm. But now even that had passed and her face was locked into a mask of haughty indifference. Only on those rare occasions when she couldn't avoid looking you in the eye, only then could you glimpse the pain.

The one time that students had to look you in the eye was when they needed a knife. It was a rule. All knives were kept by the staff and when students needed one, to cut wood or prepare the food, they had to ask you, look you in the eye as they took it and thank you. The previous week Skye had asked for a knife to make a new wooden spoon and Julia had given her one. Someone else came to ask a question and Julia got distracted and when she looked around she saw Skye had gone to one side and was sitting on the ground cutting off her hair.

"Skye!"

Julia ran to her and asked for the knife and Skye wearily handed it over and sat there squinting up at her.

"What's the big deal?"

For a moment Julia was so appalled she was lost for words. Hanks of glossy black hair lay on the ground. She had hacked away most of one side and there were jagged gaps at the back where you could see her scalp.

"What . . . why are you doing this?"

"It's my hair, I can do what I like."

"You said you wanted to make a spoon."

"You wouldn't have given me the knife if I'd told you the real reason."

"You lied to me."

"Oh, give me a break."

"No, Skye. It's important."

Skye looked away. Julia became aware that everyone was staring at them. She sighed.

"Listen, we've got scissors. If you'd asked, I'd have cut your hair."

"Why would I want *you* to cut my hair?"

Later that day she reluctantly allowed Julia to try making the best of a bad job with the scissors. While she was doing it, Julia told her that her mother was a hairdresser and joked about how her mom used to practice on her when she was a kid. But Skye didn't respond at all. Her hair was now cropped like a boy's.

The students all kept journals in which they had to write at least a page a day. At first almost all the entries were brief and stilted but as time went by most students would loosen up and some would begin to write searchingly about their life and their feelings. But not Skye. Her entries were sparse and coldly factual and gave nothing away. Julia had raised the issue two days ago during their daily one-to-one session. It was evening and they were sitting on some rocks above a small clearing where they'd made camp.

"You know, Skye, what we do out here doesn't change too much each day, does it? I mean, the basic things."

"Like what?"

"I mean, every night—well, almost every night—we have campfire and group and so on. And we eat and wash out cups and brush our teeth and drink our water. And every day that's what you write in your journal, which is fine. But maybe you could try writing about one or two things that don't happen every day. You know? Unusual, interesting things—"

Skye gave a little scornful laugh. "Yeah, right. Like what?"

"Well, like yesterday, when we saw that incredible sunset. Or today, when we had to get across the creek and we hitched up the rope and swung across. Or last week, when you cut your hair."

"That wasn't interesting. Why was that interesting?"

Julia took a deep breath.

"Okay. So, maybe then you could try writing about why you don't find any of these things interesting. About why it's all so boring to you."

"I'd have thought that was pretty obvious."

"I don't think so. Tell me."

Skye made a little snorting sound and looked away, shaking her head.

"Skye?"

Suddenly Skye turned to face her, anger flashing in her eyes.

"Listen. You're trying to be my friend. But I don't want to be yours, okay? So give me a break."

And she got up and walked away. That same evening it had been her turn again to make the campfire and as usual she'd refused to do it and the whole group circled and spent two hours talking about it to no avail.

The nightly campfire was the heart of the program. Julia had seen it cast its spell upon group after group, infecting the students with light and warmth. It was where they ate and laughed and told stories, where they discussed what had happened during the day and where even the hardest kids seemed able to open their hearts. But on every night that it was Skye's turn to make the fire, the group sat in darkness, ate their cold cornmeal or oatmeal in silence and turned in early. They resented it, some of them deeply, but they had grown tired of telling her so. Apart from the staff, the only friend she had by now was Byron. Skye had rejected him many times but still he stuck by her and defended her.

Julia had spent many hours discussing Skye with the program therapy team and spent many more on the phone back at base, during her breaks, talking with Skye's probation officer and case manager and various psychologists and counselors who had worked with her. Several times she had also tried calling Skye's mother. The woman sounded disconcerted and vague, as if it were difficult to remember who Skye was. She was obviously on some sort of medication. Once she had started sobbing and another time hung up. The last time Julia called, it was Skye's stepfather who answered the phone. When Julia said who she was, he started shouting and said no, she fucking well couldn't talk to Skye's mother and who the fuck did she think she was calling up and upsetting everyone like this?

During her last break, after Donna Kiamoto's party, Julia had spent a whole day with Glen Nielsen, discussing what was to be done. They agreed that it was time for something radical. They would take Skye on a "quest."

The quest was the program's ultimate tool, used only when there was some sort of deadlock that normal techniques seemed unable to break. The student was removed from the group and taken by two staff members on a two-day journey that was both physically and psychologically grueling. Its effects could be dramatic and so, deliberately, was its initiation. Which was why Glen was coming out now, at the dead of night, to join them.

At least, he was supposed to be. He'd said he would be there at three and it was now after three-thirty. Then Julia heard the snap of a branch down by the creek and she peered through the shadows and saw a figure. She eased herself silently out of her sleeping bag, put on her boots and made her way down the slope toward him. The air smelled sweet and resinous.

"Hey, I'm sorry. I got lost."

" 'Wilderness Director Gets Lost.' That's a good story."

"Tell a soul and you're fired."

They stood awhile, talking in whispers about what Glen was going to say to the group. The owls had started hooting again. Julia was feeling nervous.

"Boy, I hope this doesn't freak her out."

"It will, a little. And that's good. Are you ready?"

SKYE WAS RIDING. She had never been on a horse in her life, but without any fear or effort or anything, she was riding and going fast. She was on a shiny black horse and they were going at a lope across a hillside. The hill was smooth and rounded and velvety, a curve of long green grass that rippled and flurried with the wind. The sky was an immense arc of clear blue and she put her head back and felt the sun warm on her face and felt her hair streaming out behind her. There wasn't a saddle, there weren't even any reins, she was just holding onto the horse's mane and she didn't really have to do that, she could let go, she knew she could, and so she did and spread her arms and it felt like she was a plane and she could turn the horse just by leaning one way or the other.

There was a figure in the distance ahead of her, standing there, waiting, where the rim of the hill met the sky. She was too far away to see who it was, but she knew it was a man. He seemed to be wearing some kind of long dark coat. Then, as she got nearer, he lifted his arms and opened them toward her and she saw that it was her father. She hadn't seen him for many years and she could hardly remember what he looked like but she was certain it was him. He was calling out to her.

"Skye? Skye!"

Then suddenly his face changed and she was looking up and there were two faces staring down at her out of the night sky and neither one of them was her father and she screamed.

"Skye? It's me, Julia. And Glen. It's okay."

Skye sat up, rubbing her eyes.

"What's going on?"

"You were dreaming."

Skye looked around her. The other kids were sitting up and looking at her.

"We're going to do something special," Glen said. "Can we have some light here?"

Julia had a flashlight and Katie, Laura and Scott switched theirs on too. Skye shielded her eyes. Her head was still swirling with dream and she felt bewildered by all these people who'd suddenly appeared.

"What's going on? What time is it?"

"Okay, everybody," Glen announced. "I'd like everyone to circle up here, please. Quick as you can."

There were murmurs and groans, but in a minute everyone was standing in a circle. At night they all had to hand in their boots and pants to deter them from running away, so some, like Skye, now stood with their sleeping bags around them and some were just bare-legged. When everyone was silent, Glen went on.

"Okay. I'm sorry to wake you up like this, but I've come out here tonight for a very important reason. Can anyone tell me what that reason might be?"

There was silence.

"Anyone like to guess?"

Mitch put up a hand.

"Mitch?"

"Skye. It's gotta be something to do with Skye."

"Good. That's right. I'm here because of Skye."

Skye stared at the ground. She was shocked but damned if she was going to show it.

"Can anyone tell me more?" Glen went on. "Mitch?"

"Because she's spoiling things for everyone else."

"She's not!" Byron said. "She just won't play their game that's all. People do things their own way and I figure it's, like, up to her, you know? And it's tough sometimes, for all of us. But specially her." He seemed to run out of steam and stopped a moment. "Anyhow, she's not spoiling things for me."

"That's 'cos you've got the hots for her."

"Mitch, that's inappropriate," Scott said.

"I agree," Glen said.

He asked Mitch to apologize and then thanked Byron and asked if anyone else wanted to speak but nobody did. Then he announced that he and Julia were going to take Skye away on a "quest" and he asked if anyone had any idea what that might be. Wayne put up a finger.

"Like, looking for something? Like *Dragon Quest* or something." There was laughter. Wayne grinned at Mitch and Paul. "It's a video game. You have to find, like, this sacred key."

"Uh-huh," Glen nodded. "That's exactly it. We're going on a journey of our own for a couple of days to help Skye find a key."

Skye raised her eyes to the stars. Jesus, she just couldn't believe these guys. They never knew when to quit. It was all so embarrassing and stupid.

"A *key*?" she said. "A key to what?"

"What do *you* think?" Glen asked.

"I haven't the faintest idea. And you know what? Tell you the truth, I don't give a—" She looked down. "I don't care."

Glen nodded thoughtfully.

"Okay, Skye. Then, we'll have to try and find the key to that too. So, if you and Julia would get dressed and gather all your gear, we'll be setting off in five minutes. Thank you all. I'm sorry we've disturbed your sleep, but this is an important moment for Skye and we wanted to share it with you. Maybe you would like to wish her well."

The only ones who did were Byron and the staff. The rest just shuffled their feet and muttered, which as far as Skye was concerned was fine. They could all go screw themselves.

She got dressed and pulled on her boots and got her stuff together. Her heart was beating hard and her head whirling and screaming with all kinds of different things. She felt mad and proud and scared and defiant all at the same time. If they thought they could break her like this, they had another think coming.

They hiked single file, Glen leading the way with his headlamp and Julia behind. Skye wondered where they were taking her but she didn't want to give them the satisfaction of not telling her so she didn't ask. They were heading down through tall trees into a valley and she could hear water somewhere below them in the darkness but they never seemed to reach it. Then they bore left and walked a more level route that seemed to head up the valley, the water still rushing below them. They walked in silence, just the crunch of their boots on the pine needles. It surprised her that neither of them spoke, because she had expected them to start banging on at her right away, but maybe that wasn't the idea.

Soon it began to get light and through the gaps in the trees to her right she watched the other side of the valley rear out of the gloom, a wall of dark and dappled green a mile high, laced with strands of mist and patched with pale rock and she watched the sky above it turn from the blue of night to the kind of pearled pink she had only ever seen on the inside of a seashell.

She had no wristwatch and no notion of how long they hiked but it was many hours. They headed downhill again and out of the trees and into a meadow filled with wildflowers and came at last to the water. It was a narrow creek of tumbling foam and dark swirling pools which looked as if they would suck you down to hell itself. By one of these pools there was a shelf of rock and here they stopped and put down their packs. They gathered wood and Glen lit a fire and cooked oatmeal and raisins and they sprinkled cinnamon and brown sugar on it and it tasted good and warm and comforting.

They ate and still nobody spoke but Skye had a hunch that it wasn't going to be long before they started in on her and she steeled herself. She looked up along the valley and in the far, far distance saw a mountain shaped like a pyramid and Glen saw her gazing at it and told her that was where they were headed. It looked about a million miles away and Skye thought at first he must be joking but he wasn't.

Then he started telling one of those dumb stories the staff always told when they wanted to teach you some great lesson about yourself or Life with a capital L or whatever. This particular dumb story was called "The Wolf and the Rock" and it was about a little wolf cub called Nooshka-Lalooshka. Give me a break, Skye thought, do I look like I'm five years old? One day this wolf cub was chasing a chipmunk and ran into a rock and really hurt himself and all the other wolves laughed at him.

"The chipmunk got away and Nooshka-Lalooshka felt embarrassed and mad and he told the others that he'd meant to crash into the rock and it hadn't hurt one little bit. So they said, okay, if it didn't hurt, do it again. And so as not to lose face, he did. And this time it hurt even more and he got this big bloody bruise on his chest but the other wolves roared with laughter and said how funny he was and how tough he must be."

No prizes for guessing who this is supposed to be, Skye thought. Glen looked at Julia and asked if she'd like to take over. Skye figured they must have rehearsed all this between them, how they'd break her down. It seemed like a pretty feeble start, although, despite herself, she always liked these stories and was already interested in what happened to the dumbass wolf. Julia took up the story:

"And from then on whenever the wolves got bored, they'd say, hey, Nooshka-Looshka, do your rock trick for us! And if he said he didn't want to, they'd taunt him and tell him he was chicken and so to prove he wasn't, he'd crash into the rock again. And his wound never had time to heal and as he grew older it got worse and worse and infected his leg so that he began to walk with a limp and he got thinner and thinner too because soon he couldn't run fast enough to keep up with the pack when they all went hunting. The others gave him a little of what they caught but only on condition that he'd do his rock trick for them and so he'd do it, just to get fed, still pretending it didn't hurt, until one day he found he couldn't run at all and could only, kind of, collapse onto the rock instead of crashing into it and the other wolves got bored and said it wasn't fun to watch anymore.

"They told him he was of no use to the pack because he couldn't hunt and now that he couldn't even entertain them, why should they feed him? And they banished him from the pack and Nooshka-Lalooshka limped off, alone and forlorn, into the wilderness."

Now it was Glen's turn again.

"Well, he got thinner and thinner and sadder and sadder. And soon he didn't want to go on living. So he found a cave which he thought would be a good place to die and he lay down and waited. And every time the sun came up he thought, this day will be my last. Then, when death was nearly upon him, one morning, he woke up and there was this little pile of nuts right in front of him, right at the end of his nose. And he thought, that's weird. He sniffed at them and they smelled good. And he had just enough strength to eat them and they tasted good too. And he felt a little better and slept all day and when he woke up there was another pile of nuts there and he ate them, wondering who had put them there. And it happened again and again, every time he fell asleep, until one morning he pretended to be asleep but kept his eyes just open enough to keep watch."

"And after a while," Julia went on, "he heard a scrabbling and a huffing and a puffing and he saw this little old chipmunk, sweating and staggering along, carrying a great armful of nuts and dumping them down in front of him. And Nooshka-Lalooshka opened his eyes and said, hey! And the chipmunk nearly jumped out of its skin and fell over and said, please, please don't eat me! And Nooshka-Lalooshka said, why would I want to eat someone who has saved my life? And he asked the chipmunk why would he be so kind to a wolf when everybody knows that wolves eat chipmunks? And the chipmunk said it was because once, long ago, a wolf had been very kind to him and instead of eating him had let him go and crashed into a rock, just to make some other wolves laugh."

Julia smiled. Both of them sat looking at her and for a moment or two nobody said anything.

"Is that it?" Skye said.

"Unless you want to take it any further," Julia said.

"Like, the wolf grabs the chipmunk and bites his head off."

"If that's how you want it to go."

Skye looked away and stared at the mountain. There was another silence.

"So I guess I'm supposed to, like, 'identify' with someone in that story?"

"Well, do you?" Glen asked.

Skye thought for a moment, then shrugged.

"Yeah. I'm one of the nuts."

Julia burst out laughing and then Glen started laughing too. Skye looked at them in amazement. Hell, it wasn't that funny. But they didn't stop. Julia's shoulders were shaking helplessly and the more she laughed the more Glen laughed. Skye tried to keep her own face stony straight but it was really hard with them both going on like that and soon she just couldn't hold out any longer and she felt her lips begin to twitch and stretch into a smile which she tried to correct but couldn't and then it spread into a grin and soon she was laughing too. And it felt so strange, as if some alien power had taken her over and was shaking her insides around, unlocking something there. The three of them just laughed and laughed and went on laughing.

Then something even stranger happened. Although Skye was still laughing, she felt a heaving in her chest, like ocean waves breaking and shaking her whole body in a way that was both happy and sad, desperately sad, at the same time. And she felt tears start in her eyes and begin to sluice down her cheeks and she heard her own laughter turn itself into a kind of convulsive animal howl. And all the time this welling, rising, shocking release inside her, like a volcano bursting and pouring out of her in these great shuddering sobs. She cried for herself and for her whole life and the mess she'd made of it and for her mother and all that they both had suffered and for all the terrible things she'd done, like killing that young cop on the highway. And she remembered her dream, her long-lost father standing on the hill with his arms reaching out to her and she cried for him too. For all this, for all these people and deeds and misdeeds, she tilted her streaming face to the sky and wept and howled.

So blinded was she by her own grief that she didn't see them shuffle close but she felt their arms slip around her and take hold of her. It was the first loving touch of another human being that Skye had felt for a long time and she had neither the strength nor the will to resist. They hugged her and she could tell that they were weeping too and although it struck her as strange that these two people she barely knew and to whom she had shown only contempt should shed tears for her, she didn't fight them or doubt them. And for a long time the three of them clung together and wept together like survivors of a woeful storm.

THEY REACHED THE PEAK of the mountain an hour before sunset the following evening, just as they had planned.

In two days they had walked twenty-eight miles and talked many thousand times that many words. Julia had been on three quests before but none had been like this one with Skye. It was as if a dam had broken inside the girl and sixteen years of repressed pain flooded forth.

She talked about her father leaving and the dream she'd had the night before and about her mother's drinking and slow descent into depression and despair. She talked about the men her mother brought home to the trailer who all ended up yelling at her and beating her and sometimes beating Skye too and how she couldn't understand what her mother saw in them, especially the one she'd gone and married who beat on her more than all the others combined.

She talked about how she'd started staying out all night, hanging out downtown by the railroad with all the other lost souls because she was too afraid to go home to the trailer. And about how she'd gotten into drugs so that she didn't have to think about these things. First glue then pot and poppers and speed and then pretty well anything anyone came up with, except crack and heroin, which made you mad and killed you. And about how she'd gotten into thieving, which was the only way to get the money for the drugs except, of course, for dropping your pants for some filthy old pervert which was what some girls her age and younger did but she never had and never would.

And while she talked they hiked steadily west up along the valley following the bends of the drainage, sometimes clambering over rocks and sometimes taking a winding trail through the trees. And always ahead of them was the mountain and always below them the rush and babble of the creek. Sometimes the mountain would drop out of view behind a ridge or a forested bluff only to reappear half an hour later, bigger and clearer. And as they walked, the words just poured out of her. And so did the tears. Julia had never seen such epic weeping. Soon on Skye's cheeks there were great pale patches where the tears had washed away the grime. Every so often she would start sobbing so badly that they would have to stop and Julia and Glen would circle up and hug her till it subsided and then on they would go.

The first evening they had camped by the creek and Skye made her first bow-drill fire. She did it without any help from either of them and with such little effort it looked as if she had been doing it all her life. She grinned cheekily as the flames leaped and said see, she wasn't that dumb after all, she'd watched and knew all along how to do it.

They cooked a stew of tofu with peppers and rice and while they ate, the sun lowered itself behind the mountain and Skye looked up and pointed. Directly above them and flying west was a perfect V of geese, so high that the undersides of their wings still caught the sun and glowed white against the coral of the sky. When it was dark and the fire had crumpled to its embers, Julia asked Skye what had happened on the day the young police officer died and for a long time Skye said nothing, just stared into the embers. Then she took a deep breath and began to tell the story. She spoke in a low, steadied voice that cracked only when she came to how the man's arm had gotten trapped behind Sean's seat and how she'd seen the look of pure fear in his eyes.

And now, the following evening, they were coming up the shadowed side of the mountain toward the summit. It was a hike, not a real climb, and when they were only a little way off Glen told Skye that when they reached the top there would be someone waiting to meet them. Skye wanted to know who it was but all he and Julia would tell her was that it was someone she'd never met.

A few weeks ago Julia had called the number Connor had been given by his Blackfeet smoke jumper friend and found herself talking to John Standing Bird. He turned out to be a lawyer who had devoted his life to working with young people on the reservation, trying to give them a sense of belonging and to kindle in them an interest in Blackfeet history and culture. Julia had told him all about Skye and without even having to be asked, he said he would be happy to help in any way he could. When they decided to take Skye on a quest she called him again and together they came up with a plan. All day she had been excited about it but now she was feeling anxious, wondering if it was such a good idea after all.

The final slope to the summit was smooth and easy with a well-worn trail that curved up and around its southern side. And as they came around they saw the sun again, going down in a blaze of orange and red and purple and saw the silhouetted figure sitting on a rock staring west. John Standing Bird turned and saw them and he rose and came to meet them and Julia introduced Skye and they all shook hands. He was tall and broad-shouldered and had the sort of face that was difficult to age. Julia figured he was probably in his mid-forties. His hair was streaked with gray and he wore it in long braids. He had on a black hat with a wide, flat brim and a white shirt buttoned to the neck and a red and black blanket patterned with running buffalo was draped loosely over his shoulders. Skye shook his hand nervously, darting a sideways frown at Julia. John Standing Bird smiled and kept his kind black eyes fixed on her.

"I've heard many good things about you, Skye," John Standing Bird said. "It's good to meet you."

Skye didn't seem to know what to say but it didn't matter. John Standing Bird suggested they join him on the rock to watch the sun set and by the time it had gone in a sudden last explosion of light, the mood among them was calm. John Standing Bird had gathered some wood and he asked Skye if she would light the fire and Skye got her bow-drill set from her pack and did so without any demur. Julia and Glen went down to the tree line to gather more wood while the other two made supper and when they returned Skye was chatting away as if the two of them were old friends.

Julia had given John Standing Bird the name of Skye's mother and he had done some research and over supper he told Skye the line of her family and where they had come from. He told her about the Oglala and what a great and proud people they had once been and how one of the greatest warriors of all, Crazy Horse, was an Oglala. He asked Skye if she had heard of him and Skye said of course she had, every idiot had, but she'd had no idea that she belonged to the same tribe and she grinned at Julia and Glen and said how cool was that? John Standing Bird nodded gravely and said he thought it was pretty damn cool and Skye said he shouldn't cuss and now he had to give twenty alternatives, which he duly did.

He went on to tell many stories about the Oglala and how they used to live and what had happened in the end to Crazy Horse, how he was betrayed by his own people and murdered. Nobody now knew what he looked like, John Standing Bird said, because he had never allowed his photograph to be taken. Not once did Skye take her eyes off him. She hung on his every word, her forehead puckered in a little frown and her mouth slightly open in a sort of subdued wonder.

After the last story and when the last piece of wood had burned they watched the distant red and green flicker of the aurora borealis streaking the northern sky. It was the first time Julia had seen it and the sight moved her to tears. Something inside her had been rubbed raw by the past two days and Skye saw her crying and put an arm around her and that only made her cry more.

The following morning the four of them walked down the mountain and two miles west to where John Standing Bird had left his truck.

He drove them along logging roads back to within a couple of miles of where they knew the group would now be. He got out of the truck so they could say their goodbyes and Julia and Glen thanked him. He said he hoped he would see all of them again and he held Skye's hand in both of his and said that maybe, when her time with WAY was over, she might like to come visit with him up in Glacier. She said she would like that. Then he handed her a book, saying he thought it might interest her. It was called *Black Elk Speaks* and was all about her people, he said. Skye muttered her thanks and seemed unable to look him in the eye. It was obvious that she hadn't been given many gifts before.

They watched him drive off and stood staring after him until the dust drifted away.

"Shall we go join the others?" Glen asked.

Skye nodded.

NINE

HENRY'S WAS a murky corridor of a bar at the far end of North Higgins. It was one of those mysterious places whose parts didn't add up to its whole and whose whole wasn't to everyone's taste anyhow. What it lacked in decor it more than made up for in what some called atmosphere and others just plain noise, much of which was generated on any given summer's night by smoke jumpers.

There were signed pictures of legendary "Zoolies" behind the bar that ran along the right-hand wall and served just about every variety of microbrew beer known to man. For those who for one reason or another (mostly one reason) found it hard to stand, along the left-hand wall was a row of tall wooden tables where you could lean or perch precariously on stools. And it was at one of these, this particular summer's night, that Connor Ford and Chuck

Hamer sat staring morosely up at the TV news, counting all the money they weren't earning.

There were helicopter shots of a blazing mountainside and a plane flying in low and dumping a red cloud of retardant. Chuck Hamer called for quiet.

"Firefighters from all over northern California have been unable to put out the blaze that has now been burning for five days," the reporter was saying. "And so today saw the arrival at Redding airfield of sixteen smoke jumpers from Missoula, Montana."

There was a raucous cheer from the bar. And there they were, stepping down from the plane and coming toward the camera and there was Ed among them. He had on his best movie-star face, a kind of shy but resolute grin and Connor noted that there was a touch of war-hero swagger in his walk. As they filed past, the reporter called them "this elite corps" and there were more cheers in the bar. Then there was a little interview with Hank Thomas, who said something modest and meaningful about there being a job to be done and they were just glad to be able to help. Everyone cheered again.

"A man's gotta do what a man's gotta do," Chuck declaimed.

"Glad to help," someone else mocked. "And gladder still to get the overtime."

Connor had done his best to persuade the personnel officer that his ankle was good enough for him to go with them. It was ten days since his fall and the swelling was almost gone, leaving a violent purple and yellow bruise. He'd spent all that time doing tedious maintenance work, mainly repairing torn parachutes and he was getting bored and restless. He'd had physical therapy every day for the last week and managed to cajole a reluctant fitness release from his doctor. But yesterday he'd taken the mandatory P.T. test at the base which involved running one and half miles in eleven minutes and when the foreman saw him hobbling off he called him back and said sorry, the leg clearly wasn't yet mended and there was no way he was going to Redding.

The news moved on to another story and everyone in the bar started talking again. Connor took the last swig from his bottle of soda. He hadn't touched alcohol since the night of Donna's party and still felt embarrassed that he'd made a fool of himself. He couldn't remember too much about it except being carried up the stairs and then going on about how beautiful Julia was. It was nothing but the truth, but he wished he hadn't said it and hoped he hadn't said more. Chuck Hamer cuffed him gently on the shoulder.

"Cheer up, old buddy. Doesn't look like much of a fire anyhow. Those Californian firefighters are just a bunch of wusses. Why don't you let me get you a proper drink?"

"Thanks, Chuck, but I think I'll be heading home."

"Cowboy, I'm worried about you. Early to bed, no booze. You're not even chasing women this year. What in hell's name's the matter with you, boy? Turning into a monk or something?"

Connor smiled and stood up and put on his hat.

"It's called enlightenment, man. Pure enlightenment."

Outside the night air was balmy and felt wholesome to his lungs after the smoke of the bar. Apart from a beggar who often hung around the corner of Broadway, the street was deserted. Connor walked across to Worden's Market and bought himself a chicken sandwich and some apples and a carton of milk and then strolled down toward the bridge, looking idly into the store windows. There was a little place that sold used books and magazines and never seemed to shut and on impulse Connor went inside. He'd occasionally found interesting books on photography here. The guy who ran it knew him and said hello.

He spent about ten minutes browsing the

shelves and finding nothing and he was about to leave when a book caught his eye. It was about an English photographer called Larry Burrows who had taken some of the most famous and powerful pictures of the Vietnam War and lost his life doing so. The book had full-plate color pictures, some of which Connor hadn't seen before. He bought the book for five dollars and would have paid a lot more.

The beggar on Broadway was a young man about Connor's age. He had torn pants and no shoes and a straggly beard decorated with crumbs from his last meal. Connor asked how he was doing, which he realized straight away was a pretty dumb thing to say. He gave him the chicken sandwich and the guy, who would no doubt have preferred cash, looked so disappointed that Connor handed over the apples too.

The apartment seemed oddly quiet without Ed, who was always yacking on about something or singing when he wasn't yacking. Connor undressed and took a glass of milk and the Burrows book to bed.

He didn't know much about Burrows except that he'd taken many extraordinary pictures for *Life* magazine and that he'd died when a helicopter in which he and some other photographers and journalists were traveling was shot down in Laos. The book described him as diffident, modest and brave, a man of integrity whose heart was touched deeply by the suffering that he sought out and recorded for the world to see. Connor read it from cover to cover in a couple of hours and was greatly moved. There was one picture he kept turning back to.

A group of South Vietnamese soldiers were standing around a young Viet Cong who was on his knees. He had a rope around his neck and his black shirt had been ripped off and hung around his waist and his hands were tied behind him. You could see from the marks on his face and his body and from the way the soldiers were holding their rifles that he had already taken a severe beating. Technically, like all Burrows's work, the photograph was flawless. The composition was immaculate. But it was the young man's eyes that gave the picture its power. There was fear there for sure but there was courage too, as if he had somehow managed to transcend the pain of torture and the certainty of imminent death.

Long after Connor had put the book down and turned out the light, the image stayed in his mind and he wondered whether he himself could summon that kind of courage or the kind that Burrows must have had to look horror in the face again and again without fear or flinching. And somehow, for the first time, he knew with absolute clarity that one day he would find out.

ANOTHER WEEK WENT BY and Connor spent most of it doing odd jobs around the base, trying not let the boredom gnaw at him too badly. Ed was still down in Redding with the other lucky sonsofbitches, earning a ton of overtime and hazard pay. But on Tuesday evening he called to say the fire was under control and the word was that they'd be back for the weekend. He asked how Connor's ankle was and Connor told him it was okay and Ed said good because he had a plan which he'd already talked over with Julia: a canoe trip in Idaho, on a stretch of the Salmon River that he and Connor had done a couple of times before. Connor thought it sure sounded better than sewing parachutes. Ed said he'd try to hitch a ride with a fire crew from Boise who were heading home on Friday.

By the time Julia got back to Missoula on Thursday evening Connor had it all sorted out. He'd borrowed a pair of canoes and a second tent, gotten the camping gear ready and bought food. Julia was tired but in good spirits and he poured her a glass of the red wine that he'd bought specially that afternoon and made her sit down while he cooked supper. And while he busied himself in the cramped kitchen area, she sat back with one leg hooked over the arm of the couch and told him all that had happened, about the quest and how Skye had broken down and then the walk to the mountain and how "utterly amazing" John Standing Bird had been.

Julia's face was tanned and dirty from all her hiking and her hair had gone all straggly and she'd tied it up with a pale green bandanna. Connor had never seen her looking so lovely. And he tried not to, but he couldn't help thinking how like a couple they were, her talking about her work and him cooking supper just for the two of them. It was such a simple domestic scene and he knew it meant nothing, but the feelings it stirred in him were new and powerful. He wondered if he would ever find someone like Julia and doubted he would but he didn't allow the thought to sadden him or spoil the moment.

He'd bought a fillet of salmon and panfried it so that the skin was seared but the flesh was still moist inside. They ate it with salad and some baby potatoes, and Julia said it was the best salmon she'd ever tasted. Then they had blueberries and cream and coffee and sat talking and drinking their wine. Connor took it easy because he didn't want to make a fool of himself again. They sat talking a long time, although Julia did most of it. Connor listened, half hearing what she said but mostly enjoying just watching her.

The Larry Burrows book was on the table and she picked it up and started asking him about it. As she flicked slowly through the pictures, Connor waited to see if she would say anything about the one that had most affected him, but she only looked at it awhile and moved on. She stopped at one in which a young girl was crouched over the body of her mother and howling distraught at the camera.

"Do you think it's heartless to take a picture like that?" she said.

"You mean rather than help her?"

Julia nodded, still staring at the child.

"No. A picture never tells what happened next. A lot of photographers help people when they can. Burrows almost adopted one of the kids he photographed. But the most important thing, I guess, is to show the world what's going on."

"I guess."

She asked if she could borrow the book and Connor said sure, and then she asked about his own photography and whether she could see some of his work. He mostly kept it at the ranch and hardly had any pictures with him except those he'd taken of his mother at the rodeo, which he'd processed only last week. A couple of them weren't bad and he got them out and Julia studied them carefully. He could see she was impressed.

"Wow, Connor. You're really good. I had no idea."

"Thanks."

"No, I mean . . . Oh, that sounds so rude, doesn't it? All I meant was, I hadn't seen anything before—except that terrible one of the elk on fire. When I say terrible, I mean, it was really good, you know. I just . . ."

Connor let her dig herself deeper. She was blushing under her tan and he grinned and said it was okay, he knew what she meant. The phone rang and Julia reached for it like a drowning man for a life belt. It was Ed.

Connor stood up and started clearing the dishes. He listened to her telling Ed some of the same things and found himself trying to detect any difference in her tone of voice, some greater intimacy perhaps, but he couldn't.

Julia handed him the phone and said she was going to have a bath, always her great treat after eight days in the backcountry. Connor sat down on the couch and listened while Ed told him about the fire and tried to wind him up with more overtime bullshit, saying he couldn't decide whether to go for a Merc or a Lexus. Finally they got serious and talked about the arrangements for the following day. The idea was to put the canoes in the river at a little town called Stanley. One of the Idaho firefighters with whom Ed had gotten friendly lived near there and was going to give him a lift from Boise airport. He figured they would get to Stanley around two o'clock.

As he undressed in his room, Connor could hear Julia in the bathroom humming a little tune and he could hear the splash of the water as she washed herself in the tub and he had to try hard to censor his thoughts. He heard her brushing her teeth and then opening the bathroom door and switching off the light.

"Connor?"

"Yeah?"

"Thanks for a great supper."

"You're welcome."

"Goodnight."

"Goodnight."

THE TOWN OF STANLEY sprawled in a broad green bowl of a valley some six thousand feet above sea level, guarded to the north by the White Cloud Mountains and to the south by the Sawtooth whose daggered peaks were sheathed all year in snow. The river curled through meadow flats where cattle grazed alongside deer and elk to the hum of bumble-bees and the lazy flap of a heron's wing. Here and there among the buttercups hot springs gurgled and steamed and Connor had always thought they were a kind of whispered hint that the idyll on show was not to be trusted and that the river's true nature lay in the seething rapids and thundering gorges that were to come and for which the Salmon was revered.

Stanley was a five-hour drive from Missoula and they arrived an hour early and pulled up close by the river and unloaded the canoes and all the gear onto the grassy bank that sloped down to the water. The canoes were Old Town fifteen footers, both in good condition, one red, the other green. The camping gear and food were stowed in black waterproof duf-fel bags.

Julia got out the Burrows book which weighed about a ton and a half and wasn't ex-actly the best kind of book to bring on a canoe trip. Connor teased her for it and she laughed and settled herself on the grass to read while he took the truck around to the parking lot behind the Mountain Village Mercantile where they had arranged to meet Ed.

Connor was wearing only shorts and a pale gray T-shirt but in the thin mountain air the midday sun felt hot. He watched it shimmering along the blacktop as he walked around to the front and up the steps of the store. It was built of logs and had a long porch with an ice machine on it and a pay phone. Going inside was like stepping into an age gone by. There were old guns hanging on the wall and an ax and an ancient ox collar and the place seemed to sell anything a man might need, from a pair of pants to a pastrami sandwich. What Connor needed right now was a couple of cold sodas.

The woman behind the counter served him with a smile and asked where he was headed and Connor said they were going to canoe down to Challis and would it be okay to leave his truck out back in the lot and she said that was fine. She had just baked some chocolate-chip cookies and they smelled so good that Connor bought some and he bought some oranges too and thanked her.

When he got back to the river he saw Julia had taken off her T-shirt and was wearing a black swimsuit which she must have had on underneath. She was wearing sunglasses and had taken off her sandals and rolled up her shorts. Her legs were long and tanned but her ankles and feet were pale from wearing hiking boots all the time.

"I see you like sun," he said.

"Love it. They say it's bad for your skin, but I don't care. It's my Italian blood. My mom's the same. Ed says I'll wind up looking like a handbag."

"Does your mom look like a handbag?"

"Yeah, but a really classy one, you know?"

Connor laughed. He sat down beside her and they drank the sodas and ate the cookies and watched the sun spangle on the water. Connor told her that as a young man his father used to come down to these parts to fish for sockeye.

"They used to come upstream to spawn. They go this bright red color. I remember Dad saying there were so many, the water looked like blood."

"They don't come anymore?"

"No. They built these dams downstream to make electricity and though they help some fish get up here, it's nothing like what it was."

"Why do people allow that kind of thing?"

"I guess they figure electricity's more important than fish."

He peeled an orange and gave her half and

she said what a beautiful place it was, and Connor pointed out some of the peaks he and Ed had climbed over the years.

"You know what they call this river?"

"You mean apart from the Salmon?"

"Yeah. It's called the River of No Return."

"Because the salmon never came back?"

Connor smiled. "Because when Lewis and Clark reached here, they got stuck and ended up eating their own horses."

"So it was the horses who never came back."

Two o'clock came and went and they sat waiting and talking for another hour and Ed still didn't arrive. They'd agreed that he would call the Mercantile if there were any problems and Connor walked over there a couple of times but there were no messages. Every now and then a car would appear in the distance and he and Julia would stop talking and watch it come wavering and wobbling toward them through the liquid blacktop mirage, thinking it might be Ed, but it never was. A little after three they walked over to the Mercantile and stood in the shade of the porch and there they waited another hour, talking all the time and drinking more soda. And still he didn't come.

Though she tried not to show it, Connor could tell Julia was worried and he was wondering himself why Ed hadn't called or gotten someone else to. He went over to the pay phone and called the smoke jumper base in Missoula. The operations office told him that the California fire had flared up again overnight and that Ed and the others were still needed. Julia was listening and had gathered what had happened but they didn't have time to talk about it because as soon as Connor hung up, the woman came out of the store and said there was a call for him inside.

"Connor?"

"Hey, Ed. I just called the base and heard."

"Man, I'm so sorry. I'd have called sooner but things have gone crazy down here."

"You okay?"

"Yeah, I'm fine. Just pissed as hell I can't come with you guys."

"Well, the river isn't going anyplace. We'll do it another time. We'll just head home."

"Are you kidding? Do it. You'll have a ball. How's the water looking?"

"Good."

"Then go for it, man. Julia'll love it."

Connor hesitated. He wasn't sure Julia would want to if it was just going to be the two of them. She was standing beside him.

"Listen, Ed. Talk to Julia, she's right here."

He handed over the phone and while they talked he wandered around the store, pretending to look at things but really just listening. She asked how Ed was and if he was being careful and he was obviously telling her how sorry he was not to have made it to Stanley and how much he missed her. She said she missed him too.

"You bet we're going to do it," she said, looking at Connor. "Connor says it's called the River of No Return, so he's not allowed to quit."

They said their fond goodbyes and told each other to take care and then Julia called Connor to the phone again.

"Ed?"

"So you're going to do it, okay?"

"Well, if Julia wants to—"

"Of course she does. What's the matter with you, man? I know I'm the one with all the paddling skills, but you'll get by."

"As I recall, you're the capsize king."

"Listen, I've got to go. You have fun, you hear? And take good care of my girl, okay?"

Connor promised he would.

They were on the river within half an hour. He gave Julia the choice of which canoe they would take and she chose the red one. They put the green one back on the truck along with some of the gear they now wouldn't need. The woman at the Mercantile said she would keep an eye on it until they came back on the bus on Sunday night. They bought a bag of cherries and the last of her cookies and thanked her and headed for the river.

They were almost there when they heard the woman calling after them. Connor went back. She was holding something out to him.

"Your girlfriend left her sunglasses."

Connor nearly corrected her but didn't. He took them and thanked her again.

They put on their life vests and took off their shoes and stowed the two black duffel bags between the two seats. Then Julia climbed in and took the forward seat and when she was settled Connor pointed the canoe out into the stream and pushed off and stepped aboard. And they slipped slowly out into the body of the river and let the current take them.

The water was clear and cool and swifter than it had looked from the bank. Dark fronds of weed undulated like mermaid's hair and darker shapes of fish darted and skewed away in panic as the canoe and its shadow upon the riverbed slid by. The sun had lost its brazen heat and as it angled lower it lit the back edges of the grass and flowers along the western bank and turned to gold the clouds of newly hatched flies that pirouetted above the moving glass of the water. Along the bank cattle lifted their heads from their drinking to watch them pass, the water falling in sunlit drops from their glistening pink noses.

They had talked for many hours and it was good now to be silent and to listen to the swoosh of the paddles and the sounds of the wilderness around them. Julia paddled in smooth, strong strokes and he could tell she was no novice. She had tied up her hair again with the bandanna, and no matter where Connor looked his eyes kept coming back to the nape of her neck and the little brown smudge of a birthmark that showed above the sunbleached red of her life vest.

They left the lushness of the valley pastureland and the river narrowed and ran faster and the banks grew steeper until soon they were passing through a winding canyon of stone crested with serried ranks of Douglas and alpine fir and the fading blue of the sky above. Only when the river twisted west did they see the sun and when they did, the water before them was turned to molten gold.

They watched an osprey hanging high in the gorge and saw it tuck its wings and fall like a rock to the river and scoop a fish writhing fat and silver in its talons then fly away downstream. Once, rounding a bend, they came across a family of river otters tumbling in the shallows and when the cubs saw them they splashed for safety to their mother who didn't move, just lifted her chin and showed the paler fur of her neck and watched the canoe go by. Julia turned around and smiled at him and Connor smiled back and neither of them spoke.

They came to a place where the river spread and ran in a long curve of breaks and pools. There was a bench of rock that ran along the southern bank some ten or twelve feet above the water and Connor recognized it as a place he and Ed had camped before. They dragged the canoe from the water and hauled the bags up to the bench and while Julia gathered wood and made a fire Connor took his fishing rod and a couple of flies and waded into the shallows.

There were flies skitting over the water and fish rising all around him and on only his second cast he hooked one and Julia, watching from above, let out a whoop and he looked up at her and grinned and the fish jumped and shook its head and he almost lost it. It was a fine west-slope trout of around two pounds and they cooked it on a spit of wood over the fire and its flesh was as pink as the gathering night sky and tasted pure as the river itself.

They ate the rest of the cookies and some cherries and Julia challenged him to a pit-spitting contest, claiming she was the world champion pit-spitter. She bet him a dollar that he couldn't hit a particular rock down by the river in three goes and he took her on and missed every time. Then she bet him another dollar that she could hit it three out of three and she did. So Connor took her on again, with a different target this time, and twice more she beat him. By now he was laughing so much that he couldn't arrange his mouth to spit properly but even so he challenged her again, double-or-quits, to a long distance pit-spit which he was sure he'd win. But even though she was laughing as much as he was, she beat him again and at eight dollars down Connor called it a day.

After that they sat by the fire, not saying much, just watching the light fade on the river and the sky go from pink to blue to star-washed black. Connor had worried over how they would sleep and had brought both tents and he offered now to put one up for her. But Julia said to hell with tents, if anyone was used to sleeping in the open she was and on a night like this, in a place like this, that was the only way to go. So they spread their sleeping bags by the fire and Connor bear-bagged the food and went off to hang it in the trees so she wouldn't be embarrassed if she needed to undress.

The fire burned low and they lay looking at the stars and Julia asked him if he knew their names and was surprised that he knew almost all of them. He told her about his father and his star stories.

"Sounds like your dad would have made a great teacher."

"He would have. I imagine you're pretty good too."

"No. I get too involved. Like I have with Skye."

"That can't be a bad thing."

"Yes it is. It can be."

"Way I see it, she wouldn't have turned around if you hadn't cared so."

"Caring is different. Oh, I don't know."

There were two falling stars in quick succession and Julia said they must both make secret wishes and Connor didn't make the one he truly wanted but instead simply wished that the three of them would all be happy, whatever might befall them. They were silent awhile. Then Julia spoke again.

"That book of yours, about the war photographer?"

"Larry Burrows."

"Uh-huh. Is that the kind of work you want to do?"

He wondered how she knew what he had scarcely admitted to himself.

"Maybe part of me does, yeah."

There was a long pause.

"Connor?"

Something earnest in her tone made him turn to look at her and in the dying glow of the fire he saw her dark eyes were fixed on him.

"What?" he said.

"Don't. Please don't."

TEN

THE FIRE on Snake Mountain which was to change so many lives so utterly started with a single shaft of lightning. It struck on a still and moonless night, high on a ridge of pale rock and paler grass, where a dead lodgepole pine, long stripped of bark and bleached by several summers, tilted like a bowsprit over fathoms of forest. In the fractured moment of the flash the tree stood frozen in a negative of neon bone against the black of the night. A trail of tiny tongues of flame licked and flickered along its stem and the ground around it shook and small rocks broke from the earth and rolled and clattered down into the forest.

There were witnesses no doubt to this sudden splintering of air and wood, but none that was human. Perhaps, below among the trees, the elk jerked sideways from their feeding or an owl swerved in its flight and missed its prey or a passing wolf froze in the shadowed huckleberry and angled a yellow, unreflecting eye at the sky. But the rocks soon came to rest and silence settled once more. And the only hint of what had taken place and what was yet to come was the curl of smoke that issued but briefly from the charred cleft of the pine.

The sun rose on a world that seemed unchanged. It climbed vast and red from behind the mountain and as the light crept across the land a pair of ravens flew in from the north and settled like spectators on the old lodgepole.

The mountain earned its name not for its rattlesnakes, of which there were indeed many, but for the zigzag pattern of ridges and gullies seismically etched upon its western flank a hundred million years before. Its higher and lower slopes were thick with lodgepole and Douglas fir and its middle was girthed with runs of sliprock and wide patches of sunbaked grass bestrewn with boulders. The ridges ran down and across the mountainside in spines of pale limestone and the gullies between them were tangled with scrub like the wire-filled trenches of some long-abandoned war. As they made their descent, both ridges and gullies converged into a single steep-sided scoop of a valley which funneled, some four thousand feet below, into the north fork of the Hope River.

This was what the ravens sat surveying, and when the sun had revealed every part of it and the show was over, they opened their wings and in a few languid flaps crested the ridge, their raucous calls carrying far in the still of the morning. They banked right and flew south and then east again over another ridge and then down and around into a long winding canyon.

Skye heard their croaking and looked up and watched them pass overhead and go swerving away along the canyon.

"That's what I'm going to come back as."

Julia was standing beside her, watching them too.

"As a raven?"

"Yeah. Wouldn't it be cool to fly like that? Next time around, that's me."

Julia shrugged. "I don't know. That's what I was last time. The flying's good but the food's terrible. All that rotten meat. Yuck."

Skye laughed and looked at her. "You're funny."

"Well, thanks, pal."

"No, funny's good."

The weather had reverted to the remorseless dry heat of the early summer, and Julia had changed their routine to allow for it. The group rose early now and hiked while there was still a trace of cool in the air. By eleven when it was too hot to go on they would find a sheltered spot and stay there until around four when the heat began to subside a little. They spent the time productively, reading and writing in their journals or doing construction or art projects that involved the whole group. Yesterday they had painted each other's faces.

It had been Skye's idea and had anyone made the same suggestion a couple of weeks ago, she would have sneered and dismissed it as kindergarten bullshit. Which had been more or less Mitch's reaction yesterday. Instead of getting into a fight, Skye patiently sold the idea.

"I don't mean paint your face like a chipmunk or some nerdy clown or something," she said. "You have to paint it in two halves, one side what you used to be and the other what you are now or what you want to be."

Lester said he didn't get it and so Skye went through it again more slowly and simply until the penny dropped and he grinned and said cool, let's do it. They had only one mirror, so they did it in pairs, telling each other what they wanted. Skye had Byron paint the left side of her face dark blue with tears of blood dripping from one eye and the corners of her eye and mouth turned down. The right side was yellow with stars of red and orange and green on her forehead and cheeks and the other corner of her mouth lifted in a great beaming smile. Only when they were all finished did they get to look in the mirror. Skye told Byron he'd done a good job.

Today they had settled in the shade of some old cottonwoods that grew along the banks of a dried-out creek and they ate a late breakfast, then wrote in their journals for half an hour. The creek bed was lined with rocks of strange shapes and colors and the banks were littered with dead wood and Julia suggested they use both the rocks and the wood and anything else they could find to make a sculpture. They sat for another half hour discussing what it would be and nobody seemed able to come up with an acceptable idea.

Skye had read John Standing Bird's book three times over and her head was full of Black Elk's accounts of her people, so she said why didn't they make a statue of Crazy Horse? She told them a little about him and they all seemed to think it was a good idea and off they went to work, scouring the creek and its banks for materials.

They found a limb of a fallen tree that was shaped like a horse's body and head and propped it on four stacks of flat rocks for its legs.

Julia got out her box of paints and they painted their palms and made prints on the horse's flanks and on its neck. They found another limb, forked this time, for the warrior's legs and body and lashed a branch across it to make his arms. While some worked on the construction, others went off to forage for more exotic things to decorate it with.

Skye wandered along the creek in search of something to make a war bonnet. They weren't supposed to go out of sight of the staff but as she got to a bend in the creek she spotted something just beyond it, up among the rocks and without thinking made her way toward it. It was the bloody remains of a bird, some kind of grouse, she thought, which must have been killed in the night for the blood was fresh. She plucked its wing and tail feathers and picked some long stems of dried grass and sat on a rock, braiding them to make a band for the feathers.

"Hey, look what you found. Cool."

She looked up and saw Mitch grinning down at her.

"Yeah, I just . . . found them."

"Can I help?"

She thought of saying no because she couldn't stand the guy, but since the quest she had resolved to be friendly to everyone. As it turned out, it didn't make any odds because he just sat down beside her anyway. He picked up some of the grass and made a futile attempt at braiding it.

"Look," she said. "I'll show you."

She put down her own grass and took his and got the braid started.

"You gotta keep it tight, otherwise the feathers will just fall out."

"Right."

"Here."

She handed it back to him and because she didn't want to lose the tension in the braid, she kept her fingers on it while he took hold of it. As he did so their hands touched and so did the insides of their forearms. Skye's instinct was to release the braid, but he said not to and that it was slipping open, so she kept her hand there and their flesh continued to touch.

"Your skin feels real good," he said.

"What?"

She snatched her hand away. The braid uncoiled in his hands and he stared at it for a short while then slowly looked up at her and smiled and shrugged.

"It does," he said. "It feels beautiful."

Looking her in the eye, he reached up and ran the backs of his fingers down the bare skin of her upper arm. Skye froze. And he seemed to take this as some kind of consent because then he reached up and stroked her cheek. And still she stayed frozen. She could feel her heart pounding. He was looking at her in the same slow-eyed way her stepfather did when he came home late reeking of drink.

"Come on, it's okay," he coaxed, glancing over her shoulder. "No one will know, we can go up there behind the rocks."

Skye knew they were out of sight of the others. She could hear their laughter and it seemed a long way off. Mitch lowered his hand and touched her breast and something exploded inside her and she swung at him with the back of her hand and hit him hard in the face.

"Jesus!"

He staggered to his feet, clutching his nose.

"You little bitch!"

"If you ever lay a finger on me again, I'll kill you."

She too was on her feet now and she grabbed the feathers and turned and headed back along the creek. She thought he might come after her and she wanted to run but something told her not to, so she just walked as fast as she could and didn't once look back.

"You little whore-bitch! I wouldn't touch your squaw pussy with a ten-foot pole."

"Lucky you've only got a little teeny-weeny one then."

IT WAS MORE THAN TWO WEEKS since the canoe trip and Julia had spent much of that time replaying it in her head and wondering how she could have allowed it so to unsettle her. She had lain awake at night, worrying while everyone around her slept and Lester babbled on in his dreams. She had scrutinized her feelings, trying to apply the dispassionate logic of her years of studying psychology. And when that failed, she tried anger instead and chastised herself as a fickle, shameful creature for allowing such thoughts into her head about her lover's best friend. But that didn't work either.

Not that Connor had done or said anything deliberate to prompt all this. He had behaved impeccably. She had already been aware of his sense of honor and loyalty to his friend and she could imagine how shocked he would be to know that she harbored such feelings for him. But the truth was that ever since she had first laid eyes on him, that evening at the airport, something inside her had turned.

His mere presence seemed to affect how she

behaved and what she said, as if everything were somehow for his benefit. No man had ever had this effect on her before. It was the way her mother was about men, always smitten and wobbly at the knees over some new lover, who inevitably turned out to be as big a scoundrel as the last. Julia had always loftily regarded this as a weakness whose genetic code she was grateful not to have inherited. But now she wasn't so sure.

She repeated to herself, again and again like a mantra, that it was Ed she loved—and she did, she really did. But on the river that weekend she hadn't been able to take her eyes off Connor. She could remember everything he had said, every little thing he had done. There was a kind of quiet centeredness about him that moved her. She'd watched him fishing that evening, with the golden light shimmering on the water around him, and thought how graceful and beautiful he looked. Worse still, lying next to him by the fire, with their bodies only a few inches apart, she had kept imagining what it would be like to kiss him and to have his hands on her and she'd felt a physical longing for him that shocked her and shamed her.

Ed had flown back to Missoula on Sunday and was there in the apartment to greet them when they arrived back from Idaho. He had supper waiting for them and gave them both such a warm welcome and it was wonderful to see him again, wonderful. And when they made love that night, she told him again and again how much she'd missed him and how much she loved him and realized that it wasn't Ed she was trying to convince but herself. And, try as she might, she couldn't block Connor out of her head and kept picturing him lying there in the next room.

She had hoped that coming back to the group would bring some relief from all this mental turmoil. But if anything it had grown worse and was in danger sometimes of marring what should otherwise have been a time of great fulfillment. For Skye's transformation had transformed the whole group. Since her quest she had become its center. She was joyous and vibrant and considerate to everyone around her, staff and students alike. Julia had never witnessed such a change. It was as if the girl had been reborn.

So, now, as soon as Skye arrived back with the feathers, Julia knew something was wrong. The face was locked in its old frown. When Julia asked her if she was all right, she just gave a curt nod and didn't reply. A few minutes later, Mitch walked in. He did his best to hide it but Julia could see his nose had been bleeding and when she asked him what had happened he said he'd slipped and knocked his head on a tree. Later she saw him talking quietly with Paul and Wayne, who kept looking over toward Skye while they listened.

By now the sculpture was looking magnificent but Skye seemed to have lost interest. Instead, Byron had taken the lead. He got everyone to contribute something colored, a bandanna or even just some strips of paper, and these were all tied to Crazy Horse's body. Lester found the skull of a badger and Scott some broken antlers and, along with Skye's feathers, they used them to make an exotic headdress. And all the while, Skye sat to one side, sometimes watching and sometimes staring off into the distance. Every so often Julia would try to involve her but it was no good. When the sculpture was nearly done and the others were busy making final touches, Julia walked over and sat down beside her.

"So what do you think? Not bad, huh?"

Skye looked across at the sculpture.

"Yeah. It looks great."

Her voice was lifeless and little and Julia looked her squarely in the face and saw there were tears in her eyes.

"Okay. Tell me what happened."

Skye shook her head and looked away. And the tears started to roll and she wiped them viciously away. Julia reached out and gently put her arm around her shoulders, half expecting to be shrugged off, but instead Skye turned to her and put her head on Julia's chest and put her arms around her and sobbed. Julia stroked her hair and held her.

"It's okay, sweetheart, let it go. Just let it go."

She glanced toward the sculpture and saw that Mitch and Wayne and Paul were staring at them. As soon as their eyes met hers, they looked away. Katie came over and asked if everything was all right and Julia said quietly that it was. Skye murmured something.

"What, honey?"

"I just get everything wrong."

Julia tried again to find out what had happened but Skye wouldn't say and soon she stopped crying and gathered herself. And by four o'clock, after they had eaten and set out on the trail again, leaving Crazy Horse behind them proudly guarding the creek, she seemed almost back to normal.

They made camp that night in a rocky bowl on the east side of Snake Mountain. While supper was being prepared, Julia walked a little way off and made the usual evening radio call back to base to let Glen know their position. She told him that the plan for tomorrow was to cross the ridge and head down to the river. Glen asked how things were going and she told him about Skye and that something had happened with Mitch but that now it all seemed to have settled down. They talked about a few routine things and Glen said that because of the hot, dry weather the Forest Service had upped the fire risk warning and that the group should take extra care with their campfires.

As they sat around the fire that evening, Julia kept alert for any sign of tension between Mitch and Skye, who was sitting beside her, but if anything was going on, neither of them was showing it. The first to speak in group was Lester. He said how much he'd enjoyed making the sculpture of Crazy Horse and made an affirmation in support of Byron, who'd done most of the work. Scott asked Skye about Indian names and how Crazy Horse had gotten his and she said she didn't know but what she did know was that he'd had other names too, Curly and His Horses Looking. Byron said that in that book she was always reading nowadays there was a guy called Refuse To Go, which he thought was pretty cool. He said he guessed they got their names from something that happened or for doing something special. They discussed this for a while.

"So what's yours?" Lester asked Skye.

"Me?" Skye smiled. "I don't have one."

"Well, I think we ought to give you one," Lester said.

Mitch whispered something to Paul, who sniggered.

"Would you like to share that with us, Mitch?" Julia said.

"No thanks, it was kind of private."

"Mitch, you know the rules. We don't do that in group. Please tell us what you said."

"It was just a joke."

"So let's all share it. Come on."

He looked at Paul, who was grinning and shaking his head, then looked back at Julia. There was a cold defiance in his eyes and Julia suddenly knew she'd made a terrible mistake in pushing him.

"Okay, if you really want me to, I said, seeing the two of you cuddling this afternoon, Skye ought to be called Munches On Beaver."

Paul and Wayne laughed but otherwise there was a stunned silence. It took Julia a moment to believe her own ears. Everyone was looking at her and Skye.

"Mitch, that is so out of order," Scott said and

at the same time Byron said it was a mean and shitty thing to say and several others agreed. Skye had already gotten to her feet and was walking away from the circle.

"Hey, man, it was joke, that's all."

"It's not a joke, you asshole," Byron said.

"Hey, dude, just 'cos you've got the hots for her."

Byron made a lunge at him and Scott had to restrain him. Julia was on her feet too now and she called after Skye, who paid no attention. She turned on Mitch.

"Mitch, you and I are going to have a long talk about this."

He held up his hands, all innocent. "Hey, I'm sorry, okay?"

"No, it's not okay."

And before he could reply, she asked Katie to come with her and the two of them hurried off after Skye.

They found her and spent the next hour trying to comfort her. Eventually they persuaded her to come back to the circle where the others were all waiting. Mitch's face showed that he had taken a serious drubbing while they had been away. Skye sat looking into the fire while he apologized to her and to Julia for what he had said, then Paul and Wayne apologized for laughing. Skye nodded but didn't say a word or even glance at them. It was as though the door had closed again inside her.

Nobody felt like talking anymore and they put out the fire and, as usual, Katie and Laura and Scott collected everyone's pants and boots and they settled down for the night. Julia and Katie lay either side of Skye. She said she was tired and wanted to go to sleep. She gave Julia a brave little smile.

"Thank you," she said softly.

"What for?"

"For believing in me."

Julia reached out and stroked her hair.

"You're a wonderful person, Skye."

"I'm not. I blew it all."

"You didn't. These things happen. What other people say doesn't change the way you are. Remember what we always say? It's just part of the journey. Life isn't about what happens to you, it's about how you handle what happens. And the way you've been handling things is awesome."

"Maybe."

"Believe me."

They said goodnight. Julia watched her for a long time, staring blankly at the sky. Then at last Skye closed her eyes and turned on her side and only when Julia was certain she was asleep did she allow herself to think of other things. And thinking, by habit now, of Connor, she drifted into sleep herself.

UP THE MOUNTAIN and over the ridge, little more than a mile from where the group was camped, the lightning of the previous night had nestled all this time in the old lodgepole's desiccated heart, a cocoon of dull heat that neither glowed nor any longer smoked. And had the wind not risen that night and funneled upward through the pine's riven stem, along crevices carved in it by ants and mites, then this pupa of fire might well have died. Fanned by the breeze however, it fed on fragments of resinous wood until it glowed and grew and glowed yet brighter. And at last, in the witching of the night, it hatched.

The grass and scrub around and beneath the old tree were dry and brittle and rustled in the wind and when the stem torched, its entire length was engulfed within seconds and flaming fragments fell upon the grass which torched as well. And as the lodgepole's limbs came asunder, they fell and rolled downhill, laying trails of flame in their wake which spread and joined and spread yet farther until the entire slope was ablaze.

Had none of the rolling limbs of flame

reached the forest, the fire might have starved and died, but the largest found a steeper route and crashed and cartwheeled deep among the trees, sending showers of sparks as it went. And so parched was the forest that every spark found an eager host and every host became a fire of its own until all conjoined and roared as if in remonstration that want of water should have forced them to drink this other fatal element instead.

WHETHER IT WAS THE SMELL of smoke that woke her that morning or some other more mysterious summoning of her senses, Julia would never know. But as soon as she opened her eyes she knew something was wrong. When she smelled the smoke, her first thought was that they had failed to kill the campfire and with a pang of panic she sat up in her sleeping bag and peered through the muted light toward the place where they had sat last night. All was still with not even a wisp of smoke to be seen and now when she sniffed again the smell had gone. She must have imagined it or smelled traces of campfire smoke on her clothes or in her hair and in her half-awake state turned it into something else. She breathed out in relief and again lay down.

But something still seemed wrong.

Or at least different. Maybe it was the stirring of the trees. There hadn't been so much as a breeze for many days. And she had almost convinced herself that this was all that was bothering her, when again she smelled smoke. She sat up once more. Everyone around her was still asleep. Skye was buried deep in her sleeping bag, as she often slept, with the top pulled right over her head. Julia looked at her watch. It was a little after five-thirty. She slipped from her sleeping bag and stood up. She took her shorts and boots from the locked duffel bag that she used for a pillow and put them on then headed off up through the trees.

There was a narrow trail made by deer and she followed it for about half a mile, glancing up from time to time through the pines that towered above her, their tops swaying back and forth in the wind. The smell of smoke was growing stronger all the time. At last she saw a clearing ahead of her and as she came to it and stepped out of the trees, she got her first clear view of the sky and of Snake Mountain rearing above her, the sun just catching its eastern tip and lighting the cloud that was drifting away behind it. And Julia was just thinking how beautiful it looked when she noticed that the sky elsewhere was clear and that this wasn't a normal cloud, but a windblown column of smoke and she felt a chill of dread run over her.

She ran back down through the trees as fast as she could safely go. When she reached camp nobody had stirred. Holding her finger to her lips, she gently woke Katie and Laura and Scott and mouthed to them to come with her. They huddled out of earshot of the students and Julia told them in a whisper that there was a forest fire and that they should get everyone up and dressed as fast as they could, but not to panic them.

"It's on the other side of the mountain. If we hike out the way we came, we'll be fine. Any questions? Okay. You get everyone moving. I'm going to call Glen."

She took out the radio and was walking away from them, adjusting the controls, when Katie came running after her.

"Julia! Julia!"

Julia turned and waited for her to come close. Katie was still wearing the T-shirt and underpants she slept in.

"Skye's gone."

"What?"

"She must have slipped away in the night. She stuffed her pack into her sleeping bag. She's taken my boots and pants and gone."

ELEVEN

ED WAS floating in a fabulous palm-fringed pool in California. The sun was dancing on the water and at the far end of the pool there was a long white house and a terrace of exotic flowers and he could hear the ocean nearby and he knew he'd really made it big as a composer because it all belonged to him—well, maybe not the ocean, but everything else did, including the beautiful woman sunbathing naked on the terrace. He was gliding slowly toward her and the water felt silky and sensual and he knew exactly what he was going to do when he reached her. Then a phone started ringing. Until that moment he'd had no doubt whatsoever that the woman was Julia, but now the damn phone was messing everything up and when she lifted her head and smiled at him—whoa there! It was his mother.

He opened his eyes wide and in the same instant the phone stopped ringing and he heard Connor in the living room, answering it.

"Hello? Hi, Hank. Yes, he is." There was a long pause. "Okay, I'll tell him. We're on our way."

He hung up and a moment later appeared in the doorway of Ed's room.

"Ed?"

"God, what time is it?"

"Time to get your chute on, old buddy."

"Where's the fire?"

"In the Lewis and Clark. Snake Mountain."

Ed sat up.

"That's where—"

"I know. Julia's fine. They're on the other side of the mountain and moving out. But one of the group's missing."

IT WAS KATIE who first found Skye's footprints. She recognized the tread pattern of her own boots in a place she hadn't walked, in the dust at the start of the trail that Julia had taken earlier up toward the ridge. While Katie put on Skye's pants and boots, Julia grabbed a day pack and quickly put together what they might need: some food and water, a map of the mountain, a compass and a pair of binoculars. Now the two of them were following Skye's tracks up through the trees. It was hard going. The trail was mostly covered with pine needles and sometimes they would lose the footprints for as much as twenty or thirty yards before finding them again in a patch of dust.

In a series of radio conversations, Glen and Julia had worked out a plan: Scott and Laura would hike out south with the rest of the students while Julia and Katie began searching for Skye. The Forest Service and the police had already been alerted. The fire had been reported just before Julia first radioed in. It had been spotted by two wildlife biologists flying the continental divide. A planeload of smoke jumpers was on its way from Missoula.

"Your boyfriend's on his way to save you," Glen said. "It's so romantic."

She nearly snapped at him but didn't. She knew he meant well, but it wasn't a time for jokes. And she had no idea whether it was true. It was over a week since she had been able to speak to Ed. She didn't know how recently he or Connor had jumped and how high they therefore were on the jump list. For all she knew, they might both have been sent down to fight fires in California. She half hoped they had.

Katie was going on and on about how guilty she felt for not stowing her boots and pants securely, which was one of the basic WAY rules. Julia had told her three times already that she shouldn't be too hard on herself and that it could happen to any of them. But as they followed Skye's footprints up the trail and came out into the clearing, she lost patience and stopped.

"Listen, Katie. You feel bad, I feel bad. I should have seen it coming. We should have put her on watch and taken it in turns to sleep. So let's just take it as read that we both feel guilty and get on with the job of finding her."

It sounded sharper than she had intended. Katie looked chastened and just nodded and they didn't speak again for a long while except when they lost Skye's tracks and split up and one of them hollered to say she had found them again.

What Julia had said about her own feelings of guilt wasn't the half of it. Although she still didn't know what had happened yesterday between Skye and Mitch, she knew it was her fault that they had been allowed to wander out of sight. If she had been more vigilant, none of this would have happened. She also reproached herself for letting things become so tactile with Skye. Lately they had become almost like sisters, often putting an arm around each other. She hadn't thought about it, as she should have done, it just seemed so natural, but it was this that had no doubt prompted Mitch's lesbian taunt. In hindsight, Skye's transformation had seemed such a breakthrough, after all those weeks of tension and heartache, that Julia had allowed the mood to become too relaxed. She had forgotten how easily things could go wrong.

And things didn't go much more wrong than this—a student missing on a burning mountain. Julia didn't consider herself religious. Since falling foul of the nuns at elementary school, she was about as lapsed as a Catholic could be. But looking up toward the ridge and seeing the plume of gray smoke that stained the sky behind it, she found herself muttering Hail Marys to the rhythm of her footfall.

Three-quarters of the way up to the ridge, the trail turned to gravel and rock and the footprints vanished. But the terrain on either side was so harsh that Julia doubted that Skye would have deviated. It depended on what the girl had in mind. Kids on the run in an unknown mountain wilderness usually did one of two things. They either followed a drainage down in the hope that it led to a road or headed for a high place in the hope of getting their bearings and spotting the best route of escape. Skye's tracks so far suggested the latter. But there was another possibility which Julia hardly dared contemplate; perhaps the girl was looking for another kind of escape, a more permanent one.

Julia thought about their last conversation and how Skye had thanked her and said she felt she had blown it all. Now the words echoed in Julia's head like a valediction and even though the morning sun was already warm, the memory made the sweat at the back of her neck turn cold.

They were coming now to the ridge and as they walked the last few steps, the other side of the mountain revealed itself and for the first time Julia saw the fire itself and the damage it had already done. For perhaps a thousand feet below where they stood, the land was a smoking wasteland, the trees broiled to charred spikes that still smoldered in the wind. Below that, beyond one of the many rocky spines that traversed the mountain, the forest was as yet untouched. But farther down, just before the trees gave way to grassland and the scrub-filled gullies converged, there were pockets of white smoke where sparks must have carried and caught.

The main fire had been driven north and east across the mountain by the wind. Julia could see it about half a mile away, a tall front of flame moving steadily away from her through the trees. She had never seen a forest fire before and she found herself oddly mesmerized. It seemed somehow animate, even the sounds it made, the roar and crackle and rumble, like some insatiable beast rampaging through the trees. She dragged her eyes away from it and scoured the slope back and forth for any sign of life but saw none. She got out her map and worked out exactly where they were.

"So if you were Skye, standing here, what would you do?" she said.

Katie didn't answer at once and Julia turned and saw she too was transfixed by the fire. She looked very frightened.

"Katie, we're safe here. Ed always says it's like with money, if you're in the black, you're okay. Everything around here is black and burned. We're safe."

Katie nodded.

"So what would you do? Where would you go if you wanted to get out of this place?"

"We don't even know she came up here."

"Assuming she did. Where would you go?"

Katie considered for a moment. She looked at the map and then pointed to her left down the southern section of the mountain face where the unburnt gullies and spines of white rock funneled down toward the river.

"Down there, I guess."

"Me too. I'd head for the river."

That is, she added to herself, assuming I wanted to survive. They stood staring down the mountain while Julia tried to figure out a route. Unlike the east side of the ridge, where they had camped, there was no obvious trail. They had no idea what time Skye had sneaked away. If the fire was already burning by the time she reached the ridge, maybe she would have turned back. But they had found no footprints heading back down. The chances were that she had gotten here before it started.

Then the thought occurred to Julia that perhaps, in some vengeful brainstorm, Skye might have started the fire herself. She doubted it, but it was possible. But then, there were a hundred other possibilities. They knew nothing. The only course, Julia resolved, was to follow her own instinct. And her instinct was the same as Katie's: Skye would have headed down the left-hand side of the slope, following the diagonal spines toward the river. If the fire had already been burning, this would have seemed the safest route. If the fire hadn't yet started, it would still have seemed the most logical.

"Come on, let's go."

They hiked along the ridge until they were above the edge of what had been burned. The first of the spines was directly below them and its white rock stood out starkly beside the black of the burn. To reach it they had to clamber down a short but steep fall of loose rocks then lower themselves feetfirst past a small overhang. Then they were on the spine and the going was easier. The rock was smooth but not slippery and the gradient was gentle. Sometimes Julia felt as if they were descending a broad white staircase, bordered to the right all the while with the black carpet of the burn.

"Look, what's that?" Katie said, pointing ahead.

On the black earth, some fifty yards below, something white was fluttering and at first Julia thought it might be a wounded bird. They scrambled down toward it and as they drew closer she saw it was a book. It was lying open with the wind strumming its pages and long before she picked it up Julia knew whose it was. It was only a paperback and from Skye's avid use of it the covers were battered and creased. The pages were singed at the edges from the heat that lingered in the scorched earth. Julia flipped to the title page and saw what John Standing Bird had written on it.

For Skye McReedie.
These are your people.
Welcome home.

SKYE HEARD THE PLANE just in time, a moment before she saw it. It was coming from the south, flying low above the river and as its nose appeared around a bluff she dived for cover. Had she been walking on top of the rock they would surely have seen her, but luckily she'd just dropped down to cross one of the gullies and so she plunged into the bushes and stayed put until the sound of the engines melted into the dull roar of the fire.

She rolled over on her back and lay there, panting and looking at the sky through the dry leaves of the willow scrub and realized she wasn't scared anymore. Not like she'd been when she first came over the ridge and saw the fire. She'd stood watching it awhile, wondering if she should go back and warn the others, then deciding not to and persuading herself there was nothing to be scared of. The worst that could happen was that she might die and she didn't give a shit about that. She really didn't. What was the big deal about dying? It was just bang and then nothing. Just plain black nothing. It sounded like bliss. Then she'd had a sudden flash of the young cop they killed and the terror in his eyes as he was being dragged along beside the car and she slammed a door in her head and refused to go there. But it must have affected her because after she'd set off down the mountain, the fire kept on scaring her, the sound of it more than the sight.

But now she was okay. She was even starting to think how good it was to be on the run again. For a while, these last two or three weeks, she thought she'd found somewhere she belonged. But it had turned bad, just like everything always did and the best thing was to get the hell out of it.

She sat up and cautiously raised her head above the bushes, like a rabbit peering from a hole. The plane had gone but she knew it was probably looking for her and would be back. She was thirsty and reached for the knotted red T-shirt that she was using for a bag. All she had in it were her water bottle, Katie's headlamp and her book and now, reaching into it, she found that the book was missing. She gave a little moan and her shoulders slumped. She cursed out loud and then thought what the hell, what did it matter? All that Black Elk stuff was just bullshit anyway, just their way of trying to fool her into thinking she had something to be proud of.

The water bottle was almost empty and she drained it in one swig and threw it away and still felt thirsty. Her own gray T-shirt was sweaty and torn so she untied the knots in Katie's red one and put it on instead and threw hers and the headlamp into the bushes. Katie's boots were about a half-size too big for her and she had painful blisters on both heels, but there was nothing she could do about them. She stood up and looked down the mountainside. She felt as if she'd been hiking downhill forever, but the damn river didn't seem much closer. At the top she'd kept well to the left and started following these weird platforms of rock, but lower down they kept going off at funny angles and took her too close to the fire, so now she was going to try cutting across them and head directly down the slope.

The gullies were of different depths and widths but all were filled with the same tangled scrub that was as high as Skye's hips and sometimes her shoulders. Now and then she found a trail that must have been made by animals, but mostly she had to wade through it and soon her arms were scratched and bleeding and she had to hold them aloft to protect them.

Soon she heard the plane again, and she ducked down and watched it through a gap in the bushes. This time it dropped a pair of pink and yellow streamers which snaked through the air over to her right where the fire was. The plane disappeared again, but in a short while it was back and dropped two more, blue and pink this time, and then did it a third time, two blue ones, by which time Skye was not only puzzled but also a little freaked. It was like they were playing a game. She figured the streamers must be some kind of signal or marker or something.

Each time the plane disappeared she stood up and headed off down the mountain again. By now her arms were covered in blood and she had nothing to wipe them with. The next time the plane came, it flew in a lot higher and this time, instead of streamers, it dropped two people on parachutes and she wondered if they'd been sent to find her or if it had something to do with the fire. Then it came back and dropped two more and then the same again and again until it seemed like a whole goddamn army was being flown in. She watched them floating down, drifting across the mountain, blue and white and yellow. They looked real pretty but no doubt the sonsofbitches all had their beady eyes spying for her so she stayed crouched in the bushes until she was sure the last of them had landed. She couldn't see where they came down, but it was definitely a lot farther up the mountain than she was and that was good because it meant they probably hadn't seen her.

When she stood up again the air felt cooler and the wind was stronger and seemed to be coming from a different direction. It rattled the dried leaves of the scrub and felt good on her face and on her bleeding arms. Away on the horizon there were some weird clouds building up. The sky seemed to be boiling.

She set off again. The river was at last starting to look a little closer. What exactly she was going to do when she reached it, she had no idea, but something would happen. Something always did.

THEY HAD MADE RADIO CONTACT with Julia on their very first pass across the mountain. What with all the engine noise, it was only Hank Thomas who got to hear her voice, but he relayed what she said and Ed felt a great rush of relief that she was safe. Connor grinned and gave him a pat on the back. Julia told Hank where on the mountain she was and on the next pass Ed and everyone else peered out of the windows and saw two tiny figures fifteen hundred feet below, standing on a strip of white rock and waving frantically.

Hank asked her if she had any idea where the

runaway girl was and Julia said she hadn't but that she thought she must be somewhere between her and the river. But even though on every subsequent pass, every jumper on board scanned the mountain, no one had caught a glimpse of her.

The jump spot was a patch of grass and sliprock below the tail of the fire. Ed and Connor were jumping last stick and by the time they reached it, the others had stowed their jumpsuits and parachutes. They did the same and then the firefighting equipment came in and everyone tooled up and gathered around Hank Thomas. He was talking with Julia on the radio and looking at the map while she gave him the map reference of where she and Katie were. Ed was struck by how professional she sounded. The voice was level and precise and betrayed no fear. But somehow it was like listening to a stranger.

"What's the girl's name?" Hank asked her.

"Skye. Skye McReedie."

Ed looked at Connor. They both knew how attached Julia was to the girl and how thrilled she had lately been at Skye's progress. It made the calm, professional way in which she was talking to Hank all the more impressive. Hank asked her if she'd seen any sign of the helicopter search and rescue team that was supposed to be on its way. Julia hadn't and Hank said he was going to radio right away to see what was keeping it. Meanwhile he would send three of his jumpers to help her and Katie look for the girl.

"Julia, one more thing. You see those thunderheads bubbling up over there to the northwest? There's a cold front coming in. The wind's moving around and it's going to blow stronger. We've all got to keep alert to that. This old fire could start fooling around and moving any which way. We don't want anyone taking any risks. Do you copy?"

"Copy."

"Good. Julia, I've got someone here who wants to say hello."

He grinned at Ed and shoved the radio in his hand.

"Julia?"

"Ed! I didn't know you were there."

"Are you okay?"

"I'm fine. Just worried about Skye."

"She'll be fine. We'll find her."

"Is Connor with you?"

"Yes, he is. Here's Hank again."

Hank took the radio.

"Julia? Stay where you are. We're on our way."

They signed off and, before Ed had the chance to ask, Hank named him, Connor and

Chuck Hamer as the three he was sending to help in the search. Hank and the other four jumpers would cut a line around the fire's eastern flank.

As the three of them moved away into the forest, he heard Hank start to make the call to find out where the hell the helicopter rescue team had gotten to.

IT TOOK THEM TWENTY MINUTES to hike across to where Julia was. They headed up along one of the strange spines of rock that they had seen from the air. Connor could see how this one had acted as a natural fire line. The mountainside above it was black, with the charred totem poles of burnt trees still smoking, while the forest below remained unburned. Connor didn't know why, but ever since his first glimpse of the mountain from the plane, something about it made him feel uneasy.

They walked single file with Connor in the lead. Once he stepped up onto a ledge and almost trod on a rattlesnake. It ignored him and slithered off, heading with speed and purpose away from the fire. Then up ahead he spotted Julia. She was sitting on a platform of rock with Katie and he called out and they waved and came running down toward them. She was wearing shorts and her pale gray T-shirt was patched with sweat. Ed ran ahead to meet them, taking off his hard- hat, and he and Julia flung their arms around each other and held each other while Connor and Chuck walked toward them.

Julia turned to Connor as he came near and hugged him too and he held her tight and was almost overwhelmed by the feel of her and the smell of her and at having her just for that moment there in his arms. They stepped apart and she looked him directly in the eyes and maybe he imagined it, but there seemed for a moment to be some message there for him but he didn't know what it was. She smiled bravely and looked away and he could see the tension in her face. She said hello to Chuck and introduced Katie who promptly burst into tears and clearly needed someone to hug too and chose Chuck.

"Hell," he said. "Why can't I always have that effect on women?"

They spread the map on the rock and had to hold it down because the wind was whipping around them now. The thunderheads were moving in fast. Julia showed them the route she thought Skye might be taking and where they had found the book. She suggested they fan out across the slope and move down in a line, keeping radio contact. Katie was the only one without a radio and when Connor suggested that she should team up with Chuck, she looked relieved. As they were about to move out, Hank came on the radio and said the rescue helicopter had lost radio contact and no one knew where it was. For the time being, he said, they were on their own.

The idea was that they were going to move down the mountainside in a line, as straight as the terrain allowed. Ed was going to take the northern end, nearest the fire, Julia next, then Connor, with Chuck and Katie taking the southern end. Ed stayed where he was and wished them luck as Connor and the others set off to take up their positions.

Chuck and Katie hiked on. Connor walked beside Julia.

"Oh, Connor," she said quietly.

She took a deep, shuddering breath and kept her eyes straight ahead. He could tell she was right on the edge.

"We'll find her."

"If anything happens to her, I'll never forgive myself."

He put a hand gently on her shoulder and she pressed her hand on his hand but still didn't look at him.

"It's all my fault."

He wondered what had happened to make

Skye run but it didn't seem the time to ask. She took her hand away and so did he.

"You know what I keep thinking about?" she said. "That elk you took the picture of. The one with its antlers on fire. I can't get it out of my head. I don't know why, but every moment I think he's going to step out in front of me."

Connor didn't know what to say. He'd had the same thought himself but it wouldn't help to tell her and they walked awhile without speaking. The wind rushed around them and rustled the huckleberry along a rim of forest below and it seemed to Connor that the sound issued from some joined but desolate corner of their two hearts.

"Connor?" She was looking straight at him.

"What?"

"Tell me it's going to be all right."

"It is. I know it is."

It was the first time he had lied to her. And it wouldn't be the last.

TWELVE

SKYE WATCHED the anvil clouds moving ever nearer. They were the color of gunmetal seamed with a sickly yellow and as they came they seethed and merged and lightning flickered from their joined belly like the tongues of angry serpents.

How many gullies she had crossed, she didn't know. But now the land was tilting and sending her across toward a vast curving valley of grass and boulders which seemed the best way down to the river. The valley was fringed on both sides by unburnt forest. She stopped in the shelter of a leaning rock to catch her breath. Her blisters hurt and her knees ached from hiking downhill for so long. The inside of her mouth felt like sandpaper. God, what she'd give for some water.

She turned and scanned the mountain for any of those people who'd come in on parachutes, but there was still no sign of them. The fresh wind had caked the blood on her arms and they itched and she stood scratching them and watching the clouds roil and the sun searching for cracks between them, sending patches of golden light scudding across the shadowed land.

The fire was hidden from her now by a low shoulder of the mountain. Oddly, the sound of it seemed louder and for the first time in a long while she could smell smoke. And as she looked over the forest below her, away to her right, she saw a white swirl of it coming around the shoulder and then the wind catching it and drifting it fast and flat over the trees and toward the valley. It didn't occur to Skye that this was something she should worry about, for by now she was surely far enough down the mountain to be out of danger. Directly below her there was a steep slope of loose rocks and she considered going down it and cutting through the trees to meet the valley lower down. But though it would no doubt be quicker, the slope looked too dangerous. Instead, she would stay high and cross over to join the valley at the top where the gullies linked up. The decision seemed to fuel her resolve and she set off again at a jog.

IT WAS ED who saw her first. He had just checked in with Hank on the radio and been told that there was still no word on the helicopter and that back at base they were starting to think something bad had happened. Hank said the wind where he was didn't seem to know what it was doing. If those goddamn thunderheads started spitting lightning, he said, all hell could break loose. Just as they were signing off, down the mountainside and away to his left, Ed caught a glimpse of red.

At first he thought it was a deer or maybe even a grizzly, but it was too red for either. He reached into his personal gear bag for the small pair of binoculars he always carried, but when he looked through them all he could see was trees and smoke drifting across them toward that huge valley that funneled down to the river. Then he saw another flash of red and this time he saw it was a figure. He reached for his radio.

"Julia, this is Ed."

For a few moments there was no reply.

"This is Julia."

"Is Skye wearing red?"

"No. Gray T-shirt, blue pants."

"Ed. This is Chuck."

"Go ahead, Chuck."

"The girl took Katie's red T-shirt. She might be wearing it."

Ed didn't have a map and it was tricky describing exactly where it was that he had seen her. He got Julia to study the map for him and from what she told him, it became clear that the lay of the land meant that none of the others yet had a view of where he had spotted Skye. She was still a long way off, maybe a mile or more. But of all of them Ed was the farthest down the mountain and easily the nearest.

While they were talking, Skye dropped out of sight again. But Ed was sure she must be heading across to the top of the valley. He asked Julia to hold on a minute while he scanned the land with the binoculars. Presumably because it was an easier route and perhaps because it made her feel safer, Skye was staying above the trees. Maybe if he were to take a shortcut diagonally down through the forest, he would be able to drop into the valley below her and cut her off. Julia checked the idea out on the map and said that there was a creek he would have to cross just before he reached the valley, but it certainly looked possible. She said that while he did it she and the others would head down toward the top of the valley.

When he reached the edge of the forest Ed could see why Skye had chosen the higher route. The land fell away steeply down to the trees in a six- or seven-hundred-foot run of broken shale tufted with sage and stunted limber pine. Had he glanced at the clouds or at the thickening drift of smoke above the forest, Ed might have had second thoughts. But he had run scree slopes as a boy and could remember the thrill and the part of him that was still a boy took over and without further hesitation he launched himself off the edge.

With his first stride, it all came back to him. The trick was to go for it. The rocks slid with your boots and you had to be fearless and trust the slide and go with it. He tilted himself forward and soon he was striding like a giant, each step taking him another twenty or thirty feet. He felt like whooping but contained himself. Then, about halfway down, his foot caught in a clump of sage and he went head over heels and slithered the rest of the way on his back with rocks cascading and clattering all around him and over him.

He came to rest at the edge of the forest and stood up gingerly, half expecting to find he had broken some bones, but he seemed to be in one piece. The world around him was blurred. Then he realized he had lost his glasses in the fall and he delved into his personal gear bag for his spare pair.

Once he had them on, he squinted back up the slope. It looked terrifying. Even if he wanted to, there was now no going back. He was feeling a little shaken and weak and knew he had to eat something. He took out a power bar from his pocket and ate it, looking around him to get his bearings. He was sheltered from the wind down here but he could hear it rushing in the treetops. He looked up at them and was just registering how low and black the clouds above them seemed, when the air around him cracked asunder in a searing flash of white light. Ed shielded his head with his arms and dived to the ground. And there he stayed, curled like a fetus, until the shock subsided and his heart started beating again. He sat up.

"Holy shit," he said.

It was the nearest he had ever come to being struck by lightning and he threw back his head and laughed out loud in some crazy mix of defiance and relief that he was still alive. Where exactly it had struck, he couldn't see. Maybe it was somewhere higher up the slope.

He had just gotten to his feet when he heard Julia calling his name on the radio. He tried to reply but she obviously couldn't hear him because she just kept saying *Ed, do you copy?* over and over again. Maybe he'd damaged his radio when he fell or possibly the lightning had damaged it. He shook it and banged it but still he couldn't make himself heard. Whatever had happened, it was no time to be hanging around.

He holstered the radio, checked his compass and walked into the forest.

The going was tougher than he'd hoped. There was a tangle of blowdown and a thick undercanopy of huckleberry and sometimes he had to take detours from the direction he knew he should stick to. And all the while the wind whooshed above him in the treetops. There was a smell of smoke but he thought it was still only the smoke from the fire across the mountain. Then, all of a sudden, he heard a sound that told him it wasn't.

It started in a low roar and grew steadily louder, like a train thundering toward him through a tunnel. And Ed knew at once what it was and he felt a first jab of pure fear. He peered to his right through the pillared ranks of trees and saw nothing, not even smoke. Then he heard the first tree explode and then another, and he felt the fire's heat and knew that it was close and coming closer at great speed. He started to run.

JULIA DIDN'T SEE THE LIGHTNING strike but she heard its hellish crack and its echo rolling like fearful gossip across the mountain. Then, as she climbed out of the gully that she was following and got her first full view of the forest, she saw a small patch of fire among the treetops that even while she watched began to spread like a cancer of flame. And as if by some converse law of reciprocity she felt a cold dread multiply within her.

She was already having to fight hard to keep panic at bay. Her rational side was still in control but only just. And when she saw the fire and realized that Ed was somewhere near it or, heaven forbid, beneath it, the animal in her almost won, but she kept its silent howl within her. She could scarcely believe it was happening. Until just a few hours ago, everything had been golden. How could the world so suddenly have betrayed them?

She tried calling Ed again on the radio and could hear Connor and Chuck trying too. But still there was no reply. She called Connor.

"Connor, do you see the fire down there?"

"Yeah, I see it."

"That's where Ed is."

"Yeah. Don't worry. He knows what to do."

His voice was calm and clear. He asked her how far she was from the head of the valley and she told him that she could see it and that it would take her about five minutes to get there. Connor said he should be there in ten.

Neither of them could see into the valley yet, so nor could they see Skye. Julia signed off and started to run.

AS SOON AS CONNOR SAW the valley open up below him and saw the fire away to the right moving steadily toward it through the forest, he knew exactly why this place had made him feel so uneasy. And he was sure there were other smoke jumpers on the mountain who had seen the valley from the plane and had the same thought but not wished to utter it. Every smoke jumper in Missoula, every smoke jumper in America, knew what had happened all those years ago at Mann Gulch.

On August 5, 1949, just a hundred miles from where they now were, thirteen smoke jumpers had died when a fire chased them up a drainage very like the one Connor was now looking at. A long-overdue monument to their memory had only recently been erected at the base. The details of what happened at Mann Gulch were etched in every jumper's mind. Just like here, there had been a river at the bottom of the drainage and the geography had conspired to create its own wind so that the valley acted like an immense chimney sucking the fire up it in a rolling explosion of flame faster than any man or beast could ever run.

Connor had already called Hank and told him what was happening and Hank had sent out an emergency call for helicopters to evacuate them. He told Connor meanwhile to get everyone away from the drainage and back up into the black where the earlier fire had passed through, or, if that wasn't possible, into rocky terrain where the fire would have less fuel. It was common sense and Connor didn't need telling.

There was Julia below him now, heading down into the valley and there, way below her, was Skye, her red T-shirt vivid against the flaxen grass. The fire was directly to the girl's right and moving in fast. Connor guessed it would take fifteen minutes to reach the valley, maybe less. And somewhere, in that burning forest, was his best friend.

Connor scrambled down the slope as fast as he could, stumbling on loose rocks and snagging himself in the scrub. He pulled out his radio and kept going as he spoke.

"Julia, this is Connor. You mustn't go down there."

"What?"

"Turn around and get out of the valley."

"What are you talking about? I can see her. She's right below me."

"Julia, this is Chuck."

"I hear you, Chuck."

"Connor's right. Don't go down there. Once the fire gets in there, it'll come racing up toward you. I'm getting Katie out of here right now."

Julia was staring back up the mountain at Connor. He wasn't near enough to see but he could imagine the anguish on her face. Then she looked down the valley again and above the rush of the wind he could just hear her calling Skye's name, again and again. But if the girl heard, she gave no sign. She just kept hiking down the valley. Once more Julia looked back up toward him and Connor knew she was deciding and knew also which way it would go. And sure enough she turned and started to run down the valley, calling to Skye as she went.

Connor yelled for her to stop and said the same, as calmly as he could, over the radio. But she paid no attention. And now he was running, leaping over scrub and rock, with stone and debris avalanching with him, his eyes darting from where he trod to Julia and Skye and from them to the advancing fire.

And, to his dismay, he now saw that the fire was starting to crown. The top of a flaming tree separated and lifted itself like a torch clean out of the fire and flew ahead with the wind to start another fire in the unburnt trees. Suddenly the sun found space among the clouds and the valley was riven with a band of shadow from the smoke that drifted over it. Julia was in the shadowed part but Skye in her red T-shirt was beyond it and for a moment she was bathed as if in some biblical painting by a shaft of golden light.

And hurling himself down toward this place of doom and devastation, Connor prayed out loud that Ed, wherever he might be, had found some haven and that all of them would live.

ED'S FIRST THOUGHT was to head downhill and get below the fire. But the forest floor seemed to flatten and the fire seemed to be spreading as fast in that direction as it was elsewhere. Then he thought of heading back up to the scree run but concluded the fire might head him off, so instead he turned south again and ran as fast as he could toward the creek that Julia had told him about.

He could hear the fire rampaging behind him and the roar as tree after tree torched and the boom of sap exploding. Sometimes the fire seemed to accelerate and gain on him and although he didn't look back he knew that this was when it found a stretch of scrub or a patch of dried-out huckleberry. By the time he reached the creek he could see the flames only fifty yards behind him and could feel its heat, raw and intense, surging like a bow wave before it.

It was both more than a creek and less than one. What water there normally was had long dried into its bed of boulders. But its northern bank was a sheer cliff of about forty feet upon whose rim Ed was now standing, acutely aware that each second he hesitated might be the one that cost him his life.

His first thought was to clamber down it but the cliff face looked loose and treacherous and the rocks below unforgiving. There were dead trees down there too that had toppled down the cliff. Their branches bristled like spears. Ed had a rope and though it wasn't long enough to get him all the way to the bottom, he figured that he'd be able to jump or scramble the rest. He pulled the rope from his bag and looked for the best place to tie it.

All but one of the trees stood back too far from the edge. If he roped it to any of them he would be wasting fifteen feet that he couldn't spare. The only alternative was the tree that leaned perilously from the very edge of the cliff, as if contemplating the leap that its old neighbors had already taken. Half its roots were exposed to the air but when Ed leaned against the trunk, it seemed stable enough and with the fire booming and crackling only thirty yards away now, he had no choice. He threw the rope around it, made it fast and maneuvered himself out over the edge.

He had barely begun to rappel down when he heard the crash. It was directly above him and as he looked up he was showered in sparks and flying embers. He ducked but managed to keep his grip on the rope and when he looked again he saw the base of the tree was wreathed in flames. The crown of another tree had flown ahead of the main fire and landed there. The rope was already burning. He loosened his grip and let it run through his bare hands and felt it searing his flesh as he spiraled down, with flaming fragments falling with him.

But the tree to which he was tied was tinder dry and the fire hot and hungry, and it ate the rope faster than gravity could take him down and when he was not yet halfway, the rope melted and snapped. Ed lunged and clawed with both hands at the cliff face but the rocks crumbled under his fingernails and all he succeeded in doing was to flip himself over so that now he was flying facedown like a chuteless sky diver.

The fall lasted no more than two or three seconds, but each seemed stretched to a small eternity. He watched the ground swirl slowly into focus below him. He heard his radio crackle and Connor calling his name again. He noticed the beards of lichen on the rocks and the smoke curling from the fallen embers among them. And the last thing that he saw and would ever see was a red butterfly lifting from the spear branches of the dead tree and fluttering away.

JULIA WAS RUNNING as fast as she could down through the long white grass. She kept shouting Skye's name and her voice was beginning to crack and she knew anyway that it was pointless because even as each cry left her lips it was swept away on the wind and lost. Above the unburnt trees that topped the right-hand ridge of the valley a column of smoke reared like a writhing black dragon, its belly undulating and mottled with the orange glow of the fire. Skye, not more than four hundred yards below her now and running too, kept glancing up at it and once in doing so she tripped on one of the smaller boulders and fell headlong but scrambled to her feet and kept running.

"Skye! Skye!"

So far the girl hadn't once looked back and

she didn't now. Perhaps she didn't even know that Julia was there behind her. But now suddenly she stopped in her tracks. All as one, with a boom that seemed to shake the whole mountainside, the trees along the right-hand ridge exploded into flames. Julia also stopped and for a few moments the two of them stood transfixed. Connor was calling her on the radio.

"Julia, stop! Turn around. You haven't got time."

She looked back up the slope and saw him hurtling down toward her in long strides. He was a hundred yards away and gaining fast. She turned back and saw that Skye had at last seen her. Julia waved to her, signaling to her to come back up the slope and Skye stared at her for a moment then turned to look back down the valley and at the burning trees then again at Julia.

"Come on, Skye! For godsake, come on!"

The grass below the trees had caught fire now and fanned by the wind the flames were spreading in diagonal lines into the valley as fast as if they were following trails of gasoline. And above them now the tops of two flaming trees and then a third lifted off and flew like comets across the black backdrop of smoke down into the middle of the valley. They came to earth only twenty yards below Skye and cartwheeled as they landed, sending showers of sparks into the grass.

Skye took one look and immediately turned and started back up the slope. At last, Julia thought. At last, thank God.

EVEN AS HE RAN, Connor knew there was no way they could get out of the valley in time. He could see the wind whipping the fire that had been started by the flying crowns, driving it up the valley toward them. The place was exactly like Mann Gulch, he thought, just one enormous chimney. He could feel the searing blast of heat on his face. The girl was going to die. But there was a chance, just a chance, that he could save Julia.

She was only twenty yards ahead of him but, damn it, now she was off again, running down toward Skye. The slope was steep and the poor girl, three hundred yards below, maybe more, was stumbling as she tried to retrace her steps. Behind her now the three fires had become one and, sucked by the wind, the flames were raging through the grass and closing on her fast. Connor knew there was no hope for her and none for any of them if they tried to help her.

"Julia!"

At last he caught up with her and as his hand closed on her shoulder she wheeled around to face him. Her eyes were wild and the dirt on her face was streaked with sweat.

"Julia, listen. You can't go down there."

"Look at her! We've got to help her!"

"No. She's not going to make it. And if we go to her, neither are we."

She tried to break free but he twisted his hand in the shoulder of her T-shirt to lock his grip and then hooked his other arm around her waist.

"Let me go, damn you!"

She lashed out at him and he ducked, and as she leaned over him he came up again and hoisted her off the ground on his shoulder. Her feet were pointing uphill and she started to kick and hammer at his back with her fists and she was screaming and swearing at him but he managed to hold her in place and set off back up the slope.

"Don't look back," he said. "Don't look at her."

"You bastard! You fucking bastard!"

Connor pictured Skye behind, watching them desert her. The flames must be licking at her heels by now, ready to devour her. He pulled a shutter down in his mind and closed it too as best he could to Julia's punches and curses and tried to think instead only of their survival.

"Let me go! Let me go!"

One man had survived the Mann Gulch fire: the only one who hadn't tried to outrun it. Connor had already chosen the spot. On his way down he had run past a cluster of boulders and decided that it was the only place where they stood a chance. It was about twenty yards up the slope but with Julia putting up such a struggle it was hard to move fast. The smoke was thick and rolling around them now. He had his right arm clamped around Julia's thighs and was using his left hand to steady her, but now he took it away and reached into his pocket for a fusee to have it ready for when they reached the boulders.

Fifteen yards to go. Twelve. Ten . . .

Julia gave a terrible scream and kept on screaming and he knew that the flames had caught up with the girl and engulfed her and that Julia was watching her die.

"Don't look, Julia. For Christ's sake, don't look."

The scream turned to a wail and he felt her body writhe and convulse on his shoulder as if something inside her were dying too.

And now they were there and Connor lowered her so that she stood with her back propped against the nearest boulder. Her eyes were clenched and her face was distorted. Her mouth gaped in a soundless, desolate cry. She didn't struggle anymore, just let herself slide slowly down the rock and crumple to the ground.

Connor left her there and lit the fusee and it flared brightly in his hand. There were three large boulders and a few smaller ones and they formed a triangle two yards across. There was grass between them and it was this that Connor first lit. It caught fire with a rush and burned fast and fiercely and the wind whipped it through the gaps between the boulders and soon the slope above was on fire too. Connor watched it go and only hoped that by now Chuck and Katie were well clear.

He peered through the smoke below and saw the whole valley was alight. A low wall of flame was rushing up toward them. The grass between the boulders had finished burning now and he walked into its smoldering remains and stamped it out. He could hear Julia moaning on the downhill side of the boulder where he had left her and with the fusee still flaring in one hand he ran around and found her slumped there sobbing. With his free hand he grabbed her wrist and dragged her a few yards down the slope and then he lit the grass between himself and the boulders and waited until it had burned.

The boulders now stood in a patch of smoking black some fifteen yards across. Connor threw the fusee uphill beyond the boulders and then knelt beside Julia and gathered her in his arms. She thrashed at his face and chest with her fists as he lifted her.

"You bastard. You let her die. Why did you let her die?"

Connor didn't answer. He just let her hit him and carried her between the boulders and set her down on the black earth. He took out his water bottle.

"Okay, I'm going to pour this over you."

"Fuck you."

He pulled a bandanna from his pocket and wet it, then he drenched Julia's head and shoulders and emptied the rest over his own and threw the bottle away. The smoke was thick now and they were both coughing. It stung his eyes and through it he could just make out the red and orange of the fire. He figured it was about thirty yards away. Its roar was as loud as a dozen jet engines and the air so hot he could feel his flesh roasting.

He took out his fire shelter and shook it open. It was a small tubed tent of aluminum foil. Connor had never had cause to use one before and was skeptical about how much use it would be in a fire. Jumpers called them shake 'n bakes and joked that all they did was cook you crisp like a turkey. But it was worth a try. He laid it out on the ground and opened it up. The wind rattled the foil.

"Julia, stand up."

She didn't move, so he hoisted her to her feet and leaned her against him, supporting her with one arm, for she seemed unable to stand. She was still crying, but silently now. The shelters were designed for one person but Connor figured there was just enough room for them both. He managed to lift it above them and pulled it over their heads and slid it down over their bodies so that they were cocooned. Then he put his arms around her and lowered her gently until they were lying together on the ground. He handed her the wet bandanna.

"Put this over your face."

She wouldn't, so he did it for her. Their bodies were pressed tightly together and he could feel the shudder of her sobs. And as the roar of the closing fire grew louder and louder, he circled her with his arms and held her against his chest and waited.

PART TWO

THIRTEEN

CONNOR HAD flown into Kentucky twice before, once in thick fog and once in a blizzard. This time, as the plane started its descent, he was hoping to get a look at the land, which everyone said was great horse country. But Lexington lay shrouded in a low layer of cloud and when they dropped below it, all he could see through the rain-streaked window was a blur of sodden pasture and a highway jammed with cars, all with their lights on even though it was only three in the afternoon.

He wondered if she would be there to meet him.

It was late February, and in the six months since the fire he hadn't seen her once. When Ed's condition had stabilized, she had flown back with him to Kentucky and had stayed with his parents while he was in the hospital. Now that he was convalescing at home, Julia spent her weekdays working in Boston and came back here every weekend—except the two that Connor had come to stay. On both occasions she had stayed in Boston, allegedly because of work. By now Connor had gotten the message.

At first he had kept on trying to phone her. In Boston all he ever got was her answering machine and she never returned his calls. Twice she happened to pick up the phone at Ed's parents' house and on both occasions it was like talking with a stranger. She was polite and distant, relating Ed's progress in a voice devoid of emotion. Yes, the burns were healing fine; yes, the broken hip too; in fact, he was walking almost without a limp now, and, no, there was still no progress with his eyesight.

In his fall Ed had suffered retinal hemorrhages in both eyes. The doctors said that it was somehow connected with his diabetes. He'd apparently had some recent eye trouble that he hadn't disclosed in case they stopped him from jumping. The chances of it happening in both eyes at the same time, however, were a million to one against. Connor didn't ask too much about the medical details, not that they would have meant a lot to him. All that mattered was that his friend was now blind and seemed almost certain to stay that way.

To those who knew him less well, Ed's response to what had happened to him might have seemed unbelievable. Connor spoke with him on the phone two or three times a week and his mood was rarely less than ebullient. Once his hip had mended he spent a month at a rehabilitation center for the blind and came back with hilarious accounts of mishaps and mischief. There was a young Swedish orientation and mobility instructor there with whom he and a couple of the other guys seemed to spend most of their time flirting.

"Connor, man, I tell you. She had the sexiest voice you ever heard. Her real name was Trudi but we all called her Greta, because she sounded just like Garbo. One of the things they teach you, to find your way around a place you don't know, is to have someone draw a map with their finger on your back. And we'd all be, like, 'Hey, Greta, I've forgotten the map, can you do it again? No, lower, lower! You know, maybe it'd be better if you did it on my thigh?' "

He said it was marvelous what license you had as a newly blind person, you could put your hands anywhere and pretend it was an accident. Last week he had been going on about all the new computer gear he was getting to help him in his composing. It had specially modified braille keyboards and screens that talked to you. The software was so sophisticated that all you had to do was hum it a tune and it would record it and score it and play it back to you.

"It's incredible. Once I've gotten the hang of it, I'll be able to give it just a rough idea for a song—you know, love song, kinda smoochy, a little sad maybe—then go have a cup of coffee, read the newspaper, come back and find it's composed the whole damn thing. Maybe even an entire musical."

Connor didn't push to find out what was going on behind this brave face. He could imagine though. He knew that both Ed and Julia had been having some kind of post-traumatic therapy. It had been offered to Connor too, back in Missoula, but he hadn't followed it up. He didn't see the point. What had happened was done and nothing could change it. He could handle it himself.

The strange thing was, he and Ed hadn't yet really talked about the fire. Ed was always so determinedly upbeat that Connor didn't feel able to raise the subject. What he most wanted to ask was about Julia and why she was avoiding him, though he had a pretty good idea. Ed had once let slip that the fire on Snake Mountain had left her with wounds worse than his own. It seemed that she blamed herself for what had happened not just to the girl and to him but also to the five who died when the search and rescue helicopter crashed into power lines.

Ed had sounded thrilled when Connor asked if he could come to see him in Kentucky again. He promised that this time he'd be there himself at the airport to meet him. Connor wasn't counting on Julia being with him. She would probably make another excuse and stay in Boston.

But he was wrong. As he came through the gate with his old leather duffel bag slung on his shoulder he saw her, though if Ed hadn't been standing next to her with his arm linked in hers, Connor might not have recognized her. Her hair was cut short and she was pale and much thinner. There were dark rings under her eyes. She was wearing boots and a long black coat with the collar turned up and she looked beautiful and tragic at the same time and at the sight of her Connor felt a cold stone turn slowly over in the depths of his chest. She saw him and waved and he saw her whisper to Ed, telling him which direction to face and Ed dutifully lined up and beamed and waved too.

"Hey, cowboy! Over here!"

Ed was wearing dark glasses and an old yellow ski jacket that Connor had seen him wear up many a mountain. He too had lost weight and there was something about the way he stood, a slight, self-protecting hunching of his shoulders, that made him look frail. But the burn scars on his face had calmed and looked a lot better. Connor walked over.

"Hey, old buddy," he said. "When's this darn state of yours gonna get itself some decent weather?"

He put down his bag and took Ed by the shoulders and the two of them stood there hugging each other for a long time. Connor had to fight hard not to let tears well in his eyes.

"Hey, man, it's good to see you," he said softly.

"It's good to see you too, man." He laughed and held Connor at arm's length as if inspecting him. "And see? I still say 'see' and I'm not going to stop. Anyhow, in my head I can see you. And you're still an ugly sonofabitch."

Connor laughed and turned to Julia.

"Hi, Julia."

"Connor." She nodded. "How're you doing?"

"Good. How are you?"

"I'm fine. Thanks."

Neither of them seemed to know what to say or do next, whether to kiss or hug or even shake hands. Connor took the plunge. He stepped closer and put his arms around her and kissed her cheek and the smell of her came back to him in a rush. She didn't hug him back, just briefly touched his shoulders and he felt that this was more a signal that the embrace should end. He let her go and looked into her eyes but she looked away almost at once.

"You had your hair cut," he said dumbly.

"Yeah. Well, it was all singed and frazzled, you know. . . ."

Connor felt dumber still.

"Suits her, doesn't it?" Ed said, grinning. He ran his hand up the back of her head and ruffled her hair and Julia dutifully smiled.

"Yes, it does," Connor said.

There was another beat of awkward silence.

"So. Did you check any luggage in or anything?" Julia said.

"No, this is it." He picked up his bag.

"Well, what the hell are we waiting for?" Ed said. "Let's go get this cowboy a beer!"

They walked slowly across the concourse, Ed in the middle, with his arm linked in Julia's, while people scurried past and around them as if they all knew of some emergency that hadn't yet been disclosed to the three of them. They stepped out into the dank and gloom of the afternoon and Julia went off to fetch the car, leaving Connor and Ed standing in the shelter of the pickup zone with the rain gusting beyond in great swaths and sparkling in darts across the headlight beams of the cars. Beside them a young couple stood locked in each other's arms, kissing passionately, the woman telling him in gasps how much she loved him and how badly she had missed him. It made Connor feel uneasy and saddened him too, though he didn't know why.

"How do you think she looks?" Ed said.

"She looks great. A little tired maybe."

"Yeah. She works too hard. She's been incredible."

There were so many questions Connor wanted to ask but they all seemed wrong.

"You know, man, she feels so bad about what she said to you."

Connor knew what he meant but felt he should pretend not to.

"What do you mean?"

Ed sighed. "Well, she told me how she swore at you and said it was your fault that the girl . . . you know."

"Hell, she didn't know what she was saying. I never thought she meant it."

"That's good. Because she knows you saved her life and that you had no choice about the girl."

"Well, maybe."

"No, Connor. No maybes."

Ed fumbled for Connor's arm and grasped it tightly, pointing his face at where he thought Connor's was, as if trying to look him in the eyes.

"You had no choice, man. Any of us would have done what you did. Or tried to. The truth is, most of us would have failed and died."

The official inquiry into what happened hadn't published its final report yet, but Connor already knew that this would be its verdict too. It didn't make anything feel any better.

After what seemed a long time, a black Jaguar slid up to the curb and through the tinted glass Connor saw Julia lean across and open the passenger door. She too was wearing sunglasses now which, given that it was almost dark, struck him as strange.

"Here she is," he said and steered Ed gently toward the car.

DINNER AT GRASSLAND—or Château Tully, as Ed called it—was at seven-thirty prompt and it was considered bad form to be late. If you were, Ed's father didn't make a fuss about it, he would just raise an eyebrow and give you one of those indulgent smiles that made you feel about two feet tall and a total failure. Ed, in the family tradition of giving almost everything an acronym, called them SAPS: "such a pity" smiles. He'd had to put up with them all his life. Julia was heading for a SAP this evening. It was already twenty past and she was still soaking in the tub, trying to summon the strength to face Connor again.

The guest suite was about as far removed from the reality of her weekday life as it was possible to get. The bathroom was walled and floored in streaked cream marble, the lighting discreetly recessed, the tub the size of a small swimming pool. The Boston apartment that she shared with Linda and to which she gloomily flew back every Sunday evening was cold and cramped and drafty, which seemed to do nothing to deter the platoons of mice and cockroaches that tried to share it too.

Ed had first brought her to Grassland on their way to Montana the previous spring to meet his parents. And from the moment they landed at the airport, the culture shock had set in. Raoul, Ed's father's driver, was there to meet them with his dark suit and black necktie, ushering them with a diffident smile into the back of a Mercedes spacious enough to throw a party. Julia got the giggles—until they turned off the highway and, as if by magic, a pair of enormous crested wrought-iron gates whirred open and the car purred up a driveway that wound through parkland until there in front of them was this pillared palace and by then she'd stopped giggling and her jaw was just hanging loose. There were fountains and peacocks and a whole army of servants. She told him she'd had no idea she was dating Rhett Butler, for heavensakes, and Ed just laughed and kissed her and said frankly, my dear, he didn't give a damn for any of it.

Since their sons had left home, Jim and Susan Tully had the entire west wing to themselves, with staff and guests housed in the east. There were at least four guest suites and when Ed, on that first visit, had led her along the cream-carpeted corridors to the best of them, Julia whispered that she'd better leave a trail of peas because otherwise she would never find her way out again. When he opened the door to the suite and she saw the yellow silk wallpaper and drapes and Chinese rugs and the views of rolling pasture from its tall windows, she was speechless.

Now she almost took it for granted. Grassland felt like her second home and she had grown fond of Lexington. The people had a kind of old-fashioned courtesy about them which, having grown up in the cutthroat bustle of a city, Julia found both curious and comforting. And the more she got to know Ed's parents, the more she liked them. The accident had drawn the three of them close and Julia could tell that they adored her, especially his mother, who now treated her like the daughter she had always wanted.

Susan's bravery over what had happened was almost as daunting as Ed's. The shock and sorrow of seeing a favorite son blinded and burned were more than Julia could imagine, but Susan had kept her grief well hidden. Outwardly, from the start, she had been strong, practical and cheerful. Julia had drawn on this and tried to emulate it and, most of the time, succeeded. No one, not even the trauma therapist she had been seeing in Boston, knew what was going on inside her; of the terrible dreams she had, of the demons that came to visit her in the dark, dread hours of the night to squat on her chest as if they would flatten every ounce of breath from her lungs.

She had always thought she would be good at therapy, and perhaps if she had found someone whom she trusted more, she might have been. The therapist she had seen was a Dr. Schroeder, a small, delicate man with soft white hands and unsettling beady black eyes. His slow nod, presumably intended to convey understanding or sympathy or to coax more revelations, had the opposite effect. Several times she had been on the brink of telling him something important, then seen the nod and the inscrutable avian stare and a gate would come crashing down. Finally, during one of their weekly sessions, he called her Gloria and that was it. To get her name wrong was perhaps excusable, but *Gloria*? She never went again.

The burden of guilt that she now carried sometimes seemed so heavy that during those bleak winter weeks, she feared her knees might buckle beneath it. Her mother's attitude didn't help; she belonged to the school of thought that considered cheery denial to be the appropriate way to handle such things. Whenever the two of them spoke, either on the phone or on Julia's rare visits to New York, she always had some helpful homily to hand. It was just an accident. Nobody was to blame. It was time Julia moved on. Once she even said that there was no point in crying over spilled milk. Julia could barely believe her ears. *Spilled milk?*

Her work at the institute was a dependable distraction. But at any time one of her pupils might say something or look at her in a particular way and suddenly she would see Skye's face superimposed and hear her voice and Julia's heart would lurch and start to race and she would have to struggle for breath. It was Linda who helped her through those wretched weekdays; who cooked for her and brought her cups of hot chocolate and came and sat on her bed and hugged her when she heard her crying in the middle of the night. Linda was the only one who seemed to understand about the guilt.

Ten days after the fire, while Ed was still in intensive therapy, Glen Nielsen had driven Julia, Katie, Scott and Laura over to Billings for Skye's funeral. They made up more than half the congregation. All through the service, Skye's stepfather kept looking at her and afterward, outside the church, he strode over and called her a murdering bitch and said she had a hell of a nerve showing up. He started to yell and two of his friends had to restrain him.

"You didn't even leave us a decent body to bury!"

They led him away. For many days afterward, Julia could barely speak.

In Boston, on her way to and from the institute, she had to pass a Catholic church and occasionally, after school, she would stop and go in and sit at the back. Usually the place was empty, though sometimes there were vagrants sheltering from the cold and perhaps a figure hunched in prayer among the pews or lighting candles of devotion. Julia thought of doing both these things herself. She even thought of seeking out the priest and asking if he would hear her confession. But then, what would she say?

Bless me, father, for I have sinned. I killed a beautiful young woman on a mountain and blinded my boyfriend. And, oh yeah, five search and rescue helicopter guys died as well.

How many Hail Marys would it take to be absolved of such sins? she wondered. To seek forgiveness seemed almost obscene. For some sins there could be no forgiveness. And even if God, assuming there was one, forgave her, how could she forgive herself? What right did she have even to pray or to light a candle? Instead, she simply sat and stared from the darkness toward the pool of light around the altar and at the shining gold and blue and white figure of the Blessed Virgin with her puzzling smile and at Christ above, forlorn and crucified, blood dripping from his wounded flank and down his face from the crown of thorns. Julia stared and stared, hoping to feel something. Not forgiveness, not pity even, but perhaps some soft radiation of comfort. But she felt nothing.

The water in the bathtub was cooling now and she tilted back her head and wet her hair and quickly washed it. Then she hoisted herself out and wrapped herself in one of the Tullys' thick towels and dried herself, thinking about

Connor and wishing she'd stayed in Boston for the weekend or gone to see her mother in New York.

She had done her best to conceal how much she wanted to avoid him. Ed had only sensed it the last time Connor came to Kentucky when again she had made herself absent. He asked her why and she told him it was because she was ashamed of how she had behaved toward him on the day of the fire. It was the truth, but not the whole of it.

Secretly Julia was more ashamed of what she had felt for him last summer and of what, if she were to allow herself, she still felt for him. Even before the fire, these had seemed like a betrayal of Ed. Now they seemed little short of monstrous. Julia knew where her duty lay and so long as Connor was out of sight and many miles away she could bury her feelings for him and get on with looking after Ed.

But at the airport it had all come flooding back. The sight of him walking toward her, the way he'd looked at her with those pale blue eyes, the sound of his voice. She had hoped to God that he wouldn't hug or kiss her and when he did and put his arms around her, she felt something break inside her and it was all she could do not to collapse and cling to him and cry on his shoulder. She managed to hold back the tears until she went off to get the car. In the parking lot she'd sat with her head bowed on the steering wheel, sobbing.

At least now she felt a little stronger. She dried her hair and dressed quickly in a pair of black velvet pants and the dark green cashmere sweater that Ed's mother had given her at Christmas. Before the fire she had rarely bothered with make-up, but nowadays, without it, the sight of her face in the mirror scared her. She was all gaunt cheeks and cavernous eyes and with her short hair she felt she looked like a cancer victim or a survivor from a prison camp. As she was making herself up in the bathroom mirror, she heard Ed's special little knock on the bedroom door, the one he used when he came to her room at night after everyone had gone to bed.

"Milady?"

"I'm in here."

"Milady's presence is eagerly anticipated in the banqueting hall."

"I'm coming."

He was practicing using his cane and she heard him tapping his way across the bedroom and saw him appear in the mirror behind her and stop in the bathroom doorway. He had nicked himself shaving and there was a dried trickle of blood on one cheek. She turned and went to him and he propped his stick against the wall and took hold of her and kissed the side of her neck.

"You smell so good, I could eat you."

She smiled and stood still while he slowly moved his hands up her body from the back of her thighs all the way to her shoulder blades and then under her arms to hold her breasts.

"Just checking you're suitably dressed," he said.

"Uh-huh. And?"

"Feels okay to me."

She could feel him stiffening against her stomach. She reached behind her for a wash-cloth and dabbed the blood from his cheek.

"Damn, did I cut myself?"

"Just a little. There. All gone. Come on, let's go down."

"What, now? Right here? Okay."

"Downstairs, smarty-pants. Have you had your shot?"

"Yes, Mom."

"Have you told him yet?"

"No. I thought we'd tell him after dinner."

BEING BLIND, so far anyhow, didn't seem to have a lot to recommend it. But there was one thing that Ed had noticed: he was always as horny as a hound in a hot tub. He'd heard say that with loss of sight one's other senses became heightened and this was all he could put it down to, unless one of the umpteen pills he now had to take had some wondrous side effect that nobody had dared mention. With all the work he was doing, learning how to live in his new benighted world, he often got very tired. But he was never too tired to make the trip each night to Julia's room. He even joked with her that he didn't need a cane to find his way there because the one he was born with was out there in front doing it for him.

It wasn't as if his sex drive before he was blind had been stuck in first gear. Far from it. There had been scarcely a night when he and Julia hadn't made love. But now that he could only feel her and smell her and taste her, he felt turbocharged, as if those particular veins were filled with some new high-octane fuel. Not that he considered himself a great lover. He knew that he was sometimes too eager and often too quick. But he liked to think he was generous and that what he lacked in finesse he more than made up for with diligence.

With his broken hip and all those weeks that he'd had to spend in the hospital and at the rehab center, it was a long time before he and Julia had been able to make love again. At the center he had been plagued with worry that she might not find him attractive anymore. He had mentioned this to one of the counselors and the guy tried to reassure him, saying it was common for newly blind males to feel this way, that losing one's sight could have an emasculating effect. Far from reassuring him, this had made him even more worried and by the time he came back he'd managed to work himself up into a frenzy of self-doubt.

But Julia had dispelled it. That first night back at Grassland, he had fumbled like a freshman on his first date but she held him and helped him and he could feel how much she wanted him and ever since it had been as good as ever, better even. Apart from his own heightened senses, the only change he noticed was in Julia. There was something in her lovemaking that hadn't been there before, a kind of sad intensity into which she somehow seemed to disappear.

The others were all at the table when he and Julia came into the dining room. He heard the scraping of chairs and knew his father and Connor had stood up.

"Sorry we're late," he said. "It's my fault. I nearly cut my head off shaving."

"Why don't you use that electric shaver I got you?" his mother said.

"I like to live dangerously."

There was a moment of silence. Julia steered him to his chair and took her place beside him.

"Come on, let's eat," his father said. "Connor here is about to die of starvation."

He called for Annie, the Filipino cook who'd been with them since Ed was a child. They sat chatting while she brought in the first course. Ed sniffed the air. It had become a ritual that he always tried to guess what was being served.

"Okay, Annie. Let's see. Smoked salmon and—"

Annie laughed. "You'll never get it."

"And . . . those old socks you threw out last week."

She slapped his hand gently and put his plate in front of him.

"Cucumber and mint surprise."

"Cucumber that smells like socks, that is a surprise."

While they ate, Ed's father asked Connor about his flight from Montana and then launched into a tedious monologue on the merits of various airlines. He asked Julia which airline she used from Boston and Julia replied politely. It was the first time she had spoken and Ed wondered why she was being so quiet. Probably bored half to death by the conversation. It was time to liven things up.

"Hey," he said. "Did you hear about that

flight attendant who got caught banging—sorry, Mom—having 'intimate congress' with a passenger the other day?"

"Nope," Connor said. "But I've a feeling you're gonna tell us."

"Well, if you insist. They fired her and you know what? Ticket sales went through the roof. Every flight fully booked. Now they call it 'the airline that gives a fuck.' "

"Ed, please!" his mother said. "Connor, what can we do with this boy?"

"Well, Mrs. Tully, I hear the white slavery business is still pretty big in some parts of Asia."

"That's a good idea. We'll sell him."

"Oh, please," Ed said. "What kind of price would you get for a blind, diabetic, failed composer."

"What do you mean failed?" his mother said.

"Mom, it was a joke."

For a while everyone was silent. Annie came in to clear away the plates. Then Ed's father spoke up.

"So, Connor. What do you think about this pair of lovebirds here getting hitched and all?"

Ed felt like kicking him under the table. But it was too late.

"I'm sorry, Mr. Tully?" Connor said.

"These two . . . Hell, Ed, haven't you even told your best friend yet?"

Ed took a deep breath.

"You guys are getting married?"

"We were keeping it as a surprise for later. Thanks, Dad."

He reached for Julia's hand and found it and felt a tension there that surprised him. Perhaps she was just annoyed, as he was, at his father blurting out their news. He clasped her hand in both of his.

"Yes. I picked my moment, got her exceedingly drunk, popped the question and, incredible as it may seem, she said yes."

He leaned toward her and they kissed each other on the lips.

"Well," Connor said. "That's great. Congratulations."

"Thanks, man."

"Isn't it wonderful?" Ed's mother said. "We're all so happy."

"The cat seems to have gotten Julia's tongue," his father said.

"I'm sorry. I don't know what to say."

Her voice sounded strange but Ed figured she was simply embarrassed. He came to the rescue.

"How about that you're really, really lucky, given all the thousands of beautiful and talented women you had to compete with, to have snared such a fine figure of a man."

Everyone laughed.

"I think you should propose a toast, Jim," his mother said. "Before you put your foot in it again."

"You bet."

Ed could hear them all picking up their glasses.

"To Julia and Ed."

His mother and Connor repeated it. The glasses clinked.

"And health and happiness."

CONNOR WATCHED HER SITTING on the rug in front of the great fireplace. He and Ed were sitting in an imposing pair of leather armchairs, high-backed and deeply studded, facing one another across the hearth, each cradling a globed glass of Jim Tully's finest brandy. Julia had her back propped against Ed's legs and was staring into the fire and Ed was absently stroking the nape of her neck while he finished another story. Connor could see she wasn't listening and he wondered what she was thinking.

They were in what Ed's father called the den, though it was twice the size of most living rooms. There were two leather-topped tables stacked with books and the walls were lined with hundreds more, many of them ancient and bound in hide. Ed maintained that his father had bought them by the yard and never read a single one. The floor was a patchwork of old oriental rugs onto which four tall brass reading lamps with green glass shades cast pools of light. Above them the room remained dim and shadowy and the firelight flickered on the ceiling.

Ed's parents had gone to bed, so now it was just the three of them. Suddenly there was silence and Connor realized that Ed had asked him a question.

"Sorry, man, I was just thinking about something. What was that?"

"I said, we're really sorry about the way you found out. We wanted to tell you ourselves."

"Hey, that's okay. I'm just real happy for you both."

Julia turned from the fire and looked at him. Twice at dinner he had caught her staring at him, but on each occasion she looked away immediately after their eyes met. Now she held his gaze steadily and he knew she was gauging whether he had spoken the truth. He tried to read what else was in those dark eyes apart from sadness, but he couldn't. And this time it was he who first looked away.

"When's the wedding?"

"The last Saturday in June. I need to get a little fitter first. You know, for the honeymoon."

He laughed and Julia pulled a face and tapped him on the knee like a schoolmarm. "I've asked all my friends but nobody seems to want to be my best man, so I wondered if you'd do it."

"I'll have to see if I'm available. Where's it going to be?"

"Here. We wanted to do it in Montana, but until we've found a place, we figured it was simpler to do it here."

"Found a place? You mean you're coming to live in Montana?"

"Hey, pal, it's a free country."

Connor looked at Julia and she smiled and gave a little shrug.

"That's great." Connor tried to sound enthusiastic. "Where?"

"Oh, somewhere around Missoula, if we can find the right place. Listen, sorry, guys, I've got to go take a leak. I'll be right back."

He put down his glass, found his cane and stood up. Julia started to get up too, offering to take him, but he declined sharply, saying that he could find his own way to the john, for heaven's sake. It was the first glimpse of irritation Connor had seen. Julia settled down and looked into the fire again while the tapping of Ed's cane faded across the hallway.

"Julia?"

She turned to him and there was such a tragic

look in her eyes that it took him a moment to go on.

"Are you okay?"

She gave a little shake of her head. "Not really. But I'm getting there."

He held out his hand and she hesitated then took it and held it in both of hers. Her skin felt cold.

"I'm sorry I never returned your calls."

"That's okay."

"I guess I just didn't know what to say. I was so ashamed about what I said to you that day. I didn't mean it."

"I know. It's okay."

"You saved my life. And I know I should . . ."

She swallowed and shook her head and looked away into the fire.

"Tell me."

"I just . . . sometimes wish you hadn't."

Tears broke from her eyes. Connor leaned forward and clasped both her hands in his.

"Julia, what happened wasn't your fault."

Out in the hallway a door clicked and again they heard the tap of the cane. Julia took her hands away and wiped away her tears. Connor's voice was low and urgent now.

"You mustn't think that. You did all you could."

She gave a wry little smile.

"Sure."

Ed came into the room and Connor watched him find his way without falter to his chair. Silence hung over them like a shroud.

"Okay," Ed said. "So either you're asleep or you were talking about me—which is fine. What better subject is there?"

"Don't flatter yourself," Julia said. Her voice was instantly, startlingly cheerful. The only hint of what had just passed was the smudged mascara under her left eye. "Anyhow, we've been talking about you all evening. You haven't asked Connor a single thing about what he's up to."

"True. So what's hot in Montana, cowboy? How's the photo business?"

"Oh, pretty much the same as ever. It's okay, I guess. I've sold a few pictures. Truth is, it's time I moved on."

He took a sip of brandy. They were both waiting for him to continue.

"Connor, you're such a pain in the ass," Ed said. "When you say something like that, all casual, like it's nothing at all, it's a sure sign that there's a major life-change about to happen. For heaven's sake, move on where?"

"I'm going to travel a little."

"That's great. Where exactly?"

"Europe first, then Africa maybe."

"Great. To take pictures?"

"Uh-huh."

"So, where in Europe exactly?"

Connor knew Julia was staring at him. He was avoiding her eyes.

"Come on, man. What's the big secret?"

"I'm going to Bosnia."

"Wow. You got, like, an assignment or something?"

"No, I figured I'd just go."

"What, you can go to a war zone, just like that?"

Connor shrugged. "I guess I'll find out. I'm just going to play it by ear."

"Wow! Well, good for you, man. When do you go?"

"Well, I was figuring on leaving pretty soon. Now I guess I'll have to kick my heels till after this darned wedding of yours."

He had made it all sound more definite than it was, or at least, than it had been. He'd been thinking about the trip for some time and had done his research. But it wasn't until just now, hearing that the woman he loved was to be married, that he knew for certain that he would go. Julia hadn't said a word nor taken her eyes off him. And at last he looked at her and smiled but she didn't smile back.

Had he thought about it and had Ed been able to see, he would never have done what he then did. Quite on impulse, he leaned forward and wiped the mascara from Julia's cheek. And she closed her eyes at his touch and silently bowed her head.

FOURTEEN

THE HOUSE that they found in Montana stood above a rocky bend of the Bitterroot River, with the forest rising steeply behind it. It was on two floors and built of logs and had an acre and a half of land laid largely to grass. There were apple trees and pear trees and the side of the house that looked down on the river had tall glass doors and a deck and a yellow rambling rose run riot. The place had been built nine years ago by a couple who were sculptors and there was a long barn that they had used as a studio. One of their pieces, an elaborate totem pole carved from a pine tree thirty feet tall, stood at the foot of the lawn so that the scowling eagle at its top glowered east over the river like a sentinel.

After the wedding they had spent ten days lying on a beach in Mexico. Ed took along a stack of novels on audiocassette but couldn't stand the music they plastered on, so he got Julia to read to him from her book, *Madame Bovary*, and was soon concocting a musical version of it called *Oh, Madame!* Sometimes he would fall asleep while Julia was reading and she would stop and gaze at the pelicans patrolling the shoreline in lazy squadrons and making their comical crash-dives into the surf.

Tanned and refreshed, they flew directly to Missoula to start looking for a house. She had expected that it would take many weeks to find somewhere that they liked, but they found it on the third day, which was just as well because house-hunting with Ed was a tiring business. He wanted every detail described. What color were the kitchen walls? What could you see when you looked out the bedroom window? Did the river look good for fishing? Could she see any trout rising?

"Hundreds," she said. "They're monsters. There isn't room for them all. They're even sunbathing on the bank."

The downstairs was one big living room with a wood floor and Ed stood there and sang so that he could get an idea of the acoustics. The realtor, a jovial woman of about fifty in scarlet lipstick and big gold earrings, thought it was hysterical. Especially when Ed got her singing too.

"Hmm. Most impressive," he said. "The Maria Callas of Missoula."

His parents had given him a new piano as a wedding present, a sleek black Yamaha baby grand. He asked Julia where it should stand, saying it had to be somewhere that had a view of the river. The realtor caught Julia's eye and Ed somehow sensed it and explained to her that even though he couldn't see it, it was important to know it was there. The obvious place was by the glass doors that led out onto the deck.

And that was where, nine months later, it now stood. Ed had made it the center of what he called NASA control—the complex of keyboards, screens and computer equipment that did indeed look capable of launching a small missile. On the piano's lid, among the stacks of braille sheets, each with a different object upon it for identification, stood the silver-framed black and white picture that Connor had taken of them at the wedding. In it Ed was laughing—no doubt at one of his own jokes—the Kentucky sun flaring like a starburst in his sunglasses, while Julia, looking sideways at the camera, kissed him on the cheek. It still struck her as odd that Ed had never seen nor ever would see how they had looked that day.

There was, however, something more profound about the image that struck her only later. With its devotional kiss, the pose somehow symbolized the compact they had made, or rather, the compact that Julia had made with herself. It was straightforward enough. She had caused Ed to lose his eyesight, so now he would have hers. This didn't mean that she had married him merely from a sense of duty. Nor that she didn't love him. Of course she did. And her admiration at his courage, his lack of self-pity and his unflagging optimism grew with every day she spent with him. All of this was there in the picture as a daily reminder to her that this was how things were and would be; that this was now her allotted life. That the photograph also showed her looking sideways at Connor was something she refused to allow into her head.

They had moved into the house at the end of September. Both of their mothers came to stay for a few days to help them get things straight, and although they were about as different as two women could be—the southern belle and the Italian hairdresser from Brooklyn—they got along famously and laughed so much that for a while after they left the place seemed empty.

Those first few months had been hectic. The local Blind and Low Vision Services had sent rehab and orientation and mobility counselors to help them. They adapted the kitchen, marking the stove and the microwave and food containers with little rubber dots and magnets so that Ed could figure things out. They pruned the rose and the fruit trees so that he wouldn't catch his face on them and then erected posts with a rope strung between them all the way from the deck down to the river and along the bank, so that he could safely go there by himself.

Ed wasn't the only one having to learn a new way of living. Though they were nothing by comparison with Ed's, there were many minor readjustments that Julia too had to make. Such as remembering not to leave things lying around in odd places where he might trip or knock them over, not to leave doors or cupboards ajar in case he walked into them, always to put things back in exactly the same place so that he could find them. By far the most difficult thing she had to learn was the fine line between when to help him and when not to. It was painful to stand by while he got frustrated and furious with himself, to watch him fumble or even fall, but she knew that sometimes she must. By the time winter came, however, they had worked most things out and these bad moments were fewer and farther between.

It was Julia's first Montana winter and it gave little compromise. The first snow came in

October and kept topping itself up like an over-attentive waiter. Far from feeling trapped or isolated or even depressed by it, as she had feared she might, Julia loved it. They wrapped up warm and went for long walks under clear alpine skies. They even tried cross country skiing, Julia going first with a set of bear bells pinned to her back and Ed trying to follow the sound. He kept going too fast and crashing into her and they wiped out in some truly spectacular falls but ached more afterward from laughing so much.

Their evenings were spent cocooned together on the couch by the big log fire, reading and listening to music or, if Ed insisted, watching a favorite old western or musical on TV. He would make her give a running commentary about what was happening on the screen. Sometimes she would tease him by inventing characters or pieces of action, but he knew most of the movies so well that he would cotton on right away and grab her and tickle her and make her beg for mercy.

Thanks to the generosity of Ed's father and to the smoke jumper insurance money, they had few financial worries. Julia hadn't worked since giving up her job in Boston the previous spring and although she intended to find a new job, she was still relishing the freedom to read and potter and to get back to some serious painting, which she did most mornings in the barn studio. Ed, however, was a lot less comfortable about relying on charity (especially his father's) and was keen to demonstrate that he could support himself. The long-term plan was still, of course, to make it as a composer, but meanwhile he was determined to go on teaching piano.

Back in the fall he'd put an ad into *The Missoulian* and it conjured over a dozen would-be pupils. Word-of-mouth soon conjured more than he could handle. Nearly all were children who came to the house after school. And having them around the place, hearing their voices and their laughter and seeing how much fun Ed had with them, Julia knew it wouldn't be long before he raised the subject of having children of their own.

It happened on the night after Thanksgiving. They had made love on the couch beside the fire and were lying in each other's arms. Julia was watching the snow fall in slow, fat flakes outside on the deck.

"So, what do you think?" he said.

"You mean out of ten? Mmm, I'd give you a four, maybe five."

He dug his fingers under her arms. "You know what I mean."

She did, though quite how was a mystery. She often seemed able to read his thoughts and only hoped it wasn't mutual.

"Isn't it a little early? I mean, shouldn't we get a little more settled?"

"I don't know. I feel pretty settled."

"Well, so do I, but . . ."

"Listen, if you're not sure, that's cool. We'll wait."

She thought about it all night and all the next day. She wanted children just as much as he did. What was the point in waiting? They had always used condoms and the next time they made love, she silently stopped him as he reached for one. Neither of them said another word about it, as if by some tacit accord that to do so might jeopardize their efforts.

Now, more than four months later, Julia still hadn't conceived. And although she knew that these things took time and that some couples could indeed spend years trying, an irrational voice had started to nag her that there was something wrong. Having started unsure, by now she could feel herself becoming almost obsessed with having a child. And ten days ago, without telling Ed, she had gone to see her doctor and had him run some tests. Today she was going to find out the results.

The omens that early April morning all

seemed good. Ed woke her with a cup of coffee and she lay in bed with the sun streaming in and Neil Young booming on the downstairs stereo while Ed did his morning workout. Then he cooked some delicious blueberry pancakes for breakfast and they ate them in the sunshine at the long pine table and talked about the summer and where they might go for a vacation. Ed liked to start his workday by playing something on the piano and today he chose one of her favorite pieces of Schubert. Julia cleared the dishes and put on her boots and coat and kissed him goodbye, saying she was going into Missoula. It was a Friday, when she normally did the weekly food shopping, so he didn't ask her why. Outside, for the first time, there was a palpable stirring of spring. The snow had all but gone and crocuses were pushing through the weathered grass.

The clinic was in a long, low building on the south side of town, not far from the mall. In her eagerness, she arrived twenty minutes early, before the place had opened, so she walked over to the mall for a cup of coffee and a newspaper and came back to wait in the car.

She looked first, as now she always did, for any stories about Bosnia. She prayed every night for Connor's safety. All they had heard from him since the wedding was a couple of postcards, the last one from Sarajevo just before Christmas. Both were brief and chatty and gave nothing away. Last week Julia had seen a report on the TV news about what was now being called "ethnic cleansing" and how in Sarajevo snipers were randomly killing civilians. But today there was nothing in the paper and although she knew it was silly she decided to take this as another good omen.

One of her mother's many homilies was that a woman should always have a female doctor and that if for some reason you absolutely had to have a male, you should make certain to get a young, good-looking one, because all the old, ugly ones were frustrated and lecherous. Julia's was suave and handsome but pushing sixty and she didn't know where that left her. His name was Henry Rumbold, which Ed said reminded him of one of those old-fashioned cure-all tinctures they used to sell from the back of wagons in the days of the Wild West—*Dr. Henry T. Rumbold's Remarkable Throat, Bowel and Boil Remedy*. Julia had never since been able to look at the man without thinking of it.

The waiting room had been given an early spring makeover in primrose yellow and still smelled of fresh paint. Apart from a woman with a small child who had a streaming nose and a rather unsettling rash, Julia was the only one there. Dr. Rumbold came out to find her and ushered her into his office, asking how she was and how Ed was and saying, thank the Lord, it seemed as if winter was at last on its way out. He motioned to Julia to sit down in front of his desk and settled himself on the other side of it. He put on some rimless spectacles and, for what seemed an eternity, shuffled through the papers before him. Julia sat and watched, deciding that her mother was right, at least in part. Dr. Rumbold was clearly a frustrated thespian. He surely knew already what the damn notes said, so all this fussing around was purely for dramatic suspense. At last he looked up over his glasses and delicately placed his hands flat on the notes.

"Well, we've got the test results back," he said.

What an asshole, she thought. "And?" she said sweetly.

"Frankly, Julia, you're in great shape."

"Hey! You're sure?"

"Absolutely."

She immediately forgave him everything.

He went through the details with her but Julia was too elated to pay much attention. He wound up by giving her all the usual guff about how being anxious could often make it more difficult to conceive and Julia made a feeble joke about how she would try not to get anxious about getting anxious. And that was it. He showed her to the door.

"Of course, it takes two to tango," he said, almost, it seemed, as an afterthought. "And if it still isn't happening, maybe Ed should come in and we could run a few tests on him too."

"Oh."

"But I'm sure you'll find that won't be necessary."

"No. Right. If we tango enough."

She tramped around the supermarket, trying to find her earlier high spirits, as if they might be stacked on a shelf somewhere, but they seemed to have sold out. She filled the cart with all kinds of things they didn't really need, telling herself to cheer up, for pete's sake, she'd gotten a double thumbs-up, she was a proper, paid-up, functioning female.

By the time she reached the checkout she was feeling a little happier. She waited in line, watching the other women, all of them older than her, waiting patiently with their loaded carts. Maybe it was time she quit being a lady of leisure and got herself a job. After all, Ed was fit now and working and knew the house well enough not to need her hovering over him all day. He had said so himself. Maybe she would start looking. The decision made her feel better still.

"Julia?"

She looked around. A young man was standing behind her, next in line. He was tall and cute, with long dark hair, and he was vaguely familiar but Julia couldn't place him. He grinned.

"Hey, it is you. I thought it was."

"I'm sorry, I—"

"Mitch."

As he said it, she recognized him and she tried to look pleased to see him.

"Hey, Mitch! I'm sorry. Your hair's different. Longer."

"Yours sure isn't."

"Oh. No. So how've you been?"

"Okay."

"Are you working?"

"Yeah. It sucks. I'm getting a band together."

Somehow it didn't surprise her. They chatted while Julia went through checkout and she remembered how much she disliked him. Until the band got famous, he was working in a garage where he was supposed to be learning how to be a mechanic. All the people there were apparently either deadbeats or assholes. Julia toyed with the idea of asking him for twenty alternatives to that. He walked with her across the parking lot and stood watching while she loaded the groceries into the back of the Jeep and climbed into the driver's seat.

"So, did you have to go to jail or anything?" he said.

"What?" She wondered if she'd heard him right.

"You know, for what happened with Skye and all."

"Go to *jail*?"

"Well, you were the one supposed to be in charge."

Julia looked away across the parking lot for a moment and took a breath.

"No, Mitch. No one went to jail. I'll see you around."

She started the engine and shut the door. As she drove away she saw he was grinning.

SOMETIMES THE SILENCE was good.

Such as now, when he was alone and calm and the morning sun was slanting warmly in on his face through the glass doors and he could just sit there, dead still, at the piano and picture the particles of dust hanging and glinting in the beam.

Of course, it was never truly silence. The house was always talking to itself, the creaking of wood and pipework as they swelled or shrank, the click of the kitchen clock, the periodic jump-start judder and whir of the refrigerator. Outside, he could hear the drip, drip, drip of snow- melt from the roof and every now and then, out on the road, the whoosh of a passing car or the rumble of a logging truck.

Then there were those times when the silence wasn't so good.

When it seemed to close in on him like a murderer with a pillow come to smother him and he'd have to do something quick before it got to him, sing or yell or scream or clang the keyboard like a mad organist in a horror movie. Oddly, it happened less when he was alone than when there were people around.

Early on, when he was recovering at Grassland, it had been fairly frequent. He and his parents and Julia, and sometimes his brothers too and their wives, might all be sitting at the dinner table and there would be a lull in the conversation. And in those few brief moments of silence Ed would suddenly feel the panic rising in his chest like a tide of black and he would start jabbering like an idiot, talking utter nonsense or cracking terrible, self-flagellating jokes, comparing himself with Job or Jude the Obscure. Even though they laughed politely, nobody—not even he—thought it remotely funny, but he had to do it just to save himself from drowning.

He knew it had worried the hell out of his parents and Julia too. They probably all thought he was going crazy, but he couldn't help it. He'd tried once to explain it to Julia, but the closest analogy he could find was that it was a little like claustrophobia.

These moments were rare now. In fact, he hadn't had a serious one since they moved to Montana. He was aware, however, that his constant babble and banter with Julia was a precautionary defense against them. He had always talked too much, but now he sometimes caught himself, heard himself, going into overdrive. Julia always seemed to sense it. And if she were near she would reach out and lay a hand on him or come across the room to him and hold him and say hush, I'm here, it's okay.

It wasn't just to do with staving off those black, life-denying silences. Ed was aware of how "wonderfully" everyone thought he had "coped" with what had happened to him. Of how impressed they were with his "bravery" and constant "high spirits." Of course, he could have simply collapsed in a heap and sobbed all day long or shot himself. And, heaven knew, there had been many times when he had felt like doing all of those things. But the truth was, he didn't really see the point. He knew that his greatest enemy wasn't blindness. After all, he'd discovered at an early age, with his diabetes, that his body could let him down. No. Despite the grim jokes about Job and Jude, he knew that his greatest enemy by far was self-pity.

Let one ounce of it into your head and wham, before you knew it, your whole system would be taken over. It was like heroin or some shocking virus that multiplied in your veins and left you withered and crippled and wishing you were dead. Or like a malign goblin, squatting in the corner of the room, watching you with cold eyes and waiting. And the only thing you could do to keep him at bay was to act the whole time as if you were happy, as if being blind were merely an inconvenience and—you know what, guys?—what with all these new toys to play with and all these new things to learn, hell, it was actually *fun*! If you could make him believe that and believe that no matter how long he hung around he hadn't the slightest chance of climbing into your head, then maybe, just maybe, the little bastard might get bored and go away.

It was this same creature who, in Ed's lowest moments, whispered to him that Julia didn't really love him, that she had married him only out of guilt or out of some warped sense of duty or even—most absurd of all—for the money he might one day inherit. Luckily, however, Ed wasn't blind enough or dumb enough to take such taunts to heart. He'd lost his sight but not his insight. Nor, miraculously, his self-esteem.

Whether he would have found the strength to be like this without Julia he wasn't sure, but it was doubtful. Perhaps some slighter version of himself might have slithered through and scraped together something sad and shadowy that passed for a life. As it was, Julia had taken him by the hand and led him ever toward the light. And though all he could see of it was the faintest amber glow, which was probably only an odd, vestigial memory of sight, he could feel its warmth on his face and the power of its healing. Not only was she his eyes, she was the source of his inspiration, of his courage and of his will to survive. In the seamless dark of his days and his nights there was no end of him and no beginning of her. They were one and the same and indivisible.

FIFTEEN

THEY SAW the smoke from a long way off, rising like a tilting black tower from behind the ridge at the head of the valley. The road that was leading them there was narrow and pitted with tank tracks. Sometimes the valley sides would close in on them and the road become winding and steep and shadowed and the river they were following would funnel and drop out of sight and even over the strained engine of the old VW bug they could hear it thundering in falls a hundred feet below. Then the land would flatten and open itself again to the cloudless spring sky and the river would calm and curl away to their right through sunlit meadows of lush new grass with the forest rising beyond, a dozen shades of green.

They had the windows down and the fraying cloth sunroof rolled right back and the air that gusted in was cool and smelled sweet. Sylvie's dyed blond hair was blowing crazily over her face, and every so often she would take a hand off the steering wheel and tuck the loose strands back behind her ears, but in a few seconds they escaped again. All the way she had kept asking Connor to light cigarettes for her but only ever smoked them halfway because the last bit, she said, was the bit that killed you. From someone who had risked death on a daily basis for the past twenty years, Connor thought this was interesting. She had several cartons of Marlboros stowed under their camera gear and flak jackets on the backseat so that she could hand them out at roadblocks. Three times in the last hour they had been stopped by hatchet-faced Serb militiamen and she had joked and flirted with them in her husky Parisian voice, then handed out packs of cigarettes and in no time at all they were being waved through.

Sylvie Guillard was pushing forty and was photographing wars while Connor was still in fourth grade. She was with the famous Magnum agency and her fearlessness was as legendary as her talent. There were stories about her riding into battle on the front of tanks and walking out into the middle of a firefight just to check the light. How many of the stories were true, Connor had no idea. He had been aware of her since he arrived in Bosnia in the fall. She was little and skinny and something of a fantasy figure among the male journalists in Sarajevo, who seemed to find her sexy and terrifying in equal measure. She was known as a loner, which made it all the more surprising that lately she had taken Connor under her wing. He hadn't so far managed to sell many pictures, but had it not been for Sylvie's help he wouldn't have sold any.

Quite why she should bother remained a mystery. The war photographers he had met in Bosnia were mostly friendly and decent people. But when it came to business they were furtive and fiercely competitive. To share what would otherwise be an exclusive was unheard of, if not downright crass. Yet at three o'clock that morning Sylvie had knocked on his door at the Holiday Inn and told him to get his gear together. She had gotten a call on her satellite phone from one of her many mysterious contacts, telling her that the Red Cobras, one of the most feared Serb paramilitary groups, were moving in on Muslim enclaves in these hills. The informant said she should get out here fast.

With roadblocks and diversions the trip from Sarajevo had taken nearly five hours and during that time Sylvie had told him about the Cobras. Their leader was a charismatic fascist called Grujo, a meat wholesaler with a penchant for expensive cars and low-tech weaponry. He apparently liked to execute his Muslim enemies with a crossbow and then personally scalp them. The trophies were said to flutter proudly from the aerial of his black armor-plated Range Rover. Connor said the guy sounded like a madman but Sylvie shrugged.

"Such guys are rarely mad. As an explanation, that's too easy. It is like an excuse for the rest of us."

As they neared the end of the valley now, they passed a string of houses that had been burned and deserted but there was no sign among them of either life or death. At the valley's end the road grew steep, and they started to climb through the shadowed cold of the forest in a slow zigzag of bends, the roar of the engine bouncing off cliffs of wet gray rock and echoing away through the trees.

They could smell what had happened before they saw it. Even as the road leveled and they emerged from the trees into the sunlight they knew from the sour charnel waft in the air that more had burned here than houses.

It was—or had been—more a hamlet than a village. Just a cluster of a dozen small dwellings and barns in a shallow bowl of meadow filled with spring flowers that shimmered pink and white and yellow in the sunlight. The smoke they had seen from down in the valley was thinner now and seemed to be coming mostly from the blackened wreck of a tractor lying on its side.

Sylvie stopped the car a hundred yards short of the first building and switched off the engine and they sat awhile, staring ahead and listening, but all they could hear was the hum of insects among the flowers. A white dog ran across the road on some private mission and it saw them and stopped and gave a single halfhearted bark then disappeared behind a stone wall into a small orchard. There were two dark shapes among the blossom and though they were partly concealed, Connor knew what they were.

Still without speaking, they reached into the back of the car for their camera bags. The door of the VW creaked as Connor opened it and got out and they walked slowly side by side along the road toward the blackened buildings, taking pictures, their boots scrunching on the gravel.

There were charred mounds lying in the grass beside the road with flies already busy around them and it took Connor a moment to realize that they were cattle with the remains of torched tires around their necks.

The first human bodies were a little farther along the road, lying outside what had once been their home. While Sylvie photographed them, Connor walked across the road and into the little orchard.

There were two of them there, hanging by their wrists from the bough of an apple tree. A mother and her teenage daughter, Connor guessed. The girl was naked and the woman wore only a ripped and bloodstained blouse. Both had been mutilated in ways that, even as he photographed them, Connor wished he hadn't seen.

In the past months he had taken pictures of enough corpses to haunt a small gallery and he no longer wanted to be sick when he saw them through the camera's eye. He still felt both pity and revulsion and hoped that he always would. But as he went about his business, he kept these feelings, if not capped, like a lens, then at least filtered. And what he mostly now felt was a growing sense of wonder that human beings were capable of such casual, even gleeful, atrocity.

At first, it had bothered him that he could do it. That he could think about the way the light played on a dead man's skin or glinted in an unseeing eye or on a pool of blood. That he could look upon some child's father or some mother's child with the warmth of life still ebbing from them and at the same time scroll through the myriad tiny calculations that would make the image good or bad; the choice of lens, of exposure, of composition. Perhaps some vital part of him was wrongly wired or had been cauterized. But then he concluded, like so many before him, that these were the very distractions that made it possible to document the horror laid before him.

The sunlight dappling on the blossom around the woman's head had a terrible beauty to it and Connor took more pictures than perhaps he should have. Sylvie joined him but shot only a few frames and then moved away up the street and he wondered if this was some kind of acknowledgment that the scene belonged to him or a tacit criticism that he was lingering too long.

They counted fifteen bodies in all, some barely recognizable as such. Five of them had been scalped. There were probably more among the smoldering black tangle of the houses. The last two were sitting side by side, a small boy and an old man, frail and wrinkled, with a wispy gray beard. Their backs were leaning against the outside wall of a whitewashed barn and from a distance it looked as if they might have sat down there to have a chat. Above their heads, in splashed red paint, someone had written *BALIJE*, an insulting term for Muslims, and a coiled cobra, its head reared and ready to strike.

They were photographing this when they heard the trucks.

"Give me your film," Sylvie said.

She was unscrewing the cap to the center stem of the telescopic aluminum tripod that she always carried.

"Quick, come on. All of it."

He handed her the rolls he'd shot, even the one still in his camera, and she slid them roll by roll along with her own inside the hollow tubing. She capped it again and then quickly fished half a dozen rolls from her bag and handed them to him. They were tail in, as if exposed.

"Put them in your bag."

They could see the trucks now, coming toward them across the meadows. They loaded more film into their cameras and started taking pictures of them. There were two jeeps, an armored car and a big open-backed farm truck. There were twenty, maybe thirty men, bristling with AK-47s and RPGs and shorter, stubby automatic rifles of a kind Connor hadn't seen before. When the soldiers saw the cameras they began to shout and point.

The convoy pulled up about twenty yards away from where they stood and the men scrambled out. Most of them were dressed in black fatigues or leather jackets. Some wore forage caps and helmets with the Red Cobra insignia painted on them, others had red bandannas and all had bandoliers of shells slung across them and pistols and knives and grenades at their belts. At least half a dozen were heading toward them.

"Remember," Sylvie said quietly. "They're our friends in Jesus."

Connor felt his heart quicken and it worried him a little as it had before that it wasn't fear he felt but something closer to excitement.

From the way he looked and the way he walked it was clear which one of them was in charge. He was a man of about Connor's age, thickly muscled and taller than the others. His hair was cropped close and he wore aviator shades and a tight black T-shirt with NIRVANA emblazoned on it in silver lettering. Whether this was a spiritual state to which he aspired or simply his favorite band, there was no telling. He had a Scorpion machine-pistol holstered on one hip and a long hunting knife on the other. As he came up to them Sylvie greeted him warmly in Serbo-Croat. He stopped close in front of them, looking down at her with contempt and when he spoke it was in English.

"Who are you? What are you doing here?"

She answered in Serbo-Croat, getting out her cigarettes and offering him one as she spoke but he declined with a curt shake of his head. He asked her who had given them permission to be here and again he spoke in English, to show, perhaps, that he wasn't going to be charmed. He had a deep voice and a mobsterlike American accent, as if he'd watched too many Mafia movies. Sylvie stuck to her Serbo-Croat and though she spoke too fast for Connor to understand much, he heard her mention the name Grujo a couple of times, dropping it casually, as if they were friends. The man didn't seem either impressed or unimpressed.

"Give me your papers."

They handed him their passports and Connor got out his UN press card, the only other official-looking document he possessed and about as useful as a ticket to a canceled ball game.

"Good band," Connor said as he handed it over.

The man looked at him sharply. "What?"

Connor nodded at his T-shirt. The man stared at him for a moment but said nothing. Beyond him Connor could see other soldiers loading bodies into the back of the truck.

"You're American?"

"Yes."

"What newspaper?"

Connor knew he should probably pretend to be some big-shot Magnum photographer like Sylvie but he couldn't bring himself to do it. He shrugged.

"Any that's interested. Mostly none."

Sylvie started to say something, but the man cut her off, nodding toward the bodies of the old man and the boy.

"The American people, they are interested in this *balije* shit?"

"Hell, I don't know. I am."

"Oh. Really?"

"Uh-huh."

"So, what is it you find interesting?"

Connor could sense Sylvie stiffening beside him. But he held the man's gaze without flinching and shrugged.

"I guess what mostly interests me is what kind of man it takes to murder and torture women and children and defenseless old men."

The man looked at him and Connor searched for the eyes behind the sunglasses but all he could see were his own staring back at him. Sylvie started speaking, still in Serbo-Croat, but her voice lower and more urgent than before and again he heard her mention Grujo. The man kept his eyes on Connor while he listened.

"Give us your film."

Sylvie went on talking, calmly but forcefully,

telling him she wasn't going to and explaining why. He told her again to hand it over and kept on telling her and at last reached for her camera bag and Sylvie exploded, swearing at him in several languages and he shouted a command and all hell broke loose.

They grabbed them both and shoved guns into their faces and pinned their arms behind their backs. Then they ripped off their cameras and their bags and took out every roll of film and smashed the cassettes under their boots and unraveled the film to the light and then opened their cameras and did the same again. And all the while Sylvie screamed and spat abuse at them.

Then, at the man's command, they were shoved forward and marched off down the road with guns sticking into the back of their necks, past the truck now stacked with bodies and past the orchard where the blossom now hung innocent and empty and with every step Connor felt more and more convinced that they were going to be taken behind a building and shot.

But they were only taking them to the VW.

The soldiers searched the car for more film but found none. They helped themselves to the cigarettes and gave them back their papers and their camera gear, including the tripod, and told them to get in and go. Sylvie turned the car around, keeping up her torrent of threat and abuse through the window. By now the men were all laughing and jeering.

As they dropped out of sight into the forest, she slapped the steering wheel with the palms of her hands and threw her head back and started to laugh. She looked at Connor and he smiled but said nothing. He would have liked to share her exhilaration but he couldn't. He was in shock.

In his head he was still walking down that road, past the orchard and the burnt-out houses and the butchered bodies, certain that in a few moments he too would be dead. And what shocked him was the discovery that he hadn't cared.

THEY CHOSE A DIFFERENT ROUTE back to Sarajevo but it took even longer. They passed trucks of dead-eyed refugees and the rubbled remains of villages, shelled and burned and abandoned. There were many more roadblocks than there had been that morning and once they had to wait three hours while their papers were taken away and checked. Then they got stuck behind a UN food convoy, blocked in some kind of standoff with the JNA, the Yugoslav People's Army. The UN soldiers were British and Sylvie and Connor sought out a senior officer and told him what they had witnessed.

By the time they made it back to the Holiday Inn it was getting late. They drove down the ramp into the basement and parked and when they went upstairs they found the lobby and bar buzzing with news about Grujo and the Cobras and their latest spree of ethnic cleansing. A news agency guy, worse the wear for whiskey, was telling everyone in a loud voice that the area where it had happened was sealed off and nobody was allowed in. Connor and Sylvie didn't say a word. They bought two beers and went up to their rooms to dump their gear.

The lab she used was a short walk from the hotel, or rather, a short pray, duck and run across three streets surveyed by Serb snipers, who were probably all by now too drunk to shoot straight, but you never could tell. They processed the color first and then the black and white. The place was cramped and Connor perched himself with his beer in a corner and let Sylvie do most of the work. It was hot and they had taken off their jackets. Sylvie was wearing a flimsy sleeveless top and Connor couldn't help noticing that she wasn't wearing a bra. She caught him looking once and didn't smile, just went back to her work.

She dried the negatives with a hair dryer she had brought along and laid the negatives out on the light box and the two of them had to squeeze side by side to view them. Many of the images were too explicit and horrific for most papers to publish and she seemed to know at a glance what was good and what wasn't. Connor found it strange that it was harder to look at these images now than it had been to look at the real thing and when he told her this she shrugged and said it was simply a matter of adrenaline.

The shots she had taken of the old man and the boy with the Cobra on the wall above them were much better than his and so were most of the others. But when they got to one of the black and white rolls that Connor had shot in the orchard, Sylvie let out a low whistle.

"Which one," she said. "Tell me."

"The best shot, you mean?"

She nodded and stood back to let him study them. There was a sequence of five frames in which the two women were partly in silhouette. He said it must be one of these and she nodded and asked him again which one was the best. Connor said he didn't think there was a lot to choose between them and she said he was wrong and told him to make some test prints.

Even as the image was coming through on

the paper Connor knew which one she meant. You could see the girl was naked but, apart from their faces and arms, both she and the woman were discreetly veiled by shadow and somehow this made what they had so clearly suffered all the more appalling. The sunlight on the blossom behind them and above them where their wrists were tied was exquisite and shocking.

"That is the picture of the day," she said. "Maybe even of the year."

"I don't know about that."

"Please don't think I would bother to flatter you."

He looked at her and smiled. She finished off her beer. He was aware of her watching him while he lifted the print out and placed it in the fixer tray and started tidying things up.

"Okay," she said. "Now let's go earn you some money."

They gathered the negatives and locked the place up and walked to the corner of the first of the three streets they had to cross to get back to the hotel.

"This time we don't run, okay?"

Connor shrugged. "If you say so."

She took his arm and they stepped out and walked slowly across. Their footsteps echoed in the darkness and Connor pictured himself in some young Serb's nightscope and again it worried him that he didn't care. They did the same on the next street, only slower. And again on the last one, slower still.

"You're not afraid?" she said.

"Maybe if I was smarter I would be."

"Some days you just know you're not going to die."

"You think so?"

"I'm certain. Look."

She made him stop. They were in the middle of the street. She turned her back on the snipers and kissed him hard on the mouth and then laughed.

"You see?"

When they reached the hotel they went straight up to her room and she took off her jacket and her boots and got out a bottle of whiskey and poured them each a glass. She sat cross-legged on the bed and lit a cigarette and asked him about his agency in New York. It was the same one that had sold his picture of the Yellowstone fire, but since he had been in Bosnia they had done little for him. Sylvie said they were shit and he should leave them. She reached for her satellite phone. She made a call to Paris and two more to New York and by the time she was through Connor had a whole new deal.

They got out her scanner and her laptop and

sat beside each other on the bed while they scanned the negatives into the laptop, some of hers and some of his, then sent them like magic over the satphone. She poured them another whiskey and they clinked glasses and Connor thanked her and she gave him one of those funny French shrugs of hers and said it was nothing.

Then the hotel power crashed and everything went dark and Sylvie lit the three candles that were on the bedside table. For a while neither of them spoke, just sat and sipped their whiskey, listening to the distant thud of shells landing somewhere across the city and the lonely wail of an ambulance siren.

She was leaning back against the headboard and he could tell from the look in her eyes what she wanted to happen next. She reached out and stroked the back of his head and his neck and for a while they stared at each other. His hair had grown long and she twisted it in her hand, almost hard enough to hurt.

"I try to make my hair this color, but it never works."

"Your hair looks fine."

"We're like twins."

He smiled. She put down her glass on the bedside table and he did the same and she moved across the bed toward him and kissed him. Her mouth tasted of whiskey and cigarettes and there was a kind of violent hunger in the way she kissed that almost unsettled him. She leaned back against the headboard and stretched her arms above her and he lifted her shirt and hoisted it over her head and pinned her wrists high against the wall with one hand while he kissed down the insides of her arms and her neck and under her arms where there was a dark stubble and the smell of her was strong and thrilling and then he kissed her small breasts with their hard, dark nipples.

She was breathing fast and she lowered her arms and reached with both hands for the buckle of his belt. He raised himself to his knees and she opened his pants and tugged them down around his thighs and took him into her mouth and it was such a long time since Connor had been like this with anyone that he could only bear it for a few moments and had to stop her in case he came.

She laid her head back on the bed and he pulled off her pants and her panties and then took off his shirt, watching her and noticing how the skin stretched pale and pellucid over her ribs to the rhythm of her breathing and how her hipbones jutted like cliffs above her concave belly with its triangle of thick black hair. He was about to take off his boots and the rest of his clothes, but she told him not to and opened her legs wide and hoisted her hips at him and told him to fuck her, to fuck her now.

She shouted so loudly as he went inside her that it almost unsettled him and she did it again every time he moved on her, but soon he was lost in the want and the feel of her. In a low and urgent voice she told him to fuck her hard and she kept saying it, louder, telling him to do it harder, to hurt her. And though he knew he fell short of what she wanted, Connor did as he was bidden and shocked himself that he could for he had never made love in that way before.

It was only later, when they lay spent and sore with their mingled sweat cooled to salt upon them and Sylvie asleep, curled like an orphan across the tangled bedding and the gray dawn bleeding through the drapes, it was only then that Connor understood.

It wasn't love that they had made nor yet some deviant subspecies of it. It had been more a quest for affirmation, a kind of desperate animal craving. And although he sensed it in Sylvie far more powerfully than in himself, he knew its seed was in him and that it would grow. Having steeped themselves in death, they needed to exorcise it, to assert their aliveness. Pain was the province of the living and was thus part of the process. They had screamed with their flesh and whatever else they might be made of, though to whom or what beyond themselves he knew not, that somewhere, somewhere, amid the mayhem and the horror was a core of humanity that was raw and fierce and primordial.

THE PICTURE OF THE WOMEN in the blossom found its way onto the front page of newspapers all over the world. Sylvie flew home to Paris the following week and then was sent at once to Africa. Connor missed her. He didn't see her again until August when she came back to Sarajevo. But it wasn't the same. She was cool toward him and a little aloof and he wondered if he had done something to offend her. Maybe she resented the success she had helped him have.

The following week he caught a piece of shrapnel in the back of his right leg and was flown in a UN Hercules to a hospital on the Croatian coast. Sylvie had gone north for a few days and he never got to say goodbye. It was only a flesh wound but the doctors suggested he go home to recuperate and suddenly the prospect appealed. He flew to Frankfurt and while he waited for his connection in the sterile limbo of the transit lounge he tried to call Sylvie from a pay phone but got no reply.

New York was hot and humid and everyone seemed mad or miserable. When he hobbled into the offices of his new agency, they greeted him like a war hero. He wished he could have felt like one, but all he felt was empty. One of the editors, Harry Turney, took him to lunch in the smartest place he had ever eaten. He was a tall man with gentle eyes and reminded Connor a little of his father. Connor ate like a starved wolf and still felt hungry. As the coffee was being served, Turney said he was sorry to hear about Sylvie. Connor asked him what he meant.

"You haven't heard?"

"Heard what?"

"It was in yesterday's *Times*. She was with a Reuters reporter somewhere up north, near the border. They drove over a land mine. Both killed outright."

SIXTEEN

JULIA TOOK the steaks and the chicken legs out of the marinade and put them on the big wooden tray along with the salad and all the relishes. Donna Kiamoto had already ferried the rest of the food out onto the deck where they had set up the table. Julia could hear from the kitchen that she was having trouble guarding it from ever-hungry smoke jumpers. She could also hear Ed out there, making sure everyone knew the plan. He had been through it twice already as well as telling each one of them individually when they'd arrived, but he was doing it again just in case.

"So, we're all hiding out here, Donna's behind the drapes over there, the front door's open, the place looks deserted, in he comes. And Donna, be careful he doesn't see your reflection in the glass, okay? As he comes into the living room, Donna gives the signal and I start to play. And you guys better keep quiet, do you hear? No more beer for anyone who giggles or breaks wind. Ve have vays of making you restrain yourselves. Hank and . . . who? Oh yeah, sorry. Phil. You guys unroll the banner—and make sure it's the right way up, okay? He may not be bright, but he can read."

"Julia, how do you manage to live with this guy?" Hank Thomas asked her as she came out onto the deck with the tray.

"Earplugs."

She could hardly find her way to the table through the smoke. Chuck Hamer was supposed to be in charge of the barbecue and was making a pretty dismal job of it.

"Hey, Chuck, I thought you were supposed to be a firefighter? What the heck's going on here?"

"Honey, I get paid to put 'em out, not start 'em."

"Baby, you can light my fire," Ed sang.

Having lectured the troops, now he was fiddling with the amplifier for his electric guitar. Julia watched him for a moment and had to smile. He was in full buzz mode, happy as a puppy, and he looked boyish and cute in his baggy shorts and the yellow and black Hawaiian shirt she'd bought him for his birthday. He had wanted to frizz his hair into a Jimi Hendrix

Afro but she'd managed to talk him out of it. He'd settled instead for purple shades and a bandanna.

Poor Connor. He thought he was just coming over for a quiet supper with the two of them and Julia still wished he were. But Ed had insisted they lay on this surprise welcome-home party. Julia argued that having just been wounded, it was probably the last thing he would want, but Ed had spoken to him on the phone at his mother's place and said he sounded fine. There were about twenty guests, mostly Connor's old smoke jumping buddies and their assorted spouses and lovers. All had been strictly instructed to arrive early and park next door at the Robertsons' place so that Connor wouldn't see the cars.

At least he was going to see the place at its best. It was a perfect September evening, balmy and clear, with just a hint of fall in the air. There were apples on the trees and the rambling rose above the deck had flowered a second time and was a blaze of yellow. Anyhow, she reasoned, it was the kind of party that would more or less look after itself. Entertaining smoke jumpers was more a matter of quantity than quality: a big steak and plenty of beer was about as sophisticated as it needed to be.

Nevertheless, Julia had wound herself into a

state of mild hysteria about it. She wanted everything to be just right. She had cleaned the place from top to bottom, put flowers in every room and spent far too much time and money getting all the food and drink. She had even bought French champagne and baked a cake and decorated it with a little toy camera.

For days she had been worrying about what she was going to wear and then worrying about why she was worrying about it. What was the big deal? It was only Connor, for heavensake. It was odds on that most of the women would be in jeans and T-shirts, like the men. But for reasons she didn't let herself explore, she wanted to wear a dress. Nothing in her closet seemed right so she ended up going into Missoula to look for something new.

She found it right away in a store on North Higgins. It was a simple three-quarter-length shift in a shade of pale blue that flattered her tan. She tried it on and groaned when she saw how well it suited her. In fact, damn it, she looked fantastic. But it was a hundred and twenty dollars! Out of the question. Completely ridiculous. She didn't need it. She thanked the assistant and walked out, got back in the Jeep, sat there awhile, got out again, went back to the store, dithered like an idiot for another fifteen minutes, then bought it, persuading herself that it was really an investment, a dress that would be useful for all kinds of other occasions, such as . . . whatever. She hadn't treated herself in a long while, so what the hell.

But she still didn't tell Ed. Not because she thought he would mind. On the contrary, he liked her buying new things for herself. Earlier in the evening, when they were getting ready and he asked her what she was going to wear, she even lied, telling him the dress was an old one that she'd forgotten she had and found at the back of the closet. Touchy-feely guy that he was, he did, however, notice that she'd also had her hair cut and her legs waxed.

There was one more tray of food left in the kitchen, and while Julia was on her way to fetch it, Donna came running through the front door. Ed had posted her at the end of the driveway to keep watch.

"Does he still drive that old Chevy?" she said.

"I guess. A pickup, pale blue."

"That's it. He's coming."

Donna ran out and told everyone and Julia followed with the tray and helped her hide behind the drapes. She went to stand beside Ed.

"Where's my guitar? Julia?"

"Don't panic. I'm right here."

"I'm not panicking."

She handed it to him and he looped the strap

over his shoulder and lightly touched the strings to make a final check on the amplifier.

"Hank? Have you guys got that banner ready?"

"Yessir."

"Okay, smoke jumpers. Stand ready."

They all froze and after a few moments heard Connor's truck pulling up in the driveway, then the clunk of the car door and footsteps on the gravel.

"Jeez, Hank, it's your mother-in-law," Chuck whispered and everyone told him to shush.

There was a knock on the front door and a long pause.

"Hello?"

At the sound of his voice, Julia felt something quicken within her.

"Hell, no, it's that old girlfriend of yours. She's got a gun!"

"Shhhh!"

She could hear his footsteps coming into the living room now.

"Ed? Julia?"

Donna nodded from her spy hole and Julia touched Ed on the shoulder. And on cue he made the guitar howl and launched into the Jimi Hendrix version of "The Star-Spangled Banner" (quite why, Julia had no idea). Hank and Phil, on chairs either side of the doorway, unfurled the banner. Julia had written "Welcome Home Connor" on it in red and blue glitter-paint and dotted it with silver stars. And suddenly there he was below it, wearing his old cowboy hat and giving everyone that slow grin of his and shaking his head. His blue eyes scanned the faces and found hers and stayed.

Ed stopped playing and everyone cheered and gathered around him.

"Dear Lord," he said. "You guys are harder to shake off than a tick on a dog's backside."

"That makes you the asshole, cowboy," Chuck said.

"Hey, Chuck, how're you doing? Hank, Donna . . ."

He shook hands and hugged everyone, leaving Ed and Julia until last. Finally he came smiling toward them. She noticed he was limping a little.

"Julia, who *is* this weird dude you're standing next to? I mean, is this Rockin' Rudy in person or what?"

"My man." Ed put his fist to chest.

"Hearts of fire!" They high-fived and Connor took off his hat and the two friends hugged each other.

"You sly sonofabitch," Connor said. " 'Just come on over for a little supper.' "

He planted his hat on Ed's head and turned at

last to Julia and she knew there was something different about his face although she couldn't work out what. He was thinner and his eyes seemed deeper set.

"Hi, Connor. Welcome home."

"Hell, it's not as if I've been gone that long."

"It just seems like it."

They put their arms around each other and she felt his hands grip her back and hold her firmly for a moment and all the breath seemed to leave her lungs. She knew she should say something light and funny but even if she could have found the right words, she had lost the power to utter them. She worried that her feelings might be obvious to the others and quickly let him go and hooked her arm under Ed's.

"Just look at the pair of you," Connor said. "And look at all this." He gave a sweep of his arm. "The river down there, apple trees, the roses and all. You got your own little Garden of Eden here."

"Julia as Eve, I can buy," Hank Thomas said. "But if that's Adam, I'm Bambi's mom."

"In those shades he looks more like the serpent," Donna said.

"Here, Donna," Ed said. "Have an apple."

The banter went on and grew cruder and Julia dragged Chuck away to the barbecue and told him to get the meat going and then went inside to fetch the champagne. When she came out again they were all teasing Connor about his "war wound" but he was giving as good as he got, spinning a story which she only partly caught but seemed to involve him single-handedly taking on the entire Serbian army. Ed opened the champagne and when all their glasses were charged he proposed a toast. And as Julia uttered his name with the rest of them and drank his health, Connor's eyes again settled on hers and stayed and she had to look away.

CONNOR WATCHED HER as she walked ahead of him up the stairs, watched the way her hips moved inside her dress and how she trailed her left hand with its plain gold wedding band on the banister. The light outside was fading and the skin of her bare shoulders was dark against the pale blue of the dress. She looked more beautiful than ever, even than on those lonely nights when he'd lain awake listening to the shell fire and thinking of her. Even more beautiful than she did in the picture that he always carried in his billfold, the one Ed had taken of the two of them on the day they went climbing. The one in which they were smiling at each other and looked, for all the world, like a proper couple.

Ed had put some Bob Marley on the stereo in the hope that people might start dancing, but everyone was enjoying sitting and chatting out on the deck and on the grass below. Julia had lit candles out there in glass sleeves and set some more in the trees and everything looked magical. Connor had asked if he could take a look at the house and so she was giving him the tour. They'd started out in her studio in the barn and she'd gotten embarrassed when he told her how much he liked her new paintings. Now they were back in the house. Everyone else was still outside.

As she reached the top of the stairs, she turned to look at him. He hoped that she hadn't caught him looking at her hips that way.

"It's a great place," he said clumsily.

"Yeah. It works real well for us. Though it'd be easier for Ed if we lived in town."

"Why's that?"

"Oh, you know, he could be more independent, find his own way around more. He has a map of Missoula in his head, whereas out here it's all new and . . . well, kind of riskier, I guess is what I mean. Not that it stops him doing things, mind."

"I can imagine."

"Like the other day. This summer we've been running together. The trails are pretty good and he knows them by now and when I'm with him it's perfectly safe. Well, one evening last week, I've been into town, I'm driving up the gravel road out there, coming around the corner and there's this, like, apparition, in an orange hunting vest, in the middle of the road, running right at me. Guess who. He's got his cane out in front, sweeping it from side to side, and this isn't some gentle little jog. He's going like flat-out."

Connor laughed. He loved the expressive way she used her hands when she was telling a story like this. He figured it must be the Italian in her.

"So I stop the car and he comes running right up to me and hits the front of the Jeep with the cane and stops with his hands on the hood and do you know what he says? He says, 'Well, that's a dumb place to park!' I mean, Connor, what can you do with the guy?"

"Keep him in a cage or something."

"I tell you, one day. Did he tell you his latest plan?"

"Nope."

"Rock climbing. He took this course down in Colorado where they teach blind people to climb. When your leg's better he wants the three of us to do that same peak, you know? Where we took all those pictures of each other?"

"Sounds great. Give me a week and I'm up for it."

She cocked her head to one side and put her hands on her hips.

"You know what? You're as bad as he is."

They smiled at each other for a moment, Bob Marley singing away downstairs, telling everyone not to worry, everything was going to be all right. Julia switched on the landing light and he wished she hadn't. The twilight was more intimate.

"Come on," she said. "I'll show you the rest."

There were three bedrooms and a bathroom. One of the bedrooms was half stacked with unpacked boxes, the other half taken up with weights and a bench where, Julia told him, Ed worked out each morning. The second room was prettily decorated with yellow wallpaper and a dark blue quilt with a towel neatly folded upon it and Julia said this was where he would be sleeping tonight, if that was okay. He said he hadn't figured on staying over and she looked genuinely upset so he said he would, if she was sure it was convenient. She gave him one of her schoolmarm looks.

"Connor, it's convenient. Okay?"

She showed him the bathroom and lastly led him into the main bedroom. It smelled of her. The bed was set beneath the window and covered in a plain white cotton throw and he imagined her lying there and stored the image in his head. He could tell which side she slept on from the stack of books and the little collection of creams and lotions. There were pegs on the wall where she hung her jewelry and there was a big painting which though he'd seen little of her work he somehow knew was hers. It was like a cave painting of running deer and matchstick men on horses chasing them with spears and bows and arrows and it was painted in earth colors, red and black and orange and amber.

"This must be one of yours."

"Oh, that. Yeah."

She looked embarrassed again and he didn't know if it was because of the painting or because they were in her bedroom.

"It was just a phase. Something I was playing around with, you know. It doesn't really work."

"It's good."

"Oh no. I mean, thanks, but it's not. Really."

"Ed told me you're teaching again."

"Yeah. It's great. Only part-time, you know. I do three days a week at this little elementary school in Missoula."

"Teaching art?"

"Uh-huh. But mostly wiping noses and hosing them down after they've thrown paint all over each other."

"Sounds like fun."

"It is."

They stood without speaking for a moment, still staring at the painting.

"He was really worried about you, you know?" she said. "We'd hear about all those awful things going on out there, not knowing where you were or anything and we—Ed, I mean, he just got a little worried. Silly, I know."

"You didn't get my cards?"

She laughed. "Oh yeah, 'Weather terrible, wish you were here.' "

"I'm sorry."

"Anyway. Here you are."

"Here I am."

They stared at each other for a moment. Then, suddenly, she gave a little smile, a distancing kind of smile, like a shutter coming down.

"I'd better go and see if everyone's okay out there."

"SO ARE THE SNIPERS always there watching?" Ed asked. "Just waiting for somebody to cross?"

"You don't know until the bullet hits you. Some of the side streets off Snipers' Alley, you can go for days without a shot being fired. Then, bam, somebody gets killed. I guess for the snipers it's a kind of game."

"Killing total strangers."

"Worse than that. Some of these people they're killing were friends and neighbors before the war. Now they're just Muslims and fair game. Like they're not human beings anymore."

They were lying in the grass down by the river, just the two of them. Above the babble of the water, they could hear the others talking and laughing up at the house. Someone had put on one of Ed's old Doors albums. He had been trying all evening to talk with Connor on his own and eventually had to drag him off down here. For the last half hour he'd been asking questions about Bosnia and picturing in his head the stories Connor told him.

"Do you wear, like, a flak jacket or something?"

"At first I did. But not later on. They're kind of heavy old things."

Somewhere upstream among the cottonwoods a duck cackled in alarm.

"Fox on the prowl," Connor said.

"Or a coyote. We hear them yipping up there in the forest some nights."

They listened but heard no more.

"You've gotten yourselves a great place here."

"Yeah, we're real lucky."

"Have you had a go fishing? Looks like there's some good spots here."

"A few times. I had the trees cut back a little so I don't get myself in too much of a tangle. But, you know, if you can't stalk them and land a fly on their heads, it takes the fun out of it a little. All I can do is cast into the broken water, let it drift down and hope something takes it. They're here okay though. Brownies, cutthroat. Bill Robertson, the guy who owns the place over there, hooked himself a three-pound rainbow the other day."

As if to make the point, a fish rose somewhere across the water. They both laughed.

"And how's the music going?" Connor asked.

"Oh, you know."

"Well, if I did, I wouldn't ask."

Ed smiled. He didn't want to talk about it but it seemed unfair not to after the interrogation he'd just given Connor. He sighed.

"Well, to be honest, it's not going at all."

"Julia says you play all the time."

"Oh, sure. I play. I've even done a couple of gigs in a bar in town. But I haven't written anything in over a year. Anything worth keeping, anyhow. I just seem to have . . . I don't know. Lost it."

"It'll come back. You've had to learn a whole new way of doing it, I guess."

"Oh, sure, but that's not it. I've got the best equipment money can buy and I know my way around it. It's not that. I guess I've just had to accept that I haven't . . . got the talent."

"Man, you've got more talent than anyone I know."

"Well, that's nice of you to say it, but you know as much about music as I know about photography."

"I know you're good."

"Connor, do you know how many goddamn musicals I've written?"

"No."

"Eleven. And God only knows how many other bits and pieces. And every single one of them has been rejected. Not once, not twice, lots of times. I haven't had a single thing performed since I left college. And there comes a point when you have to get real. It's not going to happen. And, in the letters that come back, do you know what I hear now? Embarrassment. It's the same with my agent—that's a laugh—my non-agent. He doesn't even take my calls anymore. And when I do manage to get through to him, I hear the same thing. He's embarrassed. It's true. I've become an embarrassment."

He could tell from Connor's silence that the

poor guy didn't know what to say. He reached out and found his friend's shoulder and held it a moment.

"Do you know how proud I've been of you, just going out there and making a go of things? Man, I was proud. That picture of the women? I know it. I know what it looks like. I had Julia describe every single little detail of it and I know how extraordinary it is and I was so proud. And you know what? I was jealous as hell."

"Ed, I just got lucky. Like I did that time at Yellowstone. I stumbled across a moment and took one good picture. What you're trying to pull off is a hell of a lot more difficult."

"Hey, please. Don't patronize me."

"Patronize you? Jesus."

They sat silent for a while. Ed could imagine Connor shaking his head and staring out across the river. He felt like kicking himself for saying that. It was the first time in ages that he'd allowed himself to be hijacked by self-pity. Up at the house Chuck Hamer was finishing a joke and everybody groaned. Ed reached out and found Connor's shoulder again. After a moment Connor put his own hand on Ed's and said he was sorry if that's how it had sounded.

"No, man. I'm sorry. I just find it hard sometimes to hold it all together, you know? Hell,

I've got so much to be thankful for. I've got Julia, this fantastic place. And you know what? I'm a great piano teacher. I used to find teaching a real drag, like it was something I had to do until the musicals clicked through. But now I enjoy it, I really do."

"That's good."

"Yeah. It is."

He paused. He hadn't intended telling anyone the true cause of his low spirits. But sitting here with his best friend, he suddenly wanted to share it. He swallowed.

"Did Julia tell you we've been trying to have a kid?"

"No. Hey, that's great."

"Yeah. In theory. We've been trying for almost a year and nothing's happened."

"Well, I'm no expert. But that's not so long, is it?"

"Well, maybe. Anyhow, last month I had this minor problem with my diabetes. No big deal, it turned out that I just needed to increase the amount of insulin a little. But when I was having it checked out, the doctor, who's a really good guy, you know, up-to-date with all the latest research and things, asked me if we were going to have children. And I said yeah and told him how we'd been trying but it hadn't happened yet. And I made some stupid joke, like, maybe my sperm were all tired from having to work so hard, 'cos, boy, you know, when I say trying, I mean it. We've really been going for it—thermometers, calendars, the whole deal.

"Anyhow, then he asked me about when my diabetes was first diagnosed and if I'd ever had any immuno-suppressant treatment. And I said hell, I don't know, I was only a little kid at the time, why? And he ummed and aahed and hedged around and finally I forced him to tell me and he said apparently some of the drugs they used in those days had been found to have an adverse effect on fertility.

"So, you can imagine. Right away I call my mom and sure enough she says yeah, I did. I had like a blitz course of these immuno-suppressant things. Seems the doctors thought they might be able to knock the diabetes on the head or something. So I go back to my doctor here, he gets me to jerk off, runs the tests, looking for all these squirmy little Eds swimming around down there under the microscope and you know what? Zilch. Blanks, man. I fire blanks."

"You're sure?"

"Oh yeah."

"Can they do anything about it?"

"Not a thing."

Again, they were silent for a moment.

"Have you told Julia?"

"Not yet. I only found out at the end of last week. I just haven't had the balls to do it yet. So to speak."

He laughed and felt Connor's hand grasp his shoulder.

"I mean, I know we can adopt and all, but . . . I guess it's just the shock, you know." He paused. "Well, hey! There's a party pooper if ever there was one. I'm sorry, man. I shouldn't have—"

"Don't be sorry. I'm glad you told me."

Ed felt for his watch and pressed the button and the little robot voice told him it was ten-twenty-six-pee-em.

"Sorry, Hal? What was that again?"

It was a silly trick but it always got a laugh. He pressed the button again.

"Ten-twenty-six-pee-em."

"That's cool," Connor said.

"Yeah. The kids I teach all want one. Hey, tell me. Can you see the moon?"

"Uh-huh. It's not much of one."

"Two days old. And now, ladies and gentlemen, for his next trick, The Amazing Tully is going to point right at it."

He reached out to his right and found the last post of the rope rail to get his bearings and make sure he was facing in the right direction. Then he pointed at the sky.

"There. Am I right?"

"Absolutely. That's pretty good. How do you do that?"

Ed touched his temple like a mystic. "Ah, my friend. These are powers vouchsafed only to the chosen few. Will you draw me a map of the stars?"

"Sure. Where?"

"On my back."

Connor knelt behind him and while the river rippled by charted with his finger every planet and star he could name, which was many. While he was doing so he saw a falling star and told Ed and described it and traced its arc on his shoulder blade. And in the darkened dome of his skull Ed could see it and see them all, bright and silver and shimmering and he secretly shaved from them a sliver of their light and stored it in his heart.

SEVENTEEN

JULIA STOOD back and watched them, marveling at how such a small number of six-year-olds could make such a vast volume of noise. They were spread out along the back wall of the playground, all wearing their red and blue painting smocks. There was more chalk on their faces and smocks than was on the wall. It wasn't every day that law-abiding junior citizens were given license to deface state property and they were sure making the most of it.

Julia had gotten the idea for the project after talking with Connor about her cave painting in the bedroom. The outside of the school was being redecorated and she asked Mrs. Leitner, the principal, if her first-grade class could do a little decorating of their own before the painters got there. They had spent the previous week talking about cave painting and looking at some reference books that Julia had found in the public library. She'd handed out photocopies of some Native American pictographs in Idaho and of some extraordinary rock paintings recently discovered in France.

Today came the climax, with the kids being let loose on the playground wall. Julia had divided the wall into eight different "caves" and the kids into eight "cave families." They had to imagine what they had been doing that day and depict it in colored chalk on their stretch of the wall.

Mrs. Leitner had said it was a great idea but had failed to realize that it would be taking place right outside the room where she taught fourth-grade math. Julia had told her cave kids that they should communicate with each other exclusively in cave language, which seemed mostly to consist of loud shrieks and grunts. This was a decision she was now coming to regret and, judging by her rueful glances through the window, so was Mrs. Leitner.

Some of the children's pictures were impressive. Most had opted for hunting scenes, with deer and wolves and bears and woolly mammoths and lots of little human beings, though it was sometimes unclear who was hunting whom. Others had gotten a little more surreal. Julia had to point out to Lucy Kravitz that

Batman and Robin probably weren't around in those days and that cooking was generally done by fire, not by microwave.

Now the noise was again reaching Mrs. Leitner-alert level. Julia clapped her hands and called out and told everyone to gather around. She put a finger to her lips and spoke in an excited whisper.

"Okay, listen up. Here's the deal. I've just been up the hill and there's this big, hairy sabertooth tiger up there. And he looked really, really hungry."

"You should be telling us this in cave language."

"Lucy, I know. But this is an emergency, okay?"

"No, 'cos you wouldn't be able to say that either."

"Well, let's just pretend I'm more highly evolved."

"What does that mean?"

"Smarter. Okay, that's enough already. So we keep on with the drawing but now we have to be really quiet. Quiet as cave mice. Because I think he's out there now, prowling around outside the caves. And, boy, is he hungry."

Of course, she'd forgotten, as one easily could, about Kane Feldman. He was a taciturn, sensitive boy with a permanently runny nose and he promptly burst into tears. Julia bent down and gave him a hug. She asked him if he would like to be the tiger and he sniffed and nodded and at once stopped crying.

"Okay. And, heck, these guys look pretty tasty, so I'll be a tiger too."

The others went back to work and she held Kane's limp little hand and they started to prowl.

But even while she prowled, half her mind returned to what had been preoccupying her all morning and all through the night. She thought about Ed and his astonishing suggestion.

They had spent the previous evening with Connor at The Karmic Moose, where Ed occasionally played piano and sang. It was a smarter place than Henry's but not much. It was a Thursday evening and there weren't too many people there and things got off to a rocky start when Ed introduced himself as Missoula's answer to Stevie Wonder.

It was the kind of self-deprecating joke to which he seemed more and more prone nowadays and it went down like a lead balloon. Julia was sitting at the bar with Connor and they heard someone beside them mutter that if that wasn't racist, it was in darned poor taste. But things picked up. Ed played all his best numbers, from Cole Porter to Dolly Parton, and by the end of the last set the crowd had grown and was calling for more.

The two weeks that had passed since Connor's party had been an emotional roller-coaster ride. Ed had told her about his sterility immediately after Connor left that Sunday evening and they spent that night and almost every waking hour since talking about it. Together they went to see Ed's doctor who solemnly confirmed the diagnosis and when they got home, Ed broke down and cried. Since then, however, he had been strong and positive and so had Julia. It was sad, she told herself, more than sad. But there was no point drowning in it. And the solution was simple. They would adopt. After school each day, she researched it. Dr. Rumbold told her about an agency in Helena who arranged these matters. Julia called them and fixed an appointment.

Ed had intended to cancel his gig at The Karmic Moose, but when the time came their feelings had calmed and they agreed that a night out would do them both good. They called Connor. He drove over from Augusta and after the gig took them both around the corner for supper at The Depot.

It was almost like old times. Connor was in good spirits. He looked less strung out and said that his leg was as good as mended. He'd already been riding and said he was ready to do that climb whenever they wanted. Ed was still on a high from his gig. He had them and the waitresses and all the people at the surrounding tables in fits of laughter. Flushed and happy, they said goodbye to Connor in the parking lot and agreed that, weather permitting, they would do the climb a week this coming Saturday.

For the first few miles of the drive back home, Ed didn't speak, and for a while Julia thought he had fallen asleep. Then, out of the blue, he said it.

"How would you feel if we asked Connor?"

"Asked him what?"

Ed paused. "If we asked him to . . . If he'd be prepared to father a child for us."

Julia almost drove off the road in shock.

"What?! You're kidding. Are you serious?"

One look at him told her that he was.

"Jesus, Ed."

"No, hang on a minute. Listen. Stop the car here."

"Ed, come on. Really."

"Please. Julia, stop the car."

"I think I'd better."

She pulled off the road and turned off the engine but left the headlights on. Ed reached for her hand and held it in both of his.

"Ed, I can't believe you mean this."

"Hang on. Just listen to me for a moment."

"Jesus, Ed."

"Listen. I've thought about it a lot and—"

"Great. Well, don't waste any more time on it, okay?"

She pulled her hand away and folded her arms.

"Julia, will you just shut up and let me speak? We've got a choice here. We both want a child, right? So. We can either adopt, the child of two total strangers. And—don't get me wrong—if that's what you want, that's fine. Or we could have a child who is much more truly ours, a child who'd at least have the genes of one of us." He lifted his hand and stroked her face. "Yours."

Julia sighed and looked away down the beam of the headlights along the empty road ahead.

"And this is a child who could grow inside you. We could share all that and watch him, or her, grow. Share all the things that couples share. It'd be our child, Julia. In a way an adopted child could never be. Don't you see that?"

She didn't reply. She was too shocked to think straight. A car went by and she watched its taillights until they disappeared around the bend ahead. Ed went on, calmly.

"And then the only question is, who would be the biological father?"

"And you want it to be Connor. Jesus, Ed! What gives you the right to choose? Do I get a say? Or is this just some kind of buddy thing between you and Connor?"

"Come on, Julia. I'm not saying it's my choice. If you hate the idea, we can go to some sperm bank or whatever the hell they're called and you can pick a flask. Pick some hunky quarterback for the Grizzlies. Or, hell, let's just adopt."

"Have you and Connor talked about this?"

"Of course not."

"You promise me?"

"Julia, for godsake, what do you think I am?"

"Ed, drop it. The answer's no, okay?"

She started the engine again.

"Fine."

She pulled out onto the highway.

"I mean, seeing as this all sounds like a done deal, you know, a good-ol'-buddy smoke-jumper thing, hell, forget the sperm banks and flasks and things, let's just get him over and he can jump on me and get the damn thing done properly."

Ed didn't reply and she drove for a while in

silence, stunned at what she had just said, wondering what deranged part of her had spat out those words.

"Sorry," she said at last. "I didn't mean that."

"I'm sorry too. Let's just forget it. It was a bad idea."

They didn't speak again, not even after they reached home and went upstairs to bed, not even to say goodnight. Julia must have slept, but if she did it was sleep of only the thinnest kind, a fitful, skimming semi-sleep in which Connor and Ed and the knowing faces of unborn infants flitted like phantoms.

They were still flitting in her head while she drove wide awake to work and still there now despite the renewed din of the children.

At last the bell rang to signal the end of school.

When the kids had dumped their smocks and disappeared, Julia returned to the playground to clear up the chalk. She saw Mrs. Leitner heading out toward her and braced herself for a reprimand. Sally Leitner was a small, tidy woman of about fifty with steel-rimmed spectacles and an allegedly formidable temper which Julia might soon be able to verify.

"Sorry about the noise," she said.

"That's all right, honey. I could see they were having fun."

They walked together beside the wall, Mrs.

Leitner looking over her glasses at the cave families' efforts.

"Hmm," she said at last. "They're good. I think we'll leave them there."

AS SHE DROVE HOME, with the sun lowering itself toward the mountains, Julia went through it all again for the umpteenth time.

What she had been trying to figure out was why she had reacted with such vehemence to Ed's proposal. It was clearly something to do with her secret feelings for Connor, which only seemed to grow stronger every time she saw him and which she still considered a shameful betrayal of Ed. In some illogical way, she had taken what he said as if it were an accusation, as if he knew all about it and she had responded with the instinctive, defensive violence of a woman charged with adultery.

But, dear Lord, to have Connor's child . . .

Would that not seal the betrayal in blood, make it many times worse? Or was it simply that she didn't trust herself? That she feared how the world might change if she were to have his seed within her, to feel it stir, to give it life and bring it forth into the world and nourish and protect it. Julia started to shake.

She was approaching the place where she and

Ed had stopped to talk last night and now she stopped again. She got out and crossed the road and stood for a long time staring down at the river. Some of the trees were starting to turn. And slowly, in the golden light, she began to understand. Like a storm passing, all the doubts and fears that had swirled for so many hours in her head stilled and dispelled and she knew, calmly and with utter clarity, what she wanted.

She couldn't have Connor, but she could, if he agreed, have his child. A child that would be part him, part her and, for Ed, the greatest gift imaginable.

CONNOR SCRAMBLED UP into the sunlight and onto the ledge and as he did so he heard a croak and a flap of wings and saw the raven he had disturbed launch itself into the void. He secured himself to the anchor point that was already wedged in a crevice.

"Taking in!" he called.

He peered down into the shadow of the chimney and saw Ed on another thinner ledge some thirty feet below taking the rope from his belay system and saw Julia a little lower and to one side watching him too. Connor began hauling in the loose rope hand over hand until he felt it go tight.

"That's me!" Ed called.

"Climb when ready!"

There was a short pause and he saw Ed preparing himself and saying something to Julia that Connor couldn't catch, then he pointed his face up at Connor and called.

"Climbing!"

"Okay!"

Connor began to take in the slack, watching Ed all the while in awed silence. No stranger would ever have guessed that he was blind. He had done the climb several times, but there was a lot of mountain here, far too much for a man to remember every crack and crevice. He was literally feeling his way and only twice had they had to call out to help him find a perversely placed handhold or foothold. The part of the climb that had so far posed the most difficulties was oddly the most flat, the field of boulders that looked like dinosaurs. But even there Ed had done it by himself, guiding himself among them with a special collapsible cane, a kind of long ski-pole made out of flexible carbon fiber. He had stumbled a few times and fallen once quite badly, but he made it across without help from either of them. The climb had taken longer than last time, but not much. And now they had just one more pitch to the summit.

It was one of those perfect early fall days that

Connor sometimes shot for tourist brochures, the sky vast and cloudless, a limpid lazuline blue and the air blood-warm without a whisper of wind to chill it. The green ocean of the forest was dotted with islands of amber and rust and here and there a yellow splash of cottonwood or quakin' asp. The higher peaks around them and others far away had their first sprinkling of snow.

Connor had driven over the previous evening to stay the night at Ed's place so that they could get an early start. And as soon as he arrived he'd sensed something different in them, a slightly strained atmosphere and he wondered for a while if he had interrupted some kind of dispute. Ed was much quieter than usual and over supper there were even moments when no one seemed to have anything to say. Connor put it down to it being the end of a busy week. Maybe they were both simply tired. Or worried about the climb.

Julia had turned in first, leaving Connor and Ed to finish their wine by the fire, and they had chatted for a while about nothing in particular. Connor wanted to ask if he had told Julia about the results of his tests, because it had occurred to him that this might be the cause of the tension, but the moment didn't seem right.

He imagined that by morning the mood

might have changed. But it didn't. Driving down and on the hike to the rock face and ever since, during the climb, the three of them had hardly spoken except to utter the routine climbing calls. But as far as Connor was concerned that was fine. It was good sometimes for friends to be silent together, especially on a day like this. He just hoped that the two of them were okay.

Half an hour later they reached the top. And watching Ed's beaming face as he stepped up onto the platform of rock, Connor felt greatly moved. He hugged him and congratulated him and they did their Hearts of Fire routine. Ed asked him to take him over to the little pinnacle and he placed his palms on it, then turned and stood with his back pressed to the rock as if surveying the horizon. Connor looked at Julia. She was watching Ed and wiping away tears and grinning all at the same time. She turned to look at Connor and he smiled and she made a face and he could tell that she was cross with herself for crying.

"Pictures!" Ed said. "We gotta take pictures!"

He made a joke about how honored they were to have such a big-shot photographer on hand and Connor played the role and lined them up, bossing them around like a prima donna and making pretentious observations about the light. Then, just as last time, Julia took some pictures with her camera, then propped it on some rocks and set the timer and ran to get into the picture. She stood next to Ed so that he was in the middle but Ed said that was wrong, she had to be in the middle and they changed places just in time before the camera flashed.

"Now I have to take one of you two," Ed said.

Connor handed him the Leica and helped him position himself. Julia watched him walking back toward her and there was some message in her smile that he wished he could decipher but couldn't. As he came near she reached out and put her arm around his waist, drew him close and he put his around her shoulders and she looked up at him with that same look in her eyes.

"Am I pointing the right way?" Ed called.

"Down a little," Connor said. "And a little to your right."

"Okay?"

"Perfect."

"Man, you're going to be mad when my picture's better than yours. Okay, big smiles now . . ."

Just as before, they sat in the sun and ate their picnic and afterward Ed made Julia describe the view to him in all its detail, the precise colors of the fall, which mountains had snow on them and which didn't, the exact location of the sun and the angle of the shadows. And when she had finished he sat in silence, picturing it all in his mind's eye and Connor watched him and wondered how true the picture was. And then he looked away and stared out across the land and thought of the last time that the three of them had sat here and how full of hope the world had been.

"Connor?" Ed said.

Connor turned and saw they were both staring at him. Ed had his arm around Julia's shoulders.

"Yes?"

"Julia and I have something to ask you."

He could see in their faces that it was something that mattered and he told him to go ahead. Ed swallowed. He was all darty-eyed and nervous and started talking in a rambling way so unlike him that Connor started to feel anxious himself. Ed said how fond he and Julia were of him, how he was—hell, he knew he was—their best friend. More than that, how he'd been best man at the wedding and all, and how much, well, how much they'd all shared.

And the more he rambled, the more Connor grew confused, wondering what on earth could be coming. He looked at Julia and she seemed as nervous as Ed. She couldn't even look him in the eye.

And now Ed was going on about how they'd been trying to have kids and how they'd just discovered that this wasn't going to be possible and how they'd been talking about adoption—which was probably, in the end, what they were going to do—except . . . Except there was this other possibility they'd discussed, well, not really a possibility, really just a kind of crazy idea . . .

And Connor suddenly got it. A full twenty seconds before Ed actually found the words. And while he waited for him to utter them it was like hearing a train coming toward him through a tunnel, the rush of air getting louder and louder in his head.

"And we just wondered if you . . . I mean, we feel kind of embarrassed asking, more than embarrassed. I mean, if you think it's a terrible idea, all you have to do is say no. Because we treasure your friendship more than anything. You know that. But we wondered if you would be . . . I mean, if you would consider being, the father—the biological father—of our child."

The train hit him and for several long moments Ed's words floated like slow-motion debris in the air between them. From somewhere far below them in the forest came a strange sound which he then dimly recognized as the bugling call of an elk.

Connor took a deep breath. "Well. I don't—"

"Really, man. It's okay, honestly. It's a hell of a thing to ask and the chances are you won't want to. And that's absolutely okay by us. Isn't that right, honey?"

"Absolutely."

Ed kissed her cheek and she gave an embarrassed smile. Connor had been staring at her. She was still avoiding his eyes. At last she seemed to find the courage to look at him and the connection set something reeling inside him.

"I mean, listen, man," Ed went on. "It was just an idea, you know?"

"Ed," Connor said. "Will you just stop talking a moment?"

When he started to speak, Connor had no clear idea of what he was going to say. He was too stunned to think straight. He found himself saying that Ed sure knew how to shock the hell out of a man and they all laughed in a kind of nervous release. Then he told them he was moved and honored that they should ask this of him and that they were the two people in all the world that he cared for most, all of which was true. But bringing a child into the world, he said, was no small matter and he asked if he could take a while to think about it. They said in unison that he should take as long as he liked.

Coming down the mountain took almost as long as going up. They had to concentrate hard on the rappels, guiding Ed precisely so that he didn't injure himself. Connor was grateful that there was no time for small talk, which would have seemed phony after what had been said at the summit. Even on the hike back to the Jeep, they hardly spoke. On the journey back to the house, with the night closing in, Ed did his best to lift the atmosphere but, for the first time Connor could recall, things between the three of them seemed a little forced. He wished he could give them an answer right away but there were too many things racing around in his mind and in his heart and he just couldn't.

They asked him to stay over but he made a lame excuse about having to get back to his mother's. He put his gear in the back of the Chevy and the three of them stood there awhile, looking at the sky, their breath making clouds on the chill air.

"Looks like it's going to freeze," he said.

Julia kissed him goodbye and went into the house and he knew she was doing it so that he and Ed could be alone for a moment. He got into the truck and rolled down the window. Ed put his hands on the sill.

"Listen," Ed said. "I just want to say again. Whatever you decide is fine. I really mean that. It's a hell of a thing to lay on you like that."

"Tell me one thing. Is Julia as sure about this as you are?"

"Completely."

Connor didn't say anything for a moment. Ed reached into the car and put his hand on Connor's shoulder.

"Take your time, you hear?"

"I'll call you."

He started the engine and turned the truck around and called goodbye. As he drove away he looked in the mirror and saw Ed through the billowing smoke of the exhaust, standing there and waving, the light on the wall behind him flaring like a halo.

EIGHTEEN

THE FIRST time he'd seen it, he thought it was smoke, but by now he could normally tell the difference. You would see it swirling in a black cloud above the canopy of palm and eucalyptus. And then you would get a little closer and start to hear the cries and that was when you realized that the cloud was a living thing consisting entirely of birds. Vultures and kites and crows mostly, though there were others circling and shrieking around them that Connor couldn't name, smaller, more timid ones, who no doubt knew their place in the pecking order. But by the time you were that close, you had no need of sight or sound, for the smell alone told you where the bodies were.

It had been like that this morning. He and the other journalists had followed the soldiers along the strip of rutted red earth that wound toward the village through plantations of banana and avocado. It was early and mist lay laced on the hillside terraces that rose steeply on either side of them. Every so often the officer in the leading vehicle would raise a hand for the convoy to stop while a party went ahead to remove a land mine and Connor and the others would wait in their Land Rovers in the gathering heat and listen to the radio spewing forth its vitriol, urging on the Hutu killers to leave no grave half full, let not a single Tutsi cockroach stay alive.

They left the vehicles at the edge of the village and continued on foot. There was a small boy standing alone in the middle of the street wearing only a T-shirt spotted with blood and he stayed still as a statue, watching them walk toward him. The officer squatted beside him and asked him some questions but the child seemed to have been struck dumb and he turned and walked away up the street and they followed. And all the while the smell grew stronger.

They walked slowly between houses wrecked and pockmarked and empty of all but ghosts and past the scattered remnants of loot outside, a crumpled bicycle, a woman's shoe, a yellow toy trumpet, toward the church with its whitewashed tower and its living black tower of birds above. And the soldiers and Connor and the other journalists, all except the boy, covered their mouths and noses with bandannas or whatever else they had.

In the grass and dust yard of the church stood a white cement figure of Jesus with his arms spread in welcome and the boy stopped beside it and would go no farther and Connor photographed him and then photographed the dogs and vultures that came hurtling from the open doors of the church and photographed the soldiers chasing them and yelling and shooting at them but mostly missing.

Inside the church the air was hot and putrid and humming with flies and Connor tried not to let too much of it into his lungs or too much of what he saw into his head while he photographed the bodies. They were heaped among the pews and up the aisle and along the walls which were painted with blood and fractured by gunfire. There were more women than men although some were so maimed it was hard to tell and there were children and babies and severed limbs tucked among them.

The sun was streaming in upon those who lay in sacrifice before the altar through a tall stained-glass window which had been strafed with bullets yet somehow held together. Kendrick, the British TV reporter, was asking everyone to stand clear so that he could do a piece to camera before the sunlight shifted but

Connor ignored him and finished what he had to do and left.

Outside, a young soldier was throwing up and Connor stood behind him and held him by the shoulders for a while without saying anything and then walked back down the street. Other villagers had appeared by now and were talking in hushed voices with the soldiers and as he looked he saw others emerging like wide-eyed phantoms from behind the houses and from among the trees.

Connor photographed them while the soldiers handed out food and water from the trucks parked in the dust yard of the burnt-out school. There was a big baobab tree there, the kind that some said God had mistakenly planted upside down with its roots in the air, though to Connor it seemed no mistake at all in a world turned that way too.

He sat on a low mud wall and stared at the hills above the village. The mist had burned off the terraces by now and he could see trees sprouting like reaching hands from the hilltops. Behind them the clouds were stacking, ready for the rain that fell without fail every afternoon. It was one the lushest countries Connor had ever seen and in this part of it almost every available inch seemed to be cultivated. But the bananas and avocados hung rotting on the trees and the only crop being harvested was human.

For three days now he had been with this same contingent of the Rwandan Patriotic Front, pushing steadily south and west. And although he still photographed the bodies they came across, he had long ago stopped counting. He had seen them bloated and jammed like timber along the banks of the rivers while freer ones twirled slowly past as if in some silent aquatic ballet that only they could hear. He had seen them hacked in their hundreds in ditches and streams and papyrus marshes and around their ransacked homes and seen them stacked in citizenly fashion by the roadside. In Bysenguye, the town through which they had passed yesterday, he had seen garbage trucks collecting them. And he had photographed them all and sent the pictures from his scanner spinning home across the heavens, through God's own backyard, where maybe some of those same murdered souls stood waiting.

Now it was night and the village was throbbing with its new population of relief agency workers, journalists, human rights monitors and assorted bureaucrats, all here to document the demise of the old one. They had been arriving all afternoon and in the rain their trucks had churned the street to a river of red mud. Some busied themselves with the survivors while others huddled in groups, smoking and talking in low voices as if scared that they might somehow wake the dead. It was cooler now and the smell of death had been drowned by the fumes of the generators and of some of the trucks that kept their engines running. A group of investigators had gone up to the church and dressed themselves in white overalls and hooded masks and rubber gloves and boots and gone inside. They were still in there, working by floodlight and from where he now stood, beneath the baobab tree, Connor could see their shadows through the windows looming like monsters on the blooded walls while they catalogued the dead.

He and some of the other journalists were gathered around the young RPF lieutenant who had been assigned to brief them about what had taken place, though by now most of them knew.

The lieutenant said they had so far counted two hundred and nine bodies, all Tutsis. Many of them were from Bysenguye, the nearby town where Connor had seen the garbage trucks. When the *interahamwe*, the Hutu death squads, started work there, these people had sought the protection of the mayor, Emmanuel Kabugi, a cultured and respected man, a Hutu, but one whom all Tutsis had always considered their friend.

On his advice they had evacuated their families and fled here for sanctuary. One of the young priests, he assured them, was a personal friend and would see that they came to no harm. On the following day, when they were all safely gathered inside the church, Emmanuel Kabugi arrived with the *interahamwe*, some armed with guns but most with machetes. Both he and the priest, who on command had unbolted the doors, personally took part in the massacre.

That night most of the journalists went back to a hotel in Bysenguye but Connor and the other half dozen who had been traveling with the RPF stayed in the village. They set up camp in a couple of the gutted houses that still had roofs and before they turned in Kendrick produced a bottle of brandy and some metal tots. Someone lit a gas lamp and they all sat around it on the bare cement floor, drinking. Kendrick was plump and florid and in his late forties, with thinning gingery hair and he seemed to assume that being the oldest "Africa hand" among them gave him the right to lecture them. His producer and crew were younger and quieter and

Connor got along well with them, as he did with the two others, Anna and Reiner, who were both news agency reporters.

In the short time he had spent around journalists, Connor had met some he liked and many he didn't, but it was always the pompous ones he disliked most, the ones who'd seen it all and done it all and couldn't stop telling you. He had learned to keep his own counsel and listen and he was aware that he was usually seen as a loner. Most of the journalists—at least, most of those who were writers, rather than photographers—had been to college. And at first Connor wondered if it was this that set him apart. But then he came to realize that it was simply in his nature to be that way and concluded that when his mother had called him The Watcher, she was probably right.

He sat now watching Kendrick. The sweat on his pink cheeks glistened in the cold light of the gas lamp. He was ranting on about how democracy didn't work in Africa and how dumb it was for western governments ever to have thought it would. To "your average African," he said, democracy was just an alien abstraction. All the money for famine relief and other aid simply went into the pockets of ministers and officials who all had vast Swiss bank accounts. He'd seen it happen all over Africa.

He'd even talked about it with Nelson Mandela, whom he had interviewed many times and talked about as if he were a personal friend, which was more than a little hard to credit. Connor couldn't bear to listen anymore. He quietly got up and headed for the door.

"So our American cousin disagrees?"

Connor stopped in the doorway and looked back at him.

"Hell, what do I know?" he said. "Maybe you should go ask those average Africans lying around in the church up there."

He strolled out of the village past where the soldiers were camped. Some of them had lit fires and were sitting around them singing and tapping out rhythms. One of the sentries told him not to wander too far and he said he wouldn't. He just wanted to get away from the lights and the fumes and the din of the generators.

He followed a dirt trail that led away from the road and meandered through the banana groves until it broadened into a grassy clearing. There were some rocks there and he sat down on one of them and listened to the pulsing clamor of the insects and frogs all around him and filled his lungs with the rich damp smell of the red earth. The clouds had cleared and there was no moon and he spent a long time trying to figure his way around the stars of this strange new hemisphere but couldn't. He needed a map, like the one he had drawn on Ed's back last fall. And then he thought, as he did every day and every night, of Julia and of his child that was in her womb.

He hadn't spoken to them since Christmas. He'd phoned them from Nairobi where he had gone after things became too dangerous in Somalia. Ed told him that Julia was two months pregnant. She had conceived after the first insemination from the deposit Connor had left at the clinic before he flew out to Africa.

"It's like it was meant to be," Ed said.

They had written him a letter via his agency telling him but, like much of the mail they forwarded to him, Connor had never received it. Then Julia came on the line and wished him a merry Christmas and he could tell from her voice, from both their voices, how full of joy they were. And he tried to sound that way too and to say all the right things and only hoped that it sounded more convincing to them than it did to him. The truth was that he didn't know what he felt. Even now, after months of thinking about it, he still didn't know.

He was happy, genuinely happy, that his gift had brought them such joy. And there were times when he drew strength from it. Walking among the dead, as he had today in the church, as he had almost every day, he would force himself to think of this new life convolving so many thousand miles away, this flame of future amid all the dark denial and it gave him hope and courage.

But in his heart there was also a hollowing sense of loss which, try as he might, he couldn't dispel. And sometimes it seemed that the giving of his seed had left him spent and purposeless and more starkly alone than ever.

As he walked back past the soldiers' camp he saw a figure emerge from between the trucks and come toward him. It was the young soldier he had seen being sick outside the church. He had a piece of paper in his hand and he held it out and Connor took it.

"They say he ran away to Goma with all the others," the soldier said. "If you go there, maybe this helps you find him."

Connor wanted to ask what he meant but the soldier turned and quickly disappeared again between the trucks. Connor got out his pocket flashlight and in its beam saw that he had been given a torn piece of newspaper. It was a photograph of a man in a white shirt who seemed to be presenting a prize to a strikingly beautiful schoolgirl. He was smiling benignly. The caption below said he was the *bourgmestre* of Bysenguye, Emmanuel Kabugi.

JULIA LAY DEAD-STILL, watching in wonder as the dome of her belly shifted shape and moved from one side of the bathtub to the other. Of course, she had heard about babies kicking, but she'd always thought this must be an exaggeration and that actually it would be like a little tickle, something you really had to concentrate on to feel. Not like this. Oomph. There it was again. The little rascal just wouldn't keep still, she was swimming widths, making ripples in the water, for heaven's sake.

"Whoa there!"

Ed was standing naked at the basin beside her, shaving. He had gone back to wet shaving and, curiously, although he did it entirely by feel—and perfectly safely—he still stared at himself in the mirror. The spring sunshine was angling in on his butt through the open bathroom window.

"On the move again?"

"Bigtime. We're training for the Olympics here this morning."

He put down his razor and knelt beside the tub. Half his face was still covered in foam. He put his hands on her belly and they waited for another movement. The birds outside were at full throttle.

"He's gone all shy," Ed said.

"No she hasn't."

"Come on, tadpole. One more time for Daddy."

At her last scan they'd shown her a picture of the fetus and asked her if she wanted to know what it was going to be and she said it was okay, thanks, she already knew—it was going to be a baby. They all laughed and left it at that but actually, even though she didn't want to be told, she did know. She'd never had any doubt. It was going to be a girl.

Quite how she knew, Julia wasn't sure, except that it had something to do with Skye. She didn't think about her so much anymore. For about a year after the fire Skye had been there all the time in the corner of her mind, not threatening her or accusing her or even looking sad, just sitting there quietly. But with time, the image had faded and now appeared only when summoned in Julia's prayers or darkly magnified in those treacherous, sleepless recesses of the night.

Sometimes, of course, it could be summoned by chance, such as when she came across someone who looked like Skye. One of her third-grade pupils had an older sister who collected him after school and who looked so like Skye that the first time Julia saw her, she almost fainted. Mostly, however, she believed that she now had the issue under control.

It wasn't that the guilt had diminished. She had come to the conclusion that guilt was made of some utterly imperishable matter upon which time and happiness had not the slightest corrosive effect. She had read an article in a magazine (one of the many she now bought, to look for Connor's pictures) about a policeman who had been shot in the head with a bullet that was made out of titanium or something similarly exotic. The guy was alive and alert and seemed to be functioning fine and so rather than risk the damage of surgery, the doctors had decided to leave it there. Apart from the odd headache and some minor distortion of his vision, he apparently now led a normal life.

Reading the piece, Julia had decided that this was how it was with her. Except, of course, she had two titanium bullets—one for Ed and one for Skye. They were there constantly lodged in her head and they changed the way she viewed the world and caused her pain. But it was a pain to which she had grown accustomed.

Guilt could be as simple as that. There didn't have to be anything maudlin or self-pitying about it. It was a fact and you lived with it and dealt with the consequences, a kind of contract under which your actions led to inevitable obligations. Those to Ed, she was already fulfilling, by devoting her life to him. Now it was Skye's turn. Julia was responsible for the loss to the world of a young female life and therefore she must restore one. And although she knew it wasn't remotely rational, this was why she had convinced herself that the baby, now seven months grown in her womb, was a girl.

Ed, of course, had different ideas. The Montana wing of the Tully dynasty, he grandly declared, needed—and would have, damn it—a male heir. He even had a name ready. In honor of his father's grass-cutting empire, the boy would be called Mower. In the event of her being wrong, Julia hoped to God that this was only a joke. Tadpole was bad enough.

He still had his hands on her belly.

"He's gone to sleep."

"No . . . Here we go again."

"Wow! Look at him go. That's my boy! What does that feel like? That must feel so weird. Is it like, all kind of squirmy?"

"No, not really. More kind of . . . fluttery."

"Fluttery."

"Yeah. Kind of swimmy-fluttery."

"But not squirmy."

"No."

"Here he goes again!"

She watched Ed grinning, his eyes flickering a little as they did nowadays. She wondered sometimes, when he had his hands upon her like this and felt the baby stir, whether the joy it so clearly gave him was tinged in any way by the fact that the child wasn't truly his. Of course, it was his, in almost every other way imaginable. And Julia did all she could to make him feel it was. Nevertheless, she thought there must still be some faint residue, not of doubt and certainly not of jealousy, but perhaps of some mild variant of regret.

It was something that they had never discussed. Almost from the start, Ed had been incredible. After Connor called to give them his decision and while they were waiting for the first insemination, which had to be done at the optimum hour of the optimum day of the month, Ed had seemed troubled and restless and she had half expected him to change his mind. But when she asked him if he was still sure about going through with it, he told her not to be stupid, of course he was, so she never asked again.

The day she told him she was pregnant hadn't started well. She'd left a tube of hair removal cream on the bathroom shelf where they kept their toothbrushes and Ed brushed his teeth with it, which didn't put him in the best of moods. He got dressed and stomped off downstairs for his breakfast and while she carried out the pregnancy test in the bathroom she could hear him grumbling on about how he couldn't even taste his goddamn granola.

She stood there by the toilet, watching the strip change color, though it was only confirming what she already knew, and she didn't say a word. She went downstairs in her bathrobe to the kitchen and found some of the little adhesive dots that they used for labeling things and she wrote "baby" with them on her belly. Ed asked her in a grouchy voice what she was doing.

"Nothing. Just labeling something."

"Bit late, isn't it? Write napalm, that's what the damn stuff tastes like."

She applied the last dot and then walked over to the table where he sat hunched grumpily over his granola. She perched her backside on the table and took hold of his hand.

"Aw, come on Julia, give me a break, will you?"

"Put your spoon down."

"Listen, it really isn't funny, okay? My mouth feels like it's been nuked."

"Poor darling."

She opened her robe and guided his hand toward her belly.

"Honey, I'm really not in the mood, okay . . . what the hell's going on here?"

He had found the dots.

"Just so you know what it is," she said.

She watched his face change as he traced the dots with his fingertips.

"Oh boy," he said. "Are you sure?"

"Oh girl. And yes, I am."

He got up and put his arms around her and they hugged each other for a long time and when at last he let go she saw there were tears on his cheeks.

"Sorry about the toothpaste," she said.

He slipped his arms inside her robe and held her by the hips and kissed her and then he bent his head and kissed her breasts and with the dots still stuck to her belly he opened her legs and made love to her right there on the kitchen table. And possibly she was mistaken, but that day—and many more since—she had the impression that as well as raw desire there was some deeper impulse at work, some unconscious need perhaps to assert his presence within her too alongside Connor.

They spoke of Connor often, wondering where he might be and what he might be doing. At Ed's insistence, a photograph of the three of them—the one taken by timer on the climb last fall—had been blown up and now hung framed on the living room wall. Ed said he wanted it to be there for Tadpole/Mower to see, right from the start, so he would know the setup: Mom, Dad and Bio-Dad. He said that Connor had the better title; Bio-Dad sounded like a superhero. Julia said she thought it sounded more like a detergent.

There was a network of friends and family (Fords, Tullys and Bishops) who kept their eyes skinned for Connor's photographs and whenever somebody saw one in a newspaper or a magazine there would be an instant round of phone calls. Connor's mother had phoned only the other day to tell them to buy *Newsweek*, but warning, at the same time, that it wasn't a pretty sight. Julia went out and bought a copy.

Mrs. Ford was right. It was another of his pictures from Rwanda, a church floor carpeted with butchered women and children, sunlight pouring in on them through a broken window. Julia took one glance and that was enough. She couldn't even bear to read about it. A million people murdered in a month. One TV anchorman, clearly out to prove he was smart enough to work a calculator, said this meant that a hundred and fifty-five people had been killed every minute, almost a thousand every hour of every day. While UN troops stood powerless and watched and men in suits in Washington debated the finer points of whether or not such killing amounted to genocide.

Julia and Ed hadn't seen or spoken to Connor's mother since the previous summer and it was good to hear that gravelly voice again. They talked for a while about Connor and both moaned about how hopeless he was at keeping in touch. Then Julia suddenly realized that she had no idea whether or not the woman knew about the baby and, more important, about Connor's role in it.

"So tell me, honey, how's it going? You're what, six months gone now?"

"Seven, good as. And I'm fine, thank you. Since I stopped throwing up the whole time."

"Yeah, that sucks, I remember. I was sick as a coyote with Connor."

There was a little pause. A pregnant one. Julia wondered what to say.

"I should've called or wrote you," Mrs. Ford went on. "Guess I didn't know if I was supposed to know."

She still hadn't said quite enough to indicate if she had the whole story.

"Connor told you then?"

"Sure he did. Tell you the truth, I was against the idea."

"Oh."

"Yeah. Hell, I'm only just turned fifty. That's no age to be a grandma. Even a surgate one or whatever the hell it is."

"Surrogate."

"That's it. I mean. What's that going to do for my image?"

Julia laughed with relief.

"Honey, I'm truly happy for you."

"Thank you."

"You're welcome. Now go buy that magazine."

The bathwater was growing cold now and the baby had finished her workout or maybe just gotten bored. And so had Ed's hands. They were wandering up toward her breasts, which were now enormous, with nipples the size of small Frisbees. Ed called them Boobs 'R' Us and seemed to think their sole purpose was for him to play with. She slapped his hand.

"Hey," she said. "Cut it out. I'll be late for work."

NINETEEN

THE CARGO planes came all day and all night, lowering themselves out of the cloud like vast avenging birds and coming in over the lake to the black shore where a million lost souls had made their camp. At night you could see their lights skewering down toward the airstrip and hear the backroar of their engines and sometimes the clouds would part and give a glimpse of the great volcanic cone of Nyaragongo, ten thousand feet above it all, rumbling and glowing in a red miasma, as if gathering itself for judgment day.

The planes brought grain for the living and quicklime for the dead. And for the hundreds of thousands who hovered in between they brought clothes and drugs and blankets and tents and trucks and a whole circus of salvation to hand them out. They brought doctors and nurses and aid workers and a thousand other nameless officials from a hundred different agencies. And then there was the other circus, the three-ringed media horde who had hurried here to hustle and haggle and get in the way and then hurl their words and pictures like spears across the ether at the calloused conscience of a world that watched bemused.

Connor was bemused too. So was almost everyone he had met here in Goma, be they doctor, aid worker or journalist. The million Hutus assembled on this vast plain of sharp black lava were refugees. The name itself prompted pity and most no doubt deserved it. Their wretchedness was etched in their faces as they waited in the food lines or squatted by their paltry, evil-smelling fires, watching their children die from cholera. But among them were those—how many, nobody knew—who deserved no pity, for they had shown none; they were the very same people who had carried out the genocide over the border in Rwanda.

Everyone knew they were here. Connor had photographed the stacks of machetes and nail-studded clubs that had been confiscated at the crossing point and knew it was only a fraction of what had slipped through. Their owners didn't bother to hide but instead flaunted themselves and their weapons to bully their way to the best of the spoils. And this was why Connor thought there was a chance, just the faintest one, that somewhere among them he might find the *bourgmestre* of Bysenguye.

He had been searching now for the best part of a week. He kept the newspaper picture of Kabugi in the top pocket of his vest, protected in a clear plastic sleeve and he showed it to people everywhere he went. And every time they looked at it and shook their heads and handed it back. Even the name of the town didn't seem to ring any bells.

In the eyes of some he asked he saw them pondering what rare kind of fool would set himself such a quest and he had many times wondered the same himself. Why should this man's murders matter more than the multitude of others? Was it simply that he had a name and a face and that Connor had seen the nameless faces of his victims and photographed his handiwork? What, in any case, would he do if he found him?

He didn't know. But he had started looking, so he would finish. There were six camps and he had combed all but one. Now he was on his way to the last.

It was late afternoon and a breeze was blowing warm and damp off Lake Kivu, flattening the smoke of the campfires into a gray shroud and for a few welcome moments diluting the fetid crepuscular air. Connor was walking along the trail of black lava dust that wove through the camps. He heard the sound of an engine behind him and stepped aside. It was a white Land Cruiser, one of the many that had been flown in to shuttle the aid workers and medics around the camps. He expected it to go past but it pulled up alongside him and the driver, a blond young man with a beard, offered him a lift. Connor thanked him and climbed in the back.

There was a young woman sitting up front and she turned around in her seat to talk to him. She was Dutch and the man was Norwegian. They were both paramedics working for an agency based in Stockholm. They asked him whom he worked for and where he was going and Connor told them that he worked for himself and that he was looking for refugees from a place called Bysenguye. The name meant nothing to them, nor did the name Kabugi. He showed them the picture but neither of them recognized him.

The woman, whose name was Marijke, was about to hand it back when she frowned and took another look. She pointed at the schoolgirl to whom Kabugi was handing the prize.

"I saw that girl this morning," she said.

"You're sure?"

"Yes. I remember thinking how lovely she was."

She said they had been giving shots to a crowd of children at one of the other camps—one which Connor had already visited—and the girl was among them. The man asked why Connor was looking for Kabugi and he told them. Marijke said that if he could wait half an hour while they delivered some supplies, she would take him to where she had seen the girl.

He had to wait longer than that, and by the time they had found their way back to the place it was getting dark. They parked by one of the feeding stations and walked over to an improvised tent made of crates covered with plastic sheeting. It was where the refugee leaders for this part of the camp had their headquarters. Connor had been here two days ago and remembered the icy stares of the young men when he had asked about Kabugi. None of them had spoken English and since Connor spoke no French the encounter hadn't lasted long.

The faces they saw when they went inside now were different and less hostile. Marijke greeted them brightly in French and got a response that was almost friendly. It seemed they recognized her from that morning. Connor couldn't understand what she was saying but he heard her mention the name of the town. The one who seemed to be their leader waved an arm as he replied. Marijke translated for Connor.

"He says the people from Bysenguye are camped half a mile from here."

"Can he take us there?"

She asked him and the man shrugged and nodded.

They followed him on foot through the labyrinth of smoke-veiled paths, past bodies neatly bundled in rush matting for collection and naked children sifting the filth for food, scenes that Connor had photographed all week and of which the world by now was doubtless growing weary. At last they came to a large tent of pale blue plastic and the man told them that this was where they would find those in charge of the Bysenguye refugees and he left them there. Connor found the flash in his camera bag and fixed it to one of the Nikons that hung around his neck.

Inside, there was nobody to be seen. There was a table made out of crates with a gas light upon it and piles of papers weighted with stones and a bowl that was being used as an ashtray with a half-smoked cigarette burning on its rim. The place was full of crates and bags and boxes, many of which looked unopened. At the back of the tent was a long flap of plastic and from behind it came the sound of laughter and voices and an odd metallic scraping.

Marijke called hello but no one came and so Connor walked to the flap and opened it. And staring right back at him was Emmanuel Kabugi.

He was standing in a narrow, improvised courtyard that was walled with crates and lit by another gas lamp and he looked as if he had just stepped off a golf course. He was wearing neatly pressed slacks and a spotless white sports shirt with a little crocodile logo on it. He was taller and more imposing than he looked in the picture.

There were four other men, all younger and more poorly dressed, sitting or standing around him and there were two women, both of them young and pretty. One of the men was sharpening a machete and laughing with one of the women but when he saw Connor he stopped doing both and suddenly there was silence, all of them just staring at him and at his cameras. Kabugi suddenly smiled and said something in French, but as Connor turned to Marijke for a translation he spoke again, this time in English.

"Can I help you?"

"Emmanuel Kabugi?"

"Yes."

Connor introduced himself and showed him his UN press card. The man with the machete said something in Kinyarwanda and Kabugi turned to him sharply and replied with what was clearly a reprimand. Connor had been wondering whether to ease his way by pretending he wanted to talk about food distribution or conditions in the camp. But he'd never been too good at lying and when Kabugi asked a second time if he could help, he reached into his bag and pulled out the picture of the church massacre that he'd ripped from a magazine. He handed it to Kabugi.

He looked at it and the others looked over his shoulder and when the man with the machete saw what it was he started shouting at Connor. Kabugi told him to be quiet and studied the picture again, sadly shaking his head.

"Why do you bring me this?" he said softly.

"You don't need reminding?"

"These were my people, many of them my friends. How could I forget?"

He handed the picture back, but Connor wouldn't take it.

"Which of them did you kill? I mean, personally."

Kabugi frowned. "What?"

"I guess it's a little hard to tell with them all hacked up like that."

Connor was aware of Marijke shifting nervously beside him.

"Come on, man. You were there. You sent them all to the church and then you came with others to murder them."

"You are mistaken, sir."

"No, I'm not. There are witnesses. I spoke with them. You did a pretty good job but not quite good enough. You missed some. They saw you."

"Then they are mistaken. Of course, I heard what happened and it made me very sad and very angry. These people were killed by the RPF to blacken our names and to seduce foreign journalists such as yourself into supporting them. Why would I do this? Why would one kill one's own people?"

"I don't know. Why? You tell me."

Kabugi stared at him for a long time. Then he scrunched the picture into a ball in his fist and dropped it on the ground. He lifted his chin a little.

"Do you know who I am?"

"Sure I do."

"I am the *bourgmestre* of Bysenguye. I am an

educated man. I have studied literature and art and philosophy at the university of the Sorbonne in Paris. I go to Mass. I pray for my enemies. I have devoted my life to the service of my people. I tell you this, you understand, not to boast, but so that you may know to whom you speak. You understand?"

Connor shrugged.

"When the army of the cockroaches drove my people from their homes, I helped them and protected them and led them to safety. Many died on the way, children, babies, trampled underfoot in their terror. And now we are here in this lower circle of hell and we have nothing, not even our dignity."

He spoke quietly and precisely but with a gathering intensity. There was something chilling in his eyes now and Connor had to summon all his strength to hold his stare.

"And you dare to come before me with your false accusations and your high moral outrage while outside our wives and our children lie dying in the dirt from cholera and starvation?"

"All I come with is the truth."

"The truth? What do you know of truth? What do you know of my country, of my people? How long have you lived there? A week? A month? If the truth is a loaf of bread and you pick up a crumb, do you have the truth? If not the truth, then it is as worthless as a lie. You are American, I think."

Connor nodded.

"Then tell me, what is the 'truth' about your country? About your people? About the millions you have murdered, the millions of my people that you stole and turned into slaves? Many of whom are still your slaves. Tell me the truth about them."

"You want to make a speech, that's fine by me. I just came to take your picture."

Kabugi didn't seem to hear. His anger was uncoiling and wouldn't be stopped.

"The truth is that there is no truth. Only crumbs. You have yours and I have mine. But I have more of them and mine are gathered with knowledge and experience, not under a false banner of piety and prejudice. So I will share them with you. These Tutsi cockroaches and their Belgian paymasters want to turn us, to turn my people, once more into slaves, to reimpose their old feudal domination over us. And in the face of this what are we supposed to do? Tell me. Please tell me."

Connor nodded at the machete.

"Hell, I guess you just hack 'em all to pieces. Is that the one you used? Or is that his? I guess you'd need a fair few."

Whether or not the man holding it understood, he stepped toward them, but Kabugi held out an arm to stop him. Marijke touched Connor on the arm.

"I think we should go now."

"I think she is right," Kabugi said.

"Sure," Connor said. He lifted his camera and started to focus, and immediately two of the men came at him. One tried to grab him but Connor lashed out at him and shoved the other away. They started to come at him again but Kabugi shouted and they stopped. Connor adjusted his camera.

"I mean, hey, seeing as you're such an upright pillar of society and a hero and all, you surely can't mind having your picture taken, can you?"

He didn't wait for an answer, just took the picture. The flash seemed to startle and freeze them and he was able to take two more before Kabugi gave an order and they grabbed Connor's arms and Marijke's too and pushed them roughly back toward the tent flap. One of them tried to take his camera but Connor lashed out again and swore at him and was amazed at the effect it had. As he was being pushed through the flap he managed to twist around and take a final picture of Kabugi. The next thing he knew they were sprawling in the dirt outside the front tent, looking up at the amused and puzzled faces of the small crowd that had gathered.

Driving him back to his UN tent, Marijke said he sure knew how to give a girl a good night out. He said he was sorry and then for some reason they both started to laugh and couldn't stop. The lens and the flash of his camera had been broken. But the body had stayed shut and the film was safe.

He left Goma the next day, hitching a ride to Nairobi on a relief agency plane. As it banked away over Lake Kivu the clouds cleared and Connor craned his neck to look back toward the camps. He watched the sun and shadow chasing each other across the living sea of victims and killers and across the flanks of the volcano smoldering in judgment above. And he thought of what Kabugi had said about truth and wondered if he was right. Maybe there was no such thing.

When he checked into the Norfolk Hotel they handed him the mail they had been keeping for him. He thumbed through it while he followed the boy carrying his bag to the room and found what he was looking for, a white envelope from Missoula, Montana, addressed to him in Julia's broad, elegant handwriting. He didn't know why, but he didn't want to open it right away so he showered and washed his hair, sluicing away the smell of death.

And only when he had dried himself and combed his hair and put on some fresh clothes and settled in a chair by the window, with the evening sky glowing pink and orange above the silhouetted palms, did he open it.

There was a letter and a photograph of Julia sitting up and smiling in a hospital bed with Ed perched grinning beside her and the baby wrapped and pink and crumple-faced in her arms.

The letter said that she had been born on the fifth of July, weighing in at seven pounds and twelve ounces. After debate, verging on divorce, they had settled on calling her Amy. Her middle name was to be Constance, which was as near to Connor as they could think of. Julia hoped that was okay. They wanted him, of course, to be the child's godfather and were going to wait until he next came home to christen her.

TWENTY

A SIX-FIGURE salary and a fancy new Manhattan lifestyle didn't seem to have altered Linda Rosner at all. In fact, from the various combinations of black clothes that she had been wearing all weekend, Amy's newly recruited godmother appeared to be revisiting the Land of the Neo-Gothics. Nor did her lawyerly qualifications seem to have instilled in her any kind of verbal restraint. In church yesterday she had taken one look at Connor and sotto voce to Julia adjudged him as fine a piece of ass as she'd seen in years. The only discernible change was that instead of rolling her own cigarettes, she now bought them ready-made, long and thin but still with licorice paper. She had one dangling from her lips now while she stacked the dishwasher. Across the kitchen Julia was fixing coffee.

The christening, for which Linda had flown

in on Friday, had evolved into a weekend party marathon and this was the last lap: Sunday supper for what Ed called "Amy's inner circle—parents real, godly and grand." Assembled around the candlelit table outside on the deck were Ed and his parents, Connor and his mother and Julia's mother, Maria. By the sound of it, they still hadn't run short of conversation.

Ed's dad had taken a serious shine to Connor's mother and all evening had been asking her about her golden days on the rodeo circuit. Susan Tully and Julia's mom hadn't stopped talking all weekend. And, since Linda had left the table to help Julia in the kitchen, it sounded as if Ed was at last getting a chance to talk with Connor. Amy was upstairs, asleep in her crib.

"He doesn't even have a girlfriend?" Linda said.

Julia shrugged. "Not that I know of."

"Why?"

"I don't know. Ask him. Tell him you're available."

"Yeah, but the thing is, I wouldn't be any good at all that outdoors stuff. I don't do outdoors. I mean, horses? Can you see me and a horse within a hundred yards of each other?"

"I know what you mean. You're dropping ash into the dishwasher."

"Babe, it's a dishwasher."

"Put the glasses on the top, you'll get more in. Anyway, he's never here. He's always in Africa or somewhere."

"He says he might buy an apartment in New York."

"He said that?"

"Uh-huh. So maybe I wouldn't have to come out here and play Annie Oakley. I could just be, like, his indoor city squeeze or something."

"Excuse me? 'Squeeze'?"

"Or something."

"That won't clean if you put it in that way. Look, let me. There. You know, he can probably hear every word you're saying."

"I hope. It'll save time."

Linda leaned against the divider, smoking her cigarette and sipping a glass of wine, while Julia rearranged the dishes.

"Well," she went on, dropping her voice now. "All I can say, babe, is that you sure picked some good genes there."

Julia gave her a look. When Linda was on this kind of riff, there was no knowing where she might take it.

"I mean, I tell you, in your shoes, I wouldn't have bothered with all that clinic shit. I'd have insisted on firsthand delivery."

"Linda. That is so out of order."

Linda held up her hands. "I know. I'm sorry. I don't know what came over me."

"I mean. Really."

There was a pause. The last of the coffee gurgled through the machine and Julia lifted the pot and put it on the tray with the cups.

"Didn't you even think about it though? Be honest."

"Linda!"

"Sorry, sorry."

Julia felt herself blushing and saw Linda register this. She silently cursed herself for being such an open book. On cue, as if to rescue her, Amy started to cry upstairs. Julia asked Linda to take the tray out to the deck and hurried up to the bedroom.

Amy had her own room but had been evicted for the weekend. Only her godparents were staying at the house, Linda in Amy's room, Connor in the guest room. Everyone else was at the Red Lion in town—all except Connor's mother, who had to get back to the ranch. Amy's crib was temporarily parked in the corner of Julia and Ed's room and as soon as Julia appeared above it the baby stopped crying and gave a burbling, gummy grin.

"You little monkey. You just wanted company, didn't you, huh?"

She lifted her out and snuggled her and breathed the wonderful, sweet milky smell of her. She carried her over to the window and stood there in the dark, looking down at the table on the deck where everyone sat talking while Linda poured the coffee. Jim Tully was still locked in conversation with Connor's mother and Susan was still talking with Julia's. Connor had moved into Linda's seat to sit next to Ed who was at the head of the table, telling a story, the candlelight flashing in the lenses of his dark glasses. He wore them nearly all the time now because he didn't like people to see the way his eyes flickered.

She couldn't hear what anyone was saying and she found herself staring at Connor. It was exactly a year since they had last seen him. He looked different. He was tanned and his hair, which he wore shorter now, was bleached almost white. But it was more than that. He looked older or maybe it was just more serious or sad. There were lines around his eyes and Julia wondered if this was only from squinting in the African sun or from what he'd had to squint at.

As if hearing her thoughts, he suddenly looked up and even though she had thought herself invisible in the darkness he saw her and smiled. And no one but she saw him do so, just the two of them together in that moment. She smiled back and not for the first time that weekend felt something quicken within her, which, whatever it was, she hastily repressed. And she turned away and sat on the bed and uncovered her breast to feed Amy and soon, in the streaming intimacy, found calm and comfort.

LINDA HAD STOLEN CONNOR back again and was asking him about his work. And from her voice Ed could picture the expression on her face. Those big gray eyes fixed on him, leaning close, hanging on his every word, going *Reeeally? How fascinating? You diiid? No! Wow, that must be soo dangerous!* As he stood up to go find Julia, Ed couldn't resist saying:

"Hey, Linda, you used to do some nude modeling at college, didn't you? You should get Connor to take some pictures of you."

"Edward!" his mother called from across the table. "You're outrageous."

"I know. I have nothing to declare but my outrageousness. Is she blushing?"

"As a matter of fact, I am," Linda said.

"Hey! Well, that's a first."

He went into the house and called Julia and she answered from upstairs. He found her in their bedroom, trying to settle Amy who sounded as if being settled was about the last thing on earth she had in mind.

"Did you feed her already?"

"Yeah. She's wide awake."

"Bring her down."

"Do you think?"

"Yeah, come on. It's her party after all."

Ed carried Amy out onto the deck and all the women started oohing and aahing and competing to hold her and Ed said he was going to have to organize some kind of ticketing system. He held Amy's face to his ear as if she were whispering something to him.

"Really? Okay, you're the boss. You know whose knee she says she wants to sit on?" He started humming the theme tune from *The Godfather* and handed her to Connor.

"I made her an offer she couldn't refuse," Connor said.

Ed cuffed him over the head, harder than he should have. "Hey, pal, that's my line. If you're not careful, you'll be sleeping with the fishes tonight."

The joke didn't come out well either. His voice had a harsh edge to it. He found his seat and reached for his wineglass. It wasn't where he had left it.

"Hey, did someone move my glass?"

Nobody heard him. He tried not to get annoyed when trivial things like this happened, but that's how he felt. Maybe it was the wine. He'd had quite a few glasses already. Maybe someone had deliberately removed his glass to stop him having more. It was the kind of thing his mother would do. He asked again, more loudly, and Linda, who had been busy making baby talk with Amy, heard this time and said she had moved it. She apologized and filled it and handed it to him then went right back to talking with Amy and Connor.

Everyone was talking but nobody was talking to him and suddenly he felt isolated and grouchy. It was stupid and unreasonable, he knew. They were all having a great time and he didn't want to be a party pooper. He sat back in his chair and drained his glass in two gulps.

Linda, with her back to him no doubt, was on his right and Maria was on his left, telling his mother all about her recent vacation in Aruba and how dreadful the food had been. He was very fond of her; she was a sweetheart. But, man, sometimes, did she go on. She could pack more words into a minute than a stockyard auctioneer.

"All they had was burgers. Burgers, burgers, burgers," she was saying. "Coke and burgers."

"So snort the coke and the burgers taste just fine," Ed said.

But Maria didn't seem to hear. Nor anybody else. Or maybe they thought the joke in such poor taste that they had better pretend not to. What the hell. Ed felt around for the wine bottle, filled his glass again and had another drink.

Suddenly he felt Julia's arms reaching from behind him around his neck and felt her face nuzzling his. She kissed him on the cheek and asked quietly if he was okay.

"Me? Yeah, I'm fine. Why, what's the matter?"

"Nothing. I just wondered."

"Don't I look fine?"

"Of course you do."

"Then what's the matter? Why ask?"

"Nothing. It's okay. I'm sorry."

She removed her arms and he could hear her footsteps going away and immediately he felt guilty for being so unpleasant. He heard Connor talking sweetly to Amy and—again he couldn't help it—but it made him feel . . . what? Angry? Not exactly. More like . . . God, what on earth was the matter with him?

Jealous.

There was no point lying to himself about it. He felt jealous. And to be honest, he'd felt that way all weekend, whenever Connor was around Amy. He resented the fact that Connor could *see* her. And that he could see Julia too. It was insane, Ed knew, but it made him feel excluded, made him feel that Connor somehow had more of them than he did. Even now he could picture Amy sitting happily on Connor's knee and people looking at them both and knowing that he was her real father. And then glancing over at poor old Ed sitting all alone and getting drunk at the end of the table and thinking, *poor guy, what a pity he couldn't do it himself, but isn't it all just lovely?* Well, it wasn't. He hated himself for feeling this way, but it wasn't.

Suddenly he realized Maria was talking to him.

"So Ed, tell me," she said. His isolation had obviously been spotted. This was charity.

"Tell you what?" he cut in. He sounded so rude and he didn't mean to.

"Don't you think Amy looks *so* like Julia?"

There was a terrible moment of silence. Ed could imagine everyone staring, aghast, waiting for his reaction. It was a fabulous double bull's-eye, drawing attention both to his blindness and his sterility. He could imagine the poor woman's face mortifying as she realized what she had said. Ed started to laugh.

"Oh, dear," she said quietly. "I'm so sorry."

Ed reached out and found her hand and squeezed it, still laughing.

"I'm so, so sorry. I just didn't . . ."

"Maria, it's okay. Honestly."

"Sometimes I'm so stupid."

"You're never stupid. You're beautiful. And I love you."

He leaned across and kissed her and he could tell she was starting to cry and he put his arms around her and gave her a hug.

"Hey, come on. Maria, it's fine. Anyway, I know she looks like Julia. She's got that same little tummy."

Everyone laughed. He could sense the relief.

"I'm just glad she doesn't look like that ugly old sonofabitch whose knee she's sitting on."

"Steady, young man," Connor's mother said. "Son of a what was that?"

"Sorry, Maggie. It's short for son-of-a-betchya-never-seen-a-woman-so-lovely."

"That's more like it."

They all laughed again and after a while the conversation picked up. Then Amy started to cry and Connor handed her to Julia in whose arms, as always, she again became calm. And after a couple more glasses of wine (and a third spilled over the table), Ed stopped feeling sorry for himself, although, through the haze of sound, he knew that the evening never quite recovered.

The next thing he knew, Julia was undressing him and putting him to bed. She plumped the pillow for him, leaning over him with those wondrous breasts brushing his face and he tried halfheartedly to kiss them but was too tired and too drunk for anything more. And the last thing he remembered was her kissing him on the forehead and saying goodnight and telling him that she loved him.

CONNOR DIDN'T KNOW how long he had been lying awake but it was certainly hours. He never liked to look at his watch when he couldn't sleep because it only seemed to make things worse. You ended up notching off the minutes and then the hours and before you knew it the whole night lay whittled in pieces on the floor. Until a couple of years ago, he'd never understood insomnia. When people said they couldn't sleep, he used to think they must be exaggerating and that all they meant was that they just didn't go to sleep right away or for so long. But now he knew. He rarely lay awake all night, but he rarely slept a whole night either.

After all the others had left, he'd helped Julia lift Ed out of his chair where he'd fallen asleep and haul him up to bed. Then they finished tidying up in the kitchen while Linda sat perched on the worktop, smoking another cigarette and doing her best to entertain them. But they were all tired and soon went up to their separate rooms.

Some time ago he had heard Amy crying but the house was now quiet again and he lay on his back with his hands clasped behind his head and watched the drapes start to glow as the moon crept around the corner of the house. There was a dull and restless aching in his chest that had been there ever since he lay down. He'd tried to push it aside and not to think about it or what its causes might be, but it was like a sore tooth that gave you no choice but to keep on probing the pain.

He'd gone over the weekend in his mind and still couldn't figure out why such a happy time should have left him feeling so low. Maybe he didn't want to figure it out because the answer might only make him feel worse. Whatever it was, he knew that something had shifted between the three of them and that it could never be the same again.

He felt it most strongly with Ed. They hadn't had a decent talk all weekend and when they had managed a few words there was something forced about it. The reason, of course, was Amy. Before he arrived, Connor had tried to prepare himself for the moment he first laid eyes on her. But there was no way he could have predicted the effect she had on him. His own flesh and blood joined with Julia's, living and breathing and cooing up at him from her crib. And the thought hitting him there and then like the blast of a bomb that neither child nor mother was his or would ever be his. And he thought, how could he have been so dumb to have done this? And yet, seeing the child, how could he not have? How could he wish such a beautiful creature never to have existed?

Until this evening Connor had held her only a couple of times and then only briefly. But on both occasions he noticed that Ed seemed uncomfortable. So when he'd handed her to him after dinner, Connor had been surprised. It seemed almost like a challenge; as if Ed wanted everyone else to think how open and easy he was about Connor's link with Amy, but that Connor himself should take care not to overstep the mark. When he cuffed him around the head, perhaps he hadn't meant to hit him so hard. It must be difficult to judge such things when you couldn't see. Even so, Connor was almost sure that beneath the jest lay some kind of warning.

He told himself that it was only to be expected, that things were bound to be a little tricky at first. Hell, it was hard for all of them. Connor himself was having trouble knowing what to think. The baby stirred strange feelings in him and watching Julia hold her stirred feelings still stranger. She looked more beautiful than ever. There was a new kind of lushness or fullness to her. She had kept her hair short and her skin was golden and lustrous.

Yesterday evening Connor had blundered into the living room and found her sitting there with one white breast exposed, quietly feeding Amy and the sight nearly floored him. She smiled and didn't look at all bothered, just said hi and he said it back and tried to look nonchalant, pretending he was looking for a glass. He went into the kitchen and found one and made a rapid retreat.

Even while he had the baby on his knee at the dinner table, he kept trying to convince himself that she wasn't really his at all, that she was Ed's and Julia's and that his own contribution was nothing more than a favor, that the genes he'd given had no more meaning, nor any less, than the gifts he had brought back from Africa, necklaces for Julia and Amy and a drum for Ed.

But he had to face the possibility that the whole thing had been a terrible mistake. Maybe he should never have agreed to do it; maybe it was going to mar their friendship forever. Yet when he found himself thinking this, he would look at Amy and all the happiness that surrounded her and he would scold himself for being selfish, for how could it all be anything other than good? No doubt things would soon settle down and seem normal. It was all going to be okay. It would all be fine.

He broke his rule and looked at his watch. It was three o'clock and he was wide awake. He got out of bed and went over to the window and looked out from between the drapes. The room was on the side of the house and looked out onto the orchard. In the moonlight the leaves of the trees and the grass below were like pewter. Maybe he would just go outside and get some air. He pulled on his jeans and his T-shirt and quietly opened the bedroom door. He could hear Ed snoring across the landing but otherwise all was quiet. He walked in his bare feet to the top of the stairs.

He saw her as he came through the living room. She was sitting outside on the steps of the deck, smoking a cigarette. She was wearing a white shift of a nightgown and was facing away from him, looking out toward the river, the smoke curling above her in the still air and catching the moonlight. She heard him and turned as he came through the open doors and onto the deck.

"How's that for luck," she said in a voice that wasn't quite a whisper. "My first cigarette in ten years and I get caught."

"It's okay. Your secret's safe."

"I stole one of Linda's."

"A smoker and a thief."

"It tastes disgusting. Funny, I always liked the idea more than doing it. You ever smoke?"

"Never could get the hang of it."

She stubbed it out on the step. He asked if it was okay to join her and she said of course it was, so he sat down beside her.

"Did Amy wake you?" she said.

"No."

"I can't wait till she sleeps through. I wasn't cut out for this three-times-a-night wake-up thing. I walk around all day like a zombie."

"Well, you look pretty good on it."

"I wish. I feel fat and frazzled."

He wanted to tell her how lovely she looked even that very moment but didn't trust himself and they sat awhile in silence looking out into the gray night past the carved eagle perched on its totem pole doing the same as they were.

"I'm sorry about Ed," she said.

"He just had a glass too many, that's all."

"No. You know what I mean. I think he's finding it all a little harder than he expected."

"I guess, having a house full of people and all—"

"Connor, you know what I'm trying to say.

It's the first time you've been around Amy and . . . well, you know."

He did but he didn't know what to say.

"She's beautiful," he said simply.

"Of course she is."

"And the way Ed is with her. He's a great father."

"Yep. He's amazing."

They were silent again. Julia was staring at her bare feet.

"Oh God," she sighed. Suddenly she stood up and stretched her arms high above her. "Will you walk to the river with me?"

"Sure."

They walked side by side through cool damp grass, following the rail of rope to the riverbank. And where the trail narrowed she went ahead and he followed, watching her shoulders dark above the moonlit glow of her nightdress and through it the shadow of her body. There was a wooden bench now in the place where Connor and Ed had lain talking a year ago and Julia sat down at one end of it and he at the other and they looked out at the river and for a long while said nothing.

"So how does it make you feel?" she said quietly.

"Amy?"

"Yes."

What was he to say? That it almost broke his heart? That he sometimes wished he had never laid eyes on Julia, for only then would he be whole again and not some empty shadow of a man, like the outline of a body chalked on a cold stone sidewalk?

"It's okay," she said. "You don't have to say if you don't want to."

"I'm just real happy for the both of you."

She looked at him for a long time.

"But?"

"No buts. That's how it is."

"Connor, you're such a poor liar."

He smiled. She was still staring at him and he held her gaze for a while but then had to look away.

"I was thinking just now about the first time we met," she said. "Do you remember? When you came to collect us at the airport?"

"I remember."

"It's weird but it wasn't like meeting you. More like recognizing you. As if we somehow already knew each other."

"I felt the same."

"You know how some people say things are 'meant to be'? Your mom, for example. She's always saying this or that was 'meant to be,' like it's written in the stars or something. Do you think that?"

"I don't know. I never used to. But now I think it might just be."

"With me it's the other way around. I used to think it was all meant to be, but now I don't." She paused a moment and looked away across the river. "I remember Skye saying one time how all the important things in life happened by accident. And I said no, I didn't think so, that in my view life was all mapped out and decided and just got revealed to us as we went along. But I don't think that anymore."

"You think she was right?"

"No. I think there are accidents and then we have to make choices."

Connor didn't reply.

"But you now think it's all mapped out?" she said.

"No. I think you're right. There are choices. It's just that sometimes the important ones aren't ours to make."

"Well, you've sure made some pretty big ones lately. Look at Amy. Look at this new career of yours. Going off to all these dangerous places, risking your life the whole time. I mean, they don't get much bigger than that."

He laughed.

"What? What's so funny?"

"Oh, I don't know."

"Come on, tell me."

"Well, it's just that I don't see it that way. I do what I do because someone else made the big choice. Not me."

She frowned at him. "What choice? Who?"

He smiled and shook his head and looked away. He had already said too much.

"Come on, Connor. You can't just leave it like that. Tell me. Who?"

He looked at her. She was still frowning at him, waiting for him to go on. And maybe because already in his heart he knew that this was the last time he would see her, he went ahead and told her.

"You," he said simply. "You chose Ed."

She stared at him in silence and even through the shadowed air between them he could see her face slowly fill with sadness as she understood.

"Oh, Connor," she whispered. "I had no idea."

"You must have."

"Never for one moment."

"Then I'm a better liar than we both thought."

"Oh, Connor."

He smiled sadly at her and waited for her to

go on, for if she felt anything of the kind for him, now was surely the time to say. But she said nothing, just sat there staring at him and shaking her head.

"I've loved you from the very first moment I saw you," he said.

"Don't. Don't say any more."

"I'm sorry. I should never have told you. And I promise I'll never say it again. But that's just how it is. And hell, I'm a lucky guy. I'm part of Amy and she's part of you. And whatever happens to me, she'll have you forever."

She stared at him and slowly lifted her hands and pressed her fingertips to her temples and he saw her mouth tremble.

"Oh, Connor. Oh God."

She closed her eyes and started to sob and the sound was so deep and harrowing that it seemed to come not from her but from some dark netherworld of long-forgotten sorrows. With her eyes tight shut she slowly opened her arms to him and he moved toward her and held her and held her head to his chest and felt her tears wet against him and felt tears of his own begin to run. She lifted her face and kissed him and said that she loved him too and had always loved him and she kissed him again and kissed his tears and Connor kissed hers.

How long they stayed like that, he didn't

know. All he could think of was that these few precious moments were all he would ever have of her and that he must live them and feel them with every particle of his being. And then store them away and treasure them for the rest of his life.

PART THREE

TWENTY-ONE

AMY CONSTANCE Tully was an angel. She even had the wings to prove it. One of them, however, was looking a little lopsided right now and neither went too well with the black Yankees T-shirt her godmother had sent her for her birthday. In truth, her whole demeanor, as she stood there on the kitchen table, sulking and kicking her heels, was something less than beatific.

"Amy, will you stand still?" Julia said, through a mouthful of pins.

"It looks yuck!"

"It does not look yuck. It looks fine. At least it will if you'll just stand still a moment and let me do it."

"I'm not going to wear it."

"You're supposed to be an angel. This is what angels wear. Honey, please! Keep still. These are pins here, one of us is going to get hurt."

"I don't care."

"Well, I do."

Julia was trying to pin the hem of the silvery skirt which Amy had decided to despise. As the daughter of the composer and musical director of the school's Christmas show, she had been able to pick her part—at least, among the supporting cast, for bigger stars with better agents from the fourth and fifth grades had bagged the leads. Six weeks ago she had unequivocally declared that she wanted to be an angel. Not a chipmunk, not an elf, not even the front end of the orca (though what the heck an orca was doing in the show, Julia still had no idea). Nothing but an angel.

Of course, seeing as the school was a multicultural, politically correct and altogether right-on kind of a place, this naturally didn't mean angel as in hovering-over-the-baby-Jesus-in-his-manger sort of angel, such as Julia herself had once been dragooned into playing when she was a kid. No, the entire show was more, as Ed had put it to Mrs. Leitner when pitching the idea back in the fall, more *pantheistic*: a spiritual celebration of nature and its bounteous wonders.

Privately, to Julia, he described it as pure eco-anarchist propaganda. Accordingly, the angels were much more of the avenging, in-your-face variety and though Ed was having second thoughts about giving them Uzis, by the end of the show they had disposed of several evil loggers and an oil slick called Mr. Gloop. And it was this, in all likelihood, that lay at the root of Amy's present tantrum. In the considered opinion of this particular seven-year-old going on seventeen, the costume was just too damn sissy.

"What's the problem here?" Ed said. He'd been sitting at the piano in the next room, trying to concentrate on some changes to the finale. "You don't like your outfit?"

"It sucks."

"Amy!" Julia said. "You do not use that word, okay?"

"Kevin Lucas says it all the time."

"Well, you are not Kevin Lucas. Ed? Will you talk to her?"

"Tell me what you don't like about it."

"It looks yuck."

"Yuck's not good enough. Tell me what it looks like."

"It's all stupid and . . . splivvy."

"Splivvy?"

"I look like Barbie," she sneered. Amy didn't much care for dolls of any sort. The only Barbie she'd ever been given was promptly decapitated.

"What color is the skirt?" Ed asked patiently.

"All white and silver and stupid." She twisted it in her hands as she said this and there was a sound of ripping.

"Okay, that's it," Julia said.

She took the pins from her lips and put them back in the box. Then she hoisted Amy from the table to the floor and unceremoniously stripped her of her wings and skirt.

"I thought it was going to be, kind of, darker," Ed said quietly. "You know, like gun-metal or something."

"Exactly," Amy sneered. She was sheltering beside Ed, with an arm hooked around his leg. "That *is* what it's going to be. I told her ten times already. First we make it, then we spray it. Okay? Jesus."

Ed held up his hands. "Okay, okay, I'm sorry."

"You shouldn't say Jesus," Amy muttered.

"Really? Why not? Kevin Lucas says it all the time."

An hour later Amy was tucked up in bed looking every inch a regular angel and happy to be one. Her cheeks glowed pink from her bath and her mop of blond curls was brushed as neatly as it ever allowed. The color was clearly from Connor but nobody had a clue where the curls came from. Ed teased her that in a previous life she must have been a flue brush. Her eyes were dark brown like Julia's and she had the same olive tone to her skin. In the wholly objective eyes of her mother, she was the most beautiful child ever to have graced the planet. Yet if asked, as occasionally she was, to say which of her parents, in character, Amy most resembled, Julia would reply without a moment's hesitation that it was Ed.

She was boisterous and funny and quick-witted and in each case sometimes too much so for her own good. Like Ed, she could floor you with a smart remark from a hundred yards and there were times at school when it landed her in trouble, especially with the more lumpish boys whose only resort, when snagged and bound by her verbal knots, was to violence.

Then there was the music. Whereas Julia could hardly hold a note and Connor, as far as anyone could recall, had never been heard even to whistle to his horse, Amy was naturally musical. She had picked up Ed's habit of singing to herself when she was doing something and when she pulled out the stops, her voice could be exquisite. Long before she was out of diapers, Ed was teaching her songs and sitting her on his lap at the piano, which by now she played as proficiently as some of his pupils two or three years her senior.

On long car journeys, the two of them would drive Julia nuts, singing every wretched song from *The Jungle Book* or *The Wizard of Oz* or, worse still, from one of Ed's old favorites like *Kiss Me, Kate* or *Oliver!* and Julia, at the wheel, would have to beg for mercy or earplugs and end up being blackmailed into promises of elaborate treats to make them stop. Ed liked to joke that some of his genes must have snuck in there after all. If not, Amy Tully was walking scientific testimony if not to nurture's triumph over nature, then at least to it having given it a damn good run for its money.

Julia was lying on the covers beside her now in the cluttered cavern of Amy's room. The multicolored wallpaper with its animal motif was all but obscured by Amy's paintings and drawings and family photographs as well as the strings of beads and necklaces and bits of ribbon that she hung from pegs just as Julia hung her jewelry. There were dozens of little glass and ceramic animals and jars crammed with feathers gathered from the riverbank and books spilling from shelves and stacks more on the floor among the jetsam of toys and discarded clothing and bric-a-brac. The mess was a first-class hazard for Ed but they had both grown tired of nagging her about it, persuading themselves that it showed character and was better than having a child who was obsessively tidy. Ed had grown used to picking his way through it like a soldier looking for land mines. Amy's bedside lamp was a large illuminated goose that Julia's mother had given her and its glow made the room feel cozy and womblike.

Together, by its light, they were reading Amy's favorite Dr. Seuss, *The Butter Battle Book*. They were best friends again, mostly thanks to the fact that after Amy had stomped off upstairs for her bath, Julia had gotten out the spray can of gunmetal paint and some glitter and transformed both skirt and wings into something that even Linda in her Neo-Gothic heyday would have proudly worn. Grinning sheepishly from the tub, Amy said she loved it.

"Sorry, Mommy."

"Give me twenty years and I might forgive you."

As usual, Julia was doing most of the reading. Amy always read more to Ed than to her, describing any pictures in intimate detail. She often read to Julia too, but with this book especially, although she knew it by heart, she preferred to listen. She liked the different funny voices that Julia put on for the Zooks and the Yooks as they escalated their crazy war over which way bread should be eaten: butter side up or butter side down.

It intrigued Julia that this was Amy's favorite Dr. Seuss, for it wasn't by a long way his funniest. In fact, it was downright chilling, telling as it did of a world sliding toward apocalypse because of a fatuous disagreement. In both of their minds there had always been an association with Connor.

Buying the book, about two years ago, had prompted a long discussion about war and why people sometimes hated and wanted to kill each other. Julia reassured her that hardly anyone nowadays expected the kind of world war that was depicted in the book. But there were wars, she said, smaller ones, that were always going on in different parts of the world. She found herself telling Amy that her biological father (Bio-Dad, thank heaven, had never caught on) often went to these places and took pictures.

"Of people fighting?"

"Uh-huh."

"Shooting each other?"

"Sometimes, yes."

"Do people try and shoot him?"

"No, sweetheart. He's not a soldier, he's a photographer. He has to be careful though."

"But he'll be okay because he's really brave, isn't he?"

"Yes, he is."

"Like when he saved your life."

"Uh-huh. That's right."

When Amy was still a baby, Ed and Julia had

spent a whole evening discussing at what age they would tell Amy about various things. They wanted her to know about having two fathers right away, before she could even begin to think about it. But they hadn't felt that way about the fire. They worried that it might traumatize the child and agreed that they would tell her when she was, say, twelve years old. It was the kind of ludicrous resolution that parents make before they get real, when they still think that they would never, ever, do such awful things as bribe their kids with candy or tell them to shut up.

And of course it crumbled. At the age of four and a half, Amy asked Ed how he came to be blind and the story—at least, a censored version of it—came pouring out. And instead of upsetting her, it only seemed to make her proud of them all, especially of her two superhero fathers who jumped out of the sky to rescue poor old klutzy mom.

Amy didn't talk about Connor so much anymore. It was hard to keep a memory alive when there were only photographs and stories and the occasional letter to feed it with. He still wrote to Amy and sent exotic gifts from far-flung corners of the world. But never once, since the christening, had he come again to see her. This seemed neither to upset Amy nor to anger her and Julia supposed that this was because it had always been that way. He had never been more than an idea, like a character in an old movie: intriguing, a little dashing and, like his photographs, mostly in black and white. Occasionally Amy would peruse Connor's pictures in magazines—at least, those that were suitable—and ask questions about him which Julia and Ed would dutifully answer, trying always to sound warm about him and never to reveal their hurt.

Among the photos pinned to Amy's bedroom wall were several of Connor, including the only one that existed of the two of them together. Taken by Julia at the christening, it showed him standing on the deck, holding this funny, chubby-cheeked cherub in his arms and smiling down at her, while Amy, ever the star, looked straight at the camera.

For a long while she and Ed had kept in touch with Connor's mother and a few times had taken Amy over to see her at the ranch in Augusta. But as the years went by and still Connor didn't come, it seemed somehow pointless. Like Hamlet without the prince, as Ed said the last time as they drove home. Maggie claimed that he never came to see her either, but Julia knew it wasn't true. Nor did Maggie any longer call them with news of Connor or to tell them of papers or magazines that had his photographs.

Perhaps he had told her not to or perhaps she knew why he kept away. Mothers were like that, Julia knew; even the mothers of monsters closed around to defend them. Whatever the reason, it was now more than two years since they had seen Maggie or spoken with her.

And with Connor it was more than seven. Amy's entire lifetime. And sometimes it seemed to Julia like the whole of hers too. They were all different people and their world a different place and the sorrow that was Connor had shifted around it like the sun. Once it had risen hot and harsh and for a while had glared down on them, impossible to behold except briefly through shielded, squinting eyes. Now it had cooled and though not set, was lowering itself through a mellowed sky, casting shadows longer yet less painful to the eye.

During the first year she had written him several letters but destroyed them all. At first she thought it was simply because she couldn't find the right words. And then she realized it was simpler still and that there were no words to find. In those days she had thought about him all the time. Barely a waking hour went by without her replaying in her mind that last image of him, sitting beside her in the cold moonlight, confessing his love and then holding her and kissing her tears.

Before he left the following day, without telling him, she had slipped a photograph into his packed bag. It was the one that Ed had taken of the two of them that last day they climbed together, when they had asked him to father their child.

She kept track of him as best she could. One way or another—mostly through the eagle-eyed Linda—she would hear about some magazine that had used his latest photographs. She noticed that he now often wrote the accompanying stories, whereas at first the words had always been someone else's. His style was simple and unflowery and she could hear his voice behind the words. The pieces that moved her most were about a little-reported war which had been going on for years in northern Uganda. Connor seemed to return there often. His most recent piece was about a rehabilitation center for children who'd been abducted from their homes and forced to serve as soldiers in the rebel army. The pictures had made Julia weep.

Only once had she and Ed drawn near to speaking the truth about why Connor had since stayed away. A brown paper package, mailed from Kampala, had arrived with perfect timing on Amy's fourth birthday. It contained a little dress—just the right size—and a shawl, both in a vivid African fabric, splashes of bright green and yellow and red and purple. Enclosed in the accompanying birthday card was a photograph of a magnificent Ugandan woman wearing the same outfit and he had written instructions, complete with diagrams, on how to twist the shawl into a headdress. Amy was thrilled. She wore the outfit for a week.

Ed was furious. Once Amy was safely out of earshot, he exploded.

"Goddamn presents!" he said. "What does he say on the card? 'Say hi to your mom and dad'? Terrific. Maybe one day he'll come say it himself. Or even pick up the phone sometime and say it. She's never heard his goddamn voice! But I guess he's just too famous and busy now for that kind of thing."

"Come on, Ed," Julia said. "Don't be like that."

"Like what? I mean, are we lepers or something? He was my best friend, for christsake! 'Say hi to your mom and dad.' Well, fuck him."

"Maybe he thinks it's fairer to stay away."

"Fairer? How the hell do you work that one out?"

"Nothing. It doesn't matter."

"No, come on, tell me."

"Well, I don't know. Maybe he thinks you might find it hard."

"What, find it hard having my best friend come visit?"

"No, I'm wrong. Forget it."

"What, like, I'd be jealous of him and Amy or something?"

"No, not exactly. Please Ed, let's just drop it, okay?"

"No, I'm interested. That's obviously what you think. That he's staying away because he thinks I'm threatened by him being Amy's biological father. Is that right?"

"Well. Maybe a little. The way you were at the christening—"

"What do you mean? Like I was hostile to him or something?"

"A little, yes."

He stood there in silence for a moment, still and inscrutable behind his dark glasses. It was as though he were staring into her head with something more powerful than vision and it unsettled her.

"You tell me this now? After four years? That I'm the reason he doesn't come see us anymore?"

"Ed, how should I know?"

"Wow," he said quietly. He shook his head sadly. "Oh boy."

And Julia at once regretted saying it and tried

to soften it by saying that it probably wasn't that after all and that maybe Connor had found it hard seeing Amy and felt it better to keep his contact with her at a distance in case he grew too attached. She babbled on for a while but could tell Ed wasn't really listening. He was quiet and thoughtful for days and since that day had never criticized Connor again.

When Julia reflected on why Connor stayed away, which she could now, though preferred not to, for it still stirred feelings that ruffled the smooth surface of her life, she suspected that both of the things she had said were true. Probably he had sensed Ed's jealousy and concluded that the best he could do for his friend was to keep clear. And probably he did find the prospect too painful of seeing his daughter growing up as someone else's. If he couldn't have all of Amy, then perhaps it was better to have none. This, Julia had little doubt, was what he also felt about her. And although he was part of her and always would be and walked daily in her thoughts, if she were honest with herself, this was how she preferred it to be. If not all of him, then none.

Julia and Amy always finished *The Butter Battle Book* in unison, putting on spooky voices as the Yooks and the Zooks menacingly fingered their new bombs, the ones that could obliterate mankind. Who was going to drop it first? *We'll see, we will see . . .* Julia shut the book.

"Zooks are dumb," Amy said.

"How come?"

"They must be. Who'd eat their bread butter side down?"

"I do."

"You do not."

"I do too. You've just never seen me."

"Okay, I'm going to watch tomorrow and if you really are a Zook, you're in big trouble."

"I'd better go make my bomb."

Julia got up and turned off the lamp and leaned over Amy to kiss her.

"Gimme a big hug," she said. "Bigger, bigger! That's more like it."

"Thanks for the costume and sorry I was mean to you."

"Hey, what are moms for?"

"I love you, Mommy."

"I love you too, baby."

KAY NEUMARK TOLD the chipmunks and the elves for the third time to cut it out. If they didn't quit fooling around and trying to trip the angels like that, she said, she would have to find others who would take the job more seriously.

It was utter bluff, of course. Both she and Ed knew only too well that every child who was remotely interested had already been enlisted, along with quite a few who weren't. Still, a first full rehearsal was always a test of nerves and so far it was going all right.

Kay was going to be credited as the director and co-writer with Ed, but she did a dozen other jobs besides. And when she wasn't helping Julia paint the set or making costumes or wiping noses or generally threatening, cajoling or encouraging the cast, she taught history and English by all accounts with the same gusto and good humor that she had brought to the show. Ed had met her a few times at school social events and she and her girlfriend had once come for a barbecue with some of the other younger staff when Julia was working part-time before Amy was born. But he hadn't really gotten to know her until they started rehearsals a few weeks ago.

She was a plain-speaking dynamo of a woman from Chicago. From Julia's description of her, Ed knew that she was in her mid-thirties, had laugh lines, cropped silvery hair and a penchant for dungarees and baggy striped sweaters. Ed knew her more for her booming voice and her smell, which reminded him of those New Age stores where they burned incense all day and where you went to buy cheap Indonesian gifts for people you hoped didn't go there too.

"All right," she was calling out now. "Let's do that one more time. And this time, Mr. Gloop, more menace. Know what I mean? Show that Orca what you're made of. Yeah! Just like that. Here we go now. Positions, please. Julia, are you ready back there?"

Julia was assistant stage manager and somewhere behind the partially painted scenery was marshaling the troops. She shouted that she was as ready as she ever would be. Ed could detect a note of suppressed desperation.

"Okay, maestro," Kay called.

Ed was sitting ready at the piano which, apart from a few taped sound effects, was all the accompaniment there was. Originally he'd had ambitions of putting together a small orchestra, but he and Kay had soon realized there was enough to drive them crazy without that. As things now stood, with just two weeks until opening night, there seemed at least a chance of avoiding disaster. That was, provided he could stay awake.

The show had turned out to involve a lot more work than Ed had expected, and nowadays, since he'd been on dialysis, he didn't seem to have the stamina he'd once had. In fact lately he felt tired more than he didn't. Maybe he was just getting old. He took a deep breath.

"Okay, one more time," he called. "Gloop and Loggers, from the top." And off they went again.

Ed had been on dialysis for a little over two years now. His annual diabetes checkup had revealed that he had abnormally high levels of potassium and protein waste products in his blood. His kidneys weren't doing a good enough job cleaning it. So now, three mornings a week, he had to go into Missoula and get hooked up to a damn machine to do it instead. He'd been there this morning, four long hours which he could have usefully filled a thousand better ways.

The dialysis unit was in a ground floor room at St. Patrick Hospital. There were thirteen chairs in a circle, each with its own dialysis machine and a TV set with headphones. Daytime soaps had never been Ed's favorite entertainment, even when he'd been able to see the pictures, so he always took along some work or a tape to listen to while the machine sucked his blood. The nurses who ran the place were great and he knew them all well enough by now to tease them. He called them The Brides of Dracula. This morning he had even had them singing one of the songs from the show. Despite the fun, Ed hated the whole process with a vengeance.

He had never been one of those diabetics who spent their lives worrying and monitoring themselves. Indeed, his attitude had occasionally bordered on the reckless, especially since he'd been living with Julia. She did enough worrying about it for both of them, always checking up to see that he'd had his insulin shots, always ready with a candy bar at the first sign of a hypo. And as she grew older, Amy was getting to be the same, so now he had the two of them nagging at him. Of course, it was great that they did. But sometimes it bugged him and he could get a little snappy about it. Lately, because of the pressures of the show, it had been happening quite a lot. Julia had warned that it might be too much for him and though he tried to hide the toll it was taking, she was probably right.

All in all, the rehearsal went well. Urged on by Kay Neumark, Mr. Gloop revealed hitherto concealed star potential and everyone went away in high spirits. Well, almost everyone. On the way home, Amy told him about a backstage drama involving one the elves who had apparently peed his pants. The chief chipmunk had said something cruel and the two of them had ended up kicking and biting each other.

Ed listened in a distracted way, tuning in and out. Ever alert to his moods, Julia asked him if he was feeling okay and he told her not to fuss, he was just a little tired, that was all. He closed his eyes and propped his head back against the headrest, thinking about the show, the music still drifting in his mind.

How ironic it was, he thought, that this was where all his grand ambitions had led. Ten years ago it had all been so clear. Without the slightest doubt about his talent, he'd had his entire career mapped out. He remembered outlining it to Connor one summer's night when they were resting out on a fire somewhere. First there would be the little off-Broadway gem that got rave reviews, then Broadway itself, then Hollywood—not just movie scores but something much more ambitious: he was going to reinvent the Hollywood musical for a whole new generation. And now here he was, nearly thirty-six years old, a blind piano teacher in a little western town, busting his ass over his daughter's elementary school show.

Surprisingly, he didn't feel one little bit cheated or bitter about it. The worst he ever got was an occasional twinge of regret. When he scanned himself for self-pity, as he regularly made a point of doing, he honestly found none. Everyone—well, maybe not everyone, but plenty of people anyhow—had these grand ideas of fame or fortune when they were young. And then as they got older they got real and settled for less. Or maybe they simply discovered that there were other things that were more important in life. And from what Ed gathered, those who did make it to the top—in the music and entertainment business anyway—generally didn't end up happier. Richer for sure, but not happier.

What was particularly ironic was that of the two of them, it should be Connor who'd ended up famous. Only the other day Julia read that he had just been awarded some major photojournalism prize. He even had an exhibition coming up at a fancy New York gallery. Yet he had never once struck Ed as even slightly ambitious. It was always Ed who banged on about all the great goals he was going to achieve while Connor just sat there and smiled and supported him. Perhaps, under that sly cowboy reticence, he had been ambitious all along and had simply had the sense to hide it. In any case, Ed didn't feel envious. Just a little, well, embarrassed.

He still missed Connor badly. He'd never had a friend so close, nor probably ever would again. And if he chose, he could easily make himself feel wretched thinking about it. But what with Julia and Amy and so much else to be grateful for, to do that seemed self-indulgent, so he rarely did.

At first he had felt angry, until three years ago, when Julia told him what she believed to be the reason for Connor's estrangement. Ed had written him a long letter via the photo agency, apologizing for his behavior at the christening. Connor never replied. For a while Ed worried that the letter had gone astray and wondered if he should write again.

But he never did. And as time went by he began to think that maybe it was all for the best anyway. Ed hadn't exactly admitted his jealousy in the letter, but the more he thought about it the more certain he became that Connor knew about it. Ed hated himself for feeling jealous. It was unreasonable and ungrateful and, above all—assuming Connor did know—so goddamn demeaning. But he couldn't help it. Once the green weed took root, rational thought just withered and died. The harsh truth was that Ed feared that Connor was more of a father to Amy than he was or ever would be and that maybe—God, this was the really sick stuff—maybe Julia felt that way too. If Connor had been constantly around these past years, the paranoia would no doubt have festered, making Ed ever more twisted and resentful. It was sad to admit it, but estrangement had probably been the only course.

It was all a mess and a muddle, as Grandma Tully used to say. But then, so was life. It was a bitch and then you died. Wow, he mused sleepily, listen to the great philosopher. Dreamily, he could still hear Julia and Amy chattering away but he was too tired to concentrate on what they were saying. His mind was floating like a butterfly from one thought to another.

Poor old Connor. Had success made him happy? Ed somehow doubted it. How could anyone do that kind of work and be happy? Maybe they should all fly to New York and show up unannounced at the opening of his exhibition? Give the great photographer a surprise. Give him a blind man's verdict on his pictures. Just *love* the texture there. And, wow, can't you just smell those dead bodies? And by the way, here's your goddaughter. Hasn't she grown?

Poor old Connor. How he missed him. What a mess it all was. What a goddamn mess, muddle and fuckup.

TWENTY-TWO

CONNOR ASKED the cabdriver to pull up across the street from the gallery and handed him a twenty-dollar bill through the gap in the security screen. The driver was a Nigerian and muffled like a mummy with a long scarf and gloves and a big woolen hat with flaps like the ears of a spaniel. On the trip down to SoHo, through the cold and the fog and the acid gray slush, he had been going on about how great it was to live in New York. Connor had been to Lagos only once and hadn't much liked it but on a night like this he knew which of the two cities he'd choose. He told the guy to keep the change and wished him luck and then climbed out into the freezing night air.

The street was narrow and the buildings on both sides were tall and grim and seemed to lean in like the walls of a black crevasse, though maybe that was just his mood. He stood in the shadows and shivered and turned his coat collar up against the cold and looked across at the big plate-glass window of the gallery spilling light out onto the grimed snow heaped along the sidewalk. There were maybe twenty or thirty people in there, sipping champagne and chatting. One or two were even looking at his photographs.

He was an hour late and almost hadn't come at all. Why he had ever let himself be talked into it, he couldn't imagine. Eloise, the gallery owner, was a friend of his editor, dear old Harry Turney, and it was hard to figure out who was doing whom a favor. Probably all three of them. Eloise had lots of fancy media connections and some of them were going to be there tonight. There was even supposed to be a TV crew from a cable channel arts show that Connor had never heard of. He was glad that there didn't seem to be any sign of them.

He'd already had an idea of what lay in store. Eloise had fixed up an interview with a new glossy magazine which, she said, was passionate about photography. The editor was a good friend.

"Believe me, darling," she said. "It's going to be like *Life,* only with an edge. They see you as the new Robert Capa. You're probably going to be on the cover."

The young woman who came to interview him looked about seventeen years old and had never heard of either Robert Capa or *Life* magazine. She asked him if he ever took pictures of famous people and seemed to lose interest once he'd said he didn't. The magazine had hit the newsstands this morning. Connor wasn't on the cover. There, instead, was a young man with a black shirt, a smug grin and a bunch of Canons around his neck. The headline said: *Shooting in the War Zone with Dino Tornari.*

Connor was intrigued. He knew most war photographers but had never heard of this one before. He turned inside to discover that the war zone in question was outside various chic Manhattan clubs and restaurants where Dino, "undisputed King of the Paparazzi," lurked to snatch indiscreet pictures of the rich and famous and for his pains regularly got beaten up.

The piece about Connor was tucked away at the back and distilled down to six paragraphs, every one containing an error. They'd somehow managed to find an old picture of him in a cowboy hat and talked about his "Marlboro man looks" and his "harrowing pictures from the heart of darkness." The only shot they had used was one he had taken of a Dayak tribesman in Borneo. The caption called the man a Rwandan headhunter. It didn't really matter. The picture was so small and poorly reproduced, even the man's own mother wouldn't recognize him.

It was Connor's first taste of being on the other end of media attention. Now, against all his better instincts, he was about to get his second. He took a deep breath and headed across the street.

Eloise Martin was one of those black-garbed New York women, so thin and chic and sharp, you felt you could almost cut yourself looking at her. Harry Turney had it on good authority that she was pushing sixty, but without inside information you would never have guessed. Her eyes were made up like a fifties jazz fan and she had an immaculate bob of black hair which she liked to toss a lot when she laughed. Harry said she was in a state of constant overhaul, a work in progress, and disappeared every spring to Rio to have some new nip or tuck. Her bond-dealing billionaire husband had once been heard to joke that when he went to pick her up at the airport he was never able to recognize her and had to hold up a sign with her name on it. Eloise divided the rest of her time, according to Harry, between art and philanthropy.

Connor's exhibition fell squarely, thank God, into the latter category. Several of the photographs were from his most recent trip to northern Uganda where he had spent two weeks at

St. Mary of the Angels, a rehabilitation center for child soldiers. He had been there several times before and regularly sent them money. The proceeds from any pictures sold from the exhibition would be going there too.

Eloise came to greet him while he was still checking in his coat.

"Connor, darling. You're such a naughty boy. There are so many people dying to meet you. The TV crew had to go but they said they'd come back."

"I'm sorry, the traffic was terrible."

"Of course. Have some champagne. It'll make you look less miserable. Don't the pictures look marvelous?"

"Yeah, you did a great job."

She summoned one of the waiters and Connor took a glass and drained half of it in one gulp. He was suddenly aware of everyone staring at him and he told himself to go easy. He felt as if he'd just checked in at his own funeral. Eloise went off to find "someone important" whom she wanted him to meet. His heart sank lower. Harry sidled up and put a consoling hand on his shoulder.

"Don't worry," he said quietly. "You don't have to stay long."

Eloise came back with a tall young woman, so mesmerizingly beautiful that Connor didn't concentrate on Eloise's introduction. All he caught was her first name which was Beatrice and that she worked for *Vanity Fair*. Eloise led Harry away, leaving the two of them alone, and as she went she gave Connor a look that was no doubt meant to tell him to make a good impression.

Beatrice seemed no better at small talk than he was and for a while it was awkward. Connor was waiting for her to ask if he ever took pictures of famous people. But instead she asked which photographers he most admired and it turned out that she knew the work of every one he mentioned. He asked her how and she shrugged and said she'd just always been interested. She had met and written about some of Connor's personal heroes, people like Don McCullin and older ones like Eve Arnold and Henri Cartier-Bresson.

She asked him if he would give her a guided tour of his photographs and although he didn't want to, especially now that he knew about her expertise, he agreed.

It had been hard enough selecting the photographs and printing them, so he had left the hanging to Eloise. This was the first time he had seen them together and in sequence. They covered pretty much his whole career and were hung chronologically, starting with his picture of Ed silhouetted against the Yellowstone fire. He had also included the shot of the elk with its flaming antlers, the one that had struck such chill into Julia. He hadn't looked at it for many years and out of superstition had never had it published. Beatrice stood silently in front of it for a long time.

"Did it survive?" she asked at last.

Connor shrugged. "I don't know. It was there, then it was gone."

"So, you were a firefighter."

"A smoke jumper."

She nodded, as if this explained something, and moved on. Sometimes she stopped and asked a question but mostly she just looked and Connor wondered if he ought to be more forthcoming and give her some background on where and how and why the pictures were taken, but he didn't.

Walking behind her, studying them in sequence, it was as if he were taking a tour of his life and seeing it with clear eyes for the first time. And as he moved from one image to the next and saw the pain and the loss and the horror in the eyes of those before whom he had stood, he felt a cold sorrow well within him. The women hanging in the blossom; the little girl in Sniper's Alley, howling over her mother's body; the Rwandan boy, wide-eyed and skeletal from hiding for two weeks under corpses; a vulture perched on the open-armed statue of Christ; the chilling stare of the murderous mayor, Emmanuel Kabugi, caught in his lair in Goma; a young Liberian rebel kneeling bound before his executioners. One face after another, staring in silence as Connor passed, watching him walk his own private catacomb, the dead and the dying and the cold-eyed killers of all colors and creeds, disposable apostles of faceless men with their gods of hatred and greed.

At last they reached the final picture. It was of Thomas, one of the children Connor had photographed at St. Mary of the Angels. At the age of ten he and his twin brother had been kidnapped by rebels who called themselves the Warriors for God. To seal the boys' loyalty, they were forced to take part in the burning of their own village and the massacre of their own people. Many months later Thomas had either escaped or been discarded to die. A government border patrol found him wandering in the bush. He was shriveled and skeletal and had lost the power of speech.

Connor stood in front of the picture for a long time, staring at it and then staring through it, at the vision of himself that was on display here and in all the other pictures he had just walked past. Something seemed to be expanding inside his chest, squeezing his lungs, making it hard for him to breathe. He felt himself sway and his shoulders start to shake.

"What were you looking for?"

He turned and saw Beatrice staring at the picture too, as if she had addressed the question to the boy. Connor swallowed. He didn't know if he could trust his own voice.

"In this picture, you mean?"

"In all of them."

It was a question so uncannily close to his own thoughts that his instinct was to brush it off, to give the standard line that they were just images, moments captured by some undefinable combination of chance and instinct that somehow ended up telling a story. But instead, as if it sprang from nowhere, he gave a different answer.

"Hope."

It was a shock to hear himself say it. God, he was feeling weird. He couldn't stop shaking. Beatrice was looking at him now, assessing what he had just said. He shrugged and went on, trying to make light of it. "Maybe not. Who knows? Hell, I don't think I'm looking for anything."

"Oh yes. I think you are. But I don't think it's hope."

"No? Well, there you go."

Connor forced a little laugh but it sounded odd. Maybe he was getting sick or something. He hadn't eaten all day. Maybe it was the champagne on an empty stomach. Anyhow, who the hell did she think she was, asking him a question like that? She'd known him all of ten minutes. But despite himself, goddamn it, he wanted to know what she thought.

"So okay, what is it I'm looking for?" he said sharply.

She looked at him for a moment and saw his anger. She smiled politely.

"I'm sorry. It's none of my business."

"No, please. Since you know all these famous photographers and what makes them tick and all, you'd be doing me a favor. So feel free, go right ahead and tell me. What am I looking for?"

She frowned. "Why are you so hostile?"

"For fuck's sake, just tell me!"

Out of the corner of his eye he saw heads turn toward them. Beatrice paused again and then said quietly and simply:

"I think you're looking for a mirror of your own sadness."

Connor stood staring at her and then nodded.

"Well, thanks. Now I know. Beatrice, it's been a pleasure."

He turned abruptly and walked in a daze toward the door. He felt tears coming. Jesus, what the hell was going on here? He heard Eloise calling after him but he didn't turn, just rummaged for his coat among the others.

"Connor? Where are you going? What happened?"

"I'm sorry, Eloise. I've got to go. I'm sorry."

He found his coat and launched himself out into the street. He took a great gulp of the frozen, pungent air and tried to gather himself, closing his eyes and putting his hands over his face. His heart was thumping like a jackhammer and he was panting and he thought for a moment that he must be having a heart attack or something. But no, he was okay. He was okay.

He put on his coat and bowed his head and started to walk.

How far he walked or where, he never knew. But by the time he got back to his apartment, the towered skyline of the East Side was streaked with crimson. As he came in from the street the doorman said hi and then frowned and asked him if he was all right and Connor said he was fine, just a little tired. He took the elevator to the sixth floor, leaning thrice-mirrored in the corner, not daring to look at himself.

The apartment was as cold as outside. The heating didn't work and he hadn't bothered to get it fixed. It was six years since he'd bought the place but the only thing he'd spent money on was converting what had once been the bedroom into a state-of-the-art darkroom. He slept instead in the long living room which, with all his camera gear stacked in cases around it, looked more like a left-luggage place than a home. It had bare floorboards, flaking gray walls and three tall windows with black Venetian blinds that were broken and dusty. The bed was at one end and at the other was a big table littered with papers and photographs and old magazines. There was a small, drab bathroom and a smaller, drabber kitchen. The refrigerator had more film in it than food. Apart from a TV, a phone and one sagging armchair, the only gestures to comfort were a couple of small rugs and a handful of carved figures that he'd brought back from his travels. He hated the place and it knew it and hated him back.

He didn't switch on the lights but went directly to the bed and lay down on his back still wrapped in his coat, his breath rising in a cold fog above him. He stared without blinking at the ceiling, watching the reflected lights of the traffic move across it, yellow and red and slowly fading as another grimy day came bleeding through the blinds.

A mirror of his own sadness.

He wondered if that was a line she always used with the photographers she met, at least, the ones who specialized in suffering. It was the kind of smart, personal remark that you couldn't really argue with. People generally assumed he must be on some personal crusade on behalf of humanity, confronting the comfortable with images they would rather not see. Indeed, there had been times, early on, when Connor had felt himself to be doing exactly that, persuading himself that even in a world overdosed on news, with images of mayhem and misery forever gushing into every home, it was still just about possible that a particular picture might make a difference. And no matter how small that difference, whether it led just one person to write a check or cast a vote or even just talk about it to anyone at all, then what he did was worthwhile.

But he didn't believe that anymore. Of course there was an element of altruism in what he did. But it was only a veneer and beneath it his motives were entirely personal. And he now realized that the reason he had reacted so harshly to what Beatrice said was that she was right. She had seen something in him that he thought he kept concealed. It lodged within him like a quiet tenant whom he never saw and it had lived there so long that he'd almost forgotten it was there.

He wondered if he would still have ended up this way if he hadn't made that choice seven years ago when Amy was born. But at the time it hadn't seemed like a choice. It was simply how it had to be, for all of their sakes. He remembered how his father used to say there was always a simple way of telling whether something you were thinking of doing was right or wrong.

"You just take a pair of scales and weigh the happiness," he said. "If it looks like it's going to cause more happiness than unhappiness, then odds on it's right."

Connor used to worry about this, long after his father had died. And he and Ed had once gotten into an argument about it. Ed had studied philosophy at college and said, a little pompously, that what Connor's father was talking about had a name, in fact it was a whole school or movement or something, called Utilitarianism. The basic idea was that things were right when they caused the greatest happiness to the greatest number of people. Connor said what, if he'd been older at the time, he would have liked to say to his father, which was how could you measure happiness? Everybody, after all, had his own idea of what it was and how it felt. And what if you wanted to do something that would make one person deliriously happy and a hundred others just a tiny little bit unhappy? Would that be right or wrong? Ed went waffling on, trying to tie him up in knots and Connor ended up losing his temper and saying the whole theory was bullshit anyway and he didn't want to talk about it anymore.

But this was exactly what he had done with Ed and Julia. He had gotten out the scales and weighed everyone's happiness. How happy would each of them be, including Amy and himself, if he came regularly to see them and how happy if he didn't but instead just kept in touch with Amy by letter, to let her know he cared and thought about her. And the scales had tilted sharply, conclusively, in favor of his staying away.

Having made his decision, he should have allowed himself to move on. He had always believed, after all, that happiness was simply a matter of choice. You could either wallow in regret, even drown in it, or you could choose not to. But he had underestimated the power of habit. Because once you'd started wallowing, pretty soon that's all you were fit for. You grew fins and webbed feet so you could wallow even better. Hell, maybe you even got to enjoy it a little. And then when you thought that was enough and it was time to haul yourself out and go walking on dry land again, you found you couldn't. You had evolved into some wretched swamp-dwelling creature that had forgotten how to do it. The daunting truth, that Beatrice had glimpsed at the gallery, was that Connor now knew no other way to be.

In the first two or three years there had been many times when he almost changed his mind about staying away. But by the time Ed's letter arrived, apologizing for how he had been at the christening, it was already too late. He had in him his mother's stubborn streak. He had made his decision and he would stick to it.

The letters that arrived two or three times a year from Amy were still the closest that he ever came to happiness. He had her picture on his bedside table, next to the one of him and Julia, that Julia had slipped into his bag seven years ago. He had made smaller copies of them and laminated them so that he could take them with him wherever he traveled. In the one of him and Julia, their faces were almost touching. Anyone who didn't know the truth would assume they were a couple. And Connor would lie there and stare at it and think of how, in another, more forgiving world, they might have been.

TWENTY-THREE

IT HAD seemed like a good idea at the time and unfortunately it was his, so he had no one else to blame. A few weeks ago in a rare moment when the show seemed to be coming together well, Ed had suggested to Julia that they should invite both their mothers to stay when it was on. It had been some while since they'd been to visit, he said, and Christmas was coming up and it was Amy's theatrical debut and anyway the two women had always gotten along so well. Actually, Ed now confessed to himself, it was pure hubris. He wanted them to see *his* show.

They had flown in three days ago and, in fairness, both had done a lot to help. They had cooked and cleaned and looked after Amy, even helped Julia make some last-minute costume alterations and ferry people and props to and from the school. But, boy, the wearying cost of it all.

Julia's mom had hardly paused to take breath. He'd always found her constant chatter funny, even endearing, but now it was driving him crazy. Of course, with justice that he should have foreseen, Julia and Amy were at school all day, so the burden was mostly his. Maria had a habit of interrupting him at his workstation just when he was in the middle of something vital and complicated. Worst of all, for some unfathomable reason, she'd started calling him Eddie, a name which had always set his teeth on edge and which, when he was a kid, would earn whoever was rash enough to use it a bloody nose.

"Eddie, would you like a cup of coffee?"

"No thanks, Maria. I'm fine, thanks."

"You sure?"

"Yes, thanks, Maria. I had one just a short while ago."

"How's the work going?"

Grit teeth, count to three, take deep breath. "It's going just fine, thanks."

"I'll leave you to it, then."

"Thanks, Maria."

Dear Lord. Even Amy knew when to leave him alone.

His own mother barely got a word in edgeways. Her side of the conversation consisted mostly of *I know. Really? Is that so? You didn't?* Ed could tell she was finding it hard too. It would have been easier in summer, when they could have sat outside or gone for walks, but the moment they'd arrived, so had the snow and they were confined to the house.

Today it all seemed worse because of first night nerves. The show was on for two nights only and it opened this evening. With one performance under his belt, Ed hoped, everything would calm down and he would again have a life and learn to love his mother-in-law. Right this moment she was sitting on the living room couch telling his mother about someone she knew who in turn knew someone who'd once spent a night with Frank Sinatra. Ed had heard the story before and knew it was long and, like Frank that night, promised more than it delivered. He tried to block his ears but still it wormed its way in.

There were only three and a half hours to go until curtain time and he still had about a hundred things to do. He'd even skipped his date with The Brides of Dracula this morning. It was no big deal. He'd missed a dialysis session a couple of times before with no serious consequences, so he knew he'd be fine. These medics always played it safe, he reasoned. Having his blood cleaned twice a week was probably more than enough. All he prayed was that Julia didn't find out, as she had the last time he played truant. She'd given him hell for days. One of The Brides at St. Pat's had phoned this morning when he didn't show up and she'd given him hell too. Ed told her he felt fine (which wasn't altogether true) and that he'd come in tomorrow instead. Once the show was done, he promised, he would go back to being a good boy.

Kay Neumark was coming to pick him up at four and he still hadn't finished half of what he'd hoped to get done. Over on the couch Frank Sinatra was still on his first martini. Ed was just putting on his headphones to block the sound of Maria's voice when the phone rang. It was Julia, calling from the school with bad news. The chief logger, clearly taking theatrical tradition too literally, had fallen over in the snow and broken his leg. Kay wanted to come and pick Ed up earlier so that they could all work out what to do. She was on her way right now.

"How was the dialysis this morning?" Julia asked.

"Fine."

"What were the readings like?"

"Julia, I'm right in the middle of something. Don't fuss. I'm fine, okay?"

For once, Maria had been all ears. When he hung up she asked what had happened and while he gathered his things together, Ed explained. He told them that he would arrange a taxi to pick them up at six o'clock and bring them to the school.

"I hope that gives you long enough to finish your Frank Sinatra story."

Maria gave an embarrassed chuckle.

"I do go on, don't I?" she said.

As he was putting on his boots, he heard Kay's car scrunching to a halt outside. He collected some candy bars from the kitchen and put them in his bag. Then he put on his coat and found his cane and kissed the mothers goodbye. His mother hooked her arm in his and walked with him to the door.

"Good luck, darling," she whispered.

"Thanks, but I think you're the one who needs it," he whispered back.

She smiled. "She's got a heart of gold."

"And a tongue of titanium."

"Shhh. Remember now. Go easy on that left hand."

"It's kind of a left-hand show."

"Say good luck to Amy!" Maria called from the living room.

"I will."

"And to Julia!"

"You bet. Bye now."

FROM THE WINGS Julia watched Amy standing center stage in the dazzle of the lights, singing her socks off. The socks, like the red and black plaid shirt and all the rest of the chief logger's costume, were several sizes too large for her, but what she lacked in stature she more than made up for in sheer pizzazz. It was the loggers' big number, "Oh please! Oh please! They're only trees!" and she was giving it everything she'd got.

Julia was astonished that the girl had agreed to do it. It had been Ed's idea and made perfect sense because Amy had lived and breathed the show for the best part of four months and knew everybody's lines by heart. But after how adamant she'd been about being an angel and the agonies of getting her costume right, Julia thought the proposal didn't stand a chance.

With Mrs. Leitner's permission they'd hauled her out of class and brought her into the auditorium where the stage was and Kay explained about the chief logger's leg. Amy stood very still and listened solemnly and Julia could tell the child knew what was coming.

"So, what we wondered, Amy, seeing as you're the only other person who knows the part, would you consider not being an angel and being the chief logger instead?"

Amy shrugged. "Sure."

"That's my girl!" Ed said.

"Can I still wear my angel costume?"

"No, sugar," Kay said. "I don't think that would work."

"Does anybody else get to wear it?"

"Absolutely not."

"Okay then."

She had half an hour's rehearsal, going through some of the moves she wasn't so familiar with and now here she was, belting out the chief logger's lines as if she'd rehearsed them for weeks. Julia had never been more proud of her and from the grin on Ed's face at the piano she could see he felt the same, as did the two grandmothers in the front row.

The auditorium was packed. Probably two hundred people, Julia estimated, with more standing at the back. Kay, who was sitting beside Ed to cue him, had announced at the start that the part of the chief logger would tonight be played by "Miss Amy Tully" who had "agreed to stand in at only a moment's notice." Naturally, the whole audience was rooting for her. When she finished her song, the cheers and applause must have sent the snow sliding off the roof. There were so many calls that Ed made her do an encore.

"That's done it," Julia said to one of the other teachers who was helping her backstage. "The poor kid'll be stage struck forever."

An hour later the show was over. And apart from a few minor mishaps—and a major one when a twelve-foot flat fell on top of the chipmunks—it was adjudged by one and all a roaring success. Amy got a standing ovation and stood there in the spotlights, squinting and grinning and a little dazed. Kay Neumark dragged Ed up onto the stage and he got a standing ovation too.

Julia watched him from the wings with tears streaming down her face and clapping so hard that her hands hurt. He stood there in his smart black shirt, buttoned to the neck, smiling and bowing and spreading his arms to include the whole cast in the applause, cameras flashing in the lenses of his sunglasses. The cast was applauding him too.

What a guy, Julia thought. What an amazing guy I married.

WELL, IT MIGHT NOT BE BROADWAY, Ed thought, but it still felt pretty damn wonderful all the same. They wouldn't stop clapping. He reached out and called for Amy and felt her hot little hand find his and everybody cheered even louder. He bent down and kissed her.

"What a star," he whispered.

"Did I do okay?"

"Yeah. You did okay."

It took at least another hour before they could even think of going home. Ed felt himself in danger of being kissed to death, but it wasn't a bad way to go if you had to. Everybody wanted to congratulate him. Someone gave him a bunch of flowers and even Mrs. Leitner gave him a kiss. Julia's mom became everybody's best friend and his own mother almost had to drag her away to their taxi, which Ed had booked so that they didn't have to hang around.

Now, at last, the auditorium was almost clear and while Julia helped the last few kids into their coats and sent them off with their parents, Ed and Kay sat on the front of the stage, sipping water out of plastic cups and going over a few things that needed fixing for tomorrow's performance.

Now that he was allowed to, Ed was starting to wilt. Before the show Julia had made sure that he had his insulin shot and sent out for some steak sandwiches and milk shakes. During the show he'd had this odd, dull ache in his chest and it was still there now. It was probably just indigestion from the onion rings that had come with the sandwiches. Onions sometimes did that to him nowadays. The show had used up a lot of his energy and he knew that he should eat something because he was finding it hard to concentrate on what Kay was saying about how best to avoid another accident with the chipmunks. He'd found a candy bar in his bag but was having trouble unwrapping it.

"Want me to help with that?" Kay said at last.

"Oh, yeah. Thanks. I'm all fingers and thumbs."

"Are you feeling all right?"

"Just a little tired."

"Listen, we can talk about this in the morning."

"Maybe that'd be better."

She went to fetch his coat and when Ed stood up to put it on he felt weak at the knees and swayed a little.

"Whoa there," Kay said, supporting him. "You sure you're all right?"

"I'm fine. It's been a long day."

"You can say that again."

"It's been a long day."

Kay laughed. By the time Julia and Amy came to find him, he felt steadier.

Outside it was snowing again. Julia said the parking lot was icy and treacherous and made him wait just inside the door with Amy while she went to get the Jeep. They stood holding hands, saying goodnight to the last few parents and children who came past. The indigestion was still there in his chest and even after eating the candy bar he still felt a little weird. Kind of fuddled and detached. Maybe he was getting the flu or something. Never mind, he would soon be home. A good night's sleep was all he needed.

"Daddy, your hand's so cold!" Amy said.

"Well, you know what they say—cold hand, warm heart."

"Mine's hot. Does that mean I've got a cold heart?"

"No. Doesn't work that way. Hey, you were so good tonight."

"Could you hear me?"

"Not at all."

"You could too!"

"You sang like an angel. Like a logger-angel."

"Come on, here's Mommy."

The snow was indeed treacherous. He slipped and almost fell while Amy led him the few yards to the truck. Julia got out and came hurrying around to help him. She didn't often treat him like an invalid but when she did it annoyed the hell out of him.

"I don't need help."

"It's slippy. You nearly fell. Ed? Look at me."

"I'm okay."

"You don't look it. What's going on? Ed, talk to me."

"Don't fuss. I'm tired, that's all. Let's just get Shirley Temple here back to her bed."

"Who's Shirley Temple?" Amy asked.

He was just starting to tell her when suddenly the pain in his chest exploded. It was as if someone had shot him or stabbed him or jabbed him with a cattle prod. He reeled backward and heard Amy cry out in alarm.

He must have blacked out for a few moments because the next thing he knew, Julia was shaking him by his coat lapels and slapping his face and yelling at him. The pain in his chest wasn't so bad now. Just a weird flooding feeling. He seemed to be lying on his back in the snow because he could feel it all cold on the back of his head and on the palms of his hands beside him and could feel the flakes landing soft and wet on his face. He imagined what they must look like, floating down at him out of the sky and for some reason he remembered as a child being driven by his father one night through a snowstorm and the sight of the snowflakes in the headlights and imagining that he was traveling through space, with all the stars and planets and asteroids gliding past. Man, did he feel sleepy. The snow seemed to be drifting over him, burying him. . . .

Julia was calling him from somewhere far away. He could only just hear her. And he could hear Amy crying and Julia shouting for her to go get help and suddenly there were several pairs of hands grabbing him and hoisting his shoulders and he was being dragged backward, his feet trailing after him through the snow. One of his shoes came off and he felt the cold of the snow on his heel above his sock. Nobody seemed to have noticed. Damn, they were his best shoes too. He tried to call out to tell them about it but he couldn't find his voice. What the hell were they playing at? It was all such a pain in the ass. All he wanted to do was sleep. If they would just leave him alone and let him sleep, he'd be fine.

THEY DIDN'T HAVE TO SAY IT. Julia already knew. She knew he was dead even before the ambulance pulled up outside the hospital and the emergency team medics came running out into the snow to meet them. Huddled in the corner of the ambulance, she'd watched the paramedics battling to start his heart, thumping his pale chest and injecting him and yelling instructions to each other over his limp body and his face fading a ghostly gray beneath the oxygen mask. She'd told them about his diabetes and dialysis as soon as they arrived at the school and in the ambulance occasionally they'd fired questions at her which she did her best to answer in a steady voice. And all the while she was praying:

Dear Lord, no more. Please, no more. Hasn't the poor guy suffered enough? Just give him a break, please. Even Job got a break in the end.

Kay Neumark had arrived with Amy just as they were wheeling him in through the doors and Julia ran and gathered the girl up and hugged her and told her, stupidly, not to worry, Daddy was going to be all right, he'd be all right.

Julia had wanted to follow the stretcher into the emergency room but one of the nurses stopped her and said it would be better if she waited here with Amy and so they'd sat with Kay and several strangers in the cold fluorescent light, holding onto each other and watching the green figures moving to and fro behind the frosted glass of the doors through which they had taken him.

And now one of the medics had emerged and was speaking to the nurse at the desk and she nodded across the room toward Julia and Amy and he turned and started to walk toward them. And Julia thought, *how do I do this? No one's told me how to do this.* She stood up and made Amy wait with Kay and she swallowed hard and walked toward him.

He was sorry, he said. They'd done all they could. He was so, so sorry.

THEY BURIED HIM the Tuesday before Christmas on a crisp and clear morning with fresh snow frosted to the branches of the cottonwoods that circled the graveyard. More than two hundred people came, crowding shoulder to shoulder into the little white clapboard church with the sun streaming in upon them through the windows. Beside the pulpit there was a tall Christmas tree strewn with silver tinsel and winking with hundreds of tiny white lights.

Ed's father and brothers and their wives and children had all flown in from Kentucky and there were doctors, nurses, smoke jumpers, old college friends, pupils and their parents and many others Julia didn't recognize. Almost everyone who loved him. Except Connor.

She had tried to reach him and left messages everywhere she could think of, asking him to call. No one seemed to know where he was or how to contact him, not even his own mother, who was here now, sitting next to Ed's parents. Julia had called the photo agency and was put through to a man with a kind voice who told her that he had no idea where Connor was. He was a law unto himself these days, the man said with a sigh, always secretive about his projects. There was no way of contacting him for he had long ago ditched his satellite phone and scanner; he didn't even have an e-mail address; sometimes he would send back film or call in but mostly he didn't; often he went missing for months.

Listening to this, Julia felt a confusion of anger and guilt rise within her. How could Connor have become like this? How could she—how could they all—have allowed this to happen? And when the man finally asked if there was any message if he did happen to call in, she let her feelings spill.

"Just tell him his best friend died."

The service started with everyone singing "Silent Night," Ed's favorite carol. Then Amy and a choir of others from the school show sang the angels' song unaccompanied, with Kay Neumark conducting.

Julia watched her daughter's face and marveled at her strength and courage, for she herself felt neither. Linda, sitting beside her, was squeezing her hand hard and both of them were trying not to cry, though almost everybody else was. Julia knew that if she started she wouldn't be able to stop. There had been enough crying already and anyhow she knew from Ed's letter that he wanted a celebration not a mourning.

The letter had arrived from his lawyer in Missoula three days ago. The lawyer explained that Ed had lodged it with him last fall with instructions that it be given to her in the event of his death. Julia made sure that she was alone when she opened it.

My darling Julia,

It may strike you as strange that I should have done this, but, as Forrest Gump might put it, life is a tightrope and you never know when you're going to topple off. I didn't want to hit the floor without saying a few things that need to be said. And, although it sounds dumb, I guess what I feel most needs saying is: Thank You.

Since that rainy night all those years ago when you stole my parking space—and my heart—I've never stopped thinking how incredibly lucky I was to meet such a remarkable woman. To list the million things I have to thank you for would take too long, so I'll just stick to the Big Ones.

Thank you for being my eyes, for being my guardian angel, for being the light of my life and the inspiration of my every good thought. For being the wondrous mother of a wondrous child. For being beautiful and loving and sexy and for smelling and feeling so good (mmm, pause for reflection . . . MMM. Okay, Tully, that's enough of that!). Thank you too for being so bighearted and generous and forgiving and patient and positive and so full of energy . . . are you blushing? I do hope so, you look so gorgeous when you blush.

I guess what I'm saying, to wrap it all up, is simply thank you for being who you are and for allowing me to share your life.

So those are the thank-yous.

That just leaves the things I want to say sorry for. So here goes.

I'm sorry for not having achieved in my work what maybe you once thought I would. I had it all worked out—the palace in the Hollywood Hills, arriving in my tux at the Oscars with you on my arm in some fabulous gold creation by Armani or whoever, smiling glamorously at the cameras. And all you ended up with was a little log cabin and a pair of muddy hiking boots. As one tree said to the other: ain't life a beech?

I'm sorry too for being such a pain in the ass, so impatient and demanding and grouchy and for getting mad at you for fussing over me when all you were trying to do was keep this poor ungrateful jerk alive. I'm sorry for being manic and telling so many bad jokes you'd already heard a hundred times over and for all those dreadful ideas for musicals—though now I come to think of it, that one about . . . just kidding. And I'm sorry I haven't been able to DO more with you, to travel more, to climb more mountains and canoe more rivers and ski more powder. Okay, under the circumstances, we've done a lot, but not as much as I know you'd have liked.

Most of all, I'm sorry I wasn't able to give you all those children we should have had. I had in mind at least a dozen. Well, okay, three or four. But maybe the fact that I couldn't has made Amy even more special. (What a dork! As if that were possible!)

While we're on the subject, I'm sorry that I deprived you of Connor. I know you loved him and probably still do. I may be blind but not to that. I always knew. I tried so hard not to be jealous, but jealousy is such a goddamned tenacious creature, like a terrier that locks its jaws on your ankle and won't be shaken off. And I'm sorry that I wasn't able to be a bigger man and to get my head around it, for all of us have lost out through my driving him away.

If it's not too late and if it makes you and Amy happy, perhaps you and Connor will find each other again one day. If so, you have my blessing. Your happiness—and Amy's—is all I pray for.

I love you so much, Julia.
Ed

Amy had finished singing now and when she came back Julia kissed her and settled her between herself and Linda and they all held hands while the preacher spoke about Ed. He was a tall man in his mid-fifties with white hair and a craggy brow that gave him the look of an Old Testament prophet. Ed had occasionally helped out with the music for church services and the two of them had gotten along well and even done some hiking together. He told the congregation that Ed was one of the finest, bravest souls that he'd ever had the honor of knowing and had touched the lives of all he met with light and joy.

One of Ed's pupils then played a piano piece that Ed had once composed for him as a birthday present. And then it was Julia's turn. She walked to the solitary sound of her own footsteps to the lectern at the front of the church and unfolded the sheet of paper that had been enclosed with Ed's letter.

The title of the poem was "Walk Within You," and whether Ed had written it himself or had found it somewhere and copied it down, there was no indication. The tone and sensibility seemed like his but there were certain things in it that suggested whoever wrote it had not been blind. She had worried whether it was appropriate to read it out to everyone. But Amy wanted her to, so she was going to try. Julia raised her head and looked out at all the faces watching and waiting, half lit by the angling sun. There was perfect silence. She cleared her throat and began.

If I be the first of us to die,
Let grief not blacken long your sky.
Be bold yet modest in your grieving.
There is a change but not a leaving.
For just as death is part of life,
The dead live on forever in the living.
And all the gathered riches of our journey,
The moments shared, the mysteries explored,
The steady layering of intimacy stored,
The things that made us laugh or weep or sing,
The joy of sunlit snow or first unfurling of the spring,
The wordless language of look and touch,
The knowing,
Each giving and each taking,
These are not flowers that fade,
Nor trees that fall and crumble,

Nor are they stone,
For even stone cannot the wind and rain
withstand
And mighty mountain peaks in time reduce to
sand.
What we were, we are.
What we had, we have.
A conjoined past imperishably present.
So when you walk the woods where once we
walked together
And scan in vain the dappled bank beside you for
my shadow,
Or pause where we always did upon the hill to
gaze across the land,
And spotting something, reach by habit for my
hand,
And finding none, feel sorrow start to steal upon
you,
Be still.
Close your eyes.
Breathe.
Listen for my footfall in your heart.
I am not gone but merely walk within you.

TWENTY-FOUR

THEY GATHERED driftwood from along the shore and carried or dragged it back to the hollow that they had made for the fire. The wood was mostly stripped of bark and bleached by sun and salt to the color of bone and once when Connor bent to lift what he thought was a branch he found instead that he had chanced upon the skeleton of some great creature half buried in the sand. He asked Kocha what it was and the old man said it was a whale. Sometimes they lost their bearings and beached themselves, he said, and sometimes they died at sea and were washed ashore, though it wasn't for these bones, but for those of shipwrecked sailors that the place was named the Skeleton Coast.

They built the fire but didn't light it, and the two of them sat on the sand with the great dunes aglow behind them and watched the sun sink vast and trembling through the salt haze and into the slate-gray ocean. Connor watched the glow of the horizon fade and one by one the stars puncture the indigo sky. With the darkness came a cold breeze from the ocean and Kocha lit the fire. The wood was dry and burned with a hunger and they stood clear, watching the fanned flames dance and flatten and dance again, sending sparks whirling away into the heavens. When the fire had settled, they spitted the fish that Kocha had caught and ate it with the last of the rice.

They had known each other for barely a week but it seemed much longer. Heading slowly north in the car he had rented in Cape Town, Connor had stopped at a roadside store for water. He had never been to Namibia before but had long ago heard of the Skeleton Coast and wanted to see it. For reasons that he hadn't stopped to analyze, he wanted to reach it on foot. He asked the storekeeper if he knew of anyone who might act as his guide and the man said he did and told him to come back the next day.

Kocha was waiting on the porch at dawn the next morning with a small backpack and an ancient Lee-Enfield rifle. He was under five feet tall and dressed in a tattered khaki shirt and pants that hung in folds from his birdlike frame. He had a haze of gray hair and a face like a weathered walnut into which his eyes all but disappeared when he smiled. He shook Connor's hand and looked into his eyes for a long time, nodding as if he understood something. Inside, while Connor bought provisions, the storekeeper told him that Kocha was a Bushman who many years ago had worked as a tracker for wealthy white hunters. His English was good, the man said, and nobody knew the land better.

The storekeeper drove them out into the desert in his own truck and left them on the brink of a lush green valley many feet below. He wished them luck and went and they stood awhile and watched the red cloud of his wake catch the climbing sun and slowly drift and dissolve until he was gone and a silence deeper than any Connor had ever known settled upon them.

The chill of the dawn was gone now and as the sun rose higher the immense plain of red gravel that stretched to every horizon began to liquefy with mirage. Below them in the valley, however, the mist still curled among the trees and they shouldered their packs and Kocha his rifle with its sling of frayed webbing and began their descent.

The valley snaked east to west in a broad green band as far as the eye could see. Kocha told him that it marked the course of an underground river which rose in the highlands many miles to the east but soon grew shy and hid beneath the gypsum crust and lichen-covered gravel. Now and then, as if to check that it was headed in the right direction, it would boldly bubble up among the trees and shrubs and for a few hundred yards run clear and cool and confident over shelves of russet rock and then vanish once more into the sand.

Many animals lived in the valley of the invisible river. Over the days and nights that followed they saw kudu and gemsbok and giraffe and zebra. On their third evening while they were making camp, Kocha heard something and told Connor quietly to come and they stole among the trees and, sheltering downwind behind some rocks, watched a small herd of elephant drinking and drenching each other at a water hole.

Sometimes, sitting by their campfire after dark, they would see hyena slinking in the shadows, their eyes glinting pale and ghostly in the firelight. And once they heard the rasping cough of a leopard and in the morning found its tracks circling not twenty yards from where they had slept. Kocha, who slept—if indeed he slept at all—with his rifle beside him, said he had seen the animal and met its eyes and knew that it meant them no harm.

The old man knew the name of every beast and bird and insect and plant, though some he knew only by the names the Bushmen gave them. The language of his people was unlike any Connor had heard, with strange clicking sounds that he tried to imitate but always failed, reducing Kocha to fits of helpless laughter. Kocha taught him many things about how the creatures that lived here survived the unforgiving heat and drought. How sandgrouse would douse their feathers with water and then fly many miles to give it to their young and how the dune beetle would stand for hours to let the mist condense upon its back, then dance to make the droplets slide into its mouth. He showed Connor how a man could survive by finding water in the tubers of plants and in secret wells that you sipped through long and hollow grasses from beneath the parched earth.

At night, sitting by the fire, Connor would ask him to tell some of his people's stories. How Kaang the Creator, who often took the form of a praying mantis, made the moon by tossing an old shoe into the sky and how the Milky Way was made by the ash of a fire tossed there to light the way home for hunters and how once all animals were friends with man and spoke his language until he frightened them with fire and they were stricken dumb and fled.

And Connor sensed that, more than the sum of all the things he learned, a lesson far greater was being disclosed, though what it was he was unable yet to say.

He had been traveling now for many months. When he fled New York, he had been closer to madness than he had ever been or hoped to be again. He left with no plan, simply with an overwhelming urge to escape, though from what he still wasn't sure, except that it was connected in some way with what the woman Beatrice had said to him that night at the gallery and the vision of himself that she had made him see in his photographs. For no other reason than that it was pretty much the farthest he could go, he had flown first to Australia. From there he had traveled in a slow curve north and west, through Southeast Asia and India and finally back to the continent that now seemed forever lodged within him, by ship across the Indian Ocean, to Africa.

He lived simply, sleeping under the stars whenever he could and traveling as the whim took him, though always to places that he had never before visited. He neither sought company nor shunned it, except that of those with loud opinions. And uncannily, again and again, he had found himself with people such as Kocha, who were linked in some ancient way to the land that they inhabited and who seemed to know time and space and man's place within both as if by some extra sense.

In what precise way these encounters and indeed his whole journey had changed him, Connor could not say. But he knew they had. It showed in his face. On those rare occasions that he bothered to shave, he was startled by the sight of himself in the mirror. He had grown thin and bony and his hair was long and tousled and bleached white by the sun. His sunburnt skin stretched tightly over his cheekbones and his pale eyes above them peered back at him like a stranger's. Perhaps it should have disturbed him, but it didn't. For it matched the inner change, the feeling that he was being slowly purged of some dark organic need that had lain curled and feeding within him for years. Where once it had been, now there was clear space. And although the scar tissue was raw and tender, he knew it was healing. Still, of course, there were times when the horrors he had seen returned to haunt him and other times when he felt the ache of losing those he loved. But he knew that these feelings were but clouds that passed and that the vessel of what, for want of a better word, he could only call his soul, though scoured and almost empty, was sound.

On leaving New York he had packed only one small bag of camera gear but despite all the extraordinary sights he had seen, he had rarely opened it. He had taken a few pictures of landscapes and temples, the kind of pictures tourists took. But never once had he photographed the face of another human being.

How much of this inner journey Kocha sensed in him, Connor didn't know. Their days had been spent very much in the moment and they had hardly talked of the past or of the facts of their personal lives. Kocha had told him about a wife, long dead, and their many children who lived somewhere far away to the east. Connor had shown him his little laminated photos of Julia and Amy but hadn't gone into any detail, nor had Kocha asked for any. Yet he suspected that the old man knew many truths without needing to be told.

Two days ago, Kocha had woken him before dawn and led him up and out of the valley. He gave no reason and Connor didn't ask for one. They walked in the cold unfolding light across the gravel plain toward a great tower of jagged rock that rose from the desert like some ancient rusting citadel. It took them an hour to reach it and by then the rising sun had set its flanks aflame. And standing at its foot and gazing up at it and at the pair of black eagles that soared silently across its battlements, Connor somehow knew that there was a secret here to be divulged.

They climbed for almost an hour, more through narrow twists and gullies with lizards skittering before them and watching with unblinking eyes from the shadows as they passed. The last gully was steep and treacherous and then suddenly the mountain opened like a flower and they were standing in a circular chamber of rock, one half shadowed and the other aglow like molten iron in the sun's slant glare.

The walls were ten or twelve feet tall and the floor was littered with rock. Connor figured that the place had once been a cave whose roof had since collapsed. The air was still and hot and the only sound was his own labored breathing. Kocha lifted an arm and gestured toward the walls and for a moment, Connor didn't understand why. He shielded his eyes from the sun and stepped closer.

Then he saw. The walls were covered in paintings in black and red and white. There were animals of many kinds, elephant and giraffe and zebra, and lion and cheetah and leopard chasing them and men with spears and bows and arrows. And interlaced among them were patterns and symbols, some clearly inspired by the tracks of the various creatures but others more difficult to decipher. He asked Kocha what these others meant and the old man smiled and said that they were ancient maps of the desert, many centuries old, and that they depicted places where certain animals and plants were to be found and the rivers and water holes and landmarks, some long swallowed by the sand.

Connor walked the circle of the walls with a mounting sense of wonder. The sun was at his back and his shadow moved slowly before him across the painted rock like a curtain of constant revelation. Then, at the exact point where the sunlit rock gave way to shadow, he saw an image that made him suddenly stop and his heart lurch and a shiver prickle the back of his neck.

It was a painting of fire. There was a grove of burning trees and bushes, and standing before them, as if he had just emerged, was a horned animal. It was no doubt meant to be some kind of large antelope, a gemsbok perhaps, or a kudu. But it might as well have been an elk, for its horns and its coat were alive with flames.

Connor stared at it in disbelief. He wanted to

ask Kocha about it but it took some time before he could trust himself to speak.

"Do you know what this is?" he said at last.

Kocha replied in his own tongue, a single word with the clicking sound. But this time Connor didn't attempt to repeat it. Kocha went on.

"Maybe you would call it the Flame Spirit."

"Is it a good spirit or an evil one?"

"It is neither good nor evil. Like fire itself. My people have a story which I will tell you. But now the day grows hot and we must go back to the shade of the valley."

Kocha didn't tell him the story that night, as Connor had expected. Nor the next. And he began to wonder if the old man had forgotten. But he didn't remind him, for in his heart there was a trace of fear that the story might turn out to be one that he would regret having heard.

But now they had reached the ocean and their journey was all but done. And with the mantis shoe moon curving high across it and the chill air filled with the rhythmic thunder and draw of the waves, Kocha leaned forward and the glow of the fire glinted in his black eyes and unprompted he began.

"Long ago, after Kaang made the world and every creature that lived there, he gave to men the gift of fire. But men grew greedy and disobedient and fought among themselves. So, to punish them, Kaang decided to take back his gift and he sent the Flame Spirit in the shape of a great kudu to run around and scoop all their fires onto his horns and bring them to him.

"Tchue, who was a great hunter and leader of his people, saw Kudu doing this and shot him in the heart with his bow and arrow. Kaang was very angry and demanded that Tchue make amends by giving to Kudu his own heart. 'But how am I live without a heart?' Tchue asked. Kaang plucked a stone from the ground and said, 'This shall be your heart.' So Tchue delivered up his heart and put the stone in its place and returned to his people.

"But because the stone was so heavy, he could no longer hunt and feed his people and they turned against him and banished him. For many years he wandered alone, eating only flies and what the crows and the jackals left. One day Kaang spied him drinking from a river and, still angry with him, hurled a bolt of lightning at him. The bush all around Tchue caught fire and the only escape was across the river. The river flowed fast and dangerously. There were some stepping stones but the nearest one had been swept away. Tchue thought that if he used every last bit of his strength he might just be able to leap to the next one.

"As he was about to jump he heard a terrible wailing and he looked down and there was a praying mantis sitting at the water's edge. 'Help me, help me!' he cried. 'Or I will drown or perish in the fire!' Tchue offered to carry him, but warned him that even with the little extra weight, he might not be able to make the jump. 'Then find another stone, you fool!' shouted the ungrateful mantis (who, of course, was really Kaang).

"Tchue looked around but there were no stones to be seen and the fire was burning closer and closer. Then he remembered the stone that was his heart. And he took it from his chest and tossed it into the water to make the first stepping stone. Without so much as a thank-you, the mantis hopped onto it and scampered across all the other stones to the far side where he disappeared into the bush.

"Tchue tried to follow, but because he now had no heart at all, he had not even the strength to make it to the first stone, his own heart. And he sank to his knees and prepared to die in the fire. Then, behind him, in the burning bushes, he heard a sound and he looked up and saw the Flame Spirit, with his blazing horns, standing over him. He had been sent by Kaang and he gathered Tchue up and put him on his back and carried him over the river to safety.

"And because Tchue had shown such great courage and generosity, Kaang forgave him and broke off a piece of Kudu's fiery horn and placed it in his chest for a heart. And Tchue went home to his people and they welcomed him as a great hero. And, with Kaang's blessing, he lit their fires again with his heart.

"And that is why when you see a kudu, you will notice how his horns have been twisted by the heat and that he bears the mark of the flames upon his sides."

He paused awhile and smiled and looked deep into Connor's eyes.

"I think maybe you know this story."

Connor shook his head.

"Not until now. Thank you."

They sat for a long time staring into the embers of the fire and spoke no more. Before they turned in, they stacked the fire with the rest of the driftwood. The wind had dropped and the flames rose without waver into the night and the two men stood back and watched. Just as the fire was settling, Kocha gently touched him on the elbow and made a little gesture with his chin and Connor turned and looked where he was bade. It took a while for his eyes to grow accustomed to the dark. But then he saw it. Some thirty yards along the shore, beyond the moonlit cage of the whale's bones, a lion stood staring back at them with mirrored eyes.

He was an old male and even by the modest light of moon and fire, Connor could see that his coat and mane were past their prime. But his manner more than made up for it and he studied them both with a regal disdain, swishing his tail from side to side. How long they stayed like that, Connor couldn't say, for time seemed suspended. Then, with a final flourish of his tail, the lion turned and made his stately way up the shore and into the dunes.

At the edge of darkness he stopped and stared back at them one last time over his shoulder. And then he turned away and was gone.

TWENTY-FIVE

JULIA PUT on the leather gauntlets, lowered the visor of her hardhat and picked up the chainsaw.

"Okay, buddy. Keep that rope taut, do you hear?"

Amy nodded. She was standing about twelve feet away, holding onto the other end of the rope that was attached to the post that Julia was about to cut down. She leaned back and took the strain and grinned.

"What are you smirking at?" Julia said.

"You. You look so funny."

"I think I look pretty darned cool."

"You look hot. You're all sweaty and yucky."

"Well, thank you, Missy Prissy. Okay, get ready."

She yanked the cord and the chainsaw spluttered and roared into life. It was a hot August afternoon and she was indeed all sweaty and yucky. A job that she had expected to take a couple of hours had taken almost the whole day. They were removing the posts of the old rope rail that Ed had always used to find his way to the river. But they had found them so securely rooted in cement that each one required a major excavation. Amy had suggested they simply cut the posts as close to the ground as possible and leave the cement footings in the ground. But Julia wanted to dig them out. Otherwise they would forever be tripping over the stumps.

Starting down by the river, they had worked their way up toward the house, refining their teamwork and technique as they went. The post through which Julia was sawing now was the last. The symbolic significance of the job wasn't lost on either of them.

People were full of wise advice about the big issues that surrounded the death of a loved one. There were books galore about the importance of proper mourning and about the open resolution of grief and guilt and anger. But it was the little things, the trivial details, that Julia found so perplexing. When was the right time to remove Ed's coats from the pegs by the door? And his muddy boots and his cane from the corner? And should she discuss it with Amy or do it furtively so that they could both pretend not to have noticed? Perhaps time alone was the judge of these things.

The first six months had been a matter of plain survival for both of them. When the shock wave of Ed's death subsided, it left Julia feeling oddly separate from everyone and everything but Amy. They clove to each other like abandoned creatures in a nest and when Julia peeped out at the world it was as if she saw it through a cold haze. She had always known, of course, that Ed's life hung by thinner strings than most, that with his diabetes there was always the chance of some perverse and potentially fatal new glitch. But she realized now that deep down she had always thought of the likelihood as remote, almost academic, like the chance of life being discovered on another planet. Perhaps she had done this to protect herself and Amy. Or perhaps it was because Ed's lust for life, his energy and optimism were simply so great that they masked the reality, for how could a man so vividly alive be at any real risk?

During those first cold months, it hadn't occurred to her to start removing or rearranging his things. It was crazy, she knew, but it seemed perfectly possible that one day he might reappear, as if nothing had happened, that she might come home one afternoon and there he would be, beaming at her from the piano, asking her in one of his impromptu librettos what kind of day she'd had. Even if it had occurred to her to move his things, it would have struck her as sacrilegious.

So his clothes stayed in the closet, his shaving things in the bathroom cabinet, his sheets of music still stacked on the lid of the piano, which Amy rarely played anymore. Julia understood why and didn't push her, hoping that in time she would come back to it. Meanwhile, the piano stood like a solemn black mausoleum, gathering a dust of memories on its closed lid. And as the months passed, so the echo of its silence grew ever more deafening.

On the night Ed died Amy had slept in Julia's bed and she'd slept there ever since. Again, Julia worried if this was right, if it would somehow hamper the child's independence. But the truth was, they both enjoyed the comfort and the company, enjoyed having someone to hug in the middle of a cold night when either one of them felt lonely or sad. At weekends they would have breakfast in bed and lounge there half the morning sometimes, reading their books and chatting. And it was while doing that this morning that Julia had casually floated the idea of removing the rope rail. It was no big deal, she said, but maybe it would give them more space, for Frisbee and ball games and so on.

"Would we get a man in to do it?"

"A *man*? Are you kidding? This is no job for a man. You and me, sister. The gals is gonna do it."

Amy grinned. "Cool."

"You don't think it matters that it was, you know, well, Daddy's thing?"

"Do you?"

"No."

"Nor me. He'd say it was the right thing to do."

Now, six hours later, the chainsaw was almost through the last post.

"Okay!" Julia yelled. "Get ready. Here she goes!"

"Timber!"

The post toppled slowly and as it landed on the grass with a thump, they both cheered. Julia killed the chainsaw and when its noise subsided they heard the phone ringing.

"Honey, would you get that?"

Amy ran up onto the deck and into the house while Julia took off her hardhat and, picking up the spade, started to dig around the foot of the post to loosen the cement footing.

"Mommy? It's for you."

From her voice, Julia knew there was something special about the call. She took off the gauntlets and stepped up onto the deck.

"Who is it?"

"I think he said he was your dad."

"Well, there's a thing."

She made a comical face and ruffled Amy's hair as she walked past her toward the deck doors, trying to look unruffled. In fact her heart was doing cartwheels. She hadn't heard from him in five years and it was probably more like fifteen since she had last seen him. When they invited him to the wedding, he had written back with some feeble excuse. He had never met Ed and never met Amy, his only granddaughter. By the time Julia picked up the phone, she was already seething.

"Hello?"

"Julia?"

"Yes, who is this?" It was mean, but she couldn't resist it.

"It's your father."

"Oh. Hi."

"Hi. How are you?"

Julia laughed. "Well, I'm just . . . Completely fine, thanks. How're you?"

"I'm okay. That was Amy, I imagine."

Imagine. Of course, that's all he could do, never having laid eyes on her.

"Yep. That was your granddaughter."

There was a pause. She wasn't going to make it easier for him by filling it.

"So, listen. I'm calling from Seattle."

"Oh, nice."

"Yeah, I'm over here for a couple of days on business. And, well, I wondered if I might hop on a plane and come down and visit with you."

It almost floored her. She couldn't think what to say. She looked around and saw Amy standing in the doorway, watching and listening.

"Of course," her father went on, "if it's inconvenient or you'd rather I didn't, I'd absolutely understand."

"No. Well. I mean, God, it's just been such a long time."

"I know. I'm sorry."

There was another pause, while Julia's mind scrolled on overdrive through all the conflicting emotions he had managed to stir with so few words.

"Listen," he went on. "I know how you must be feeling—"

"Please don't presume to know how I feel," she snapped.

"I'm sorry. I didn't mean that. Look, maybe it was a bad idea to call."

"I don't even know where you live nowadays!"

"I know."

"I mean . . . Jesus!"

She was about to ask who the hell he thought he was, calling out of the blue like this and thinking he could just breeze into their lives when it suited him. Then she turned and looked again at Amy and saw how worried she looked at hearing all this. She reached out an arm and Amy came over and nestled against her. Julia took a deep breath and said quietly into the phone:

"Come."

"Are you sure?"

"Yes. Come and see us. We'd like you to."

He flew in the following evening.

His hair was completely white and he was shorter and slighter than she remembered him. She had worked out that he must be in his mid- to late fifties but he was still a good-looking man. Above all, she remembered the crooked smile and the blue, faintly melancholy eyes. He saw her as soon as he came through the arrivals gate and headed toward where she stood with Amy tucked under her arm.

On the way to the airport and all the time they had been waiting, Julia had been lecturing herself not to cry when they met and as he drew near she could see he was fighting tears and she guessed that he had probably made the same resolution. He hugged her tightly and for a long time, neither of them saying a word, and the smell of him came back to her and it was that, more than anything, that nearly set her weeping. But they both just about held out.

She introduced him to Amy, who squirmed and gave him a coy grin. He clearly didn't know whether or not to kiss her and so he took her hand and held it in both of his and Amy, whose subtle reading of such emotional quandaries never failed to amaze Julia, reached up and kissed him on the cheek.

On the way home he sat pivoted in his seat, talking mostly to Amy in the back, about his trip and how he had been in Vancouver a few days ago and seen a rare white whale there in the zoo. He asked her about her school and she told him how she'd started horseback riding and was learning how to lope and gave him the names and descriptions of all the horses at the stables. By the time they reached home, the two of them were already friends and, while Julia made supper, Amy took him on a tour of the house, then led him down to the river.

Watching them from the deck while she set the table, Amy chattering away and holding his hand and her father in his faded denim shirt looking down at her, hanging on the girl's every word, Julia had a vision of herself at Amy's age, walking and talking with him in the park and feeling so protected and proud of him and proud too of herself to be treated seriously, not like some silly kid but like a grown-up whose views on life were just as valid as his own.

The cement footings of the rope-rail posts were still lying on the grass. Julia heard Amy telling him that they had turned out to be too heavy to shift and that Mom had been forced to concede that they did, after all, need to "get a man in" to move them. It was a hint as broad as it was unintended and when they came back into the house, Julia's father said he would see to it in the morning.

Sitting out on the deck eating their steaks by candlelight, with Amy still gabbling away, it occurred to Julia that this was the first time she had ever cooked a meal for her father and how, strangely, she felt herself to be as much his parent as his child.

At bedtime Amy asked if he would come upstairs and read her a story and while he did, Julia cleared the dishes. She went upstairs just as he was saying goodnight.

"He's lovely," Amy whispered after he'd gone downstairs.

"Yeah. He is. And so are you."

When she came downstairs her father was sitting out at the table again, smoking a cigarette. He said he hoped Julia didn't mind and she said she didn't so long as she could have one too. He gave her one and lit it for her.

"She's a great kid," he said.

"Yeah. She is."

For a while neither of them spoke. It was he at last who broke the silence.

"Julia, there's so much I need to apologize for, I guess I don't know where to start."

"Why don't we just take it as said. I guess I'm just a little puzzled about why now, after all these years."

He stared at the table for a moment. Julia couldn't stand the taste of the cigarette and stubbed it out.

"Last year I got cancer. Skin cancer, a malignant melanoma."

Oh God, she thought. Please. Not another death. He must have read the thought in her face, for he went on quickly, stubbing out his cigarette too.

"No, I'm okay. They found it early. Well actually, Claudia, my wife—"

"I know who she is, Dad."

"Of course you do. Anyway, she found it. And they cut it out and I'm fine. Really I am. But these things make you stop and think. You know? About the important things in life. And, with you and me, I don't know, I realized I'd just been so dumb. To let things go so far. Let all that time slide by. Because the more you let slide, the harder it is to reach over it. Hell, I'm not saying it very well. . . ."

Julia reached out and took his hand.

"It's okay."

"No, it's not. Julia, I never met your husband, for Christsakes. I was never there for you when things were so hard for you. I can't even pretend I didn't know, because your mother always told me. She told me what a great guy Ed was and begged me to come to the wedding and Amy's christening, even to the . . . to Ed's funeral. But I'd just let it all go so far, let it all slide, and I was just too, I don't know, ashamed or something, yeah, ashamed, to get in touch. And, God forgive me, I am so, so sorry. I feel such a goddamn fool. Because here you are, so beautiful and wonderful and Amy too. And . . . Oh boy, I'm sorry."

He turned his head away and wiped his eyes. And Julia got up out of her seat and went to him and knelt beside his chair and put her arms around him and for a long time they held each other and wept.

"I wish I could have another go at it," he said. "I'd do better next time."

The next day he helped them clear the cement boulders of the post footings and fill in the holes and then cut the posts into firewood which they stacked in the barn. He was flying back to Seattle that afternoon and from there straight back to Europe. Julia and he had only a few more moments alone before he left. Amy had insisted on making them sandwiches for lunch and while she was in the kitchen doing that, Julia and her father sat on the deck drinking iced tea.

"It's a beautiful place you've got here," he said. "Do you see yourselves staying?"

"I don't know."

"Maybe you should travel a little. It's good to travel."

"Maybe we will."

"You could come and stay with us. See Europe."

Amy appeared in the doorway with the sandwiches.

"I want to go all around the world," she said.

They drove him to the airport where he made them promise to consider coming to stay with him and Claudia in Germany. It was sweet of him but Julia knew it would never happen and suspected that he knew it too.

His visit affected her deeply. It was as though a circle had been closed. In some mysterious way, it also seemed to release her, made her feel that it was time to take a step forward. A week later she gathered Ed's clothes and shoes and gave them to a charity store in town. She cleared his things from the bathroom cabinet and boxed all the sheets of music so that they could be stored tidily in the bookshelves. And she gave his specially adapted computer equipment to the local chapter of the Association for the Blind.

School started again for both of them and Julia tried to fire herself with a new enthusiasm for her work but found she couldn't. In class, she caught herself staring out of the window and having to ask her pupils to repeat questions that in her daydreams she hadn't heard. The prospect of another cold winter and another school year with all its cyclical familiarity depressed her.

She loved Montana and if Ed were still alive, she would have been perfectly content to go on calling it home. But the truth was, it had always been more his place than hers. She couldn't see herself spending the rest of her life there. Of course, it was Amy's place too, the only home she had ever known. But the girl was young enough and bright and secure enough to adapt anywhere. As the fall closed in and the days drew shorter, so Julia grew steadily more restless and convinced that it was time for some sort of new beginning.

In her new mode of tidying and clearing,

Julia had found some big boxes of photographs that for years she had promised herself to sift through and stick into albums. It was just the job for a cold and gloomy fall weekend and Amy was excited by the idea. They went into Missoula to buy six smart albums, came home and lit the fire and then settled in front of it on the floor with the photos spread around them.

Julia hadn't realized how ancient some of them were. Some even predated her meeting Ed. Amy found a batch of Julia and Linda dressed up as hookers for a fancy dress party in Boston and laughed so much that Julia thought the child was going to do herself an injury. Julia pretended to be indignant.

"I don't know what's so darned funny. That's how we always dressed in those days."

In one of the boxes there were photos that Julia had taken as reference for her painting and among them were those she had shot on her trip to Kenya, the summer before she met Ed. Amy was transfixed. They had talked about her African adventure before but Amy now wanted to know the story behind every picture and about everything else that Julia had seen and done while she was there. One of the pictures was of some lions lazing in a tree.

"Did you really get that close?"

"Uh-huh. We were in a truck, so, you know,

we were safe. Anyway, they eat so many tourists they get bored of the taste."

"Can we go to Africa one day?"

"I don't see why not. One day."

Not long afterward Julia was sorting through some old magazines and came across the one with Connor's article about St. Mary of the Angels, the rehabilitation center for child soldiers in Uganda. She put it aside and took it to bed that night and with Amy snuggled asleep beside her, read the piece again, trying not to rustle the pages as she turned them. She found herself staring for a long time at the picture of the ten-year-old boy, Thomas, so traumatized by what had happened to him that he could no longer speak.

The first time she had looked at it, a few months before Ed died, it had made her weep, but now it didn't. In the accompanying article Connor wrote that the center was mostly funded by a charitable organization based in Geneva but that its resources were sorely stretched and that there was a constant need for "both financial and practical help."

At first Julia thought maybe she could hold a fund-raising event at the school, get her pupils to write to the children at St. Mary's, even start some kind of sponsorship arrangement. Then she read the next sentence. It quoted Sister

Emily, the center director, saying that she was always short of "properly trained and qualified staff." It set Julia's mind whirring.

That was exactly her field. She thought of what Amy had said about wanting to go to Africa. She put the magazine down, switched off the light but couldn't switch off her head. She lay awake almost the entire night thinking about it.

For days she didn't mention it to anyone. It was an absurd idea. How could she uproot them both, take Amy out of school and go waltzing off with her to Africa? What about all the danger and disease? It was out of the question.

But try as she might, she couldn't shake the idea that somehow it was meant to be. What an extraordinary experience for a child it would be, to see another continent, to get to know another culture and another people. What a great adventure it could be for both of them. And it wasn't as if it was going to be forever. A few months, a year at the most. Like a long working vacation; like working for WAY in the old days. She wouldn't even have to give up her job at the school; Mrs. Leitner would let her take a sabbatical, she was sure. They could rent out the house, which would pay for the trip. And they would both come home with their lives enriched.

By churning all this in her mind for many days and nights, Julia managed to turn what had begun as a harebrained fantasy into a serious, worthwhile proposition, bursting with benefits for all concerned; something which wasn't merely possible but which positively demanded to be done.

She agonized about how best to broach the subject with Amy or whether she should mention it at all until she had checked things out more. In the end she came right out with it. They were having supper at the kitchen table, eating one of Amy's favorites, spaghetti with pesto sauce.

"Do you remember how you said you'd like to go to Africa?"

"Uh-huh."

"Did you really mean that?"

"Sure I did. Why?"

"Well, I've been thinking about it. Maybe we should."

"You mean, like, a vacation?"

"Well, yeah. We'd certainly have a vacation. We could do a safari, see all the animals."

"Hey, Mom! Are you serious? Wow!"

"But I was also thinking that maybe I could work there for a while."

"What, we'd, like, live there?"

"Maybe. Just for a while."

“How long?”

“I don’t know. A few months, maybe.”

“Where?”

Julia had the magazine ready and pushed it across the table. Amy glanced at it and went on eating her spaghetti.

“I already saw that. Is that where you’d work?”

“If they’d have me. Did you read it?”

“Sure. I always read Connor’s stuff. Is that where he lives?”

Julia laughed. “Oh, no. I think he was just visiting. I don’t know where he is right now. Where was that last postcard he sent you from?”

Amy frowned, wrinkling her little nose. “I think it was . . . India. Is Uganda like Kenya?”

“It’s right next door. People say it’s even more beautiful. They call it the Pearl of Africa.”

“The Pearl of Africa.”

“So, what do you think?”

“About what?”

“About you and me going to help these children in Uganda.”

“I get to help too?”

“Well, I’m sure there’s plenty to do.”

Amy shrugged. “Cool.”

“You mean you’d like to?”

“Sure. May I have some more spaghetti?”

Julia found the phone number of the charity

in Geneva and called them. An efficient-sounding woman with a French accent said yes, they did indeed need properly qualified counselors at St. Mary's, in fact at the moment they were desperate for them. She told Julia that the organization had an office in New York and gave her the address and number.

Julia called Linda in New York to get her reaction, half expecting to be told she was insane. Instead, Linda asked a couple of questions, weighed things up for about a second and a half and said, "Go for it, girl." Why not bring Amy to New York for Thanksgiving, she suggested. Julia could visit the charity's office and check things out.

What Julia forgot to say was that she hadn't breathed a word about the plan to her mother who, ever since she had heard about Julia's father coming to visit, had been a little snippy. When Julia called to say they were coming to New York, instead of sounding pleased, her mother immediately took offense that they would be staying at Linda's apartment in Greenwich Village rather than with her in Brooklyn. Julia tried to explain that as it was going to be Amy's first trip to New York since she was a baby, they wanted to be in Manhattan, in the thick of it, so that they could do the whole tourist bit—Empire State Building,

Statue of Liberty, ice skating in Rockefeller Plaza.

"You know," she added unwisely. "All those things I never did as kid."

"Was that my fault?" her mother snapped. "You never wanted to. Anyhow, you go ahead. Stay with Linda. I'm sure you'll be a lot more comfortable. It's fine."

Which of course meant that it was far from fine. Julia eventually managed to mollify her, the main concession being that they would come to her place for Thanksgiving dinner. Somewhat grudgingly, Linda was invited too.

Julia wrote the charity's New York office, enclosing a resumé. She agonized over whether or not to mention at this early stage that she would want to bring her eight-year-old daughter and decided it was best to come clean. A woman with a formal but friendly voice called her two days later. She said she hoped that Julia understood that St. Mary's was, technically, in a war zone (although for more than a year things had, in fact, been peaceful), that the food and accommodation were basic and that the pay was somewhat less than basic, in other words, none.

Julia asked about the possibility of bringing Amy and the woman said it was unusual but not unheard of. However, it would, of course, be entirely at Julia's own risk and she must understand that the organization could not in any way be held responsible for the girl. Julia said fine. They arranged the interview.

Thanksgiving had never been Julia's favorite holiday. What it mostly summoned were memories of family fights. All the uncles and aunts and cousins used to come and when they had finished decimating the turkey they traditionally turned on each other. This year, she hoped, would be different.

They flew into New York on the Wednesday evening and the following day Linda drove them through a cold rain in her new black BMW over the bridge to Brooklyn. It was where Julia had grown up, but even as she pointed out the local landmarks to Amy, recounting exploits from her youth, she felt oddly detached, as if she were talking about someone else's past. Her mother's little house, with its neat handkerchief of a backyard, looked much as it always had, but still Julia could find no connection with it, not even with her own bedroom, where some of her teenage paintings still hung on the walls and a huddle of cuddly toys eyed her reproachfully from the windowsill.

Her mother had invited Julia's cousin David and his family. Brad was a year older than Amy; Becky was five. Julia had always been close to David but had never really taken to his wife,

Liz. A pert little woman, always immaculately turned out, she worked as an office manager and treated the world as if it were part of her job. She mothered her children with an ostentatious perfection that always made Julia feel inadequate.

It was the first time they had seen each other since the funeral and Liz's manner, all these months later, was still laden with a cloying sympathy that made Julia wanted to scream *It's okay, Ed's dead but we're doing fine, so act normal for Christsake!* But instead she just smiled and smoldered. What made it worse was that Julia's mother, in her new role as The Hurt One, virtually ignored her while gushing over Liz, who, of course, had come at the crack of dawn to help with the cooking and had brought gifts for everyone and was altogether utterly goddamn angelic.

Wedged shoulder to shoulder around the table in the cramped dining room, they had almost finished eating when Linda dropped the bombshell about Julia's plan to go to Africa. Julia was too far away to kick her and before she could squash the conversation, her mother pounced.

"You're taking Amy and going to work in *Africa*?"

"Mom, it's just an idea."

"It's the most ridiculous idea I ever heard. You must be out of your mind."

"I'm sorry," Linda mouthed guiltily at Julia across the table. "I thought she knew."

"Africa!"

"Maria, I'm told it's really beautiful out there," David said.

"Do you mind if we don't talk about this right now?" Julia said, glancing at the children who, sensing a scrap among adults, were all eyes and ears.

"What's wrong with Africa, Grandma?" Amy asked.

"Africa's where they made *The Lion King,*" Becky declared with great authority.

"They did not," Brad said.

"They did too."

"*The Lion King* is a cartoon, dorkbrain. It's just drawings."

"Well, that's where they did the drawings. And I'm not a dorkbrain."

She tried to pinch his leg and he punched her on the arm and she howled. Amy wasn't paying any attention. Her eyes were fixed on Julia.

"Okay, you guys," Liz called out. "Who'd like more ice cream?"

All three children fell for the ruse and she led them diplomatically out into the kitchen and shut the door.

"Everybody in Africa has AIDS!" Julia's mother now announced.

"I think there are one or two who don't," David said, giving Julia a sly wink of sympathy.

"What do Ed's parents think? I mean, I assume you already told *them*."

The barb was justified. Julia had mentioned it to them on the phone, casually, only the other day.

"They think it's . . . exciting."

"Oh, really?"

"Yes, really. Mom, please. Let's not talk about this now. It probably won't even happen."

To say that Ed's parents were excited was literally true; excited as in aroused and agitated, although their reaction had been somewhat more demure. Ed used to say that his mother spoke with subtitles which often said exactly the opposite of what came out of her mouth. It was easier to read these subtitles when she was sitting in front of you, but over the years Julia had become adept at picking them up over the phone too. So when she'd called the other night and outlined the idea to Susan, giving it as benign a gloss as possible, she knew even from the length and weight of the pause that her mother-in-law thought she must have gone insane.

"Well, Julia. What a very *interesting* thing to want to do."

"You don't think it's crazy?"

"Crazy? Well, no, of course not. I mean, I'm sure you'll have considered all the possible risks of taking Amy to a place like that."

Julia replied in the measured, positive tone that she normally reserved for the parents of her most hapless students.

"Yes, of course. But they can be minimized. And I really believe that what she stands to gain from the experience outweighs whatever small risk there may be."

The conversation ended with Susan sighing and saying that she was sure Julia would decide for the best. Maybe Julia was being paranoid, but the subtitle of that suggested that her mother-in-law was off that very minute to see a judge about a restraining order.

By now Liz had shepherded the kids with their ice cream into the living room and sat them down in front of a video. Not to miss the fun of the fight, she had come back to the table. Side with my mother, Julia silently vowed, and you're dead meat. Her mother was like a dog with a bone. In the space of about five minutes she moved in a seamless segue from AIDS to malaria and from there to war and famine and snakes and crocodiles.

"What about the cannibals?" Julia muttered rhetorically.

Linda sniggered wickedly. Julia's mother gave her a withering look and then adjusted it to icy for Julia.

"I'm sorry? What was that?"

"You forgot about the cannibals."

Her mother stared at her for a moment. Then, in a textbook display of noble martyrdom, she lowered her eyes and lifted her chin and quietly stood up.

"If everybody's done," she said, "I think I'll clear the dishes."

FIVE MISERABLE HOURS LATER, back at the apartment, Julia checked that Amy was asleep and rejoined Linda on the big leather couch. The two of them had already made quite an impression on a bottle of Jack Daniel's. Linda poured them both another.

"Seeing your mother today, at last, I understood why you guys are so goddamn good at guilt. It's like she invented it."

"Oh, she didn't mean it. It's my fault for—"

"See what I mean?"

Julia smiled.

"Listen, Julia. Don't give yourself a hard time. They may not even offer you the job. If they do, then you can decide. But, babe, it's your life. You're the only one who knows what's best for you and for Amy. And change is good, whatever. I mean, look at me. I used to be an anarchist with black lipstick and now I'm a lawyer with a black BMW. Isn't life cool?"

They talked on until long past midnight. About family and friends and work and, finally, men. In particular, Linda's apparently endless quest for one with whom she could bear to spend so much as a year, let alone a lifetime. She said that the only ones she ever liked were either gay or married. Then, as if out of the blue, she asked about Connor and whether Julia had heard from him lately.

"Not for a long time. Amy had a postcard from India a few months ago. But since then nothing. He even forgot her birthday this year. First time ever."

Linda took another drink, staring at her over the rim of the glass.

"What? What's with the meaningful look?"

Linda shrugged. "Nothing."

"Come on, what?"

"Well, one didn't exactly need a degree in telepathy to figure out what you two felt about each other."

"Don't be ridiculous. As I recall, you were the one who was smitten."

"I don't deny it. Who wouldn't be?"

"Well, me, for one. He was my husband's best

friend for heavensakes! How could you even think such a thing?"

"Hey, don't go all prim and haughty on me. All I asked was had you heard from him."

"Well, I haven't."

"Well, fine."

There was a long pause. Linda lit another of her long cigarettes and leaned her head against the back of the couch, blowing a cloud of smoke toward the ceiling.

"Is he the reason you want to go to Africa?"

Julia erupted. "Linda, for crying out loud, what's gotten into you tonight? What a totally idiotic thing to say. Of course he isn't. How could you even think that?"

"Whoa, babe. Sor-ry!"

"I mean, really, Linda. Sometimes . . ."

They changed the subject but the conversation never quite recovered. Julia went to bed feeling a little drunk and rather more foolish for having so overreacted. The truth was, beyond the fact of his being Amy's father, Connor was an issue that she had long ago trained herself to handle by denial. He had never ceased to live within her, but in a corner that she never now allowed herself to visit. When Linda had challenged her so directly about her feelings for him, it was like someone poking the scar of an old wound.

And as she lay there with Amy asleep beside her, a living shrine of their joined selves, Julia admitted to herself that her friend was right. However vigorously she had been trying to deny it to herself, deep down she knew that this urge to go to Africa was of course connected with Connor. She wasn't so crass as to imagine that they would find him there. The rational part of her knew full well that they wouldn't. Indeed, she had no idea where in the world he might be. No, it was something more complex that drew her. She wanted to see what he had seen, to take their child to a place that had moved him and be moved by it too and be connected with it and through it to him. And even though he was now a stranger and must long ago have stopped loving her, at least in this small vicarious way she might yet share this part of him.

TWENTY-SIX

CONNOR WOKE with a start and for a moment couldn't figure out where he was. He lay still and listened, staring up into the folds of his mosquito net dimly paled by the first hint of dawn. Then he heard orders being barked and soldiers running across the dirt compound outside and he remembered.

He could hear the strain of an engine making its way up from the lower camp beside the river and he quickly got up and out of the net and unrolled his jeans and shirt that he used for a pillow. By the time the vehicle roared to a halt outside with its lights slicing in through the hut's open doorway he was dressed and shaking out his boots for scorpions.

"*Muzungu*! Wake up! You must come!"

It was Okello, the arrogant young buck of a colonel who had been his chaperon for the past twelve long days of waiting. He knew Connor's name perfectly well but always called him *muzungu*, the Swahili for "white man." They had forged an instant and mutual dislike and Connor didn't bother to answer.

"*Muzungu*! Get up! Get dressed!"

He yelled some kind of reprimand at the young guard who sat all night outside Connor's hut. According to Okello, the guard was there for protection, but Connor knew that the real purpose was to stop him sneaking down into the camp to talk to the abducted child soldiers.

Okello ducked into the doorway and stood there framed and peering in, the jeep's headlights glinting on the matching silver Colt automatics holstered on his hips. He was maybe twenty-five years old, about six feet three or four and powerfully built. Connor had never once seen his eyes for they were always screened by a pair of wraparound sunglasses with reflecting snake-eye lenses. Even now, in the dark, he was wearing them, which probably accounted for why he hadn't spotted Connor sitting to one side on the shadowed mud floor, tying his boots. Okello walked over to the mosquito net and poked it with the short horn-handled cane he always carried. Connor had seen him use it once on a young soldier who had somehow displeased him.

"*Muzungu*! Wake up!"

Connor stood and picked up his camera bag and at the sound Okello turned sharply and saw him.

"You must come! Now!"

"What was the name of that charm school you went to?"

"What?"

"Forget it. What's going on?"

"You will see."

"Is it Makuma? Is he here?"

"Come, hurry!"

The compound was thronged with soldiers, some still pulling on their clothes as they ran, while those of higher rank yelled at them. In the back of Okello's jeep sat two of his henchmen dressed up like a pair of gangster peacocks in their shades and pirate-style bandannas and crisscross belts of ammunition. One was cradling an M16 and the other a 90mm rocket launcher. Connor gave them a cheery smile.

"Morning, fellas. My, do we look the business today."

They just stared through him as they now always did.

"Yep, slept like a baby. Thanks for asking."

It probably wasn't smart to tease them but he was interested to see if one day he could coax just a tiny smile. It clearly wasn't going to happen today. He swung himself up into the passenger seat while Okello climbed behind the wheel, screaming more abuse at the guard. He rammed the jeep into gear and sent it hurtling perilously through the crowd, its wheels spinning and showering all behind them with dirt.

In the dusty purple half-light, they followed the trail that climbed in a long meander to the plateau, their headlights bouncing and jagging across thickets of acacia and eucalyptus and the threadbare backs of the soldiers going the same way on foot. The trail was rutted and rocky and Okello kept his hand on the horn, yelling at those who were slow to move out of the way. Sometimes the jeep clipped or bumped them, which only made him yell louder and lash out with his cane as he passed them.

Half an hour later the soldiers were lined up on the plateau of baked earth and grass, rank upon rank of them, maybe two thousand Connor calculated, more maybe, all standing with their weapons shouldered. There were armored cars and personnel carriers and an array of artillery and mounted machine guns, all apparently assembled for inspection. During his days of waiting, he had been denied access to the younger soldiers, and even now Okello told him to keep his distance and not to photograph them. Connor scanned the rows of faces, searching for the one that was the cause of his coming here, the face he had never seen yet felt sure he would recognize. But there were too many of them and the light was still too dim.

Nevertheless he could see just how young many of them were and how they were dwarfed by their rifles. Those in front wore fatigues, most of which were ragged and many sizes too big. The clothes of those behind looked as though they had been salvaged from a garbage dump, torn and dirty T-shirts and pajama tops and pants that were frayed and caked with filth. Some had boots and others sandals made from tires but many more stood barefoot. The soldiers were mostly boys but there were girls among them too and many more behind, huddled with the sorry ranks of women who were kidnapped to cook and carry and serve as sex slaves to the older soldiers. And now all of them, every man, woman and child, stood gazing aloft as if some great truth were about to be revealed.

A few last stars still glimmered in a sky that had gone through many shades of pink and purple and now blazed in a swath of orange above the dark mountains far away to the east where soon the sun would rise. Connor didn't need to ask again what was going on. There could only be one reason for everyone to be gathered here: Daniel Makuma, The Blessed One, mystic, prophet and supreme spiritual leader of the Warriors for God, was about to descend from the heavens. It was a moment for which Connor had waited many months and he couldn't suppress a quickening of excitement.

So thick was the web of myth and falsehood that had been spun around him, that facts about Makuma were hard to come by. All that was really known was that he was an Acholi from the north of Uganda, that he was forty-two years old and that he was a distant and disaffected cousin of Joseph Kony, the notorious leader of the Lord's Resistance Army, who terrorized other parts of the north. Both claimed to be the rightful heir to the Acholi warrior-priestess Alice Lakwena, whose brutal blend of Christianity and local magic had come close, some fifteen years ago, to toppling the Ugandan government. The rebellion had been bloodily crushed and Lakwena had simply vanished.

Makuma's followers claimed that he, like Lakwena, was a medium who communed with the spirit world in many esoteric ways, often through the souls of animals, and had been instructed in a vision by the Holy Ghost, *Tipu Maleng*, to continue the holy war against the "great evil" that governed the country.

To that end, for more than a decade, he had bolstered the delinquent rabble of his rebel army with abducted children and from bases such as this, in southern Sudan, sent them forth in God's name over the border to burn and rape and murder and pillage their way across the land he claimed to love and sought to save. All this was done with the blessing of Sudan's Islamic government in Khartoum which supplied copious amounts of arms on condition that they also be used against the Sudanese People's Liberation Army which for nearly two decades now had been fighting its own civil war.

Connor knew more than he cared to remember about the methods of Makuma's army. He had photographed the charred aftermath of its raids, counted the dead and met suspected informers whose lips and ears had been removed as a lesson to others.

Until now Makuma had never once granted access to a western journalist or photographer and it had taken every atom of guile and persistence that Connor possessed to find his way through the maze of secrecy and paranoia with which The Blessed One's acolytes had surrounded him.

To make initial contact Connor had flown first to Nairobi where the WFG kept a discreet office in a dingy back room above a travel agency. There was a three-week wait, presumably while they checked him out. Every couple of days Connor would call until finally one of the officials told him that his request to meet The Blessed One was still being considered and that he must fly to Khartoum. Connor's heart sank. Americans were about as popular there as a dose of malaria but the official said he would talk to the Sudanese embassy about expediting Connor's visa application. It took another three weeks, but at last the visa came through.

In Khartoum the waiting grew worse. The people at the WFG office treated him as if he were a tiresome insect, brushing him off again and again and telling him to come back the next day and then the next and the next. He was made to fill in forms and submit his passport and a resumé and a list of the questions he wanted to ask. When, after three weeks, he at last succeeded in meeting someone of apparent authority, he was told rudely that he must not come to the office again but instead wait at his hotel. His request for an interview with The Blessed One was still being considered. He would be informed of the decision in due course. Sweet-talking the western media clearly wasn't a WFG priority.

After a month wandering the streets and communing with cockroaches in his hotel room, finally it happened. At the dead of night there was a hammering on his door and two men with machine pistols told him to pack his things and come. They bundled him into the back of a truck and drove him out of town to an army base, where an unmarked transport plane stood ready to go. He was told to climb in among the crates, a few of which seemed to contain food and the rest arms and ammunition. The flight took many hours and was about as grueling as any Connor had ever made. There were neither proper seats nor windows and hardly any air and it got so hot he nearly passed out. When he next saw the light of day it was here on this godforsaken plateau where he now stood. Naturally nobody would tell him the camp's precise location, but he knew he was in the far south of Sudan and that Uganda's northern border must be close by.

It was only on arriving that he had finally lost patience. He had been led to believe that Makuma would be here, but it quickly emerged that he wasn't. When, or indeed whether, he was coming, nobody either knew or would disclose. It became apparent that the bullying Colonel Okello hadn't been consulted about Connor's visit and consequently did his best to make things as difficult as possible. He even tried to confiscate his cameras and relented only when Connor flew into a rage. But it was hardly worth having them for he was kept under virtual house arrest and banned from taking pictures. He couldn't even take a walk or a leak without an armed escort.

Of course, Okello and everyone else assumed that the purpose of his visit was to photograph and interview Makuma. Which was fine. It was what he wanted them to think. His real mission, the vow that he had made to himself after that night of revelation on the Skeleton Coast, would remain secret until he had the chance to reveal it to the man himself.

Now, with the sun flaring up behind the mountains, a murmur spread across the waiting crowd. One of Okello's henchmen had been talking into a shortwave radio and now he called out and pointed and Connor looked away to the north and saw the lights of a plane, as bright as twinned stars, lowering toward the plateau.

The plane circled above them once and as if on cue the sun broke from the mountains and flashed on its silver wings and a moment later the plateau and all who stood upon it were bathed in a golden light. Connor marveled at the audacity of the man, that he should so stage-manage his arrival. And watching the lit faces of these stolen children, their lives benighted by this same man who now would have them see him as the Bringer of Light, Connor saw that they were indeed impressed.

With a nod from Okello, he started to photograph the plane which was making its final approach from the east. The landing strip was the shape of a vast cross marked with whitewashed stones and as the plane touched down it cast a smaller cross of traveling shadow along it and a spiraling cloud of sunlit dust behind. The plane slowed and turned in the lateral and began to taxi back. Colonel Okello shouted an order and the drums began to thump and boom and all the women and girls raised their voices as one in a sustained, high-pitched trill. Okello called for Connor to follow and set off toward the plane with a little reception committee of senior officers shambling after him.

The plane stopped and a moment later the door opened and steps unfolded to the ground. Then a small figure, dressed all in white, stepped into the sunlight and a cheer went up from all the soldiers, so great that even the drums and the ululation of the women were for a moment drowned. Makuma stood at the top of the steps with both his arms aloft and Connor zoomed in on his smiling face.

Through the lens he saw a slight and handsome man with delicate features and a neat mustache. From a long chain around his neck hung a heavy gold cross. His eyes and his smile were beatific. He lowered his arms and came carefully, almost daintily, down the steps, followed by a small group of advisors and bodyguards.

Okello walked forward in welcome and Makuma opened his arms and the two of them embraced. A pretty teenage girl in smart green fatigues was waiting with a garland of flowers and on a sign from Okello she stepped forward to place it around Makuma's neck. As he lowered his head he glanced sideways at Connor and stared straight into the lens and in that brief moment Connor caught, or thought he caught, a glimpse of something in the man's eyes far colder and more daunting than the saintly smile that lingered on his lips.

Okello was about to lead the party off on a tour of inspection when Makuma turned and walked toward Connor. Connor took one more picture then lowered his camera and shook the hand that Makuma offered.

"I am sorry that you have had to wait so long. I understand that you have been here many days."

His voice was gentle and his English meticulous.

"No problem. Colonel Okello and I had a lot of laughs."

"I am glad. Later, I hope there will be time to answer your questions."

"I sure hope so. I've got a real important one for you."

THE SUMMONS CAME AT SUNSET. Two of Okello's sidekicks picked him up and drove him along the ridge trail above the camp which Connor had been forbidden to visit. Through the eucalyptus trees he caught glimpses of the baked mud curve of a drying river and beside it a great sprawl of crumbling mud huts and improvised tents and shelters. All was veiled in a blue drift of smoke from campfires and the smell of cooking rose on the golden air and mingled with that hot and primal red-earth scent of Africa that Connor had come to love.

Sheltered among the trees at the end of the ridge and concealed beneath many square yards of camouflage netting, the officers' camp was a far more salubrious arrangement than the one it overlooked. It was a complex of grass-roofed huts and spacious tents which Connor guessed had probably been looted from some relief agency camp or convoy. As the jeep pulled up, Okello came out to meet him.

"The Blessed One is tired and we have much to discuss with him. You have twenty minutes, no more. And no photographs without his permission."

Connor didn't bother to argue. Okello led him through a labyrinth of avenues between the tents and huts and Connor could see as he passed that many were crammed with crates of weapons and ammunition and hundred-pound sacks of sorghum and lentils, stamped with the names of various relief agencies. They came at last to an earth-floored yard where two of Makuma's bodyguards stood outside a hut far grander than the rest. Okello left him there and the guards checked his camera bag and frisked him and then one of them pulled aside the drape that hung in the doorway and nodded for him to enter.

It was dark inside and there was a strange smell, a blend of incense and something musty, almost putrid. For a while all Connor could see was a cluttered trestle table with three empty canvas chairs and a single gas lamp upon it burning low. The mud floor was strewn with grass mats and animal skins. There was no sign of Makuma.

Above the chug of generators outside, he could hear music playing, something classical, a choral piece of some kind. Apart from the little he had learned from Ed, Connor knew nothing about music, yet he was struck by how beautiful this piece sounded. It was coming from a portable CD player wired to two small speakers that sat upon the table and as Connor stepped closer he saw there was a stack of discs beside it, Mozart, Bach and Brahms. The rest of the table was covered with documents and a large-scale map of northern Uganda that was spread open and had a pair of rimless spectacles lying on it.

As his eyes grew accustomed to the dark, Connor saw that the walls of the hut were hung with dark red cloth and animal skins against which leaned branches of bare white wood. And then he saw the glint of eyes and saw that there were birds on the branches and stepping closer realized that it wasn't only birds but that there was a whole menagerie of dead animals. There were stuffed heads of elephant and buffalo and zebra and many kinds of antelope, their glass eyes all staring at him. There were tusks and horns of all shapes and sizes, bundled on the floor like firewood. In the corner stood a full-bodied lioness, flanked by a leopard and a cheetah and along the wall beyond lay a vast crocodile with its jaws agape and its back piled high with chameleons and lizards and coiled snakes.

In the farthest corner was a doorway draped in zebra skin with a dim light spilling at the edges. Quietly Connor stepped closer and through the gap he saw Makuma. Still dressed all in white, he was kneeling in prayer at an alcoved shrine upon which stood a gold cross and two candles. Just as Connor was wondering if he should slip away and come back later, he saw the man cross himself. Connor quickly headed back to the center of the room and turned in time to see Makuma emerge from the zebra-skin drapes, apparently not at all surprised to find him there. He was holding a small black leather Bible.

"How much do you know of the spiritual beliefs of my people, Mr. Ford?"

"The Acholi people? Not much I'm afraid."

Makuma walked past him to the table and put his Bible down on the map. He gestured at one of the canvas chairs and took another for himself and they both sat.

"Nor did the first white men who came here. Are you familiar with the term *jok*? No? It is difficult to translate, but broadly it means a spiritual power. A *jok* can be good or evil, depending on many factors, and all have different names. When the first European missionaries came, they thought they might save more souls if they made their message appear to comply with Acholi beliefs. So they gave their Christian

God the name of a *jok*. They called him *Jok Rubanga*. Unfortunately it was not initially a great success for there was already a *Jok Rubanga*: the spirit responsible for causing spinal tuberculosis. Perhaps these poor white men were mischievously advised. Or perhaps it merely proves that one should not meddle with spirits that one does not understand. Do you believe in God, Mr. Ford?"

"I guess it depends what you mean by God."

"Ah. So you don't."

Connor shrugged. If that's what he wanted to think, it was fine. Makuma leaned back and folded his hands, staring at Connor with a smile that was both patronizing and vaguely threatening.

"Do you like Bach?"

"Is that what you've got playing here?"

"The St. John Passion."

"It's beautiful."

"Yes. Do you think such music could exist if there were no God?"

"Seems to me that many things exist, both good and evil, whether there's a God who wants them to or not. Is it okay if I record this?"

"If you wish."

Connor took his recorder from his pocket and set it beside the Bible.

"So, you don't believe in God but you do believe in good and evil?"

"I know that men are capable of both."

"And you believe that you can distinguish between them."

"Between good and evil? Yes, I do."

"But if there is no God, how can that be possible?"

Connor hadn't expected any of this. He had thought long and hard about how best to present the proposal that he had come here to make and he knew that it was important not to let himself get riled. After all these years, he was only too aware of his instinct to confront those whose horrors he had witnessed. It was a foolish and perilous flaw. And if they tried to engage him in some kind of intellectual debate, as that murderous Rwandan mayor once had, as Makuma was trying now, it somehow tapped into that old seam of inadequacy, where he was still the kid who had never been to college, and fueled his anger all the more.

It was happening now and he couldn't help himself. And in answer to Makuma's question, he opened his camera bag and pulled out the photograph. It was the one he had taken of Thomas, the dumbstruck boy at St. Mary's. He held it out to Makuma who thought for a moment and then took it. He picked up his glasses from the table and put them on and studied the picture.

"I have seen this before. I read the article and the many lies you told."

He said it simply with no hint of accusation or bitterness. He handed the picture back but Connor wouldn't take it. His blood was up and pumping hard.

"You asked me how I can tell good from evil. What was done to this boy was evil. Your soldiers murdered his mother and his father, abducted him, then forced him to go back and murder the rest of his family and friends and burn down his own village. Then they left him in the bush to die. Tell me, does that sound like evil to you? Or does your God have another label for these things?"

Makuma laid the photograph on the table and then did the same with his glasses. He gently put his palms together as if in prayer and raised his fingertips to his chin and for a long time stared at Connor. His smile had disappeared. The music was building to a climax and now seemed more ominous than beautiful. With his heart still thumping and his head screaming at him to keep cool, Connor stared back defiantly.

"Whoever told you these things was telling lies," Makuma said quietly. "We do not abduct the children who fight for our cause. They flock, in their hundreds, of their own free will, to join us. Why? Because they want to help purge our land of the great evil that has seized it. If they are too young we do not let them fight—"

"That's bullshit and you know it."

". . . we do not let them fight, but care for them and let them help the cause in other ways. Many of them are indeed orphans. Their parents have been killed by the soldiers of the government. It is the government who tortures and kills my people and who burns our villages and then, with the help of gullible western friends such as yourself, pretends to the world that we are to blame."

"I've seen it with my own eyes."

"Then your eyes deceive you. Tell me, did you come here, all this way, to interview me or to insult me?"

Connor hesitated. The music had come to an end and the only sound now was the chugging of the generators and the muted roar of the gas lamp. It was probably too late, but he took a deep breath and pulled out a sheet of paper from his pocket and held it out to Makuma.

"This is a list of some of the children who have been kidnapped by your soldiers from the Karingoa area. There are seventy-three of them. The last name on the list, Lawrence Nyeko, is the twin brother of Thomas, the boy in the picture there. Please, take it."

Makuma didn't move, so Connor leaned forward and put the list on the table in front of him. Makuma didn't so much as glance at it, just kept his eyes fixed on Connor.

"Now, I'm all set to do an interview with you and to take your picture and all. And you can say whatever the heck you like, correct all those lies you say I told about you, whatever. I'll make sure it gets printed. But what I'm really here for is to make you an offer."

He paused and pointed at the list.

"I don't know what you think these children are worth. If they're in anything like the shape of those I've met who escaped, my guess is they're not a whole lot of use to you. And maybe some of them aren't here. But those who are, I'd like to buy."

Makuma looked at him for a moment, plainly astonished. Then he laughed.

"How is it that Americans always think everything is for sale?"

"All I'm trying to buy is their freedom."

"With whose money?"

"My own."

Makuma laughed in scorn.

"You don't have to believe me. I don't give a

shit one way or the other. But the cash is ready and waiting in an account in Nairobi. I'll give you two thousand U.S. dollars for every child on that list. Payment on delivery, however you want."

Connor was ready for some proud or outraged dismissal but Makuma made no reply. Instead, he called out to summon one of the guards and waved him over to where they sat. He spoke to the guard in Acholi and then handed him the list and Thomas's photograph and the man hurried off with them.

"On behalf of what agency or organization are you doing this?"

"I told you, my own. Nobody else knows about it. And nobody needs to if that's how you want it."

Makuma considered this for a moment. Connor studied his face for a hint as to what he was thinking but found none. Makuma looked at his watch.

"Go now," he said. "We will talk again in the morning."

LONG INTO THE NIGHT Connor lay awake in his hut, shifting on his grass mat and sifting what was said. Every time he went through it he cursed himself for allowing

Makuma to rile him so. He had rehearsed his proposal many times and had gone in determined to be strong and calm and polite and instead had promptly jeopardized the whole endeavor by attacking the man. However insane the idea was, he could at least have given it his best shot. The only consoling thought he found was that even if Makuma now detested him, it was the proposal itself that mattered. Either it appealed or it didn't. Finally, as the sky was starting to pale, he fell asleep.

For the first time in a long while he dreamed of Julia. They were on a river that looked a little like that stretch of the Salmon that the two of them had canoed many years ago. It had those same tall canyon cliffs but the rock was the wrong color, not gray but the kind of red that you found only in Africa and the vegetation that towered above and into the clouds was clearly rain forest. Connor was in one canoe with all the gear bags and Julia was in another up ahead with Amy behind her and Ed in the stern. Amy was trailing her hand in the water and the mood was calm and blissful. Julia turned once and smiled at him and he smiled back and felt no tinge of sorrow or separation.

Then he was peering up at the cliff walls because he knew there were supposed to be some rock paintings hereabout, but he could see no trace of them. When he looked ahead again he saw Julia's canoe disappearing around a bend and Ed, in his dark glasses, looking back at him over his shoulder and waving for him to hurry on. Suddenly Connor knew that there were rapids ahead and a great waterfall and that he had forgotten to tell them and that you had to leave the river and carry the canoes around. And as he listened, he could hear the thunder of the water and he called out to warn them but knew they couldn't hear him and so he started to paddle after them as hard as he could, yelling for them to stop, the roar of the water getting louder all the time.

The roar woke him and it turned out to be Okello's jeep pulling up outside the hut. And a moment later the man himself was in the doorway and yelling *muzungu! muzungu!* as if it were yesterday all over again and Connor found himself wishing that it were, so he might have another chance.

He could tell at once that the mood had changed. As he stepped out of the doorway, Okello gave him a shove between his shoulder blades. Connor turned on him.

"What the hell was that for?"

"Get in."

The two henchmen in the back were grinning but it wasn't the kind of grin that he had been trying all these days to elicit. They seemed to be privy to some joke that no one had told him yet. They drove down the winding trail that led to the lower camp with birds cackling and whooping in the trees as if they were in on it too.

The camp was a lot more squalid that it had looked from the ridge. The red earth was churned to mud and the shelters were pitiful. Vultures picked at piles of garbage and the smell of human filth hung heavy in the sultry air.

Connor looked over his shoulder and saw another jeep was right behind, Makuma in the front passenger seat with his head held high, gracing all they passed with a regal wave and his sanctimonious smile. They drove through the camp and stopped at the edge of a mud clearing where a group of the youngest soldiers Connor had yet seen stood waiting on parade. He estimated that there were about forty of them and their ages ranged from maybe nine or ten to about sixteen. All but a handful were boys. On command, as Makuma alighted from his jeep, they snapped to attention and shouldered their weapons and chanted some kind of battle cry. Everyone else got out of the jeeps too and Connor stood by the hood, watching Makuma come sauntering toward him.

“These are your so-called ‘abducted’ children. There are forty-two of them. Nineteen of the others on your list are not here because they are currently serving with active units. For reasons of security, I cannot of course disclose where. The other twelve names on the list we know nothing about. Probably they were taken or killed by the forces of the government."

"I thought you told me last night that the young ones weren't used as soldiers. Some of these kids can't be more than nine years old."

"It is not a question of years but of spirit. If they are passionate to fight for the cause, who are we to stop them?"

"Is it okay if I take some pictures?"

"No."

"For reasons of security, I suppose."

"Naturally."

"A photograph would at least let their parents know they're alive. I've never seen these children. I need some way to identify them."

Makuma nodded to Okello who on cue held up the list and started shouting out the names. One by one the young soldiers piped up in answer. Connor watched, shaking his head. He had little doubt that this was a setup. The last name that Okello called was Thomas's brother, Lawrence Nyeko.

"Let me talk to him," Connor said.

Makuma nodded to Okello and the boy was

called forth. Makuma handed Connor the photograph of Thomas.

"Perhaps you need this to remind you."

Connor didn't. He knew the twins were identical and he could see the likeness in this boy's face when he was still twenty yards away. His fatigues were tattered and billowed big and as he came nearer Connor could see how his collarbones jutted and how his skeletal little wrists had sores on them. He halted before them and gave Okello a brave salute. But although he was trying to carry himself like a grown soldier, there was a child's fear in the eyes that flicked nervously from Makuma to Okello and on to Connor. Connor smiled at him but he didn't smile back.

"Lawrence?"

The boy looked at Okello, glancing at the horn-handled stick with which he was clearly acquainted. Okello spoke gently to him in Acholi and Lawrence looked briefly again at Connor and nodded. Connor held out his hand.

"Jambo. Jina langu ni Connor."

"He does not speak Swahili," Okello said. "Nor English. Only Acholi."

Lawrence looked at the hand and then at Okello who nodded permission to shake it. The boy's little hand felt cold and limp and bony. Connor showed him the picture of Thomas.

Lawrence looked at it briefly then looked up again at Okello to check how he should react.

"Ask him who this is."

Okello did so and Connor heard the name Thomas in the boy's reply but couldn't understand the rest. He cursed himself for not having learned more than a few words of Acholi. Okello translated.

"He says it is his brother, Thomas, who died a traitor and a coward."

"He didn't say that. If he did, tell him that's not true. Tell him his brother is alive."

Okello glanced at Makuma and Connor told the boy himself in Swahili but he could see that he didn't understand. The boy's eyes were darting with fear. He was obviously afraid that he might already have said the wrong thing. Okello spoke to him again and when he replied his little voice cracked and he had to pause to clear his throat.

"He says you are lying," Okello said.

Connor had had enough. "This is just bullshit. I don't know what the hell either one of you is saying, but any damn fool can see this poor kid's terrified."

"I think it is you he fears," Makuma said. He spoke to Lawrence again and the boy listened, then shook his head violently.

"What did you say to him?"

"That you had come here to buy him. I asked if he wants to be sold."

Connor shook his head and looked away. What a fool he was to think this could ever have worked.

"I will ask all of them the same question."

"Yeah, right. I bet you will."

Makuma put his arm around Lawrence's shoulders and turned him around so that he was facing the other children. He spoke for about a minute and simply from the tone of his voice Connor had a clear enough idea of what he was saying. He could imagine the pious bullshit rhetoric and the lies he must be lacing it with. The speech ended with what was clearly a question and all of the children stood silent, too terrified even to look at each other. He repeated it and still no one responded. Makuma turned and smiled at Connor with a smug regret.

"I asked if any of them want to be sold to you. And you see? Not one."

"Tell them that I will take them home. They will be with their families again. Tell them that."

Makuma spoke again but Connor knew damn well that he wasn't saying that and so he began to shout it out himself in Swahili. At once Okello turned on him and yelled for him to stop and when Connor didn't he came at him and struck him across the shoulder with his stick. Connor lunged at him but Okello's two henchmen grabbed him from behind by his arms and Okello struck him again hard across the face this time and punched him in the stomach, knocking all the air from his lungs.

Connor sunk to his knees gasping for breath and Okello kicked him in the chest and sent him sprawling backward so that his head hit the ground. Connor lay there and looked at their faces scowling down at him with the clear and cobalt sky behind. And the last thing he heard before the blow that delivered him to darkness was Makuma calling out the Warriors for God battle cry and the shrill automaton chant of the children in response.

TWENTY-SEVEN

THE TOWN of Karingoa lay at the head of a valley in that part of Uganda where the arid grass and acacia flatland of the east began to crumple and roll and grow ever lusher as it spread west toward the Albert Nile and the jungle and mountain of the Congo beyond. It was a single street of terraced stores with a church at one end and a police station at the other. In the distant days before the war it had been a sleepy, unassuming place of only a few thousand people, though many more would come daily from the surrounding countryside to trade their produce in its marketplace. Now, however, they had come to stay and Karingoa's population had grown fiftyfold while homesteads and villages for many miles around lay plundered and burned and deserted.

The government had set up "protected" camps to which they urged the dispossessed to move but many resisted for the camps were far away and riddled with disease and even there the rebels still came at night to steal their children and what little else they had. So, instead, many had flocked to Karingoa and its squalid shanty camp that now sprawled for a mile at either end of town. At least from here those who were brave enough could from time to time sneak back to their villages to plant or gather crops. And often when they did, they found children who had escaped from the rebels or been cast aside, cowering in the bush or wandering the ruins of their homes like bewildered ghosts, searching for their families.

The rehabilitation center of St. Mary of the Angels, where many of these children were eventually brought, stood in the southern outskirts of Karingoa's shantytown. Glimpsed from its gateway of crumbled stucco, the old convent building looked a proud and imposing place. It was three broad stories tall and stood square and stalwart at the foot of a gently sloping driveway of red dirt. The driveway was lined with flame trees and beyond them, on either side, were palms and giant mango trees colonized by fruit bats who at dusk would spread their large and leathered wings and clatter forth to feed. Both the convent and the chapel that slid into view alongside it as one came down the driveway were whitewashed and garlanded with crimson bougainvillea. It was only as one drew close that the impression of colonial confidence began to fade.

The whitewash was flaking and blotched by the water that twice yearly in the rainy season gushed through broken gutters from the cracked terracotta tiles of the roof. The facade of the convent building had six large windows on each floor, all with torn mosquito screens and slatted shutters whose green paint had so badly peeled that it looked like patches of mold upon the wood. In front of the building, the driveway broadened into a forecourt from which four wide steps of cracked cement ascended to a pair of hefty doors. Before the war, when St. Mary's was still a girls' school, these had always stood open. Now they were always kept closed and at night were locked and bolted.

Behind the main building was a straggle of smaller buildings that serviced the center's needs. The kitchens, from whose windows came a constant clamor of voices and clang of pots, stood around a low-walled compound enclosing three tall papaya trees and a well with a hand-cranked pump. Scrawny chickens and ducks scrabbled in the dust for scraps while scrawnier dogs lounged beneath the trestle tables of a vast open-sided tent that served as the center's dining room.

There were storerooms, a medical clinic and a workshop and a garage where a motley collection of vehicles stood in various states of disrepair. Towering surreally over them was a red double-decker bus which had been driven a decade ago on an epic fund-raising trip all the way from England. It was called Gertrude and, thanks to the loving attention of George, the center's ancient gardener, mechanic and all-around saint, was still in good working order. Beside it was a red dirt field patched with dried grass where now, in the late afternoon sunshine, the children were playing soccer and basketball. Finally, beyond it all, lay twelve acres of garden, an overgrown eden of orange, banana, mango and avocado.

Surveying this scene from her third-floor window, Julia remembered how alien everything had seemed when they arrived here three months ago and how quickly they had come to feel at home.

She and Amy had just had their daily Acholi lesson with Sister Emily and, as usual, Amy had put her mother to shame. The girl was almost fluent by now, while Julia still sometimes faltered over simple sentences and made mistakes that prompted howls of laughter from Amy and even a benevolent smile or two from Emily. After the lesson Amy had run outside to play basketball when she should really have been up here doing some schoolwork, but Julia hadn't had the heart to stop her. She could see her down there now, calling for the ball and running with the other girls, her blond curls bouncing in the dusty sunlight.

The room they shared was spartan but spacious. It had a high ceiling with a fan that didn't work and pale green walls where little pink geckos with suckered feet and bulbous eyes would hang motionless for hours. There were two metal-framed beds pushed together under one big mosquito net, a wooden desk with drawers, a couple of chairs and a giant closet that smelled of mothballs for their clothes. The only luxury was having their own shower and washbowl which were screened off in one corner. The communal toilets were along the corridor.

Julia checked her watch. She had half an hour before the English class that she had recently started teaching every other evening before supper. The class was voluntary but she made it fun and more and more children were showing up. She turned away from the window and undressed and took a shower, washing her hair and relishing the cool trickle of the water while a gecko watched her from above. Then, wrapped in a towel, she sat at the desk with the sun slanting in on her shoulders and finished a letter to Linda.

In her last letter to Julia, Linda had asked about Connor and whether the people at St. Mary's knew where he was. They didn't. But Sister Emily had more recent news than anyone. Only last fall, about six months ago, he had called from Nairobi and asked her for a list of local children known to have been abducted by the WFG. He hadn't explained why he wanted it and Sister Emily hadn't asked. She assumed it must be for an article he was writing.

It was clear from the way that she and the other nuns and counselors at St. Mary's talked about him that Connor was greatly loved. Framed photographs that he had taken of the children hung on the walls of the hallway. Julia gathered that he regularly sent money and great packages of clothing and shoes and that on his last visit he had brought them a new video and stereo system. Julia had naturally mentioned that he was Amy's godfather but not, for some reason, that he was also her father.

On hearing Sister Emily's news, she had felt such a surge of relief that she had almost burst into tears. Connor was alive. At least he was alive. But swiftly afterward came feelings of hurt and jealousy that he hadn't contacted her or his own daughter for so long. She presumed that he still didn't know about Ed's death, for surely, if he did, he would have been in touch. Julia didn't divulge these feelings to anyone, least of all to Amy, nor did she now in her letter to Linda. Connor belonged to the past and she had vowed to live in the present and not blight it by a longing that she knew she could easily summon if she let herself.

There were forty-two children at St. Mary's, two thirds of whom were boys. Of the nine counselors who worked with them, all but three were nuns who had been born and grown up in the Karingoa area. All of them had been at the convent when it was a school and had since been specially trained by the charity to work with traumatized children. Though they were Catholics, the religious tone of the place was low-key and carefully tuned so that those children who were Protestants never felt out of place.

The other two counselors were a jovial, middle-aged Swiss divorcee called Françoise, and Peter Pringle, a sweet and slightly intense young Scotsman who doubled as the center's physician. He had frizzy ginger hair and was becoming inordinately fond of Julia. He always made sure that he sat near her at mealtimes and blushed when she caught him staring at her. All the staff had rooms on the third floor, while the children slept in segregated male and female dormitories on the second. Peter Pringle's room was next to theirs. They could hear him through the wall sometimes, singing obscure folk songs rather badly in the shower, which would send Amy into helpless fits of giggles. She had nicknamed him Cringle because of his hair and did wicked impressions of him protesting his undying love for Julia.

She finished her letter and got dressed and gathered the props that she needed for her class. She taught entirely in English and if anyone asked a question in Acholi she pretended not to understand, which quite often she didn't. She always liked to have a theme and this evening's was a visit to the market. She had collected a basketload of items that the children could pretend to buy and sell and haggle over. She had about thirty things, from oranges and bananas to clothespins and combs, along with several boxes of matches to use for money. Pandemonium was guaranteed.

On her way downstairs she met Amy coming up from basketball, arm in arm with Christine, a ten-year-old Acholi girl, who had been held by the rebels for over a year and horribly abused. But she'd been at St. Mary's for two months now and was well on the way to recovery. She and Amy had become close. They were both covered in dust.

"Is it okay if Christine comes to our room?" Amy asked.

"Of course it is. But don't you forget that math, young lady."

The girls went running past her up the stairs.

"I know. I'll do it later. We're going to write a play."

"Great. See you later. And take a shower!"

"Yes, Mom," Amy groaned.

The English class went well. There was a record attendance of fifteen children as well as two of the nuns who already spoke the language but wanted to brush it up. The biggest surprise was to see Thomas there, the boy in Connor's photograph, who still after nearly two years at St. Mary's had yet to utter a word. He had put on a little weight since the time of the photograph but he was still thin and frail. He had a self-protective way of tucking his chin onto his chest so that he always seemed to be looking up from under the shelter of his brow. No one seemed to know what to do with him. Most of the children at the center stayed for only two or three months before going back to their families. Thomas had once been sent to live with an uncle but it hadn't worked out. He came back to the center after only two weeks, looking more lost and lonely than ever.

In their morning counseling sessions, Julia had tried hard, as others had before her, to encourage him to draw. And sometimes he would take a crayon from her and sit with it poised over the paper as if trying to muster the courage to begin. But he never did. Whatever lay locked inside him was clearly too terrible to release.

Throughout this evening's English class he sat watching from the back corner of the room and when it was his turn to come to the front and buy something from the market stall, he just shook his head. Julia picked up a few items and took them to him and eventually succeeded in getting him to point to a comb and pay for it with five matches. Everybody cheered and he gave a rare shy smile.

How much English anyone ended up learning, Julia wasn't sure, but they all had a good laugh which was probably more important. She ended up thoroughly exhausted and was relieved when the bell rang for supper.

As she came out into the corridor she was surprised to see two soldiers standing in the hallway, talking in hushed voices with Sister Emily. From their uniforms Julia could tell they were members of the Uganda People's Defense

Force, the government army who had a base at the northern end of town. But soldiers of any kind weren't welcome at St. Mary's. Even a glimpse of a uniform or gun could strike terror into the children's healing hearts and some had been brutalized by the UPDF almost as badly as they had by the rebels. As Julia walked toward them she heard one of the soldiers say the name Makuma but then he saw her and stopped talking until she was halfway up the staircase and out of earshot.

They were all outside in the dining tent and halfway through supper when Sister Emily joined them. She was a tall, graceful woman who was probably in her late thirties but whose gentle manner somehow made her seem ageless. Her official position was Director of the Rehabilitation Program but to the children she was the mother that many of them had lost and that's what they called her. It was rare to see her without one or more of the younger ones sheltering under her arms or clinging to the skirts of her spotless white habit.

The staff ate at a separate table from the children though everyone always ate the same meal. This evening it was corn bread, boiled cassava and a spiced beef stew. They had left a place for Sister Emily and as she sat down among them, one of the kitchen maids put a plate of food in front of her. Since the beginning of supper all they had talked about was the soldiers and why they might have come and now everyone fell silent, waiting for her to tell them. For a few moments she pretended not to notice, just crossed herself and picked up her fork to start eating. Then she looked up at all the expectant faces and feigned surprise.

"What's the matter with you all? Have the cats got all your tongues?"

She smiled and took a mouthful of food and they all waited.

"All right," she went on. "It's nothing. Just rumors. They have had intelligence reports that Makuma has been gathering a big force across the border and that he is planning some new offensive. The soldiers say that this is why everything has been so quiet these past months. Nobody knows what he intends but he is apparently under pressure from his paymasters in Khartoum to use this new force against the SPLA in Sudan not, as he would no doubt prefer, against Uganda."

"So why did the soldiers need to come to tell you this?" Françoise asked.

Sister Emily shrugged. "Because nobody can be one hundred percent certain. They want to station some soldiers with us as a precaution, to set up a camp here in the garden."

"And what did you say?" Pringle asked.

"What do you think? I said no, of course. How would it be for the children to have soldiers tramping all over the place? We have our own guards on the gates. It is enough. And anyway, what need do we have of soldiers when we have the brave Peter Pringle here to defend us?"

Everyone laughed. Pringle blushed. Sister Emily took another mouthful.

"Julia, the stew is good, no? I bet you don't have stew as good as this in America."

It was a signal that the subject of the war was closed. Julia smiled and shook her head.

"Nowhere near as good."

After supper the staff and children usually convened in the recreation room and played music or a game of some sort or watched a video. Tonight, for about the eighteenth time, they were watching one of the tapes that Julia and Amy had brought with them, *The Lion King*. Julia had seen it a hundred and eighteen times and she told Amy, whose appetite for it was insatiable, that she was going up to their room to read.

Walking through the darkened hallway to the stairs, she saw Sister Emily sitting writing by lamplight at her desk in her little office near the front doors. She heard Julia's footsteps and looked up and smiled.

"Julia, do you have a moment?"

"Of course."

She walked across and into the office and Sister Emily gestured for her to sit. On the desk between them was a tray with a blue china teapot on it with two cups and a small pitcher of milk and a bowl of sugar. The window shutters were closed and the walls bare save for a simple wooden crucifix above the Sister's chair and a framed print of the Virgin Mary above Julia's.

"Will you have some tea?"

"Thank you."

"It's Lipton's English tea, as drunk by Her Majesty the Queen of England herself, they say. I'm afraid it's one of my vices."

"I don't think it quite qualifies as a vice. Maybe if you add a slug of whiskey."

Sister Emily laughed and poured her a cup and passed it to her and then offered sugar and milk which Julia declined.

"We are all so busy that sometimes we don't get a chance to talk. I just wanted to hear if everything is all right, you know, with your work and so on."

"Well, yes. Absolutely."

"You are doing so very well."

"Thank you. I love every minute of it."

"And you are happy?"

The question startled her.

"Sure. Why? Don't I look it?"

"No. Sometimes you look very sad."

"Do I? Wow. Well, gee, I'm sorry."

"No, please, don't be sorry. In front of the children and everyone else, you always appear happy. But sometimes I see you when you think no one is looking and then, just occasionally, I think you look a little sad."

"It's my long face. Ever since I was a kid, people have always asked me what's wrong, why the long face? And I say, nothing, I was born with it."

Sister Emily smiled again, clearly unconvinced. There was a pause. They both sipped their tea.

"I hear your English classes are a great success."

Julia laughed. "Well, we sure make a lot of noise. But, yeah, the kids are doing great. I just wish I could learn their language as fast as they learn mine."

"Oh, but you speak Acholi well now."

"I wish! Amy's the one who's gotten the hang of it. All those fresh young brain cells, I guess."

"The children love having her here. It is very good for them. She is a beautiful child. She is very like her father."

Julia frowned. "You mean . . ."

"I'm sorry, I mean her—what is it she says? Her 'biological' father."

"Amy told you about Connor?"

"Yes. Was she not supposed to?"

"No. I mean, yes. It's fine. I just didn't know she had."

"She is very proud of him. And so she should be. He is a fine man."

"Yes. Yes, I know."

She couldn't think why, but the subject made her feel uncomfortable. It was somehow as if the woman knew more about her than she did herself. She took another sip of tea and decided to change the subject.

"So you don't think the war is going to flare up again?"

"I don't believe so. Karingoa has never been an important place for the rebels. If they did launch an attack, it would much more likely be directed at Kitgum or Gulu than here."

Later, as she lay reading with Amy in the lamplit igloo of their mosquito net, with the frogs and insects chirping like some demented electronic machine outside, Julia couldn't stop thinking about what Sister Emily had said.

"Do you think I look sad?"

Amy put down her book to examine her. "What, you mean, like now?"

"No, I mean, any time."

"Uh-huh. Sometimes. I figure it's when you're thinking about Daddy."

"Oh."

"Is it?"

"Sometimes."

Amy cuddled up close, laying her head on Julia's breast.

"He'd have liked it here," she said.

"Yes, I think he would."

Julia stroked her hair and for a long while neither of them spoke.

"Mom?"

"What, sweetheart?"

"Do you think you'll ever get married again?"

"Oh, I don't know." She paused. "Depends if he'll have me."

Amy propped herself up on her elbows and frowned at her.

"Who?"

Julia pretended to look all coy. Amy tickled her under her arms.

"Tell me. Who?"

"Cringle, of course."

Amy yelped with laughter. Julia told her to hush or he would hear but it was some time before they both stopped laughing. At last they went back to their books but Amy soon fell asleep. Julia quietly lifted the book from her hands and turned off the lamp. Floating on the humid air from somewhere away across the town came a muted boom of drums. And she lay there in the darkness, listening to the rhythm and the shriller pulse of the insects and trying not to think of Connor.

TWENTY-EIGHT

THEY HAD taken away his watch so he always waited for the day to show its face before he allowed himself to count it. And when at last it came seeping through the slit of the window, he would feel with one hand under the grass matting of his bed and find the shard of rock and then he would hoist the mosquito net and carefully etch another small vertical line on the hut's mud wall.

The line he had etched that morning was the last of another group of seven and so he had scratched a longer line across them all. There were eight of them now, like a small shoal of fish skeletons, each with seven bones divided by a spine; each bone a day, each spine a week. Fifty-six days. Seventy, if he counted the two weeks he had spent waiting for Makuma to arrive. He tucked the rock shard back under the mat and lay for a long time on his side staring at the fish.

He still didn't know what Makuma had in mind for him. Okello had taken pictures of him on the first day of his imprisonment before confiscating all his camera gear along with his recorder and his notebooks and pens. But Connor had learned enough about hostage-taking over the years to know that a simple mug shot was never enough to secure a ransom. Even the dumbest kidnappers knew the procedure. You had to provide evidence that the hostage was still alive, photograph or video him holding up the front page of a newspaper and this they still hadn't done. In Okello's pictures, with his face all bloody and bruised from his beating, he probably looked half dead. No one back home would be hurrying off to the bank on evidence like that.

The only clue that this was what they intended had come from Makuma himself. Lying in the dust after the beating, just as he was coming around, he had heard the man make some smart remark about being able to get a better price for an American photographer than for a few bony children. But that was the last anyone had said about it. In all these weeks he hadn't seen Makuma again. For all he knew, The Blessed One had again taken to the heavens.

At the start they had kept him cooped up in his hut. The beating had left him with two cracked ribs and for those first few days the pain had been so intense and the heat so stifling that he kept passing out. They slid his food and water under the door and it took all his strength to crawl to it or to the bucket that they gave him as a toilet. The flies on his cut face nearly drove him crazy but after a while he couldn't find the energy to brush them off. Then one morning Okello came with an officer he hadn't seen before and who had obviously had some medical training. The officer examined him and was visibily shocked by what he saw. He obviously had status too, for Connor could hear him outside afterward yelling at Okello.

From that day on things improved dramatically. The food got better and more plentiful and he was given clean water, enough to wash himself and his clothes too and twice a day he was allowed outside for exercise. The medical officer came several more times to check on him and seemed pleased with Connor's recovery. He brought him some more antimalaria pills and some iodine to purify the water and the last time he came he brought a Bible and an oil lamp to read it by. Connor thanked him and asked if he could have a pen and some paper but was told that this wasn't possible.

Since he had gotten better, it was only Okello who came to see him. The purpose of the visits seemed to be mostly to gloat and goad. Connor would hear the jeep pull up outside and the guard unlocking the padlock on the slatted door and then Okello bellowing *muzungu!* The door would swing open and Connor would step squinting into the sunlight to see old Snake Eyes lounging in the driving seat and leering at him or strutting the compound like a turkey cock, thwacking his stick against his boot tops while he accused Connor of being a spy. Mostly it was the CIA that he was supposed to be working for, but sometimes it was the British or Mossad or the Ugandan government or all of them at once, depending on what day of the week it was.

"We have gathered all the intelligence on you," Okello had said on his last visit two days ago. "All of it. We know where you have traveled, we know who you report to, who your contacts are in Kampala and Nairobi. Everything. We know that you were sent by the CIA to provide photographic intelligence that would enable our enemies to attack us here."

"Absolutely."

"You don't deny it!"

"Hell, what's the point? Sounds like these intelligence guys of yours have gotten the whole thing sewn up. Of course, the CIA's got satellites up there can photograph every inch of this place, even something as small as your dick. But hey, why bother use all that shit when they can send me here cleverly disguised as a photographer?"

Irony wasn't Okello's strong suit and he never seemed to know how to react when Connor talked like this. This time he started ranting and threatening execution and Connor quietly stood there and took the abuse, even when he came up and jabbed him in the chest with his stick, hollering at him so close that Connor could smell his breath and feel the spit upon his face. It took all of Connor's self-control not to punch him but he figured that this was exactly what Okello wanted. The fact that he seemed to need a pretext to beat him suggested that he must be under strict orders not to harm him without good reason and Connor drew some comfort from this. Even so, the encounters always left him shaky.

The marking of the days on his wall was his only indulgence, for he knew that to watch the passage of time was the surest way to slow it. Instead, he tried to occupy himself in the detail of his daily routine, in the cleaning of his hut, in his washing and his exercise. And every morning and evening he would sit cross-legged and still and silent with his eyes closed and for an hour or more clear his mind of all thought.

There was always an armed guard outside the hut and they all seemed to have been instructed not to talk or become friendly. Only one of them, a tall young man called Vincent who regularly did the night shift seemed prepared to take the risk. He spoke a little English and when he was sure nobody else was around he would ask Connor questions about America and teach him a little Acholi. He even helped him cut his hair and trim his beard.

Otherwise, apart from mosquitoes and spiders and scorpions and the occasional visiting rat, the only company he had was his Bible. He had already read it once straight through and now was going through it again, but lingering this time and savoring its stories. Neither of his parents had set much store by religion and although he had a passing acquaintance with the Gospels, he had never known till now what a treasure trove of tales the Old Testament was.

He read again of Daniel and the lions and of his three friends, Shadrach, Meshach and Abednego, who were cast into the fiery furnace and how an angel appeared among them and saved them. And he read in the Books of Samuel of the great friendship between Jonathan and David and of David's love for the married Bathsheba and how he arranged to have her husband killed so that he could marry her himself. Connor played these tales over and over again in his head like movies and at night, after he had put the Bible down and turned off the lamp, he would ponder long upon their meaning and what lessons lay in them for his own life.

When he reflected on what had brought him to this place, he knew that many would consider his mission insane and his methods reckless. Perhaps it would have been wiser over the past year to have let those who loved him know where he was and he regretted the pain and worry that his disappearance must have caused them. But he knew too that the journey he had made was part of his own private destiny and that it was somehow ordained, though by whom or what he had no idea, that he should travel its path alone and without reference.

He knew the truth of this destiny only in fragments that twirled in his mind like pieces of a jigsaw puzzle floating in a pool: the elk with its flaming antlers, the walk through the desert along the invisible river, the rock paintings, both the ones in the roofless cave and the one that hung on Julia's bedroom wall; the story of the kudu and the skeleton of the whale and the old lion staring with its firelit mirror eyes. All these images he knew to be connected and sometimes, in moments of calm, on the edge of his vision, the pieces of the puzzle seemed to float so closely together that he thought he was about to see the whole picture and at last to understand. But when he looked directly at it the pieces would twirl again and quickly drift apart. And he soon came to realize that whatever the truth might be, it was not a thing of mind but of being and that he would know it by living and not by looking.

During the past two weeks, when the guards let him out into the compound for his morning workout and for his evening walks at gunpoint through the eucalyptus trees, Connor had become aware that there were many more soldiers and vehicles around than there had been when he arrived. At night he heard the drone of planes landing and taking off up on the plateau. Some great mustering or preparation seemed to be going on. He had asked Vincent about it but the boy either didn't know or wouldn't say.

This evening however when he took his walk everything was quieter. The guard who accompanied him was new and nervous and belligerent. He kept shouting at him not to walk too far ahead and ordered him to turn back much earlier than the other guards ever did. When Connor tried to argue the guard grew angry and came at him, jabbing with his rifle. Instead of letting him sit outside to eat his supper, as Vincent and most of the other guards now let him, so that he could watch the sun go down, this tyro tyrant shoved him inside and locked the door.

Such petty assertions of power happened from time to time, and Connor always tried not to take them personally. But tonight he couldn't help it and as darkness crowded in he sat brooding and feeling cheated and bitter and sorry for himself. He tried to meditate but his mind was fizzing and wouldn't clear. He lit the lamp and opened his Bible to the Book of Exodus, where earlier he had been reading again of the great plagues that God sent upon Egypt to free the children of Israel but he couldn't concentrate and found himself reading the same verse over and over again. He undressed and blew out the lamp and lay on his bed mat in the dark, closer to despair than he had been for many weeks. Finally he fell into a troubled sleep.

He woke in the middle of the night and knew something was going on outside. He opened his mosquito net and looked across the hut. There was a slatted square of moonlight on the mud floor and as he watched he saw a shadow move across it. Then he heard voices outside. One of them was the guard's and he sounded riled, as if he were challenging someone. Connor got up and walked naked to the door and peered out through the slats.

The compound was silver with moonlight and the long shadow of a palm tree reached across it. The guard's chair stood deserted outside the hut with the padlock key dangling from its back on a string. He could still hear the voices but couldn't make out where they were coming from. He moved to another gap in the slats and craning his neck at last he saw them.

The guard was standing before a soldier much smaller than himself, prodding him in the chest with his rifle and haranguing him. Then Connor saw a third figure step from the shadows behind the guard and start to move silently toward him. He was as tall as the guard and had something long in his right hand which, as he tiptoed closer, flashed in the moonlight and Connor saw it was the blade of a machete. It glinted again as the man raised it and brought it down in a great arc toward the back of the guard's neck. The sound of the blow was shocking and although Connor couldn't see, he knew it must have all but severed the guard's head. His knees folded and his body crumpled to the ground and a dark stain began to spread from his shoulders.

The two others took his rifle and his knife and hurried toward the hut. The taller one had a bag slung over his shoulder. Connor ran to the bed and unrolled his jeans and shirt and quickly dressed. He could hear the urgent murmur of their voices outside and the rattle of the key in the padlock. Then the door swung open and the taller one stepped in and as his face turned it caught the moonlight and Connor saw that it was Vincent.

"Put on your boots, quick," he said. "Get your things."

Connor didn't ask any questions.

He found his boots and pulled them on, then bundled his few belongings in his spare T-shirt. In a minute he was outside and ready to go. Vincent had hauled the guard's body toward the hut and Connor helped him drag it inside. The short one had been kicking dust over the bloodstain and now he came toward them and Connor saw that it was Lawrence Nyeko. The boy looked very frightened. He said something in Acholi and Vincent nodded and turned to Connor.

"He asks if it is true that his brother is alive."

Connor told him that it was. Lawrence gave a little nod.

"Stay close and be quiet," Vincent said. "If they see us, they kill us all."

They ran all three across the compound and into the shadow of the trees along the ridge that overlooked the camp. Vincent went first with Lawrence close behind and Connor at the rear.

There was a trail but they kept away to one side of it, scrambling through the rocks and scrub with the insects screaming around them and the moon strobing in through the treetops.

Vincent had the guard's AK-47 in his hand and sometimes he would hold it up as a signal for them to stop and they would all stand as if frozen, peering into the dappled shadow and barely daring to draw breath. Once they startled some large animal that snorted in alarm and stomped darkly off, crashing through the bush. Vincent turned and grinned. Another time they heard a truck coming along the trail and the sound of soldiers' voices and they lay down with their faces pressed to the sweet-smelling earth while the lights swung over them.

By the time they reached the end of the ridge, the moon had angled lower and the darkness had deepened around them. The soldiers' camp was away to their right now and far behind and all Connor could see as he peered down through the trees was the pale mud outline of the dried river curving away to the east.

How long they walked, he couldn't tell. Maybe two or three hours and not a pause for rest. Only when they came to a small clearing of pale grass and boulders and a first glimmer of dawn brightened the horizon ahead did Vincent stop. He pulled a piece of paper from his pocket and handed it to Connor. There was enough light to see that it was a crude map drawn in charcoal.

"Follow the river east, but do not go too close to it," Vincent said. "Stay in the high ground, in the trees. And travel only at night."

"How far is it to Karingoa?"

"I don't know. Maybe sixty, seventy miles south of here. But you must not go south. Between here and the border there are more camps. Many, many soldiers. They prepare a great war. You must go east. Three, maybe four days. Only there is it safe to cross."

"You're not coming with us?"

"I can't. Take this."

He unslung the bag from his shoulder and gave it to Connor.

"There is a little food and water."

Then he held out the rifle. Connor shook his head.

"Take it!"

"I feel safer without it."

Vincent clearly considered this crazy and insisted that they should at least take the machete which Connor saw was still smeared with the dried blood of the guard. Vincent laid a hand on Lawrence's shoulder and said something to him in Acholi. The boy nodded and murmured a few words in reply of which Connor understood just enough to know that he was offering his thanks.

Connor held out his hand and Vincent shook it.

"Thank you," Connor said.

Vincent nodded. "Go now. Take the boy to his brother."

They went their separate ways and Connor didn't look back until he and Lawrence had reached the far side of the clearing. But when he did, Vincent had already vanished into the trees.

TWENTY-NINE

THE WAKE-UP call at St. Mary of the Angels was about as blissful as any ever devised. The dawn air was always cool and clear and still and as it filled with light so the birds began to whoop and whistle and scold each other in the jungle of the gardens. For about an hour they had the world to themselves until at six o'clock the nuns began singing in the chapel and Julia would lie and listen with Amy still asleep beside her. Only rarely did she recognize a tune for mostly they chanted African masses which were so powerful and exquisite that even the birds soon stopped trying to compete.

Slowly the old convent building would then start coming to life. There would be a first murmur of children's voices from the dormitory windows below and then the sound of doors opening and closing and the shuffle and slap of running feet along the corridors and on the stairs. Soon from outside would come the chatter and laughter as the children drifted across to the kitchen compound to wash at the pump. Normally that was when Amy would stir and rub her eyes and she and Julia would lie and talk awhile until Cringle started singing Scottish ballads next door in the shower which was their cue to get up and take a shower themselves.

But not today. For just as Cringle started up, there was a scream from outside and then a yell and soon the whole world seemed to be doing it. Julia and Amy leaped out from the mosquito net and ran to the windows and pushed open the shutters. There was a group of about a dozen excited children down in the compound and more running to join them, while out of the kitchens came a jabbering war party of maids and cooks, some armed with frying pans and brooms.

"What are they saying?" Julia asked.

"I can't hear. Let's go see."

By the time they got out to the compound there were a lot more children there, all gathered in one corner. Françoise was already there at the back of the crowd and so was Peter Pringle, his fuzzy ginger head still dripping and making splotches on his T-shirt. He turned excitedly as they ran up.

"It's a snake. I think it's a python."

"It's taken a duck," Françoise said.

"Wow! Mommy, come on, let's see!"

There weren't many animals that gave Julia the creeps and even in the presence of those that did—most especially spiders—she always tried, for Amy's benefit, to appear relaxed. Back home, if Amy was watching, she had been known to pluck big hairy ones from the bath-tub with her bare hands as if it were nothing and carry them outside to release them, saying, "There you go, little fella," when really inside she was screaming. But on a scale of terror, nothing, absolutely nothing, came close to snakes. And now her dear daughter was hauling her by the hand through the crowd toward a monstrous one.

"Amy, hold on there! Don't get too close! Amy!"

They broke through into the front row of children and there, about four yards away, cow-ering in the corner and trying to hide under a straggly scarlet hibiscus bush, was the python. It was about five feet long but to Julia it might as well have been twenty. It had a great bulge be-hind its head which was presumably its break-fast, the late lamented duck. How it could have gotten the darned thing through its nasty little mouth, Lord only knew. Two of the older boys had found sticks and were trying to pitchfork the terrified creature out into the open.

"Wow, look at that," Amy said. "Isn't he beautiful?"

"Frankly, that isn't the first word that springs to mind."

The snake was a greeny yellow with rounded dark-chocolate markings edged in white. The children were yelling at the boys who had the sticks, urging them on. And now, pushing through the crowd came Sister Emily and old George, the gardener, who was carrying a shotgun which Amy immediately saw.

"You're not going to kill it?"

He grinned down at her. "You like snakes?"

"Yeah, they're fine. Don't kill it. Mommy?"

Julia didn't know what to say. Even Sister Emily beside her seemed lost for words. To protect itself the python had coiled into a bundle and kept moving its head from side to side, keeping as low as it could. But the boys weren't going to give up. One of them hooked his stick into its coils and managed to drag it out into the open. The children were all shouting for them to kill it. Sister Emily stepped out in front of them and raised her arms and called for calm but her voice was drowned and no one paid any attention to her.

The boys were prodding the creature now and when it suddenly made a halfhearted lunge at one of them they both raised their sticks and started to beat it. Amy grabbed onto Julia's arm.

"Mommy! Stop them!" she wailed.

Julia was about to lead her away, when someone elbowed past from behind and ran out in front toward the boys. He had a piece of sacking in his hand and he pushed the boys aside and turned to face the crowd. Suddenly everyone stopped yelling. It was Thomas Nyeko.

He positioned himself between the boys and the python and for a moment there was utter silence. Both of the other boys were older and taller than he and now one of them raised his stick and tried to step past him to finish the job. A few of the children started to yell again. Thomas blocked the boy's way and as he did so he opened his mouth and shouted. The boy stopped in his tracks. It was the first time he or anyone present had heard Thomas's voice and the effect was electrifying. The boy lowered his stick and Thomas went on, not shouting now but talking, addressing everyone.

Julia didn't understand all that he said but what little she missed she found out later. He said that there had been enough cruelty and killing, that they had all seen too much of both.

There had to be an end to it. They had all known hunger too and stolen food to live and this was all the snake was doing. They should respect his courage and let him live. And he turned and threw the sacking over the python and then knelt beside it and wrapped it up. Then he stood with it bundled in his arms and came past the boys toward the crowd. And everyone stood aside for him to pass and watched in silence as he walked away across the compound and into the trees.

Until that day, all that was known of what had happened to Thomas and his twin brother had been gleaned from others: from neighbors who had witnessed their kidnapping and then witnessed their return as avenging devils with Makuma's men, killing and looting and burning the village; and from the government soldiers who later found Thomas wandering naked and near death in the bush. Now, over the weeks that followed his rescue of the python, he told the story himself.

Every child at the center had his or her own special saga of horrors, and Julia knew it was wrong to compare or to grade them. But Thomas's was about as shocking as it got and worse than anyone had suspected. The story emerged in a slow flowing of words and drawings during many hours of counseling, both in one-to-one sessions and in group sessions with the other children.

When the Warriors for God rebels came one night to his village, he and Lawrence were forced to watch while their mother was raped and tortured. Then they were forced to club her to death and afterward to do the same to their father and their younger brother and sister. The rebel leader told them that this would make men of them. They and the other abducted children were made to march for many days without food and barely any water to a great camp over the Sudanese border. There the prettier girls were given to the older soldiers as "wives." The boys and the rest of the girls were trained as soldiers.

Daniel Makuma himself gave them long lectures about the spirit world and how *Tipu Maleng* would protect them in battle. He said that they must anoint themselves with shea butter oil that he had himself blessed so that enemy bullets would bounce off them. In battle they must always run directly into enemy fire, he said, shooting as they went. Anyone who lay down to shoot or to hide was a coward and would be executed.

Their first mission after training was to go back to burn their own village and to kill their friends and neighbors. This, Makuma told them, would free them of all earthly ties and allow *Tipu Maleng* fully to embrace and protect them. Before the attack Thomas and the other child soldiers were given drugs to bolster their courage but in truth, he confessed, there was no need. He knew full well what he was doing. He wanted these people dead because they were witnesses to what he had already done to his family. By killing them and burning the village he and Lawrence hoped to erase all testimony and all memory of their first and far more hideous crime.

At the camp, he said, if any child disobeyed an order, the others were made to club him or hack him to death. If they refused, the same fate befell them. It was after one such murder that Thomas lost the power of speech. He said it was as though God had taken away all his strength. During his last battle he became so useless that the commander abandoned him in the bush. His brother, he said, was braver.

These weeks of Thomas's slow revelation affected everyone at St. Mary's, both staff and children alike, bonding them more closely than ever. Some of the older boys who had been reticent about their own crimes seemed to draw courage from Thomas and made confessions of their own. During one of Julia's morning group sessions one of the would-be python killers, whose name was Alex, admitted taking part in several rapes. To Julia's amazement, he said that one of his victims had been Amy's friend Christine. The group consisted only of boys, so she was not present to hear this. Julia asked Alex if he would like to apologize personally and he said that he would. Christine said that she would be prepared to listen.

On first coming to St. Mary's, Julia had tried to protect Amy from the rawest horrors of what had happened to the children. But the girl had become so much a part of the place that this was now almost impossible. Christine had told her much of what she had suffered at the hands of the rebel soldiers (though not, it transpired, about the rape) and Amy had asked Julia many difficult questions. Faced with the choice of whether to gloss things over so as not to disturb the child or to address the issue squarely, rightly or wrongly, Julia had opted for the latter. The two of them had since had many long discussions about what it was that might drive ordinary decent people to commit such appalling deeds.

Had she been asked to justify her decision, Julia would have argued that children of Amy's age back home saw real-life horrors unfold every day on the TV news, but in a way that was somehow anesthetized and distancing, in which both villain and victim were nameless and quickly forgotten. Here at St. Mary's, however, they were real. Amy knew their names and held their hands and played with them and watched them rediscovering the simple joys of love and friendship. What she was witnessing here was nothing less miraculous than the power of redemption. And this, Julia persuaded herself, was a rare privilege that neither of them, nor anyone else involved, would ever forget.

Even so, Julia had wondered if it would be appropriate for Amy to attend Alex's apology to Christine. She sought the advice of Sister Emily.

"Amy is what some people call an 'old soul,' " the sister said. "She has an inner strength and a wisdom beyond her years. She is part of our family and Christine thinks of her as a sister. Since you ask my opinion, I believe it would be wrong to exclude her."

That evening, after supper, all of the children and all of the staff were asked to assemble in the hall. Sister Emily announced gently that Alex had something to say and the boy stepped forward. He stared at the floor, twisting a hand in the ragged tail of his shirt and in a small voice began to relate what he had done. Julia stood and listened with her arm around Amy's shoulders. Every so often Amy looked at Alex, but mostly her eyes were fixed on her friend.

Alex said that he was sorry and that he would never forgive himself for what he had done and as he said it he started to weep and soon many of those who watched were weeping too. Christine, however, kept her composure throughout, although she seemed to find it hard to look at him. When he had finished there was a short silence and she swallowed and gave a little nod and Sister Emily went to her and hugged her and then did the same to Alex. Some wounds ran too deep for instant forgiveness, Julia reflected, or perhaps for forgiveness at all. Christine would bear the scars forever. But the boy's words might at least have helped with the cleansing.

The following day, Peter Pringle had to drive down to Entebbe airport to collect some medical supplies that had been flown in from Geneva. He returned with sobering news.

There had been a problem clearing the supplies through customs and so he had stayed overnight with friends in Kampala. A British diplomat and his wife came for dinner and talked of little else but the war in the north and how the lull of almost two years was rumored to be drawing to an end. The diplomat said that in the past twenty-four hours there had been reliable reports that Makuma and his army were on the move. And their target was not, as everyone had assumed it would be, to attack the SPLA in Sudan. They were moving south toward the border.

On his drive back north, Pringle told them, he had followed great convoys of government troops and artillery and as he drew near to Karingoa he had seen a first trickle of refugees heading on foot in the opposite direction with their children and their scant and bundled belongings.

Two nights later, as she lay in bed, too hot and restless to sleep, Julia heard a distant thudding that at first she took to be thunder. The rains were late and the land was parched so that even the hint of a cooling storm bore some relief. But it lasted only a moment. For although she had never heard the sound of shell fire, she soon knew that this was what it was and that the promised storm was of a different kind.

THIRTY

THEY DID as bidden and traveled only at night. The map was of little use but the sky was mostly cloudless and Connor steered by the stars and by the passage of the thinning moon that rose to eclipse them, casting ashen shadows across a landscape sometimes as lunar as itself. As they hiked higher into the mountains the air grew thinner and cooler and the going more treacherous. They would walk for miles, picking a route among the rock and thorn bush, only to find themselves lured by the lay of the land to the foot of an unscalable cliff or to the rim of some jungle ravine with a thousand feet of blackness echoing below. And they would have to retrace their steps and circle for many miles more before they could continue their journey east.

When they were forced into the lower land

they kept when they could in the cover of the trees and in the elephant grass that was often taller than themselves and always away from any road or trail they came across for many of these were mined and monitored. They skirted villages devoid of any life but the crows and vultures that sat atop bleached skulls and skeletons of cattle in the barren fields. Connor knew that the Dinka people who lived hereabout had suffered much at the hands of the rebels, both Makuma's and those of Joseph Kony's Lord's Resistance Army. On the second night they saw a convoy of military trucks rumbling slowly south with the dust swirling in the dimmed beams of their headlights. He and Lawrence lay side by side in the shadows watching for an hour while it passed. The boy said that he thought these were Kony's men and that there were rumors that he and Makuma were joining forces for the invasion.

When the sky began to pale they would start looking for a place to shelter for the day, some shaded enclave in the rocks or jungle glade where they could rest in safety. The food and water that Vincent had given them lasted two days and would have lasted longer if Lawrence hadn't been so thin and weak. They shared the water but Connor made the boy eat most of the food and he used the iodine to treat the open sores on his bony arms and his bare and swollen feet.

Most of the drainages they passed were dry but they found just enough water to get by. At the camp the children had tried to supplement their meager rations by scavenging in the bush and Lawrence had learned which trees and plants had leaves that were edible. When they came across one he would point it out and the two of them would stop and force themselves to eat. They ate the roots of certain other plants and sometimes even the bark. Connor had eaten many strange foods but none so desperate or foul. All tasted bitter and felt like prickled plastic in his mouth and he had to chew for a long time before he could swallow. Lawrence had grown used to it and grinned at the sight of Connor trying not to gag.

They spoke little and when they did it was mostly to confer about which route to take or place to rest. Only once did Lawrence ask about his brother. He said he had been certain that Thomas was dead and questioned Connor closely about when he had last seen him and how he had looked. He said that he hoped Connor was not mistaken and had not merely seen the boy's ghost, for it was a land now populated more by ghosts than men. Connor told him that Thomas no longer spoke and Lawrence nodded solemnly and said that he knew this and had thought the same might happen to him. He said that he and Thomas were "half of each other" and Connor didn't know if this was simply an Acholi way of saying they were twins or if the boy meant something more.

As dawn approached on the sixth day they found themselves walking along the side of a winding wooded valley. Their night's journey had been hard and they were weary and weak from hunger. The birds were starting to call and white butterflies the size of saucers fluttered before them in the half-light, startled from the dew-damp elephant grass. A herd of antelope of a kind Connor didn't recognize moved slowly off through the trees, their ears and tufted tails atwitch and Connor found himself wishing, not for the first time, that he had accepted Vincent's offer of the gun. They found a place to lay up and Connor left the boy to rest and took the plastic bottle and walked down through the trees in search of water.

As he dropped deeper into the valley bed he heard the rush and tumble of a stream and soon caught sight of it down between the trees. There was a waterfall and a dark pool below, half rimmed with rock. He made his way down and squatted there to fill the bottle, staring at the surface of the pool and at a twig that slowly twirled there. The water felt cool and soothing to his hand. It was a place where they both might bathe and wash their dirt-caked clothes then dry them in the sun while they slept.

Had he been less lost in the thought of this, he might have seen in the pool's darkened mirror a pair of eyes staring back at him. For all the while a lone figure stood watching him from the trees that fringed its other bank and watched him now as he stood again and drank and walked back up the slope to fetch Lawrence.

By the time they had drunk their fill and washed themselves and rinsed their clothes then climbed naked and dripping back to their hideout, the sun had almost risen. They spread their clothes on the bushes and settled in the grass to sleep.

Connor woke with the feeling that an insect had settled on his neck. He was lying on his back and could feel the morning sun already hot on his bare chest. Without opening his eyes he lazily lifted a hand to brush the bug away and it was then that he felt the cold hard edge of the blade.

He opened his eyes and saw the figure standing over him, silhouetted by the flaring sun behind. And for an instant as he squinted up he thought it was Lawrence. Then he saw it was a man and that the blade now poking hard into his throat belonged to a spear. The man was tall and broad and his eyes were fierce. His head was shaven and except for a loincloth he was naked. And now Connor saw there were half a dozen others with him, all armed with spears and machetes. He tried to sit up, but they started to shout so he lowered himself again and, craning his neck, saw that Lawrence too had spears at his throat. The boy looked petrified.

The men were yelling so excitedly that it took Connor a while to figure out that they were speaking a kind of Swahili. And though he couldn't make out much, he understood enough to know that he and Lawrence were suspected of belonging to the rebels. He heard Makuma's name several times and Kony's too. One of them was shaking out the contents of the bag. The discovery of the machete and Connor's Bible seemed to bolster their suspicions.

The men made them both get to their feet and it was plain from the way they looked Connor up and down that they hadn't seen too many naked white men before. He kept his eyes fixed on the one who appeared to be their leader and who still had his spear poking at

Connor's chest. Connor tried not to look as frightened as he felt and greeted him in Swahili.

"Shikamoo."

It was the respectful greeting normally used for addressing elders but it didn't seem to impress anyone, for they all began shouting and accusing them of being Makuma's spies. Connor felt the spearhead pierce his skin and he looked down to see a trickle of blood run down his ribs. He waited for them to stop talking and then told them as calmly as he could that they were not Makuma's spies but his captives and that they had escaped.

There was a gabbled conference and from the little Connor understood, it seemed that he had sown enough doubt to avoid being murdered on the spot. One of the men seized Lawrence's tattered fatigues off the bush and shoved them into the boy's face, shouting why, if he wasn't a rebel, did he wear a rebel's clothes. Connor said that the boy didn't understand Swahili and when the man ignored him the leader told him to stop. He turned to Connor and said that they must put on their clothes and come with them.

They were marched for maybe an hour down the valley with spears at their backs until they saw a cluster of mud and grass huts in a clearing above the river, sheltered by acacia and borassus palms. News of their capture had clearly gone before them for as they drew near a gaggle of naked children came running toward them, calling out *muzungu! muzungu!* and daring each other to touch Connor's arms. One even jumped to touch his hair.

They were made to sit on the ground in the shade of the palms with two of their captors standing guard and a throng of women and children who stood staring and talking and giggling. Then the crowd hushed and parted and the leader reappeared with an older man who seemed to be treated by all with great respect.

"*Shikamoo*," Connor said.

The old man nodded. *"Marahaba."*

The old man asked where they had come from and Connor told him their story as best he could in his faltering Swahili and the man watched him all the while without interruption. When he had finished, the old man asked if they had seen other soldiers on their journey here and Connor told him about the convoy. Finally the man asked when they had last eaten and Connor told him that for three days all they had eaten was leaves. The man told the crowd to disperse and left without any indication of what was to be their fate, but a short while later a woman brought them a pot of water and two bowls filled with a thick porridge which they both ate hungrily.

In the late afternoon some soldiers arrived and from the drift of their questions Connor gathered that they belonged to the SPLA. Their commander wanted to know all about Makuma's camp, how many men were there and how well armed. Connor and Lawrence told him what they knew. The commander asked why, if their destination was Karingoa, had they come this far east and Connor said they had been warned that there were troops massing in the west and only here would it be safe to cross the border.

At dusk they were taken to a bare hut and fed again. Through the guarded doorway Connor could see the soldiers across the compound talking with the old man and some of the other men but he couldn't hear what they were saying. Lawrence sat slumped and forlorn against the wall, staring at the ground. Connor settled himself beside him and put his arm around his shoulders and tried to cheer him up by talking about Thomas and St. Mary's and the kind of things they did there. His Acholi was so primitive and poor that soon the boy started to smile at his mistakes and correct him.

Lawrence asked him what kind of food they ate there and Connor told him it was always tree leaves, but plenty of them. The boy laughed. Connor asked him what was his very favorite food and Lawrence thought for a while and said with great seriousness that it was roasted goat meat and *matoke,* a mash of plantains. Once, however, his father had brought home a jar of peanut butter which they ate with warm corn bread and this, on reflection, was probably his favorite taste.

He fell asleep with his head resting on Connor's chest.

The soldiers woke them at dawn and marched them from the camp without saying where they were going, though it soon became clear that they were heading south, following the course of the river. The valley was thickly forested and the going hard and by the time they stopped to rest, the sun had climbed high and their clothes were soaked with sweat. They cooled themselves in the river and drank. The soldiers gave them some sorghum bread and they sat eating it in the shade, watching scarlet and yellow birds swoop for flies above the water.

The commander told Connor that they were close to the Ugandan border now and that he had sent men ahead to make contact with the Ugandan government forces who patrolled it. Half an hour later the men returned with a UPDF sergeant and two younger soldiers. The sergeant greeted Connor solemnly and asked the same questions that they had answered many times already. The SPLA commander led his soldiers off without another word.

Once across the border they were met by a Land Rover and driven south for many miles along dirt roads and then across dry savannah until at dusk they arrived at an army barracks. It was at the edge of a small town and Connor asked its name but the sergeant wouldn't tell him. At the barracks they were separated and Connor was led to a room with a dirty cement floor and bare walls with barred windows. There was a table and two chairs and he sat waiting for a long time until a young major in a smartly pressed shirt came in and sat in the other chair on the other side of the table and asked all the same questions again and many more besides.

The man spoke precise English and had a brisk manner in painful contrast to the slow and meticulous handwriting with which he noted every answer. When Connor told him about his botched attempt to buy back the abducted children he seemed mystified.

"But you are a photographer. Why would you want to do such a thing?"

Connor shrugged. "I don't know."

"I think you do."

"You really want to know? Well, I guess it was something to do with the fact that all these years I've made a living out of other people's misfortune. At the outset you figure the pictures might help in some way but after a while you discover they don't change a thing. I guess I just wanted to try giving something back. You know? To *do* something rather than just stand there and watch."

It was the only answer that the man didn't bother to note.

Afterward Connor was led across the compound to some sort of detention block where he found Lawrence already in the cell waiting for him. The boy looked relieved to see him and said that they had asked him questions but hadn't beaten him.

The cell had two narrow bunks. It was the first time in almost three months that Connor had slept in anything like a proper bed and even though the mattress was hard and full of lumps and the blanket mangy it felt like five-star luxury.

The next morning he was summoned once more to see the major and this time the man's manner was friendlier. He said he had made a number of calls, including one to the U.S. embassy in Kampala. Someone there had in turn managed to get hold of Harry Turney at the agency in New York and even tracked his mother down in Montana.

"Everybody thought you were dead. You have been missing for a long time, much longer than you told me."

"I was traveling."

"Where?"

"All over. Australia, India."

He didn't elaborate and the major didn't press the point.

"You and the boy will be taken today to Kampala."

"We have to get to Karingoa."

"That is impossible. The rebels have made a great push south. There is much bad fighting. The army has sealed off that whole section of the country. You cannot even get to Gulu."

Connor asked if he could call St. Mary's to tell them about Lawrence but the major said this too was impossible. All communications with Karingoa had been cut.

CONNOR SAT ON THE BED looking out over the hotel gardens and waiting for the operator to call him back. A pair of marabou storks were tumbling and flapping in the tops of a row of flame trees and he couldn't decide if they were fighting or mating or playing. Maybe it was all three.

It was late afternoon and after all the frantic activity of the past hours he suddenly felt weary. He had spent the day so far shuttling around Kampala, talking to government officials and aid agencies and people at the U.S. embassy and generally trying to figure out what to do about Lawrence. The embassy people were going to fix Connor a new passport and they let him use the phone to call his bank in Nairobi to arrange for some money to be wired. Meanwhile, so that he could buy them both some new clothes, he had borrowed money from the only real friend he had in Kampala.

Geoffrey Odong was a journalist whom he had met on his first ever visit here before going into Rwanda. He was a year or two younger than Connor and being bright and ambitious had since risen to become an assistant editor of the country's leading newspaper. Both he and his wife Elizabeth were Acholis and it was they who had first made Connor aware of what was going on in the north and about the extraordinary work being done at St. Mary of the Angels. Elizabeth worked part-time for a local radio station and they lived with their three daughters in a modest house at the foot of one of the city's seven green hills.

Connor had called them the previous night as soon as he and Lawrence arrived in the city after a sweltering and spine-jarring day's drive from the northeast in the back of an army truck. Geoffrey came at once to collect them and insisted they stay the night. Elizabeth was appalled at how emaciated they were and fed them until Connor thought the boy was going to burst. Their eldest daughter was Lawrence's age and after a shy start the two of them were getting along well. The place was small and Connor felt bad that the girls had been ousted to the living room so that he could have their bedroom. After heavy protest, Elizabeth had reluctantly conceded that he should move to the Sheraton, but only on condition that Lawrence stay on.

Connor had never much cared for the kind of antiseptic corporate luxury which such hotels seemed to deem necessary. And after his long weeks of deprivation the room with all its cellophaned frippery made him feel like a visitor from another planet. The chilled air and the white roar of the air-conditioning marooned him from the world outside and even that, the rolling acres of lush and manicured garden, the silent traffic, the white office blocks and the tree-lined hills beyond, all seemed faintly surreal.

Stranger by far was the figure he saw in the

fluorescent glare of the bathroom mirror. He had asked the concierge for a razor and shaving foam and after showering for at least twenty minutes (a luxury that he wasn't going to knock) he had slowly scraped off the scraggly beard and watched another alien version of himself emerge, this one with vanished lips and white and hollowed cheeks and his long hair wildly adrift like some fanatic frontier preacher.

He sat now with a towel wrapped around his waist and another over his shoulders, wondering if the operator had forgotten about the call he had placed or if all the lines to New York were still busy. The storks in the flame trees had been joined by four others now and they were all flapping and cavorting and he still couldn't figure out what they were up to. The clock-radio on the bedside table clicked to ten past four, which meant it was ten past nine in the morning in New York and ten past seven in Montana. His mother normally slept until eight, so he'd decided first to call Harry Turney. At last the phone rang. The operator said she had New York on the line and told him to go ahead. Connor asked for Harry Turney and waited.

"Turney."

"So they didn't fire you yet."

"Jesus, Connor! Where the fuck have you been?"

"Did you miss me?"

"Jesus Christ."

"You know, in all these years, I don't think I ever heard you swear till now."

"Yeah? Well, you save it for when you need it. What the fuck have you been doing? I mean, Jesus Christ, Connor, how can you do that? If you want to go get yourself kidnapped and killed, that's your business, but at least you might have the sense or decency to let someone know where the hell you're doing it."

"Harry, I'm sorry."

"So you damn well should be. Have you called your mother?"

"I'm just about to."

"What's the matter with you? Get off the phone and do it now. I'll call you back. I got about a thousand messages for you. What's your number?"

Connor told him and hung up, smiling to himself guiltily. He called the operator to give her his mother's number and while he waited for the call to come through dressed himself in his new shirt and pants.

His mother was a lot more forgiving. She said that she had long ago gotten used to his vanishing acts and even if it had been five times longer than any of his previous ones she hadn't been worried. Connor didn't believe her for a moment.

She wanted to know when he was coming home and he said soon, as soon as he could find a way of reuniting Lawrence with his brother. He asked her how she was and about the ranch and she told him she had found an eager and hardworking young fellow from Augusta who was helping out with the cattle. That aside, nothing much in her life seemed to have changed.

"You heard about Ed, of course."

"What about him?"

There was a long pause and he asked again.

"Son, Ed died. Christmas before last. I forgot how long you've been gone."

Connor was stunned. She told him what had happened and what a shock it had been for everyone and Connor sat on the bed and listened in a muted daze.

"How are Julia and Amy?"

"Well, heck, they're right out there where you are."

"What?"

"They're out there in Africa."

"In Uganda?"

"Yeah. At least, I think it's Uganda. Tell the truth, I get a little confused with all those different places you go to. But, yeah, she's gone out to work with those poor kids you photographed, you know, the ones they turn into soldiers. Taken Amy with her."

"In Karingoa? St. Mary of the Angels?"

"That's the place. I had a postcard about a month ago. Her mother got herself all wrought up about Amy going, but it sounds like they're having a real good time."

There was a pause.

"Connor? Are you there?"

"Yeah."

But he was too choked with emotion to go on speaking. In little more than a whisper he promised his mother that he would call again later and hung up.

An hour later he was pacing back and forth across Geoffrey Odong's cubicle of an office at the newspaper. Through the open doorway he could see the tension mounting in the newsroom as the evening deadline approached. Geoffrey was leaning back in his chair behind a desk piled high with papers. For the past twenty minutes he had been on the phone to an old college friend who was now a senior officer in the northern command of the UPDF.

Connor could hear only one side of the conversation but he had already gotten the drift. At last Geoffrey hung up. He gave Connor a gloomy look and shook his head.

"There's no way. There are roadblocks on every route into the area. You wouldn't even get as far as Gulu. They're not letting anyone near the place, least of all any journalists."

"What's happening in Karingoa?"

"He said the rebel advance has been checked, but I don't think I believe it. They're attacking on two fronts, Makuma to the northwest and Kony's forces to the east."

"How near are they to Karingoa?"

"He says about twenty miles. My guess is that they're nearer. He said many people have already left. He claims that the situation is under control but it sounds to me as if the government has greatly underestimated the rebels' strength."

Connor turned and stared out of the window at the street below. A truck had overturned and spilled its load of green bananas and all the blocked cars and taxis and buses were blaring their horns. A woman sheathed in vivid yellow was weaving gracefully through the chaos, carrying a vast wrapped bundle on her head and leading a small child by the hand. The last of the sun bathed them in a golden glow and cast their shadows long over all they passed.

"Geoffrey, I have to get to them."

"There is no way. In any case, they may have already been evacuated."

"If I know Sister Emily, they'll be the last to leave."

Connor turned to face him.

"Do you know someone who would fly me up there?"

"Don't be crazy."

"Do you?"

THIRTY-ONE

THREE TIMES now the government soldiers had come to advise them to leave and every time Sister Emily had refused. To flee from the devil, she told them, only helped him flourish; St. Mary of the Angels had stood firm against Makuma's threats and thieving raids upon the town for more than a decade and she wasn't about to yield to him now.

At first the calm and confidence that she displayed had been infectious. She told both children and staff that there was nothing to fear; that the shell fire that they could hear at night was from the government forces bombarding the rebel positions and driving them back; that it had happened before and would no doubt happen again. If things got bad, she said, they could all pile into Gertrude, the double-decker bus, and be away in minutes. Everyone seemed reassured, even inspired.

Yet as the days went by and the boom of the guns grew nightly nearer, it became apparent that this was more than another "thieving raid." On the road beyond the convent gates the trickle of refugees was swelling to a steady flood. From dawn to dusk they filed by, the twice-displaced and dispossessed, the ragged and the wretched, watching with blank eyes while UPDF trucks packed with soldiers thundered past the other way, heading north toward the battle front.

Several times Julia had found children at the windows watching all this and though she did her best to allay any worries they voiced, she had secretly begun to share them. It wasn't for herself that she worried but for Amy, who had at first seemed blithely unconcerned. With her great gift for guilt, Julia had now managed to rekindle all those early anxieties about bringing the child here in the first place. Her mother had been right. Perhaps they should go before it was too late. Ever alert to Julia's moods, Amy seemed to sense this change in her and now she too was showing symptoms of anxiety. She was quieter, always checking where Julia was; and she began to sleep poorly, cuddling close and asking often if the shell fire sounded closer.

Last night, after the soldiers' third visit and all

the children had gone to bed, Sister Emily asked Julia, Françoise and Peter Pringle to convene in her office and, after pouring each of them a cup of the Queen of England's favorite tea, announced quietly that they should consider themselves free to leave.

"I still refuse to believe there is any cause for concern. The lieutenant assured me that the rebels are being pushed back and yet still he says we should flee. I asked him why and he said because he could not guarantee our safety. I told him only Our Lord Jesus can do that."

She wagged a finger and narrowed her eyes.

"I suspect the real reason is that they want to use this place as a barracks. It was the same two years ago. They created panic and many people left." She shrugged and smiled. "Then . . . they came back."

She took a sip of tea.

"Makuma is like a frightened dog who barks ferociously. You run away, he chases you. You stand still, it's he who runs away. But, Julia, if you are concerned about Amy, then you should go. George can drive you both down to Gulu and from there you can go on to Kampala. We would all understand." She turned to Peter Pringle and Françoise.

"The same goes for both of you. We would miss you, of course, but we can manage."

There was a short silence. Pringle cleared his throat.

"Well, I can only speak for myself," he said. "But as long as you and the children are here, I'm not going anywhere."

His little declaration made Julia feel ashamed. That night, for the first time in a week, there was no sound of shell fire. Amy slept without stirring and Julia lay scolding herself for being weak and foolish. How could she, even for one moment, consider abandoning everyone? Wasn't that what she had done all those years ago with Skye? Once was enough.

She woke in the morning with a new resolve.

But it lasted only a few hours. At sunset the shelling started up again, louder and nearer than ever. And there was a new accompaniment now, a thudding sound that Peter Pringle said was mortar fire. As they were sitting down for supper in the tent, a white Land Rover came roaring around the side of the building. It skidded to a dusty halt outside the kitchen compound and two people, a man and a woman, climbed quickly out. Julia recognized them. They were Danish aid workers, a young married couple who sometimes came here to eat, but it was all too apparent that they hadn't come now for their supper.

They reached the staff table and Sister Emily and all of them stood and gathered around. The man was breathing heavily and trying with little success to conceal his alarm. The children had all gone silent and sat watching from their tables.

In a low voice he told them that Makuma had broken through and that the government forces were retreating in disarray before him. The rebels were less than ten miles away and moving steadily toward the northern outskirts of the town, looting and burning all before them.

THE MAN SAT with his bare elbows on the table either side of his beer, his bushy blond mustache propped on his cupped fists and his pale blue eyes fixed unblinking on Connor. His forearms were massive and sunburned and on the left one, above the heavy gold Rolex, was a tattooed crest of an open-winged eagle which Connor figured must be the emblem of some elite military corps. His neck was thicker than his bristled head and a thatch of blond chest hair sprouted from the collar of his dark green sports shirt.

It had taken Geoffrey just three phone calls to find the kind of person Connor needed but beyond that he didn't want to be involved. Johannes Kriel ran a small aviation company and was rumored to be involved in smuggling, gunrunning and many darker deeds beside. Connor was told to go to the Parkside Inn next to the old taxi park and find a table out on the balcony. Kriel would join him there.

When he did, the man neither said hello nor offered his hand. In a clipped South African accent he told the waiter to bring him a Nile Special and then he sat down and told Connor to go ahead and say what he wanted. He listened without any hint of what he might be thinking. But his condescending smile now, as Connor finished, told it all.

"Did anyone tell you there's a war going on up there?"

"Just get me as near as you safely can."

"Safely? Makuma's got fucking heat-seeking ground-to-air missiles."

"You know that?"

"I know that."

He took a drink of his beer.

"When were you thinking of doing this?"

"Right now."

"Tonight? You think I'm going to land in the bush in the middle of the fucking night?"

"You wouldn't have to land."

"What?"

"I'll jump. Can you find me a parachute?"

Kriel narrowed his eyes. "Are you fucking me around?"

"I'm serious. Can you?"

"Maybe." He grinned. "Whether it'll open is another matter."

"I'll give you two thousand dollars."

The man laughed and looked away and took another drink. From below the balcony came a boom and thump of rap music so loud that the air vibrated. It was coming from a white car that had pulled up at the curb. The driver had his arm dangling from the window, slapping the door with his hand in rhythm.

"For ten I might think about it."

They settled on six, although the deal almost fell apart when Connor explained that he didn't have the money to hand and would have to call his bank in New York to get it wired to Kriel's account.

He had a black Range Rover parked outside with a driver waiting, and they climbed in and headed out of the city. They drove south and then west for about half an hour with barely another word spoken until the suburbs dwindled to scrub and they came at last to a small private airstrip. It was heavily fenced and there were armed guards at the gate who touched their caps and let the vehicle pass as soon as they saw Kriel's face.

There was a small office with a flickering fluorescent strip and a private colony of mosquitoes. Kriel asked for the name of his bank and dialed the number to make sure it was the real thing. Then he handed Connor the phone and wrote down his own bank details and loomed over him listening with great attention while Connor arranged for the transfer.

When it was done he left Connor to the mosquitoes and went around to the storeroom at the back of the building to dig out the parachute and while he was gone Connor called Geoffrey who again tried to talk him out of it.

"Listen," Connor said. "If this was Elizabeth and one of those beautiful daughters of yours, wouldn't you do the same?"

"I don't know how to use a parachute."

"Well, there you go. I don't have that excuse."

"How long since you last jumped?"

"Awhile."

Connor asked him to let Lawrence know that he would come back for him as soon as he could and if for some reason he couldn't, to make sure that the boy was reunited with his brother. Geoffrey promised.

"I remember you talking about this woman when we first met all those years ago. You must still love her very much."

It was pitched as a question and Connor hesitated for it was as momentous as any he had ever been asked. Yet he felt he owed his friend the truth.

"Always have and always will," he said simply.

Kriel reappeared carrying a stained canvas bag and when he dumped it on the floor it sent up a cloud of dust.

He grinned. "Been a long time since anyone had call to use it."

Connor asked for a flashlight and when Kriel found him one he carried the bag outside and unpacked it. He hooked the end of the parachute to the wall and stretched it out to examine it. It was a basic but steerable emergency bail-out system with a twenty-six-foot conical canopy and an old-style cotton and canvas harness that had seen better days. He checked every one of the twenty-two gores and found only a couple of small holes, then followed the lines down to the connector links and the risers. It wasn't great but it was good enough. Kriel stood with his arms folded, leaning against the door frame and smirking as he watched.

"Hope you're not going to get all picky on me."

"It'll do. Is there a reserve?"

Kriel laughed. "I wouldn't worry, bro. You'll probably get shot before you hit the fucking ground."

"I'll take that as a no."

While Connor carefully repacked the chute, Kriel went back inside and when he reappeared he had a 9mm automatic holstered at his hip and was carrying a semiautomatic rifle and a black nylon jacket which he tossed to Connor.

"Put that on. You'd be hard to miss wearing that fucking shirt."

Twenty minutes later they were taxiing along the runway in an unmarked Cessna 206. All but the front two seats had been removed, presumably to make space for the contraband it normally carried. There was a cargo door at the rear of the starboard side, so jumping out wasn't going to be as tricky as Connor had expected.

They took off to the south with the black expanse of Lake Victoria stretching away to nothing below them. Then on tilted wings they circled around and headed north with the lights of Kampala to their right shimmering and winking through the hot night air. It was the first moment of stillness that Connor had allowed himself since the phone call to his mother and he realized that in his obsession to reach

Julia and Amy, he hadn't yet spared proper thought for his lost friend Ed now lost forever. And as the lights of the city suburbs faded and disappeared behind them and the little Cessna nosed its way north into the ominous night, he felt sorrow surge within him and settle like a leaden weight in the hollow of his chest.

THE BRANCHES OF THE FLAME TREES scraped against the top of the bus as it passed beneath them on its way up the driveway and the noise was so loud and shocking that some of the children sitting on the upper deck cried out in fright and ducked as if they expected the roof to lift off like the lid of a can.

Julia was sitting with her arm around Amy in the rearmost seat at the top of the stairway. Through the window to her left she saw the shadowed shapes of the fruit bats erupting from the mango trees and when she looked back she could see Peter Pringle's determined face at the wheel of the truck behind. Most of the children and staff were on the bus but the rest sat crammed in the open back of Pringle's truck. Behind that were two smaller trucks with all the cooks and maids and kitchen boys but all that Julia could see of these were the swaying stacks of luggage roped to their roofs. The center's four security guards had been allocated one to each vehicle.

When the bus reached the convent gates it had to stop for the road outside was a seething river of panic and confusion. Most of the refugees were walking or running and there were cars and trucks and vans weaving among them with their horns blaring and people clinging desperately to their sides and roofs, lashing out and kicking at others who tried to climb aboard. Julia watched a man trying to ride a bicycle, a baby squirming and screaming in one arm and two frenzied chickens flapping upside down from his belt. Oblivious to all and thundering past through the pall of illumined red dust that swirled above the chaos came the retreating army trucks packed with soldiers, the weary and the wounded, the shell-shocked and the dead.

When the crowd caught sight of the St. Mary's convoy a score or more came running and yelling and waving their arms and as the bus started to move out into the road they screamed and hammered on its sides and Julia could hear the security guard and Sister Emily below fending them off and telling them again and again that there was no room. Amy was quaking with fear.

"Mommy!"

"It's all right, honey. It's all right."

It wasn't of course and perhaps it never would be but there was nothing else to say. The girl had been so brave while they packed their things and helped everyone else get ready to leave. Julia stroked her hair and felt her burrow deeper and cling more tightly.

The bus was on the road now and George the gardener, all alone down there in the cramped driver's booth with his hand planted on the horn, was steering Gertrude south through the parting waves of people. Julia looked back again and saw Pringle and the other trucks pulling out of the gate and following. And beyond them now, for the first time, she saw the flash of exploding shells. Far away to the north the horizon seemed aglow with fire.

There was a clatter of footsteps on the metal stairway and Sister Emily emerged, beaming as if they were all on some exotic school outing. In a cheery voice she asked the children how they were doing and why on earth they were all so quiet. The children all turned around in their seats and stared at her but only a few murmured in reply. Unfazed, she looked around at Julia and saw Amy sheltering under her arm and she made a face that was sad and funny and sympathetic all at the same time.

"Amy, I think we need a song. What do you think we should sing?"

Amy gave a small shrug but didn't say anything. Sister Emily persisted.

"How about one of those English songs you taught us all? From your *Lion* film. No? Then what about the Purple Submarine?"

"Yellow."

Sister Emily frowned. "Are you sure? I think it was purple."

"It was yellow!"

"Oh well, maybe you are right. Anyway, how about that one?"

Sister Emily had clearly forgotten the tune and she looked at Julia to give a lead. And because Julia's singing talents had always been a favorite source of mirth and mockery for her daughter, she had only to sing a few bars before Amy began to grin and then to giggle. Then Christine and Thomas sitting nearby started to giggle too, not just at Julia but at Sister Emily who had the hang of the tune but not of the lyrics. On every chorus she gave the submarine a different color, and this made Amy sing ever more loudly to correct her until gradually, row by row, the other children joined in and before long the lower deck was singing too.

Even as she sang, Julia was aware that their contrived merriment was of course a kind of denial, for the children's eyes were now all turned in upon each other and not upon the fleeing crowds below who waved and clamored for help as the bus rumbled by. But, as Ed used to say, what was wrong with a little healthy denial? Her duty was to those she could help and most of all to Amy. And as she watched the singing lift the children's spirits she began to feel stronger herself. When the song was done they sang another and then another and when she looked over her shoulder Julia could see that Pringle and his passengers were singing too.

It would be all right, she told herself. They would all get through.

THE NIGHT AT FIRST was clear and the stars undimmed by a moon now carved to a sliver. They flew without lights and for the first hour kept high with the land unfurling far below, the grassland gray and the jungle black and the great still waters of Lake Kyoga gleaming like obsidian.

They sat side by side with Connor on the right and the lights of the instruments glowing between them and glinting dully on the barrel of Kriel's rifle now clamped above his head. They wore headsets so that they could talk above the roar of the engine but they rarely did except when Kriel pointed something out and told him the names of the places they passed.

As the lights of Lira fell away to their left and the land to their right grew more barren, they saw clouds ahead and Kriel said that Connor should count his blessings, for had the sky stayed clear they would have been too easy a target and he would have had to jump while they were yet a long way off. He asked where he had learned to use a parachute and Connor told him.

The clouds were coming on a light wind from the west. The first to arrive were fluffed like cotton and separate and Connor watched their shadows on the arid gray land and the shadow of the plane passing among them. But as they traveled farther north so the clouds began to thicken and darken and join and from away in the west came the flicker of lightning.

They were yet some seventy miles south of Karingoa when they got their first glimpse of the war. With the cover of the clouds they were flying lower now and through a gap they saw the lights of a great many trucks on a straight stretch of road and at once Kriel banked away west and started to climb. The next time they were able to see the road it seemed much more crowded and confused and the lights were moving more slowly. They climbed higher above the layer of clouds and saw to the north a dim red glow which as they flew nearer seemed to spread and intensify. And from his days as a smoke jumper Connor knew what it was.

Soon the canopy of cloud glowed like a vast red cauldron before them and Kriel nosed the Cessna farther to the west to skirt it. A moment later the clouds parted and they saw the town of Karingoa and the swath of flame that fringed it to the north. And even in those few short seconds before the fissure closed they saw the flash of shells and the red and crisscross streaks of gunfire in the sky.

"I've heard of a few fucking stupid ways to die, but this about beats them all. I'll come around once more and then I'm out of here. If you're going to bail out, you better get back there."

Connor looked at the dials and made some rapid calculations. They were flying at a hundred and ten knots at eighteen hundred feet, which was a lot higher than he wanted to be. The chute would be safe from as low as four hundred and the less time he was floating out there for the world to see, the better his chances.

"How low can you get me?"

"This is it, bro. They've got some big fucking toys down there and Christ knows what in the air. It's a miracle we haven't been hit already."

"If we went east, we'd have the cover of the smoke. You could get lower."

Kriel muttered some further obscenity and shook his head but it soon became plain that he was doing just that. And as they circled east around the glowing bowl of cloud Connor unbuckled his seat belt and took off the headset. As he got up from his seat Kriel held up his right hand.

"Good luck, bro."

Connor grasped the hand and thanked him.

"Now get the fuck out of here," Kriel said.

Connor made his faltering way back to the cargo door clutching onto anything he could as the plane banked and juddered through the cloud. He checked his harness then squatted down beside the door and took hold of the handle. His heart was pumping hard. He thought of the last time he had jumped, that day on Snake Mountain that now seemed more than a lifetime ago. He remembered how he and Ed had been the last to jump and how Ed's face had been so pale with worry watching the others go before him and knowing all the while that Julia was somewhere there below them in the flames, just as she was now.

"Sixteen hundred!" Kriel yelled.

Connor gripped the handle hard now and planted his feet firmly on either side of the door so that he wouldn't be sucked out in the rush of air.

"Okay!" he yelled. "I'm opening up!"

Without looking back Kriel gave him a thumbs-up.

The door ripped open and a moment later Kriel nosed the plane below the line of the clouds and Connor got a first murky view of the terrain he was going to be landing in. They were maybe two miles east of the town now and through the smoke he could see its northern part was well ablaze with the sky glowing fiercely above it. He could see the silhouetted shapes of trucks moving steadily from the north toward it. The smoke and the light of the fire made it harder to see the shadowed land that was closer at hand. He knew the layout of the town well but not the land that lay around it and all he could see of it were inky smudges of jungle and gray patches among them which he figured to be fields.

"Okay," Kriel yelled. "We're at fourteen-fifty. I'll take you down to twelve hundred but that's as low as I go. Speed one hundred knots. Get in the door!"

Connor braced himself with one hand above the frame and maneuvered himself into the doorway so that he was squatting with the toes of his boots poking out into the void. His knees were shaking and he shivered and it struck him as strange for although his heart was thumping it wasn't with fear and the roaring air was warm. Then, in the next instant, he had a sudden and overwhelming sensation that someone was standing beside him and he knew that it couldn't be Kriel. He turned and looked and saw nothing. But he felt the presence ever more keenly and whether it was real or conjured in his fevered imaginings, he knew without a shred of doubt that it was Ed.

"Twelve-fifty!"

Connor fisted his right hand and pressed it to his chest.

"Hey, old friend," he whispered in the wind. "Hearts of fire."

"Twelve hundred! Jump, you crazy fucker!"

Connor launched himself into the night with all the power he had. He felt the warm air rushing past.

"One-one-thousand . . ."

He was twisting as he fell and looking up he saw the belly of the Cessna tilt sharply away and go into a steep climb toward the clouds.

"Two-one-thousand . . ."

To give himself the best chance of not being shot he was going to wait as long as possible before pulling the ripcord. He figured he had five seconds, no more. He spread his arms like wings to find the right position.

"Three-one-thousand . . ."

He was looking down now and the upward rush of air was blasting his eyes and making them stream. All he could see was blackness.

"Four-one-thousand . . ."

He reached for the ripcord and felt a stab of panic when he couldn't find it. But then he did and he grasped it firmly.

"Five-one-thousand . . ."

He tugged it hard and felt the pins give way and then the faint flutter and pull at his back as the pilot parachute broke out, hauling the main chute after it. He braced himself and then, a moment later, felt the whack and jolt to his chest and shoulders as the canopy cracked open and filled. And then that moment of utter calm before sound began to filter in. He could hear the last fading drone of the Cessna and the boom of shell and mortar fire and now the rattle of machine guns too.

He found the toggles, which were of little use for he had only the flimsiest idea of where to steer. It took awhile for his eyes to clear and a little while longer before he realized that they had and that the reason he couldn't see much was that the air was laced with smoke. It tasted thick and acrid in his mouth and stung his eyes and nostrils and when he looked up he saw it swirling beneath the great white and orange dome of the canopy.

Even in the smoke it was still a massive billboard of a target and the chances were that someone down there would spot him. All he could hope was that whoever did was a long way off and wasn't much of a marksman. In all the years and all his work in war zones there had been many moments when he had consciously risked his life, but never had he felt so helpless and exposed. Many times he had dared death to take him and perversely it had chosen not to. Maybe it knew and had always known how little he cared, how cheap a price he placed upon his life.

Yet as he floated down through the smoke and the dark, he realized that the stakes had changed. Now he did care. He had two good reasons to live and they were somewhere out there beyond the smoke and the flame. If they were alive, somehow he would find them. And if they were dead, then death could happily have him too.

When he was still some eighty feet from the ground the smoke seemed suddenly to clear. Somewhere away to his left he heard men shouting and then caught the briefest glimpse of figures running toward him, maybe three or four hundred yards away. And then he looked down and saw the dark tops of some giant palm trees racing up toward him as if through a zoom. There was a paler space on the far side, away from where the men were, and all he could do was hope that it was a clearing. He toggled hard and lifted his knees as high as he could and the next thing he knew he was being dragged chest-high through the clattering palm fronds and then he was dropping fast beyond them. His boots hit the ground hard and he rolled and somersaulted and came to rest on his back in time to see the canopy floating down over him like a premature shroud.

He felt a jab of pain in his right shoulder but his legs were fine and that was what mattered. He found the edge of the canopy and hoisted it and froze for a moment to listen. He could hear the voices, though how close he couldn't tell for the sound was baffled by the trees, but he knew he had only seconds to free himself from the chute and disappear.

The clearing was cultivated and seemed to be in a plantation of some sort. The vegetation on the other side looked thick. Connor fumbled with the harness buckles. They were of a type he didn't know and one of them seemed to be jammed. He could hear the men's voices much closer now. He should have practiced a release on the plane and he cursed himself for a fool. In a few moments, however, he was free and he ran as fast as he could for the cover of the trees.

Once he was among the trees all he could hear was the pulsing scream of frogs and insects. The undergrowth was dense and tangled and he had to duck and crawl and stamp and scramble to make any progress at all. He had but the vaguest notion of which direction he was headed but from his last brief view of the burning town he figured he was moving south. Every so often he paused and held his labored breath while he listened for the men. But the only movement he heard was the branches that he had parted twitching back into place.

Just when he was starting to feel safer he startled some roosting birds who erupted around his ears squawking and thrashing their wings and Connor thought his heart was going to explode. He swore at them and spurred himself on for his pursuers would surely have heard them. Whether the men were Makuma's or UPDF he didn't much care. Either way they were likely to kill him before he had a chance to explain what the hell he was doing dropping in on them uninvited.

How far he traveled through the bush he had no way of knowing. Every so often through the fringe of the trees he would catch sight of the burning town and at last he saw the great water tower that stood near the marketplace and he was able to get his bearings from it and adjust his course. The shelling had stopped. Sometimes he saw soldiers, small and silhouetted by the flames as they ran across the fields firing from the hip in the way that Makuma made them. Connor saw two get hit and fall. Once he saw a helicopter gunship come swerving out of the night above them, the flames reflecting a sickly orange along its belly as it strafed the southern end of Karingoa. In the confusion he could only guess, but it seemed as if the rebels had almost succeeded in taking the town, with the government forces putting up some last resistance in its southern enclaves.

As Connor headed yet farther south, the town became obscured by trees and soon all he could see of it was the rising glow of fire above them. At last, through the darkness, he saw what he had been searching for: a pale horizontal band with the black shapes of trees beyond. It was the rear wall of the convent gardens and he jumped the ditch before it and stood with his hands pressed to the crumbling whitewash and his head bowed while he gathered his breath.

He was panting hard and drenched in sweat and his face and hands were cut and bloody from thorns and razored leaves and creepers. Kriel's black jacket was soaked and hot enough to cook him but it made him less visible and he kept it on. He rested only a short while then clambered above his bloody handprints on the wall and hoisted himself over into the garden.

The convent was burning and so was the chapel. From the shelter of the orange trees he could see the flames licking hungrily from the upstairs windows and one by one the burning wooden shutters breaking away and crashing to the ground in great cartwheeled explosions of spark. He was expecting to see soldiers but the place seemed deserted, nor was there any sound of gunfire now, only the rumble and crackle of the burning building.

He watched awhile longer, trying to picture the place as it was and to imagine Julia and Amy living there, but such thoughts seemed to belong to another universe. He walked across the playing field through flaming scraps of debris, past the looted kitchens and the smoldering shreds and poles of the dining tent and then around the side of the chapel where little flames raced along the charred rafters like gleeful demons. When he came around to the front of the building he startled a mangy dog carrying something pale in its jaws and it skittered off into the mango trees and vanished.

Connor walked up the driveway beneath the flame trees and didn't once look back at the blazing convent. As he drew near to the gates he saw that the road outside was blocked by two overturned trucks, both of them in flames. A moment later he heard the rattle of a heavy machine gun and ducked in among the mango trees and almost at once tripped over a soldier.

The man was lying in the grass under cover of the wall with his assault rifle trained on the gate. From his uniform Connor was almost certain that he was UPDF. There were others too, six or seven of them, all lying there. Connor got to his knees but they yelled at him to get down and no sooner had he hit the ground when a grenade went off between the gates.

"Come! Come! Come!"

Suddenly they were all up and running across the driveway and without a moment's thought Connor got up and ran with them. As they crossed the gateway through the clearing smoke of the grenade, the machine gun opened up again and Connor saw the dust around him kick and heard the bullets thwack against the stucco columns and go screaming in ricochet into the trees. Nobody was hit and they ran ducking and dodging among the bushes and trees, and when they got to the side wall of the convent grounds they helped one another and Connor too to scramble up and over and down into the scrub beyond. One of them had a sergeant's stripes on his sleeve. He grabbed hold of Connor's shoulder.

"You are a teacher?"

For a moment Connor didn't know what he meant. The sergeant jerked a thumb at the burning convent.

"A teacher, here?"

"Yes."

"Come now. We must go quick."

About a mile down the road they reached a small convoy of trucks that stood waiting for them under cover of some tall eucalyptus trees with the jungled hillsides of the valley looming black on either side. The waiting officers were shouting at everyone and the constant frenzied ranting of shortwave radios only helped stoke the sense of burgeoning panic. Everyone clearly wanted out as soon as possible.

Connor was the only civilian and foreigner among them but nobody bothered to ask who he was or what he was doing there so he stayed close to the young sergeant and climbed with his men into the open back of one of the trucks. As each truck filled, so it was waved out onto the road and soon Connor's too was heading off through the choking dust with the flames of St. Mary of the Angels lighting the sky behind.

The rebels seemed to have circled around the town in an attempt to cut the valley road, for along the hilltops on either side there were sporadic flashes and booms and in the headlights of the truck behind he could see the road was cratered with shell holes and strewn with the debris of evacuation and the burnt-out carcasses of cars and trucks. There were bodies too and as they went by, Connor scanned them with a growing sense of foreboding, telling himself again and again with fading conviction that the two he loved most in all the world were somewhere safe.

Some of the soldiers huddled around him were wounded and all seemed too tired or shocked to talk and just stared blankly into the night or at the bouncing metal floor. The one sitting opposite Connor couldn't have been more than sixteen years old. He was bleeding from a head wound and shivering and Connor took off his jacket and laid it gently around the boy's shoulders.

Not long after that the air above them ripped asunder and they all flinched and ducked and looking up Connor saw three fighter planes skimming the valley treetops and heading north to Karingoa. Moments later came the boom of their missiles and it echoed and rolled around the hills and all along the valley. No sooner had the sound died when more planes came screaming overhead and did the same and then more and yet more until the truck had traveled so far down the valley that their bombing was only a muffled murmur and a dim red reflection in the distant sky.

How long he slept he didn't know, but when he woke, the sky was washed with dawn. Most of the soldiers in the truck were still asleep. The clouds were low and leaden and the air was damp and smelled the way it always did before rain. Still only half awake, Connor looked back along the road, idly watching the dimming lights of the truck behind them in the convoy as it slowed to maneuver around some burnt-out vehicles.

And that was when he saw it. The convent's ancient double-decker bus.

He leaped to his feet and yelled for the driver to stop and the soldiers around him woke and some of them grumbled or shouted at him to sit down. He yelled again but the driver clearly couldn't hear or didn't care for he began to accelerate away. Connor turned and scrambled forward over the soldiers' legs and they cursed and shouted at him some more but he wasn't going to be stopped. He reached the back of the driver's cab and hammered on its rear window and then on the roof.

"Stop! You gotta stop!"

The driver didn't look pleased and yelled something back at him, but Connor couldn't hear what it was and just kept on hammering until the truck slowed and even before it came to a halt he had hoisted himself over the side and jumped down onto the road. He fell as he landed but was on his feet straight away. The driver climbed down from the cab haranguing him and many of the soldiers in the back were doing the same but Connor didn't care.

"The bus! That's the convent bus! My family!"

He turned and started to run. The truck coming toward him blasted its horn at him but he ignored it and ran past. It was no more than a hundred and fifty yards back to the bus but it felt as many miles. Gertrude lay askew with one wheel in the ditch and tilting perilously as though a mere touch might topple her. Long before he got there, Connor could see that she had been burned out. The glass of the windows had gone and the roof and uppers were blackened and buckled and only along her lower flanks were there still some patches of blistered

red paint. The lower front where once the grille had been was splayed like a charred shell-fish from some great explosion. In the driver's cab, hunched and curled, as if even now in death he sought to protect himself, was a body burned beyond recognition.

Connor braced himself to find more bodies inside. But he checked both decks and found none, nor in the burnt shell of the truck behind. The young sergeant and two of his men had arrived now to bring him back.

"We must not stop here," the sergeant said.

"You go on."

"No. You must come. It is dangerous here."

He put a hand on Connor's shoulder but Connor brushed it off distractedly and told him again to leave. His mind was reeling with images of what might have happened here. As there was only one body, maybe the others had managed to escape unscathed. Maybe they had been picked up by other vehicles.

"Come," the soldier said. "There is nothing here for you."

"They might be here. Somewhere."

"Where? Look, there's no one."

Another truck roared by along the road, sounding its mournful horn as it passed. Connor turned away in anguish and looked up at the seamless dark green jungle of the hillside, its top veiled by the lowering cloud. He felt a slow, churning sense of loss and desperation rise within him and he walked in faltering steps into the scrub at the side of the road and howled at the sky.

"Julia!"

The sound echoed along the valley and he called her name again and again so that the echoes redoubled each time. And when the last echo faded he stood and scoured the hillside for any sign of movement but nothing stirred.

Then the rain began to fall, slowly at first, in heavy drops that slapped upon the ground and upon his face and shoulders and quickly filled the air with the smell of thirsting dust.

"Come," the sergeant said gently.

Connor couldn't speak. He shook his head.

"Perhaps you find them in one of the camps."

Connor nodded and bowed his head. The rain was thicker and faster now and his hair and his shirt were already soaked. The others waiting down the road in the open back of the truck were calling impatiently.

"Come now," the sergeant said. Again he put a hand on Connor's shoulder and this time he didn't have the will to remove it and instead let himself be steered in his desolation back toward the truck.

When they were halfway there the calling of

the soldiers suddenly seemed different, as if they were no longer chiding him. And the sergeant beside him glanced back toward the bus and then stopped.

"Look," he said.

Connor turned. The rain was so heavy now and his eyes so brimmed with tears that at first he saw nothing. And then the figure standing in the scrub at the side of the road moved and he saw her.

"Connor?"

Through the rain her voice sounded small and frail and full of disbelief.

"Connor? Is that really you?"

He started to walk back along the road and his legs felt so weak that he almost stumbled. She was stepping onto the road now and walking toward him through the pale curtain of the rain.

"Julia?"

They stopped when they were still a little way apart and stood staring at each other as if they were seeing each other's ghost. Her cotton dress was ripped, her face filthy and her short hair bedraggled. Even in all his years of dreaming she had never looked more beautiful.

"Why are you . . . ?" she said. "What are you . . . ?"

"I heard you were here. I had to find you."

She shook her head slightly and then her face crumpled and he stepped toward her and took hold of her and he could feel her whole body begin to shake. And he tried to say just a little of what was in his heart but he couldn't find the words nor even the voice to utter them. He held her face to his chest and stroked her head and she slowly lifted her arms and put them around him and clung to him. She tried to say something but couldn't and just started to sob until he thought she would break.

Over her shoulder he saw the others now, emerging from the trees like wary and disheveled prey. He saw Pringle, the doctor, and Sister Emily holding the hands of two children and others following, ushered by the nuns. And hurrying past them now onto the road and running through the rain toward her mother came Amy, the daughter he hadn't held since she was a baby and who was now this tall, fine girl with a smudged and worried face and a mass of sodden blond curls.

"Mommy?"

Julia gathered her in her arms and started to explain who Connor was, but somehow the child already knew and tentatively reached out to him and took his hand. And with the rain beating down upon them and turning the road around them to a river, the three of them stood clinging to one another as if the world and whatever it might bring would never be allowed to part them.

THIRTY-TWO

IT WAS one of those crystalline Montana mornings, when the freshly fallen snow glinted in the sun like sequined satin and the mountains stood so bold against the blue of the sky that you could count every frosted crevice. Julia followed the dogs out onto the pristine planks of the new porch and closed the kitchen door behind her. Even in the cold the sawn-timber floor still smelled of resin. She stood for a moment peering at the mountains through the icicled fringe of the eaves, her breath billowing, while the two young collies squirmed and bounced around her.

"Hey, you guys. Down now. Get down."

She came down the steps and stopped again and shielded her eyes from the glare of the snow to see more clearly. The only trace of the horses were the twin tracks that led from the barn and out past the corral and then up and away in a gentle curve across the hillside and into the trees. She guessed that they would probably be coming back their usual way so she turned up her collar and headed down toward the creek.

The house that they had built stood in a low fold of the hills some dozen miles east of the massive limestone wall of the Rocky Mountain Front. The building was low and modest and made of wood and, with the smoke curling from its stone chimney and the sun flecking the pale stems of the aspen behind, it already looked as if it belonged. It had taken them more than a year to build. And with each beam and nail, each rafter and strut, so too the new construction of their lives had slowly taken shape.

THEIR HOMECOMING had been hard.

In those few days that they spent in Kampala before flying home, Julia and Amy had stayed cocooned in their hotel room, shell-shocked and licking their wounds, while Connor rushed around the city organizing things. He wanted to help Sister Emily start looking for a new home for the children of St. Mary's and then he had to reunite Thomas and Lawrence Nyeko who had both now been adopted by Connor's friends the Odongs. He even helped arrange the funeral of poor George the gardener who had taken the full blast of the mortar round and by some miracle been the sole casualty of the flight from Karingoa. The result was that Julia and Connor had scarcely had a moment to themselves. Even the airline conspired against them. There weren't three seats together, so Connor sat separately.

After his astonishing quest to find them, his desolate calling of her name across the jungle, the sight of him standing there so gaunt and filthy and wretched by the burnt-out bus, and then the three of them clinging to one another in the rain, after all this, Julia had assumed that everything was resolved and that, once they got back to Montana, she and Connor would be together and that the three of them would be a blissful fairy-tale family. But it wasn't to be like that.

While they were away in Africa, the house in Missoula had been rented out to some UM postgrad students. They were friends of friends and had left it clean and tidy and done no damage, but they had rearranged all the furniture and left the place smelling so utterly different that Amy promptly burst into tears. It no longer felt like home, she said.

Once she had found her old toys and books and made contact again with friends, she soon felt better. And whether it faded or they just got used to it, they soon forgot about the smell. But there was something more potent in the air which no amount of freshening or subtle tidying could banish. The memory of Ed was everywhere, not simply in the photographs—many of which Connor had himself taken—but like an almost palpable presence in every room.

Julia knew that Connor must sense it even more sharply than she did. She tried to view it as benign, to convince herself that they had Ed's blessing, that he would want them to be happy and to move forward, not fester like prisoners of the past, but she couldn't make the mental leap. She knew that she and Connor should talk about it, but it was too vast a subject and she worried that to raise it would somehow make her seem presumptuous.

He stayed for a couple of days to help them settle in and get themselves organized. But Julia could tell how awkward he felt. After all the trauma, Amy still needed constant comfort and even if she had wanted to, there was no way that Julia was going to let her sleep on her own yet. Connor slept in the little guest room and once Amy had fallen asleep in her arms, Julia lay wondering if she should slip away and go to him. But the risk of Amy waking and finding her gone seemed too great. And, anyhow, although she longed for him, she wasn't certain that he felt the same. On the third morning he left to go to his mother's ranch and perhaps she imagined it, but he looked relieved to be going. When he kissed her goodbye, it was on the cheek, like a friend.

It seemed to Julia, in those first desolate days, that the entire geography of their lives had been changed and that by some cruel joke no one had given them a map or a compass to steer by.

In the weeks that followed, Connor phoned every day and came often to see them. And on weekends she and Amy would drive over the divide to stay with him and his mother at the ranch. It was the cusp of spring and Connor would take Amy riding and when the weather grew warmer, the three of them would sometimes go hiking. He gave Amy a camera and showed her how to use it and he took her down to the creek and taught her how to cast a fly.

He had a way with her that was altogether different from Ed's. Amy's relationship with Ed had been full of exuberant banter; they were both great talkers and extroverts and being around them was sometimes like listening to a pair of comics competing on a talk show. Connor talked too, but his way was much more gentle and mostly he just listened, fixing her with those pale blue eyes and smiling and nodding.

Watching the two of them grow steadily closer, Julia felt happy for them both. But she couldn't quite suppress a faintest twinge of envy. For her own relationship with Connor seemed becalmed in a kind of sibling friendship. There were moments, the occasional look or touch, when she felt sure that he wanted her as much she wanted him. But neither of them seemed willing or able to step across the line. In any case, with Amy still so needy and the memory of Ed so vivid and omnipresent, the occasion never seemed to present itself.

One balmy evening in May, Connor dropped by unannounced. Julia had been busy digging neglected flowerbeds all afternoon and was blotched with dirt and sweat. He said he was on his way to Hamilton to meet up with Chuck Hamer and some of his other smoke jumping buddies and since he was passing, he thought he would call by and say hello. He hoped she didn't mind. Julia said she didn't and apologized for looking such a wreck. He said he thought she looked just fine. Amy had gone down to the river to see if she could catch supper. She heard Connor's voice and turned and waved and he waved back.

"Would you like a beer?" Julia said.

"Sure, if you're going to have one."

She went inside to fetch them and while she

was there tried to smarten herself up in the hallway mirror but decided she was beyond repair. She thought he might have gone down to the river to be with Amy but she found him waiting for her on the deck and they stood there, drinking their beers while the light mellowed around them.

"I was trying to figure out what was different out here," he said. "You took down that old rope rail."

"Oh, yeah, we did. Well, you know, it wasn't really needed anymore."

"Opens the place up."

"It does. Gives us more space."

He nodded and for a while neither of them said anything. How the conversation might have developed, she would never know, because at that moment, Amy hooked a fish and let out a whoop and they both went running down to the river to join her. She landed it with only a few words of guidance from Connor. It was a rainbow but too small to keep. Connor carefully unhooked the fly and lowered the fish gently into the water and they watched it linger for a moment as if it couldn't believe it was free, then dart away in a flash of silver.

By early June, Amy seemed to have recovered most of her old zest and confidence. She started to sleep in her own room, though the first few times she came creeping back at the dead of night to Julia's. At supper one evening she announced that the coming weekend her friend Molly was having a sleepover birthday party.

"Is it okay if I go?" she asked tentatively.

"Is it 'okay'? I think that's terrific."

"You're sure you don't mind?"

"Heck, I might even have a sleepover myself!"

"With Connor?"

Julia gulped. She laughed too loudly and felt herself blushing.

"Well, no, honey. That's not what I meant. I just said it, you know, as a joke."

"It's okay, you know. I don't mind."

Julia didn't know where to look or what to say. Amy went on.

"I mean, I thought we were all going to, like, live together."

"Is that what you want?"

"Of course I do! I love him. He's not my daddy but he is my father."

That did it. Julia got up and went to her and they grabbed hold of each other, crying and laughing at the same time. Still hugging her, Amy went on.

"You love him too. I know you do by the way you look at him."

"Do I? I mean, do you?"

"Yes. And he looks at you the same way."

"Does he?"

Amy disengaged from Julia's arms and sniffed and wiped her tears away.

"How come you guys are so dumb?"

Julia shrugged.

"Anyhow," Amy went on, with great deliberation, "I'm going to the sleepover. Okay?"

"Okay."

"Okay."

Julia called Connor that same evening and asked him bluntly what he was doing Friday night.

"Well, I've got a date."

"Oh." Julia was floored.

"With you and Amy. Aren't you coming over this weekend?"

"Amy's got a birthday party." She swallowed. "It's one of those sleepover deals, you know."

"Oh."

"So, I just wondered if you'd like to come over and I could cook us something nice to eat. Maybe cook outside if it stays dry."

"Just the two of us."

"Yes."

There was a silence. Was he teasing her? She couldn't tell.

"I mean, you don't have to," she went on. "It

was just, you know, an idea. Maybe you've got something else to do."

"What time?"

"I have to drop her off at six."

"I'll be there at seven."

Friday was slow in coming, but at last it did and Julia spent most of it feeling like a high school kid preparing for a prom and trying to look nonchalant in front of Amy. She changed the sheets and put flowers on one of the bedside tables. On the other one were some framed family photographs of her and Amy and Ed; Julia made a mental note to remove them when old eagle eyes had gone off to her party. She went into town to buy the food and to get her legs waxed and her hair cut. When she came back Amy said how nice she looked and Julia tried to act all casual and said, well, you know, it was summer and all and short hair was cooler. Amy gave her a knowing smile and said the flowers in the bedroom looked nice too.

Earlier in the week Julia had gone shopping for a new dress but everything she saw was either too smart or too fussy. So she dug into the back of the closet and found the old pale blue dress that she had bought all those years ago for Connor's surprise homecoming party. She took it to the cleaners and it came back looking like new.

She dropped Amy at Molly's house in Missoula ten minutes early and nearly got caught speeding on the way home. The weather was clear and warm and so she had decided that they would eat outside. She had already set the table and put candles all around the rail of the deck and in the trees. They were going to have tuna steaks and salad and new potatoes and then raspberries and cream. Connor would probably want a beer, but she put wine and champagne in the refrigerator just in case. She lit the barbecue and hurried inside and upstairs.

She showered and dried off and stood in front of the mirror, smoothing herself all over with some fifty-dollar moisturizer that Linda had given her. Allowing for the first effects of gravity, for a woman in her mid-thirties (okay, mid-to-late thirties if you had to be picky about it), although she said it herself, she looked pretty darned fine. She spent an unseemly amount of time deciding what underwear to put on, all the while telling herself what a fool she was being and trying to calm her racing heart and succeeding only in making it race faster. Her shoulders and arms were tanned from the recent good weather, so she ended up choosing a plain cream satin bra and panties to match.

The dress looked great. A little eyeshadow and mascara, no lipstick. Well, maybe a little.

No, better without. Turn on the bedside lamp. Would that look too calculating? Dear Lord, after the candles and flowers and champagne, if he hadn't got the message by the time they got up here, they were in big trouble. What would Linda do? Maybe she should call her. No. Leave the lamp off. On. What the hell.

She went downstairs and put a Spencer Lewis CD on the stereo. It was called *A Sense of Place*. She remembered Connor commenting on it at the christening, at least she hoped that was the one. Whatever, the music was light and airy and somehow seemed right.

It was five after seven when she heard his truck turn into the driveway. She took a last look at herself in the hallway mirror, then stood perfectly still for a moment with her eyes closed.

"Ed?" she whispered. "It's okay. Isn't it? Tell me it's okay."

She took his silence as a yes.

Connor was wearing a salmon-colored denim shirt with white snap buttons and his old blue jeans looked as if they'd come straight from the laundry. He had on his best boots too and his best hat which he removed as he walked toward her across the gravel, never once taking his eyes off her. In his other hand he had a bottle of champagne and there was a bunch of blue cornflowers tucked under his arm. When he was still a short way off he stopped and stood looking at her, smiling his slow smile.

"I remember that dress."

"Yeah. Well, you know, they're all back there inside, Chuck Hamer and the boys, all ready to surprise you again. Just thought I'd warn you this time."

"Thanks."

"You're welcome."

"You look so darn beautiful, I don't know where else to look."

Julia swallowed and smiled and held his gaze.

"Well, why don't you just keep on looking."

He stepped toward her and handed her the flowers.

"Thank you."

Her voice was so small she could hardly hear it herself. She tried to stop herself trembling but couldn't. He stepped still closer until they were almost touching and she could smell his clean soapy smell and saw him take a deep breath of her scent and lower his eyes to her lips. She opened her mouth a little, and moved it slowly up toward his and as their lips touched everything went still as if the world had stopped turning.

Their hands were too full of flowers and hats and bottles so all that touched were their mouths. Then, without a word, she turned and led him into the house. And though it wasn't what she'd planned, it honestly wasn't, she led him up the stairs and into her bedroom. She dropped the flowers on the bedside table beneath the others and to her horror saw that she had forgotten to remove the photos from the other table. God almighty, what an idiot she was. She thought about doing it now, but it didn't seem like a good idea. If he had already noticed, he didn't seem bothered.

He laid the champagne and his hat on the chair and turned to face her and they stood close, looking into each other's eyes. He traced down the outside of her arms with his fingertips and then traced up along the insides too and then took her by the shoulders and bent his head and kissed her neck and beneath her chin and along the line of her jaw.

He turned her around and kissed the birthmark on the back of her neck and slowly unzipped her dress and let it slide down her body to the floor and smoothed his hands down her back and onto her hips and thighs. She turned and kissed him and he lifted his hand and brushed the tops of her breasts and then kissed them. As he reached behind and tried to unhook her bra she felt his body quake a little and she had to help him do it and watched him watching her as she slipped it from her shoulders.

She saw his eyes flicker beyond her to the photographs.

"Connor, it's okay." She kissed him gently. "It's us now. We're allowed."

He nodded and she kissed him more deeply and soon she felt him loosen and the worry or guilt or whatever troubled him dissolve. He stroked the undersides of her breasts and then her nipples and then he lowered his head and did the same with his tongue and lips. She lifted his head and kissed him again while she unbuttoned his shirt and reached down and felt him already hard inside his pants.

"Oh, Connor, I've wanted you for so long."

"I've wanted you too. I dreamed of you like this. A thousand times."

"I dreamed of you."

He lowered her to the bed and she lay there and watched him taking off his boots and his clothes, his eyes fixed on her all the while without shame or shyness. The evening sun was angling in on him and she was struck by how very thin he was and how his pale skin bore many scars whose stories one day she would ask him to relate. When he was naked he knelt before her and ran his hands and then his lips all along the insides of her thighs and then he slowly slid off her panties and kissed her belly and opened her legs and kissed her there too.

She came almost as soon as he entered her, came in great spasms and waves that made her cry out and cry again and again. Then she felt him come too, deep inside her, as though at last he had found his place at the very center of her being, where he should always have been and where he now would be forever. And she started to sob and couldn't stop, her whole body shuddering and the tears flooding and he lowered his head and kissed them and softly rolled his face in them to mingle them with his own.

"Promise," she at last managed to whisper. "Promise you'll never go away again."

"I promise."

THERE WAS ALMOST A FOOT of new snow and it scrunched and squeaked beneath her boots. The collies ran ahead, chasing each other in flurried circles among the trees, coming back every so often to check that she was still with them. The banks of the creek were plated with jutting overhangs of ice and the water between them curled with steam and ran slow and viscous as though of half a mind to turn into ice itself.

She followed the dogs through the willow

scrub and the chokecherry along the bank, past the tangled wreckage of abandoned beaver pools and on and up and around the bend until the land flattened and opened and she could see all the way up the valley. And there they were, still a good half-mile away, coming at an easy walk along the creek toward her.

They were too wrapped up in their talking to have spotted her and she stood at the edge of the cottonwoods and watched them ride slowly toward her. Amy was wearing an old red woolen blanket coat and some battered leather chaps that Connor's mother had given her. Her cowboy hat was an old one of Connor's that he'd padded inside to fit her. It was almost as stained as the one he was wearing now with his old tan canvas Carhartt jacket. His horse was a pale buckskin and a little taller than the pretty brown and white paint he'd given Amy for Christmas. Riding side by side now with the mountains behind them they looked a regular pair of desperadoes.

The dogs blew Julia's cover. They went racing away toward the horses and as soon as Connor saw them he looked beyond them and saw her and waved and so did Amy. Julia waved back and watched them quicken the horses to a trot and then to a lope, kicking snow over the dogs at their heels.

They slowed the horses as they drew near and reined them to a halt.

"Mommy! We saw wolf tracks!"

"You did?"

"Yeah, way up past the old homestead."

"Well, you sure better be careful, dressed up in that red coat."

They both laughed. Connor climbed down and walked toward her, leading his horse.

"Hey, Mrs. Ford, I thought you were supposed to stay tucked up in bed."

"On a day like this? Give me a break."

He put his hand on the great dome of her stomach and kissed her on the lips.

"Do you want to ride?" Connor said. "I can lift you. You can ride sidesaddle."

"Sure, if you want me to have the baby right here and now."

"I don't think so," Amy said.

Julia was eight months pregnant. They already knew it was a girl. They even knew what they were going to call her. Her first name would be Emily and the middle name Skye.

Amy rode on ahead now, letting the little horse splash through the icy shallows. Connor put his arm around Julia and walked her back beside the creek and up through the cottonwoods toward the house with the horse blowing softly behind.

She wondered sometimes what would or wouldn't have happened if Amy hadn't taken the initiative and gone to that sleepover party. The important things in life never happened by accident. But even with those things that were meant to be, sometimes you had to wait awhile and then maybe give them a little nudge.